Symphony of Goode Love (Goode Love Series)

Written By: Y. Deonna

Cover designed by coversincolor

Editor: Little Pear Editing Service

This book is a work of fiction. Names, characters, places, and incidents either are products of the author's imagination or are used fictitiously. Any resemblance to actual persons, living or dead, events, or locales is entirely coincidental.

Author Y. Deonna

linktr.ee/ydeonna

Printed in the United States of America

Library of Congress Control Number: 2021905573

ISBN: 978-1-7330585-6-8

First Printing: May 2021
Crown Ruby Publishing

Scripture taken from the New King James Version®. Copyright © 1982 by Thomas Nelson. Used by permission. All rights reserved.

Synopsis

Skin the color of onyx, a voice so electrifying that it saves lives, and eyes so bright that they dim sunshine, but all Amina sees is an unattractive, unlovable, unworthy woman. The lies told to her have negatively impacted her self-esteem. After years of neglect and losing half of her family in a horrible car accident, Amina withdrew from the world and silenced her voice. However, her affinity for music could never be silenced. It is her only communication. Amid tragedy, Amina discovers the power of her voice, the beauty of her dark skin, and unexpected love, one beyond her reach yet so close. The once voiceless girl that grew into a shy woman discovers just how attractive, lovable, and worthy she truly is, but will Amina's insecurity keep her imprisoned in a loveless life?

Built like a warrior king, with a need to protect those he loves, Reth Goode is the definition of a good man. Through ambition and hard work, he is one of the youngest immigration judges to sit on the bench. Known for his devotion to family, community, and God, Reth is admired by many. To the outside world, he seems to have a perfect life. However, perfection is deceiving. One secret has forced two people to live a lie, and Reth is determined to keep until death. That is until he meets a woman who can awaken his dormant heart. The perfect picture he has painstakingly created is threatened when his eyes are opened to the possibility of good love. To her. Can a man known for his loyalty allow love to enter?

<u>Quote</u>

"We must learn to endure what we cannot avoid. Our life is composed, like the harmony of the world, of contrary things, also of different tones, sweet and harsh, sharp, and flat, soft, and loud. If a musician liked only one kind, what would he have to say?"- Michel de Montaigne

Verse of Inspiration

Psalm 126:5. "Those who plan in tears will harvest with shouts of joy."

Swahili Language: Bibi-grandmother, Binti-daughter, Mpendwa-beloved, Mpenzi-lover, Mndani -sweetheart.

Character Prounciation: Reth: Ret (h) (It's like breath but without the B) - the name means a king. (African Origin) Eleora: E-leo-ra: the lord is my light. (Hebrew origin) Kondo: (KON do)- battle (Swahili) Jotham: (JO-tham)- perfection of Jehovah (Hebrew origin) Djimon: (JEE-mahn¬) Powerful blood (African origin) Hasina: (hah-SEE-nah) "Beautiful, Good" (African Origin)

Chapter 1

"**A**mal Goode," the petite Asian nurse called, causing Amal to discard the magazine that she was fake reading on the table. It was simply a prop to distract her shaky nerves.

It had not worked.

With the grace of a pageant queen, she collected her purse and cell phone and ambled toward the now smiling nurse.

Amal did her best to return the greeting, although, she was terrified. A few years ago, she was diagnosed with cancer. It was thought that the doctors had discovered it early enough to treat and cure it. Everything was going well until she started feeling off. Not anything extremely alarming but enough to cause her concern. Today, she would know for sure.

Amal had not told her husband, her best friend, that she suspected that the cancer was back. She knew that he would only blame himself. Her heart would not permit her to upset him until she received confirmation.

Here she was, alone and about to learn if she would have to battle cancer all over again.

"Amal, I'll take you to the exam room to meet with Dr. Miller."

Amal nodded as she followed silently to the exam room, sat down in the chair, and waited. Her eyes started to feel heavy, a combination of fatigue and dread. She loathed to admit that to herself, but she was terrified.

She was frightened because if it were back, and she could not fight it off, who would take care of her daughter Hasina and Reth? Their union was not a conventional marriage, but she cared deeply for him.

"Show me what to do, Father. Let me not be led by fear or worry. You know the plans You have for me. Father, give me the strength to accept what is to come, erase my fears, and allow me peace. Father protect Hasina and Reth. Help me not falter in my faith and not to question Your plans. Help them too. I admit, I am frightened, the most frightened I've ever been. Though my mind knows that You did not give me a spirit of fear, my heart is being stubborn. Guide me, Father; get me through this so that I can get my family through it too. In Jesus' name I pray. Amen."

Just as she finished praying, a knock sounded at the door. Instantly, she grew tense and felt a sharp pain in her back, where she carried her stress. Her fate was about to be revealed, and she was unsure that she was prepared for the outcome.

∞ ∞ ∞

It was after five o'clock when Amal made it home. After leaving the doctor's office, she needed time to process the news that the doctor gave her before she shared it with Reth. Then, they would have to tell the rest of the Goode family and, at some point, their daughter. Tears welled up in her eyes as she thought of having to deal with the disease again. Something felt so different about it this time. Letting out a discouraging breath, she mentally outlined what she needed to do. First was to tell her family.

The family she married into were the kindest people she had ever met. She had a wonderful relationship with her in-laws, much better than what she had with her biological mother Dalilah St. John. Her mother cared more about money, material things, and men who could provide her with a lavish life. There was no room for her daughter, especially after her father died. However, her stepfather, had been good to her.

Delilah only reentered Amal's life when she married Reth. The only reason she came to the wedding was to brag and see how it would elevate her financially and socially, which was why Amal was not going to contact her about her diagnosis. Her heart was not in the mood for her mother's rejection.

"Mal, is that you?" The deep baritone voice dance through the hall.

Her eyes closed as he called out to her. How had she not noticed Reth's vehicle? Amal thought she had some time to gather her thoughts. Her heartbeat increased at knowing that Reth was home.

"Yes, it's me," she replied as she made her way to her bedroom. Amal quickly took off her shoes, dropped her purse, and looked for something more comfortable to change into.

She settled on yoga pants and a basic white tee. By the time she changed and stepped out of her closet, she saw Reth's well-built physique leaning on the doorframe.

"Where's Hasina?"

"She's having her music lesson at the center. Kondo took her. I think he's teaching a self-defense class tonight. What's up?" he asked, his russet eyes taking everything in. That was the lawyer in him. Reth Goode missed nothing. She knew that he suspected something was off about her. For the past few weeks, she had been unbalanced and forgetful. Reth knew her well. They had been childhood friends, so he knew when she was hiding something.

Feeling a bit exasperated, she motioned for him to enter in her space. He sauntered in, all confidence and grace. Even in his youth, he walked with that kind of confidence. It was one of the qualities that she admired in him. Her father Edmond did as well.

Amal's eyes followed his path until he sat down on the accent chair and watched her sit in the one adjacent to it. As soon as she was settled, she spoke. "Re, I had a doctor's appointment today."

There was no alarm on his face, just understanding. "Which doctor? Primary, OBGYN, or oncologist?"

See, he knew her too well. "The oncologist. I had an appointment with Dr. Miller." As soon as she spoke, she noticed the change in his demeanor. Most likely, he was upset that she went without him.

Amal observed his steepled hands and the two deep breaths he released in quick succession. He was calming himself down and mentally preparing for whatever she revealed. By nature, Reth Goode, was a protector. All his life he looked out for his brothers and protected her. To have that removed from him caused him to distress, that much she knew.

"Mal, why didn't you tell me? I would have gone with you or had my ma go. We're in this together; remember?"

They were, but again, something felt different about this time. "I know. You're right. However, I didn't want to bother you about it. You've been extremely busy with work lately, and I just didn't want to add more on you."

Reth frowned at her admission, and frustration was written across his face. "Mal, you're my wife, my family. You and Hasina always come before my career. Haven't I always made my family my priority?"

Without hesitation, she nodded in agreement. "You have,

Re. Probably more than you should. You're an incredible provider, partner, father, and friend. Honestly, I just thought it best to go alone."

"It's done now and not something to be upset over. I respect your feelings. What did the doctor say?"

"It's back," Amal almost whispered. Before she could let a tear drop, Reth was on his knees, pulling her into him. His embrace felt warm and welcoming, and for a moment, she released all the tension and just allowed herself to take his strength.

"It's okay, Mal. We beat it once, and we'll do it again. Tell me what you need, and it's done."

That broke her down. So much had occurred in her twenty-eight, almost twenty-nine, years. This was not how she thought her life would go. When she made her five-year plan, marriage was in the cards, but not this way. Everything she wished for did not happen the way she thought it would.

"I'm sorry, Re."

Reth shook his head at her, resting his forehead against hers. His large hands embraced the sides of her face. "Don't be sorry, Mal. Never apologize about something that isn't your fault."

"It is."

His russet eyes held hers, letting her know he disagreed with her. "No, it isn't. I told you that when everything went down. Remove all of that out of your mind. I need you to be at your best mentally to defeat this once and for all physically. You know that I'm with you every step of the way."

A hint of a smile graced her face. "I know. I'm grateful. What're we going to tell Hasina and the family?"

"Let's talk to the doctor about your options, and then we'll go from there. We'll get through this, Mal, just like we've done before. I've always protected you, and nothing will ever stop that."

Amal felt herself being lifted, and Reth carried her to her bed and gently laid her down.

"Rest. I'll get Kondo to bring Hasina home, and I'll have my mother bring over something to eat.

"All right."

He gently kissed her forehead and then walked out of the bedroom.

∞∞∞

It was back. The taunting of those three words turned his world upside down. It irritated him and made him feel helpless. He could not show any weakness in front of Amal, even if he were a little scared. His wife would never know.

Reth sat down at his desk, flipping through the medical contacts, and preparing to make phone calls. He had to save her.

Her suffering was something that he could not handle. Whenever she had a problem, he always fixed it. This would be no different. They had gone through this before. He just needed to reach out to some experts in the field, see if there was a medical study she could participate in, and fix her. Then everything would be well again.

Inhaling a slow breath, he exhaled even slower to calm his mind. Reth clicked the music icon on his laptop, and the smooth sound of African Jazz musician Manu Dibango filled the room.

Reth was a lover of jazz; he especially loved African jazz. It was a reminder of his culture and life history. It helped relaxed him when he felt himself getting stressed. Closing his eyes, he let the music caress his soul. He took a moment to just be and then released the stress.

Gone was the urge to make the phone calls. He needed to soothe his mind first and then he would come up with a plan to save his wife.

His russet eyes eased opened, and he opened his drawer to get his Carlos Toraño 1916 Cameroon Robusto cigar. He took a whiff before preparing to smoke it. Lighting it up, Reth inhaled and felt the smoke wrap around his lungs like a warm quilt.

Reth leaned his head back on the leather chair and forced his mind to clear. It was time to do something with his family. Hasina had been asking about going to Disney World to meet the princesses. Due do his work schedule, he had not put a lot of thought into it, but he would now. The worst-case scenario would be losing Amal, which he could not even conceive. However, the cancer was back, and he knew what that meant. So, before the illness took over, he wanted his daughter and wife to have as many good memories as he could provide.

Reth reached for his iPhone and texted his baby brother Kondo to bring Hasina home once she was done with her music class.

Once that was done, he started with phone calls.

Chapter 2

Amina smiled as the children disassembled their instruments and put them away. Goode Community Center saved her life. It allowed her purpose and was one of the few places she found solace, where she could play her music and share her passion with children who loved music as much as she did.

Here, she was safe.

"Mina, can I take the guitar home?" Benito asked.

Turning toward the voice, she answered, "Yeah, just sign it out."

Benito gave her a big toothy grin and shot off to get the guitar while she helped the other children gather their belongings.

Parents were streaming in to collect their children while the other children who rode the bus were preparing for the van line. It was chaos and excitement, and Amina loved every minute of it.

"Are you almost done?" Kalifa, Amina's friend, asked over the chaotic cacophony of little voices.

"Yeah, is BC out there?"

"I think so; well, I didn't see his car, but I saw Diego's SUV."

Amina nodded. "Let me take Hasina over to her uncle, and then I'll meet you and Benito in the parking lot."

"Okay, c'mon Benito, let's go."

Amina watched them leave and then reached for Hasina's little hand as they strolled together to her uncle. Kondo was the youngest Goode brother. There were four altogether, and they were all equally impressive. Though Amina did not say much to them, she mainly talked to their parents and their third oldest son, Jotham.

"Hasina, did you have a good time tonight? You did so well on the piano today."

Her little face brightened at the compliment. "I had fun, Ms. Mina." Her eyes twinkled before she dropped her head shyly. Amina understood; they were both timid, but music brought them out of their shell.

It did not take them long to arrive at the gym where Kondo taught self-defense. It looked as if his class was ending too. Hasina and Amina posted up on the wall and observed quietly.

"Amina."

Amina turned to her left and smiled at Jotham, or JD, as he was fondly called. He was the youth pastor and did a lot of street ministry.

"Hey, do you need me?"

"No, I was just coming to get my niece. I believe that Benito and Kalifa are waiting on you. I got this little one."

"Are you sure? I don't mind hanging with her." It was the truth. Amina adored Hasina.

"I'm sure you've been here practically all day."

"Alright. Goodnight, Hasina, and I'll see you soon." Then, she got down on her knees and opened her arms to hug Hasina and the little girl fell into her arms. "Be good, my sweet girl. I love you, my little piano princess."

Hasina giggled.

Amina got up and said goodbye to the others and then headed for the exit.

"Dang, Mina Mami, I thought I was going to have to come find you," BC teased.

Amina just shook her head at his antics. He met her halfway and reached for her book bag. She had class today and came right to work at the center. The two had not spoken for most of the day.

"No instrument today?"

"I left it at the university. You know how my dad is about music anyway."

"I do, and that's why I suggested you stay on campus or get an apartment with me, but you said no."

Amina ignored him. BC knew why she had to stay home. Someone had to supervise her alcoholic father. Besides, they were not ready to live together. BC still had some maturing to do. Plus, his grandmother depended on him to help her with Benito.

"So, you just going to ignore me like that? You better be glad I'm crazy about your quiet mean self." He smacked her butt and she yelped. He cackled hard. "That got your attention. I don't know why you stay trying me. C'mon, my little brother fussing about being hungry."

Amina got into backseat with Kalifa and Benito, and they drove off. While Benito, Diego, and BC spoke amongst themselves, Amina got lost in her thoughts.

"Kali, you up to hanging out tonight at my brother's spot?" Diego asked, looking at Kalifa through the rearview mirror.

Hearing that lulled Amina out of her reverie. She knew that Diego liked Kalifa, but she was not interested. Kalifa was fixated on her future. She did not want anyone or anything to sidetrack her dreams. Amina understood because they both had difficult childhoods, and Kalifa did not want to continue the generational curse that seemed to plague her family.

"I don't know."

"Well, Mina coming, and I know you don't want her by herself."

"I want to go," Benito chimed in with his boyish charm. His left hand swept his hair from his eyes. He was growing it out.

"Not this time, little bro. It's just for the adults," BC replied.

"Wait, that's tonight?" It had completely slipped her mind. "I don't even have a change of clothes. I can't go."

Deep down, she really did not want to go. All those people gave her anxiety. In certain situations, she was socially awkward.

BC whipped his head around so fast that Amina was scared he'd broken his neck. "You're coming. If you need some clothes, then we'll stop by the mall and get you an outfit. You owe me this. I don't bother you when you're doing your school stuff, but you need to start making time for your man," he snapped possessively.

The aggressive tone was unnecessary. By the way Kalifa was making a face, Amina knew she agreed.

Lately, it did not take much for BC to become agitated. BC was aware of her situation, and he knew she was not fond of crowds or the new people that BC was keeping company with. Instead of instigating his anger, she replied, "Okay."

∞∞∞

"I'm really tired and would much rather be at home," Kalifa whispered to Amina.

After being at school all day and then working afterward,

they really wanted to rest. Not that Amina's home life was peaceful, but she wanted her bed. Instead, she was sitting at this kickback with people she barely knew.

"Me too. I'm trying to be a supportive girlfriend. I'm sorry you got dragged into this."

"At least there's food."

Smiling, Amina's amber eyes wandered until she saw BC. He was in his element and so happy. That at least warmed her heart.

BC had a rough couple of years. During his freshman year of college and on a soccer scholarship, he got hurt. It ended his career before it started. He fell into a depression and lost interest in school. Then his grandfather died. That nearly broke him. BC was super close to his grandfather and losing him took BC down a dark path, and Amina tried to be supportive.

Honestly, Amina felt he was still recovering from it all. She did her best not to add to his stress or worry him. If he wanted her here, then she would be here. It hurt her a little that he thought she was not making time for him. She was trying.

"What y'all pretty little chocolates doing sitting here alone? I know I can't touch you," Nic stated, looking at Amina. "I can get to know you, though," he cooed, looking at Kalifa.

You would have thought Nic was a serial killer the way Kalifa reacted. Her bright eyes looked as though they would pop out of their sockets. She started to physically shake, which caused Amina concern. Kalifa always became nervous around men, except for a few, and Nic was not one of them.

Nic was a creepy jerk who made her uncomfortable. Amina did not know a lot about him, but he offended her when he said she was pretty to be so dark, followed by asking if she was, she wearing contacts and if her hair was hers. After that, she kept her distance.

Anyway, he was one of the new people that BC had started to associate with. Something about him seemed dangerous. Even though she hated to speak up around strangers, she would do so to protect Kalifa.

"Aye, Nic, that's me so move on," Diego warned.

Kalifa glanced at Amina, lifting her brow, and Amina gave her a look that said go with it. The rest the guys there would not attempt to come for her if they thought she was taken. That was one thing she learned about them. There were women whom they shared, and women who were off-limits. Diego just let them all know that Kalifa was taken.

"Okay, little brother, I didn't know. She's fine, though," Nic replied and then moved on to another group of women.

"I'm about to be sick. I'm not built for this," Kalifa exclaimed dramatically.

"It'll be okay. Let's just try to do one hour and then we can get them to take us home or at least back to BC's house."

Kalifa nodded.

Amina was so thankful she had such a good friend. Kalifa was really her only friend besides BC. They had met at the diner that Kalifa worked at. Benito loved the place, and one day, Amina and Kalifa started talking because Benito wanted something not on the menu. After that, they were fast friends.

"*Negrita, mi amor*, come dance with me," BC called out to her.

Her eyes widen at his request. Amina shook her head in the negative and mouthed "no". However, she could see by the determination in his coffee-stained eyes that no was not an acceptable response.

"Come on, *mami,* you know I love this song. You're really going to make your man dance alone?" he fake pouted as he made his way to where she was seated.

"I don't dance in public."

Pausing, BC's dark eyes scanned her body before lingering on her face. Feeling the burn of his glare, Amina met his gaze. "Mina, baby, you can dance, and you know it. Come on, for real; dance with me. Tell her, Kali."

"Just dance with him," Kalifa added. Like Amina, she knew that he would not stop until he got his way. Still, Amina made a face at her, causing them both to laugh.

"Don't worry, Mina, Kali dancing too," Diego assured.

Before Kalifa could say no, Diego had her on her feet and was escorting her to the dance floor. The look of horror on her face made Amina feel a little bad for her.

"One dance, BC." She allowed him to pull her off her seat and then he gently pulled her into his arms and started to slow dance with her.

"Now, is that so bad, Mina, baby?"

If her skin were not so dark, a deep blush would be visible. "No."

"See," he cooed as he leaned in nearer to her for a kiss.

There he was doing that again. They talked about this. One, she was not into public displays of affection, and two, BC had been attempting to push her past her comfort zone. She told him before that she was not ready for more, and she would not be ready until she was married. Call her old-fashioned, but she respected her body and did not see the need to have sex for the sake of having sex.

"*Negrita*, don't do me like that. You're making me feel rejected."

Instead of fussing, she allowed his lips to capture hers.

"Mm, you tasted so good and sweet; we need to get out of here and just be alone."

Amina dropped her head, but BC nudged her to make her look up at him.

"Why are you still so shy with me?"

"Hey, Benigno, I didn't know you were here. I got next dance, right?" the high pitch feminine voice interrupted. Amina turned slightly to her left to see Nayelis standing there as if she were not present.

Amina did not realize that Nayelis was there. She had never been before, or at least not the few times that Amina visited Bash's place.

"Nay, this is my girlfriend and she got next and the next after that."

Nayelis looked offended. "I'm sorry. I ain't know it was like that with y'all."

Hearing her feign ignorance ticked Amina off. This girl was lying. It'd been like that since BC and Amina were in high school. They were an unlikely couple. Girls like Nayelis made her life horrible in high school. She did not allow them to see her cry. When she and BC entered college, they were still a couple. Nayelis stayed in BC's face.

"It is," BC snapped, and it was then that Amina glanced into BC's eyes. There was something there, something like a warning, and for some reason that made Amina feel uneasy. However, she remained silent and just observed the interaction between the two.

The young woman finally took the hint and stomped away with an attitude. Amina just shook her head and tried to back out of BC's embrace.

"Don't do that, Mina, baby," BC warned as he pulled her back into him.

"I'm ready to leave."

BC dropped his head, annoyed. When he was upset, the tips of his ears became red, and they were now glaring like a stop sign. Amina quietly watched him calm himself. He inhaled a deep breath and slowly exhaled it. The scent of strawberry Crush soda attacked her senses. She knew if she were not present, he would be drinking beer or something harder. He did not do that around her because he knew that her father was an alcoholic.

"Don't let another woman control you, Mina. I'on even care about her. It's me and you. I'on know why you let her get to you," BC preached.

There was an unease that overtook Amina at his accusation. Never one to give into anger, she could feel her blood pressure rising and narrowed her eyes in defiance at him. "I don't know why you entertain her. This is nothing new. She's been trying me since high school. Could it be that you're giving her hope when I'm not around?" Amina quizzed, folding her arms in front of her.

BC's expression showed that he was unprepared for her outburst. He did a double take because this was not their usual conversation. Normally, she would nod obediently or just be quiet.

Amina watched as BC licked his lips as if he were contemplating what to say next. "So, you're suggesting I would cheat on you?"

Amina shrugged her shoulders and pressed her lips together, showing her annoyance. At this point, she felt that anything was possible. That girl was not coming for her and flirting with him for nothing. Cats don't come back to eat where they are not fed.

"Mina, you know better than that. I don't appreciate you even suggesting I would do that. Come on and let's go. I'm not even in the mood for this. Your insecurity is frustrating, Mina. You gotta stop acting like that! It's about to be a problem," BC fussed and then took her by the arm and pulled her with him.

Irritated and defeated by his response, Amina dropped her

head in shame. Insecurity had not entered her life until her mother died, and she had to deal with her aunt. An aunt who let her know that she was ugly and unlovable. It was hard to compete with other women whom she felt were physically prettier than her. Women that the world defined as beautiful. Women with her complexion were not viewed as attractive. Dark skin was always viewed as less than. The color of her skin spoke volumes to others about her character, her intelligence, her likeability, before she could even open her mouth to introduce herself.

"BC."

"Save it Amina; you want to go home; I'm taking you home." There was such malice in his reply that she snapped her mouth shut. Though his grip on her was hurtful, she said nothing. It was best to be quiet until he calmed down.

Chapter 3

It was late when Amina finally arrived home. They had left with Diego, dropped off Kalifa, and then headed to BC's house so he could get his car and take her home.

She silently prayed that her father and her aunt Adeya were asleep. It was easier to deal when they were occupied. For the past three months, the two of them had been getting on her nerves terribly. With one more year of college left, she would move out and get her own place. Her mother willed her the house, but she did not have the energy to fight them over it.

"Mina, you're sure about this? I can take you back to my house. Abuela loves you and would not mind if you spent the night."

Amina was happy that he was speaking to her now. After they left Bash's place, he ignored her. His concern warmed her heart. BC was worried because the lawn was littered with beer cans and liquor bottles, the aftermath of one of her aunt's parties, which meant her father probably drank himself into a stupor.

It was beyond embarrassing to be that house.

Adeya used the house as her own private club. Her friends were a bunch of drunkards and washed-out wannabes.

"I'll be fine. Just text me when you get home, so I'll know you're safe."

"I will. Bye, babe, love you." It was an automatic reply that he often said when dropping her off.

Amina smiled. "Same," she replied distractedly as she exited the car. If it 'weren't so late, she would have cleaned up the yard, but she would get to it in the morning before she headed to church.

As she was about to shut the car door, she remembered that tomorrow was the youth program and she wanted BC to come. So, Amina knocked on the window to get his attention and opened the door and asked, "Hey, will you come to church with me tomorrow? The kids I teach at the Goode Community Center, will be performing with the youth choir."

He frowned and cut his eyes at her before finally replying, "I'll try."

"Why are you frowning?" she asked, genuinely perplexed.

He released his tongue and licked his lips before responding. "Why don't you ever say you love me?"

At that question, Amina stood as still as a statue and was momentarily struck silent. Yet, the hurt look that now replaced his frown had her complete attention. "I do."

BC let out a disagreeing grunt. "No, you don't. You've been on one since we left the kickback."

Fighting the urge to roll her eyes, Amina closed them and counted to twelve. It had been a strange week with BC. He seemed to pick apart every little thing she did or did not do, as if he intentionally wanted to argue. He knew she was not into that. Talking was fine but fussing and the baseless accusations were not her style. Arguing led to physical fighting, at least in her life, and she did not want that between them.

It was bad enough what happened at the kickback. Knowing what he needed to hear, and hoping it would lead to peace, she spoke softly, "I love you too."

BC shook his head the moment the words left her lips. "Don't say it if you don't mean it," he snapped.

His reaction took her by surprised. They were having a good night, and now, he wanted to start an argument. What was really bothering him, she pondered?

"I do mean it, BC. I'm not always good with verbally communicating my feelings; you know that. It's why I write music. I wrote you an entire song to show you how I felt about you."

That seemed to calm him a little. "I know. It's just nice to hear the words."

"I hear you, and I'll do better to tell you that. I'm sorry my actions have been making you feel as if I don't love you. That's not my intention."

The need for him to reply was strong; she was awaiting his response when the porch light came on. That meant either her aunt or father was awake, and she would have to go through another round of arguments.

"I better go."

BC nodded knowingly, as she stood at stood at the opened car door. Hoping everything was okay, she shut the car door and strolled toward the house.

As soon as she made it to the door, Adeya was there glaring at her. She had her house coat wrapped securing around her ample bosom and her bonnet protecting her pink rollers. That look on her face was enough to let Amina know that Adeya was on one.

"Where yo hot tail been all night? Ain't nothing opened this late but the mini mart and legs. Lawd knows, you don't need to have no baby, unless it looks like that boy 'cause you pitch black and ugly. Your only saving grace is you ain't nappy headed. I swear I don't see how you got that fine boy. I figured he was using you in high school, but he still around, so you must be giving it up."

Amina did not even dignify her presence, let alone respond to her questions and allegations. Instead, she entered the house and went about her business.

"I know you hear me talking to you. You just as disrespectful as your whorish mother. You better be glad my brother sleep so he can't see you repeating your mother's sins. I hope you know having sex with that boy won't make him stay. He'll find something better if he hasn't already!"

Amina's blood started to boil. Her mother, Kenise, had been dead for years, and she missed her mother daily. It enraged her that Adeya spoke so harshly about her mother and was a sore spot for Amina. However, she did not want to act a fool in response to another fool. She needed to get ready for church and then go to bed.

Adeya would have to argue with herself tonight. Amina went to her bedroom and jumped into the shower and washed the pain away. The stuff she said about BC using her and finding someone else was a real fear of hers.

The verbal abuse, the taunts about her mother, the reminders that she was ugly was a daily occurrence. Every day she was battling her aunt or dealing with jealous girls who wanted her boyfriend. Then, she had to deal with a father that loved the bottle more than his life. Shaking the thoughts, she finished her shower, toweled off, and dressed for bed.

Her body ached for sleep, but she had to check on her father. Her aunt had fallen asleep and could hear her snores. That was a relief.

When Amina entered her father's bedroom, the smell urine immediately assaulted her. Careful where she stepped, Amina maneuvered her way through the labyrinth of dark yellow liquid. The carpet had long been removed from the house because Aaron had a tendency not to always make it to the toilet after one of his benders. It was covered in either vomit or urine.

Amber eyes scanned his body like an x-ray. There was no wetness on the bed. She released a murmur of thanks. Fatigue hit her like a poisonous arrow to the heart. Cleaning up her father's bedroom would have to wait until later. Mentally writing her to do list, this chore would be added to one of the many things she had to do before going to church in the morning.

"Night, Daddy," she whispered with tears in her eyes. Something had to give because she could not keep doing this.

∞∞∞

Amina awoke early the next morning and went outside to clean up the yard. The last thing she wanted was for the neighbors to see the embarrassing sight. She worked quickly and efficiently to discard the evidence of her father and aunt's depravity.

An hour later, the mess was cleaned up; her face was drenched with sweat, but the yard looked much better. Exhaling a sigh of relief, she quickly entered the house to start breakfast and to get ready for church.

Entering the kitchen, she halted at the sight of her father. Amina had yet to make her rounds to his bathroom to clean it up. Clearing her throat, she spoke softly, "Good morning, Daddy."

Aaron turned slightly; the whites of his eyes were bloodshot. His face was sagging and sunken, the past written on his skin like an ancient stroll. Her heart went out to him. Aaron was a broken man who shattered himself by seeking the bottle and not the Bible. No, she was not judging her father; she just mourned for the man and father he could be.

"When did you get in last night?" his gruff voice inquired.

It took her aback momentarily. As Aaron made it his mission not to care about what she did as long as the bills were paid, he did not bother her.

"After midnight."

"You was wit that Latino boy?"

"I was with my boyfriend BC."

He stared at her before responding. "Well, you grown, so do what you do but don't bring no baby to this house. I ain't interested in being no granddaddy."

He was not interested in being a dad either, she thought to herself. Feeling the tears prickle, Amina refused to allow them to fall. Instead, she turned to exit the kitchen.

"Amina!"

Grinding her teeth, she answered, "Sir?"

"I'm hungry. You cooking or what?"

"I'm about to cook now."

"Good; wake me up when I can eat. I got up thinking you already did it. You was making all that noise."

"I was cleaning up the yard."

He did not reply; he just turned and left the kitchen and stumbled back to his bedroom as if he had no care in the world. It chipped away at another piece of her heart.

∞ ∞ ∞

Amina entered church later than she had planned. After the disappointing conversation with her father, she felt tiny. Removing the negative thoughts, she focused on her task and was elated to see that everything was ready.

Glancing at her phone for the millionth time Amina was

disheartened that BC had yet to return her call or text. Immediately, she assumed he was tiring of her. Did she come across too needy and too insecure? That was something she would work on.

Making her way to inspect the instruments, a song nudged into her mind. Feeling as if the Spirit was leading her, Amina went to the piano used the tips of her fingers to gently stroke each key. It was as if each one held a memory. Thoughts of her mother ran through her mind, and a smile tickled her face. The carelessness of her father and rejection of BC were no longer at the forefront of her mind.

Sitting down in front of the piano, her long, delicate fingers kissed the keys, and she allowed the Spirit take over. It had been a trying week; music notes flowed through her head, as did lyrics, but the song she started to play was not her own. It was the melody of Tamela Mann's song "Potter". It was rare that Amina ever sang. It seemed she lost her voice after her mother died, but this song had meaning to her. It spoke to her soul in the same way Lauryn Hill's *The Miseducation of Lauryn Hill* spoke to her mother. Honestly, she was heavyhearted this morning. Sometimes, it was hard trying to keep it all together when she wanted to fall apart. Except, when she fell apart, there was no one there to put the pieces back.

Fear ate at her heart, fear that her father would drink himself to death. Then there was BC. His moods and demands worried her. Honestly, their relationship felt off, and it had felt that way for a while. Denial was a constant in her life; it was how she survived. To admit what she really felt would leave her with one less person in her life.

It was always something. How did it feel to wake up without worry, fear, or internal ache? That freedom eluded her. The stress of it all was getting to her, but music was her relief. Music was her therapy and her communication. Closing her eyes, the words just flowed out of her mouth. Everything she felt she poured it into the song. Lamenting, pleading, crying; it all came out when she sang. For a while, she did not hurt; for a moment in time, the cracks in her heart filled. Coming to the end of the song, she felt empty but in a good way. Relief eased over her, and a smile crept across her face as she drowned herself in peace.

"Amen. My goodness, your voice is touched by the Lord. I needed that to uplift my spirit this morning." A lyrical voice erupted Amina's quietude, causing her to turn around to see its owner. Her amber eyes widened in awe as she saw the woman standing below. Instinctively, Amina offered Amal, Hasina's mother, a shy smile.

"Thank you. I don't really sing anymore. My voice is a little rusty." Doing her best not to clam up, Amina rose quickly, attempting to make a hasty retreat. Unknown to Amal, she made Amina nervous, even though they attended the same church and Amal used to bring Hasina to her music lessons.

Shooting out her arm to halt Amina's retreat, she quickly stated, "Don't go, Amina. I apologize if I interrupted your praise session. Your voice, it just called to me. There is nothing rusty about it. The family and I were praying, and I heard you. It was as if your voice led me to you, as if God was using your voice to speak to me."

Unable to think of a sufficient reply, Amina just nodded. In certain circumstances, her shyness and nervousness could be debilitating. Amal was always kind to her. Never once could Amina recall hearing the woman say a single bad thing about anyone. However, Amina felt incredibly insignificant in her presence.

Maybe that was the insecurity that BC was complaining about. It was just another strike against her that she was dealing with. Defeating insecurity seemed an impossible feat.

Amal Goode was a woman whom other women admired. She was flawless—in looks, in speech, and in aura. There was an ease about her as if she did not have to try; she just was. This woman was Cover Girl model beautiful. Her voice was elegant and soft, like a bouquet of calla and peace lilies. She carried herself like royalty, not stuck-up, but with grace, neatness, and confidence. She exuded a quiet strength that was magnetic, all which Amina lacked.

"Will you sit with me?" Amal asked. Her makeup was immaculate, making her face glow.

It took a moment for Amina to react. Her eyes bugged out at the request. "Me?"

Amal grinned enduringly, her eyes glistening with joy. "Yes."

Nodding in agreement, Amina followed her to one of the pews and sat down beside her.

"Is something wrong?" Amina asked. More than likely, this had to deal with Hasina. Though for the life of her, she could not think of how.

"No, sweetheart." Amal's voiced hummed; she reached for Amina's hand, patting it like a caring mother. "God just placed it on my heart to pray over you. I don't know what's going on, but He wants you to know that He's with you."

Amina almost choked on her saliva. Never in a million years would she think they would be praying together. Once she got over the shock, Amina bowed her head and let Amal pray over her. They had stayed in the sanctuary for so long after praying that others started coming in for service. Amina thanked Amal for praying and talking to her. Even after walking away, Amina still felt the presence of something. Something transpired between the two of them once Amal touched her. It left her confounded.

Unable to interpret the meaning of their interaction, Amina hurried to the front of the church. It was time to welcome the children. As soon as they saw her, they bombarded her with questions. She did not mind because this was her element. Amina adored children.

"Ms. Mina, I need your help. I can't tie a tie!" Brayden's squeaky voice cried out.

Amina almost laughed at his excitement but kept it together. She went right to him and tied his tie. "All set, Bray."

A wide grin covered his face, and he winked at Amina. That caused her to chuckle at his antics. He was a good kid.

"Hey, lil'dude, don't be flirting with my girl. I'll fight for that one," BC's mellow baritone warned, causing Brayden to scurry off.

Amina turned slowly around to see not only him but Diego. "You're here!" Amina exclaimed.

"You invited me." He cocked his head to the side as he spoke to her.

"I know, but you never returned my calls."

"I left my phone in the car. I'm sorry. Good thing I got here too; I see these little boys be making plays for you. I'ma tell Benito to give me a list," he teased. Then he sauntered closer to her and pulled Amina into a hug and took a deep whiff of her.

"What're you wearing because you smell good enough to eat? And this dress. You don't need to be wearing stuff like this in church."

Amina playfully rolled her eyes before replying, "Hush. Your abuela chose this dress. The scent is Kuumba Made Vanilla Bean. Kalifa put me on to it, and I like the way it smells on me."

"I like it too. So, after this is over, you're coming home with me."

"All right, but it can't be late like last night. My aunt was upset and then this morning my dad got annoyed with me."

BC side-eyed her. "That old biddy is always on one. I've never cared for her. She's jealous and bitter. She needs to get a man so she can mind her own business."

Before Amina could reply, she felt a tap on her shoulder. She glanced up and saw that it was First Lady, Eleora Madiata Goode, a woman whom Amina adored and admired. This woman knew her past struggles and never judged her.

Removing herself from BC's embrace, she quickly introduced him and Diego. Amina silently wondered if Eleora heard what BC said, but if she did, she made no mention of it.

"Nice to meet you all. I hope you young men don't mind, but I need Amina to help me wrangle in the children and get service started. Please feel free to sit anywhere and welcome home." Mrs. Goode smiled then reached for Amina's hand and they were off.

Chapter 4

Amina got a case of bad nerves, which usually happened before a performance. It was triggered more at the church because of her family's past with the congregation. After her mother fell in love with a church member, and her father cursed the church, because of it, she carried the brunt of the shame. No one said anything to her face, but there were looks and whispers. It was not as bad as it used to be, when she first returned, but they were there. For that reason, she tried to keep a low profile while at church. It was as if they were waiting for her to mess up.

Tipping out of the sanctuary, Amina dashed to the women's restroom and ran inside the stall.

"Lord, give me strength," a familiar voice whispered, followed by the sound of vomiting.

Alarmed, Amina quickly completed her business, exited the stall, and washed her hands. Then she turned to the last stall and approached slowly.

"Ma'am, are you okay?" Amina asked the mystery woman.

There was no response for a moment, and then the vomiting started again.

Worried, Amina peeked in the stall, and her mouth dropped in surprise. It was Amal. A thousand thoughts flooded her mind, but the most pervasive was what happened since she left her in the sanctuary. When they spoke earlier, Amal seemed perfectly fine. Maybe she was pregnant?

"Oh, my goodness; let me help you. I'm going to get a wet towel," Amina offered and quickly jumped into action. Having a father who always drank beyond his limit and threw up just as frequently, she was unbothered by the sight or sound of vomit. Not even the smell affected her because she had witnessed much worse at a young age.

Amina quickly retrieved a towel, wetted it, and hurried back to Amal who was now standing by the stall to hold herself up.

Calming her own breathing, Amina reached out and steadied Amal and then assisted in cleaning her up. This was second nature to her, and her normal nervousness disappeared.

"Thank you," Amal whispered.

"You're welcome. If you're ready, I can help to take you where you need to go. Or we can just sit here together in the waiting room."

Amal smiled, latched onto Amina, and they carefully exited the restroom. They had barely made it three feet when Reth, accompanied by his brother Kondo, met them.

At the sight of them, Amina shutdown. Something about the Goode brothers made her just fall to pieces. It was unclear if it was their stature, attractiveness, or that they knew her tragic past.

Okay, that was not the full truth. Reth alone had that impact on her.

Reth's eyes went directly to his wife, and he was by her side, lifting her in his arms. Amina's heart melted at how focused and caring he was toward Amal. Briefly, she wondered what that felt like to be that safe and comfortable in loving arms.

Biting the inside of her jaw to halt those thoughts, Amina observed mutely. At this point, she might as well be invisible.

No one acknowledged her presence, and honestly, she was okay with that. If Reth had turned those entrancing eyes on her, she would have fainted or done something equally as embarrassing.

"Amal, what happened?" Reth deep timbre filled the entire hall. That man's voice was everything. It was cultured and refined with inflections of a French accent.

"I'm okay, Reth, please put me down. Amina took good care of me."

It was then he remembered that Amina was present, but not for long. He nodded his thanks and then motioned for his brother to assist him with Amal.

Amina swallowed hard and then went back to the sanctuary. She whispered a prayer of protection for Amal.

∞∞∞

"I'm taking you home."

"Reth, no. I want to watch the children perform. Hasina is really excited about this. My stomach just got queasy, but I feel better now."

Reth shook his head in disagreement, but Amal did not mind. She knew that he cared about her and was worried. He was always overprotective of her, their daughter, and his brothers. That was just who Reth was.

It broke her heart that she was causing him pain. The one thing he could not protect her from was cancer, but he was determined to defeat it.

"Fine, but the moment it's over, we're leaving so you can rest."

"As you wish." She winked at him and he offered her one of

his rare smiles.

"Come on then. Kondo went to let Ma know not to worry."

Amal nodded, and with her husband assistance, they entered the sanctuary just in time to see Hasina start playing her piano solo. Her daughter looked almost angelic sitting in the piano seat that Amina sat in earlier.

Amal closed her eyes and let the music flow through her. She was so proud of her daughter. Everything that Hasina did Amal imprinted in her brain. She knew one day it would end. It was a conversation that she and Reth had, but he always told her that she would beat the cancer. Still, she wanted to prepare her family for her departure, and she wanted to prepare her heart for the years she would miss. In her mind, that was God's grace and mercy. Where some were taken from their family without ever saying goodbye, she was able to prepare herself and her family for her departure.

By no means was she giving up. Amal had a fierce faith in the Lord. She knew that His will would be done, no matter what. Still, her eyes watered with love, adoration, and fear as she watched her only child play the piano with confidence.

When she first found out that she was pregnant, it was not excitement or even love that she felt. It was anguish, terror, and betrayal. Hasina was unplanned, not unwanted, but the circumstances of how she came to be nearly shattered Amal to pieces. Reth was there; he was always there and always sacrificing. Soon, his time for happiness and love would come, and she prayed he claimed it.

Now, seeing Hasina, who was a diffident child only comfortable around family, was now playing the piano in front of the entire congregation. Hasina's bravery made Amal brave.

Ever since Amina had come into Hasina's life, Amal saw a change in her daughter. It was a subtle change, only something a mother would notice. How beautiful it had been to witness her daughter bloom. The relationship that Amina had with Hasina and the way Amina loved her warmed Amal's heart. It comforted her in ways no one knew.

Amal did not say much, but she was observant. There was something unique and special about Amina Williams. It was in the way she loved and cared about others, the way she took extra time with all the children and poured all her knowledge into them. It was how she returned to church, even after some of the members gossiped about her parents. It was apparent to Amal that Amina had no idea how special she was, but one day soon she would.

The piano solo ended, and Hasina turned and smiled at her mother. Amal grinned back and blew her daughter a kiss.

Reth pulled her hand in his and shared in their family moment. Amal closed her eyes and said a brief prayer. When she opened them, her eyes caught the amber glint of Amina's and she offered Amal a reassuring smile.

Amal placed her hand over her heart. Yeah, there was something special about Amina.

Reth rested his head on his hand. He had put Hasina to bed after reading her two bedtime stories, and then he went to check on Amal, but she was sound asleep too. Now, he was left alone with only the silence of the house and his own thoughts. They were not good thoughts.

Today at church when Amal became ill, it upset and worried him. It was almost as if Amal was accepting her fate and refusing to fight. That could not be true, could it? Shaking the thought, he got up from the recliner and started walking the circumference of the den. His eyes caught the family covenant. In each of their homes, his parents' home included, there was a framed Goode Family Covenant, derived from Colossians 3:12-17:

Therefore, as *the* elect of God, holy and beloved, put on tender mercies, kindness, humility, meekness, longsuffering; bearing with one another, and forgiving one another, if anyone has a complaint against another; even as Christ forgave you, so you also *must do.* But above all these things put on love, which is the bond of perfection. And let the peace of God rule in your hearts, to which also you were called in one body: and be thankful. Let the word of Christ dwell in you richly in all wisdom, teaching and admonishing one another in psalms and hymns and spiritual songs, singing with grace in your hearts to the Lord. And whatever you do in word or deed, *do* all in the name of the Lord Jesus, giving thanks to God the Father through Him. GOODE-Give love. Obey His word. Offer forgiveness. Declare His Good News. Edify His ways in every aspect of life.

He paused. Beside the family Covenant was supposed to be the Goode Love Vow for marriage. Reth and Amal never took the vow because, to her, it would be a fraud and a disrespect to God, and he agreed. For her, the family covenant was enough, but his family often questioned him about it, and he never answered. He prayed he never had to tell them the truth.

The ringing of his doorbell brought him out of his deep thoughts. Shaking his head to ease the tension, he went to the door.

A smile crossed his face when he saw that it was Kondo. He opened the door and his brother had cupcakes from Tamu. Reth was not a man swayed normally by sweets, but he did enjoy a good strawberry cupcake from Tamu. He stood aside to allow his brother entrance.

"I tried to get back before you put Hasina to bed. I thought we could all enjoy something delicious."

Reth smiled. Kondo was always thoughtful. He motioned his brother to follow him into the kitchen. Once they were settled, Kondo asked, "Am I to be an uncle again? I know pregnancy can be difficult for women after having chemotherapy."

Reth stilled at his assumption. That would never happen unless they were adopting. Of course, he had not told the family about Amal's cancer returning.

"No, actually, the cancer has come back," Reth admitted.

Kondo dropped his cupcake, his mouth agape and his eyes stunned. "Huh?"

"We were planning to tell the family today, but Amal got tired. I'll share the information with the rest of the family. I don't want them thinking that Amal is pregnant."

"Brother, I'm so sorry to hear that. How can I help?"

Reth was humbled by his brother's request to assist him. "Pray. I have reached out to the specialist that Aunt Miriam knows. There aren't currently any medical trials that she can participate in. It's now in God's hands."

"Of course, I'll pray. Now it all makes sense why you were alarmed when she went to the bathroom. JD and I thought we were about to get the news that you were expecting again. Forgive me for making assumptions."

"Kondo, there is no need to apologize."

"I love you and Amal, and I'll pray without ceasing that God will heal her completely."

"Thank you; that's all I can ask."

∞ ∞ ∞

"I love you, Mina Mami," BC proclaimed as the two lay side-by-side on the blowup mattress in his mancave. "You're my one."

Amina side-eyed him and sucked her teeth. He was laying it on extra thick, which meant he was up to something. Just the other day he was fussing at her.

"What's all that for, huh? Why you always coming for me like that?"

Before she could answer him, he was on top of her tickling her. BC knew she hated to be tickled, and she did her best to throw him off.

"Stop it, BC! Please, I love you, stink head. Get off me!"

He stopped tickling her and then leaned his head down and kissed her slowly. "You going to marry me, Amina? One day, you'll be the mother of my children. You're going to be a good one, too, because you take good care of Benito. That means a lot to me. Plus, I see how you're with them kids at church."

Amina turned her head. She loved Benito, Ms. Mary, and BC. They were a great family. Family was something she missed, so when she found people she could love and trust, she considered them family. Though it was not the same as having her own; it was something.

"Babe look at me. You got that sad look. You know I don't like to see that. Why don't you let me make you feel better? You know I love you."

Amina knew his meaning, but she was not ready; not for that.

Turning her head to make eye contact with BC, she opened her mouth to deny him, but the ringing of her phone interrupted them. Silently she thanked God for the interference.

"Let it ring," BC demanded.

"I can't, hold on." Amina fumbled with the phone as BC eased off her.

"Hello?"
"Is this Amina Williams?"

"Yes ma'am."

"Hey, this is Holly at the bar. You don't know me. You usually talk to Chad, but he's not working tonight. Anyway, I know your dad. Aaron was involved in an accident—"

"Oh, my goodness." Amina cut the woman off; all her mind thought about was that her dad was going to die in a car accident like her mother and twin brothers. "Is he okay?"

"Honey, he was driving and hit another person. The police have arrested him, and he wanted me to call you."

That was all Amina heard. It played like a broken record in her mind. The woman was still talking, but Amina heard nothing. Dropping the phone, tears welled up in her eyes and fell hard. Shaking her head, she wanted it to be a lie. This was her life, a constant merry-go-round of torture.

"Mina Mami, what's up?"

Trembling like a leaf during March winds, she fell into BC's arms. "My dad was in a car accident and hurt somebody. I don't think I can fix it this time."

Chapter 5

2017, One Year Later

Amina's bright amber eyes stared into her father's strained chestnut ones. Despair, fear, and hopelessness lingered in those lifeless orbs and reflected her own. This time, she could not right his wrongs; she could not bring back the life he stole. The power to rewrite history was not her gift.

Aaron Nathaniel Williams was giving up. The past year of awaiting this trial had done him in. Nothing Amina said or did could pull him out of his depression. For one year, he had not been able to drink, so he had to feel, and she was sure he had no idea how to handle the emotions that were flowing through him. He never dealt with the loss of her mother or brothers. The alcohol allowed him to suppress the pain. Now, he was living in sober misery.

Honestly, she did not know what else to do or say.

Soundlessly, Amina prayed that the jury would show mercy to her troubled father. This man had endured torment, though much of it was self-inflicted, but he had suffered an agony most could not conceive. Right now, the jury needed to be benignant. This was one-time; Aaron needed their empathy, not their disdain.

Even as she had those thoughts, she knew how this would end. The same way everything ended in her life—badly.

For the Williams clan, good things stopped happening a long time ago. The word good seemed foreign to her defective mind. The past year was debilitating and devastating.

Still, this man, though he was cruel and unkind at times and ignored her all others, was the only living parent she had. If he were convicted, then she would be alone in the world. That sounded extremely dire. Even though her father was not the greatest, he was hers. That was how desperate she was for his love. The idea of him remaining behind bars crushed her.

Just like that, she was yanked back to the time and place where she had lost it all. The reality that half her family was dead. Her father was dying daily due to his alcohol addiction. If she were honest, she had been alone for a long time now. Childhood ended the moment death took her mother and brothers. The twins. In one day, she lost three people.

Unlocking the intense gaze with her father, Amina turned her attention to the jury. Five men, seven women, a variety of ethnicities, all with poker faces, but still she knew. They had only been deliberating for a few hours, and now they were ready to decide her father's fate, as well as her own. Right about now, she wished she had accepted Dr. and Mrs. Goode's offer to attend the trial with her. However, shame had taken over. Didn't it always?

Amina was sure they would relieve her of her position at the center, but they had not. Still, it was difficult to ask for help. The year had felt like a decade, and the few people she allowed in her small circle she distanced herself from.

That was a mistake.

There was an intense pressure in her heart as the madam foreperson began to speak. Her harsh voice was about to secure the fate of her father. Closing her eyes, Amina allowed her head to languidly roll back as she listened.

"We, the jury, find the defendant guilty of one count of

felony vehicular manslaughter." Amina felt her heart split at the announcement, and her closed eyes burst open.

She lost her mother and twin brothers to a road rage accident, and now, her father had taken the life of another due to his drunk driving.

Life fast-forwarded, the past intertwined with the present and future. How many times had she implored him to not drink and drive? How many times had she hidden the rainbow bottles of liquid poison that had stolen her father long before the judicial system? Why was she never enough? He would rather be in prison than with her. Was she that worthless to him?

Guilty.

It sounded final, like the end. She, too, would be doing time; those who judged her father would also judge her. The daughter from the rotten fruit. She was judged by sins that were never her own, first by her father and his sister and now, by these strangers.

It ripped through her veins.

Yet, she was unable to cry. Tears had not fallen since the night she received the call that her father hurt someone. Even then, they did not last long because for her, tears never made the hurt stop.

On the inside she mourned for her own family and the family who lost a loved one. Everything always happened on the inside. There was safety there, where others could not see.

Life taught her to hide her feelings and emotions.

Still, this was not the outcome she wanted for her father. Since the death of her mother, she devoted herself to being an upstanding and outstanding daughter. Amina's life mission was to make Aaron's life easy so that he would choose her and not the alcohol.

Amina failed miserably. Her father never chose her.

Daily, Amina prayed for her father. She attended church regularly until he forbade her to continue. He assumed she would be like her mother. Those were lonely years when he would not let her go to church, and she missed it immensely. Still, she prayed for him, and this was what he did with the life God offered him. He took another life. In doing that, he took her life too.

Aaron's selfishness had caused another calamity. Regrettably, another family was suffering from loss and would forever be incomplete because of his decision.

Now, Amina was the one left behind. Left to sort out the mess he created. She was the abandoned one. Always. *But why?* she mentally lamented.

To combat the sorrow that was overtaking her, the tune of Plumb's song "Need You Know (How Many Times)" whispered into her head. If she could get lost in the music, she would make it through this moment.

"I knew a black man wouldn't get a fair trial with a predominately white jury," Adeya harrumphed loudly, causing others to look their way.

Her gruff voice yanked Amina back to reality, the reality that her aunt was present. For a moment, Amina had forgotten she was there.

It was a task to deal with Adeya on a good day. A day like this would be impossible. Amina did her best to ignore her aunt's ignorance. The two did not get along, and never had, but this past year had tested all her faith. It was by God's grace that Amina had not lost her mind.

The Williams family was hanging on by a thread. It was never Amina that caused the toxic chaos. Lord knows she humbled herself repeatedly. Amina absorbed all the horrible, heinous, and cruel comments her aunt unleashed. For some reason, her aunt developed a deep hatred toward her. Amina felt that her aunt was taking out the anger she had against Amina's mother, Kenise, on her. The two were never friends. It seemed to Amina, even at an early age, that her aunt was jealous of her mother. Somehow, that transferred to Amina after Kenise died.

That was all she could rationalize. Adeya despised not being the focus of Aaron's world and acted as if everyone owed her something.

Wordlessly, Amina stood up and watched her father be handcuffed and escorted out of the courtroom by two deputies. He did not spare her a glance and for some reason that hurt.

Casting off the repudiation, Amina glanced over to see the Hernandez family; they had lost their son due to her father's stupid decision. Inhaling deeply, Amina hesitantly trudged over to the family. Their all-consuming grief was familiar.

Faintly, Amina overheard her aunt mumbling disparaging and bitter words behind her. Nevertheless, Amina dismissed her. Rarely did her aunt say anything important, polite, or meaningful. Mostly, belittling mean remarks were her expertise.

"Mr. and Mrs. Hernandez," Amina's tender voice spoke; her timbre was low, courteous, and sensitive. Empathy and remorse showcased in her hooded eyes.

Their puffy, sorrow-filled, cinnamon eyes turned toward her. Absent from their gaze was malice or rage, just curiosity and melancholy.

"I," she gulped hard before attempting to speak again. "I apologize for my father's actions. I'm as much to blame as he is. I tried without success to get him to enter rehab. He's had an addiction to alcohol, ever since the death of my mother and brothers. I know you heard that during the trial, and that in no way excuses his actions. I just...I understand your grief. I know the pain of loss and how unbearable and all-consuming it can be. I've prayed for you and your family since this horrible accident occurred. I pray one day that you'll forgive my family, this trespass against your family. I'm sorry that I was unable to get my father the help he needed to prevent this tragedy your family now suffers."

It had taken everything in her to say that. By nature, she was introverted and did her best not to be the center of attention, but this had to be done. It may not have been the popular way to do things, but it was the proper and right way to do this. Her mother had taught her that. To always do what was right, not what was popular. Since her father did not do what was right, as his daughter, it became her cross to bear.

Dropping her head in shame, Amina turned to leave the family, but Mrs. Hernandez reached out and pulled her into a motherly embrace.

"*Gracias, señorita.* You, my dear, are not to blame, but we appreciate your kindness. Promise me you'll not feel guilt over something that was beyond your control. Don't lose your life because of what another has done. Be free; we don't blame you and there's nothing to forgive."

Tears welled up and fell like a waterfall down Amina's eyes, astonishing her.

Tenderness and thoughtfulness were savagely extracted from her life, like a surgeon doing open heart surgery without anesthesia. The loss of her mother, her champion, was excruciating. Affection was replaced by insults and mental affliction. This woman, this stranger, had offered her more affection than her father and aunt combined.

"Thank you," Amina managed to speak. It was barely out of her mouth before her aunt snatched her away by her neck and smacked her hard on the back of her head. The Hernandez family gasped in horror.

"What is you doing, Pitch? You so stupid! Them people is the enemy; you don't embrace them people. They probably illegals anyway. I got the mind to call ICE on 'em. Now, my brother locked up because of 'em. We all know that the boy was drinking too, but they gon' blame the black man!" Adeya spat loudly. Her racially charged words embarrassed Amina. That young man died because of her father; it was as simple as that.

Without a second thought, Amina jerked away from her aunt and jetted out of the courtroom in humiliation, not only from the actions of her aunt, but also because she called her Pitch. It was an offensive nickname meant to humiliate and degrade Amina.

Adeya had bestowed the ugly name on her because Amina's skin was as dark as night. Sometimes, it nearly broke her spirit at how mean and calculating her aunt could be. Escaping outside, Amina dialed BC. He said he would be with her when the verdict was read but had not shown up. Over the past year, their relationship had been rocky. BC had become distant and unreliable. His inability to support her was evident now. His absence felt like betrayal.

Gazing at her phone, she realized that he had yet to return her call. Disappointed, yet undeterred, she called him again. Instantly she was sent to voicemail. Shaking the feeling of abandonment and fury, Amina marched to the bus stop and quickly hopped on the bus.

Thankfully, her professors were aware of her situation and worked with her. Tomorrow she would be in class, but now, she needed a moment to breathe.

There was one place she could go, and that was the Goode Community Center.

The ride to the Goode Community Center was swift and sightless. Then again, her mind was a river of emotions, and she was distracted. However, seeing the extraordinary building calmed the turbulence in her heart. The building was huge, modern, cutting-edge, and eco-friendly, inspired by the family visiting the Clayton Community Centre while vacationing in Melbourne, Australia. It was a project headed by the second oldest Goode brother, Djimon. He spent a summer in Australia and was inspired by the architecture. Although the Goode Community Center was the brainchild of the four Goode sons, Djimon spearheaded the building project.

The center had become Amina's sanctuary. While there, she did not have to deal with Adeya. Here, she taught the children music, and soon she would start a music therapy program to assist children dealing with trauma.

Recently, she had been accepted into the Doctor of Psychology program at UNC. It was her goal to fuse together her love for music, her past trauma, and her love for children into a therapy practice for youth. It was the only way to find purpose in her pain.

In losing her mother and brothers, she found her life's calling. The love of music and God was instilled in her through her mother. That was what she incorporated when teaching the children music. Today, she was the one seeking solace. Today, she felt all the wounds of her youth.

Entering the building, she found it quieter than usual, mainly because most of the children that used these services were still in school. Only the younger children were present, and they were most likely outside for recess. The center also took children from infant to age four for families that could not afford daycare.

Amina made her way up the steps to the second level of the building where the administrative offices were. Mrs. Goode and her husband Pastor Chiram Goode shared an office. As

Amina glanced down at her watch, she was sure the pastor was at his church office.

Making a quick left, she padded toward the last office, noticing the door was slightly ajar. Thinking that Mrs. Goode was awaiting her arrival, she entered prepared to fall into Mrs. Goode's warm embrace. Instead, she suddenly stopped in her tracks. In front of her was Reth Goode. He was the eldest of the Goode tribe. Reth was well loved and one of the youngest immigration judges in North Carolina.

Reth, well, all the Goode brothers were beyond imagination. They seemed too impossible to be real. There was not a woman in the church, young or old, who was not affected by their presence.

In Amina's opinion, Reth was the handsomest. Due to her attraction to him, she kept her distance, even though she babysat his daughter in the past. Fear that she would say something stupid in his presence or his wife's presence made her shy away.

In his company, her brain turned to Jell-O, and her voice disappeared. However, Amina adored his family. Reth's daughter was becoming one of her most promising students. That child played a mean piano and harp.

Over the past year, Reth had become elusive. Add that to the fact that he was a bit intimidating, she did her best to avoid him. There was a rumor that his wife was deathly ill. She, too, had not been seen much in public. However, Amina did her best not to listen to gossip; that led to the downfall of her mother and father's relationship; well, that and infidelity.

Decluttering her mind, Amina took in the sight before her. Reth was tall and thick. His powerfully built body was clothed in a tailor-made suit outlined by perfection. The smell of some unnamed hypnotic scent permeated the air, and she hungrily inhaled.

The scent dressed her exposed parts like a cozy fleece. In that moment, she forgot about the shame, the loss. Amina just embraced her feelings for a second before coming to her senses. It was moments like this that made her wonder if her aunt were correct. Was she broken like her mother? How was it right to have a crush on a married man?

"I'm sorry, sir. I was looking for your mother," Amina replied to the unasked question. Honestly, it did not seem that Reth was even aware of her. At the sound of her voice, he stared at her as if she were an intruder, a stranger. There was no recognition in his eyes when he glanced her way. Then again, she was not close to him. There was no need for her to be on his radar.

Still, his detachment seemed odd. Yet now was not the time to start analyzing the man she was just mentally drooling over. Reth did not seem the type to appreciate that kind of behavior.

"She's on her way back. Excuse me." His diction was perfect. Reth announced every syllable of the words he spoke. He gave words life. His voice was clear and commanding. Even though he had said nothing enduring or flirtatious, just hearing his voice captivated her.

Once Amina shook off the effect of him, she turned toward the door only to find him gone. It was a strange interaction that had her contemplating if the rumors were true. Unlike his brothers, he had not been active at church. Come to think of it, his wife Amal had not been either. Had she not been so distracted by her father's trial she probably would have noticed that sooner. Between school, acquiring a lawyer for her father, and shutting down all her social media, she had not been aware of her surroundings. Attending church over the past year had not been a priority either.

For the past twelve months she had been meandering in a haze. If she attended church she did so online. Still, it was hard not to miss Amal's presence. She was an ethereal beauty. The pair looked like they belonged together.

Countless times Amina compared herself to the elegant beauty and knew that there was no comparison. It was not even a competition. Reth Goode would never see her, think of her, or even talk to her. She was not on his level and never would be. A man like that was meant for a woman like his beautiful wife.

"Stop thinking," Amina whispered. She should be ashamed of herself. Besides, she had BC. No, BC would never measure up to Reth Goode even though that man was beyond her reach, even if he were not married. She was too young, too black, too ugly, and too awkward. That is what Adeya would say; that is what she always said.

"Amina, you're here. Come here dear and let me love on you."

Drowning in negative thoughts Amina had not heard Mrs. Goode enter the room. The cooing of Eleora's Congolese accent vibrated, making Amina smile. Just like that, she fell into her welcoming arms. Eleora ran her hands through Amina's hair to offer her comfort.

"Tell me what happened, my Song Thrush."

Inhaling deeply, Amina told all that happened in court. It felt so good to just let it all out. They talked a little more and then Amina left. She would return later as she had a class. She needed to get some work done and she still had not heard from BC. Before she could finish her thought, her cell phone rang. She looked down and saw it was BC; she quickly answered but heard nothing but voices on the other end. She kept saying his name, but he never replied, and then she heard a female voice.

They were conversing in Spanish, which she understood just as plainly as she did English. The feminine voice was saying how much she loved BC and how she missed him. So, that explained why he was ignoring her calls. There was someone else. What a perfect day it was turning out to be. He freaking butt dialed her, and now she knew for sure what she had suspected. He was up to no good.

Chapter 6

For three tortuous days, Amina dodged BC. The task was difficult as he knew her schedule. Back and forth her mind volleyed about how to confront the man she once trusted. Lauryn Hill's "Ex-Factor" was on heavy rotation. So being here right now and seeing him with another woman confirmed what she knew. Standing outside of BC's grandmother's home she stood quietly ruminating.

Mentally, she had broken up with BC and taken him back, but now she was ready to approach him. Amina's unscheduled popup was brilliant, if not calamitous. Without trying, she found him caught up in lies. They poured out of his mouth like a cold glass of lemonade on a sweltering June day. The vein in the middle of BC's forehead was pulsating, a telltale sign that he was lying through his teeth.

An explosion of dread, mental anguish, and fury unleashed in Amina's chest. Distressed flowed through her marrow as she realized she was unprepared to handle this confrontation. Maybe, she should have taken one more day to prepare.

Narrowing her gaze Amina's nostrils flared and burned as she fought back tears. This was the end. She cried more in the past week than she had since her mother and brothers' funeral. Her father was incarcerated; her boyfriend was a cheat; her aunt was an abuser and user. Amina had no safe place to just settle her spirit and release the pain that had built up inside of her.

All she wanted was a moment of peace, but peace had eluded her for years. Now this. How could he?

Incorrectly, she believed the man before her would bring her the calm she desperately needed. Benigno was never a perfect boyfriend. A woman like her was not looking for perfection, just acceptance and understanding. Throughout their relationship, he provided that. He was one of her best friends. Life was lonely, and his family filled the emptiness bequeathed by death and deception.

The Soto-Calderón family gave her normalcy and made her feel a part of something. So, she let his shortcomings slide. Not this time. His dishonesty and disloyalty were too much to overlook, especially after dealing with her father, who still would not talk to her and Adeya who never missed a chance to degrade her.

This relationship was officially done. As much as she yearned for what BC had with his brother and grandmother, her mother did not raise a fool when it came to relationships.

This was the ultimate disrespect.

Amina was an idiot for not seeing the signs sooner. It was never a sustainable relationship. Somewhere deep down, she knew it would end this way, but still, she was unprepared.

Girls adored him. He was popular and cool. In high school, he was a soccer star. Though it had been awhile since he played, he still had an athletic build. Back then, he was still into her. She was the dutiful girlfriend, attending all his soccer matches and helping him with his homework. Now it felt as if her years of loyalty were being thrown in her face.

Benigno had the most entrancing ochre eyes and hypnotizing grin. He was six feet tall and gorgeous. When he noticed her, she thought it was to make fun of her. To her astonishment, he seemed interested. Like a moron she fell for every word spoken and every promise made. For the girl that nobody cared about, his attention and persistence were everything.

Amina, the virgin. The music nerd. The one with no family. The girl with skin so dark that people made the dumbest, most asinine, banal jokes. Hurtful things like, at night, she was so black she was invisible. They called her crow and shadow. He had protected her, dared them to speak disparagingly in front of him. His protection had earned her loyalty, her love. Now, it would be one more thing to mourn, another unhealable wound to medicate.

Mentally sobbing, Amina accepted the truth. This situation was inevitable. How many times had she heard, "Why would a guy like him be attracted to a woman that looked like her?"

It should not surprise her that BC would be drawn to someone that favored him. Maybe they shared something culturally that she and he never would. Even though his grandmother was a Black woman and had raised him, her skin tone was nowhere near as dark as Amina's. She always knew she was thought of as less beautiful because of her skin tone. It never mattered when her mother was alive. It did now. Everything mattered now.

Adding insult to injury, he chose to cheat with Nayelis, a woman known to share herself freely. Apparently, that was what BC wanted. Nayelis was attractive with straight, silky dark hair. Her light ecru skin looked nearly white compared to Amina's adumbral skin tone. They were literally night and day.

Sure, Amina had long, natural hair; uncurled, it hung to her waist. It was a gift from her mother. She felt no shame in her natural hair, though some thought it was a wig. What made her stand out were her amber eyes. Most people assumed she wore contacts, but they were hers. For some reason, people assumed that Black people only have dark brown eyes or only wore wigs and weaves. The ignorance she had to deal with daily was astounding. Even in college, higher education couldn't eradicate stupidity.

Now this.

Sweat beads popped up on the top of Amina's nose, a clear sign of agitation. It wasn't just agitation or even embarrassment; she was devastated. Amina just lost her father and boyfriend in the same week. How much was she supposed to endure?

Though her heart was fractured, she refused to showcase any weakness. *Not here and not now*, she mentally chanted. Alicia Key's "Superwoman" entered her mind. This day would not end her; it would slow her down like a bump in the road, but she refused to let his actions denigrate her worth. Later, it would all come: the agony, the shame, the guilt; it always came. It was her secret and her thorn to bear. He would not get the benefit of knowing how bereft he made her feel.

Internally calming her perturbed nerves, she evaluated her current situation. This entire display was cliché and humiliating. The week had been disastrous, but she would not allow herself to act out of character for a man who felt she was not worthy of respect.

In the back of her mind, the questions flowed. Was this her fault? Had she failed him in some way? Why had he chosen Nayelis? How long had the relationship been going on? This girl clearly could not stand Amina. His lack of decorum and willing deception stung.

A part of her was upset with herself, enraged that she allowed herself to have any expectations of him. She had become too comfortable. That did not lessen the heartbreak, however.

Glaring at BC, she just could not form the words to express her internal battle. Then again, her mind did not always work in words. Her mind worked in musical notes and lyrics. Right now, Lauryn Hill's "I Used to Love Him" and for King &

Country's "Love's to Blame" played repeatedly in her head.

"Mina, you heard me?" BC asked as he slowly trotted her way. There was caution in his movements. He was unsure of how she would react. Maybe because she had gone to another place mentally.

How long he had been speaking was beyond her. His words had yet to penetrate her mind. She did that too — disassociated from the world when she needed to avoid trauma. It was a defense mechanism she developed as a child. Pulling herself back into the present, her eyes came into focus and she saw that Nayelis was barely showing a baby bump.

How she missed that before was beyond her. Seeing it now quickened her heartbeat. She was sure BC could physically see the thumping of her pulse in her neck. Sweat covered her upper lip now. She was sure her entire face was painted with sweat as her eyes narrowed on Nayelis stomach. That girl had the audacity to cup her belly. It was her way of baiting Amina. Methodically, Amina's stare rose higher until a smirking Nayelis greeted her.

"Mina, Mami, just let me explain," BC attempted again, but Amina's body was trembling too badly. There was no way she could entertain a thing he had to say.

A new wave of something indescribable released through her veins. There was no coming back from this. Adeya's words that she often used to taunt her came back to her mind. *"You too black, Pitch. Don't no man want that; you too funny-looking. All that shape wasted on you. I swear you ain't my niece. Nobody in our family is as dark as you. Truth be told, my brother probably ain't your daddy either. Ya mama was just a useless hussy messing with anyone's man. Who knows who your people are; it's not us? The least you could've done was bleach your skin. I told you to bleach your skin. Maybe that would have helped you look like you belonged to this family."* Amina fisted her hands at the memory.

"Don't cry," Amina inwardly scolded as her amber stare

oscillated between BC and Nayelis' small belly. There was an overpowering need to release the emotions that were eating away at her. The need for her piano, violin, or flute was overwhelming. It was the way she released her feelings instead using her hands for violence. Hands were created to heal, not hurt; that's what her mother often taught her. Sometimes, her father who was more obsessed with her mother than in love with her, would use his hands to hurt Kenise.

Amina learned long ago not to argue and not to hit. She used the fury that boiled in her to write music. Musical notes were already flowing through her brain. Inhaling and exhaling gently, Amina began to take small steps away from BC and his baby's mother. There was nothing to salvage here. He played her like an instrument, and she was lured in by his Pied Piper melody.

At twenty-one and a soon-to-be college graduate, how had she allowed BC to mislead her? Easy; love stopped when her mother died. Without her mother's protection, she was susceptible to manipulators and users.

Shutting down her mental soliloquy, Amina turned her attention to the front door where BC's brother Benito stood. He reminded her so much of the brothers she missed. At ten, he was a good kid. He had a learning disability, but he was one of the smartest people she ever met.

"*Negrita, mi amor*, Nay isn't pregnant by me."

"Yes, I am!" she deadpanned. Her beautiful face balled up, making her unscarred face wrinkle.

Nostrils flaring in annoyance, BC snapped, "Shut-up, Nay. You see me talking to my girl." The entire time he kept his intense gaze on Amina.

"I thought I was your girl. You're the one who says she don't put out and chu was tired of her. Talking 'bout her family issues and stuff," Nayelis argued, rolling her neck to emphasize

SYMPHONY OF GOODE LOVE

how upset she was. When BC failed to respond she continued. "What? Now I'm the problem? I thought you didn't even want her. I mean ain't chu using her because she a free babysitter?" Her long, manicured nails accented each word she spoke. Then she finished with a satisfied grin and went back to popping her bubble gum. Her fake eyelashes looked as if they were about to take flight.

The entire display was exasperating and insulting. It had lasted longer than necessary. The last thing Amina wanted was to draw attention to their exchange. Now she was in the middle of a domestic dispute. During this entire display of ignorance, she had yet to speak one word. At least she knew the truth now.

BC needed her to keep an eye on Benito. There was no reason to manipulate her love. He never had to pretend to like her. Being with Benito was a treat. She loved Benito as much as she loved her deceased brothers and would protect him with her last breath. BC's family meant something to her. For him to disrespect her and tell his, whatever Nayelis was, that he was using her, was a soul wound.

The fact that he was upset because they had not had sex did not matter. He could be mad a million times over because there was no way she was sharing that with him. She never would unless they were married. BC was not worthy of her gift. Her right hand quickly went to her left where she wore her True Love Waits ring. It was an oath she took on her fourteenth birthday. It meant a lot to her. She did not have much, in looks or love, but she would never jeopardize her dignity to be accepted by fools.

Burning on the inside, Amina ignored them both. She nodded at Benito, signaling for him to get his bag. She turned from BC preparing to leave. She and Benito were headed to the diner to eat before going to the Goode Community Center. Her growling stomach took priority over this absurdity with BC and his side piece.

"Mina, where're you going?" BC demanded, completely abandoning Nayelis. The displeasure on her face showcased her dislike of his action.

Amina just rolled her eyes at him and crossed her arms, infuriated by his audacity to question her.

"Don't do that, Mina."

She forgot that BC despised being ignored, and he abhorred the silent treatment. Still, she couldn't care less about his feelings. Accommodating his feelings was no longer a priority. Turning her back to him completely, she silently waited for Benito to come out of the house so they could catch the bus and leave.

"So, you're just going to ignore me?"

"See, she don't even love you like me. You out here mistreating me and I'm carrying your child. You just stupid!"

"*Silencio!* Don't speak another word. Your breathing is annoying me," BC growled before turning his attention back to Amina.

"Mami, let me take you and Benito where you need to go. Then we can talk about this. Nay is lying. I mean, I messed up. I made a mistake, but she ain't having my baby."

"I don't need this!" Nayelis hollered and stomped off.

The fact that BC seemed unaffected by Nayelis' departure shocked Amina. He did not even acknowledge her. Amina was not sure if that was because she caught him cheating or because he really did not care. Either way, she would no longer subject herself to his duplicity.

"Forgive me, Mina. You're my girl, been my girl since forever." He eased closer to her and attempted to pull her into an embrace, but she pushed him off.

"How would you feel?" she whispered; her voice softer than

the wind.

BC stepped closer. "Feel?" he parroted dubiously.

"If I did what you did? If I'd ignored your calls and did not support, you? How would you feel if you arrived at my house and I was with another guy and who claimed that he got me pregnant?"

A transformation overtook BC. The darkening of his eyes and white-hot anger outlining his light brown skin alerted her. The tips of his ears were blazing like a furnace. The mere idea of that must have really disturbed him. His entire faced shriveled up like a dying rose. For a moment, she felt fear. BC had a temper, one she could usually tame, but today there was no urge to pacify him. Today, his actions aggrieved her.

"Don't even play like that. You already know what I'd do. You ain't me. Don't start getting no stupid ideas in ya head," he threatened as his index finger tapped the side of her head. Then he got close to her face, completely invading her personal space, and added, "You let another man touch you and that's blood on your hands." His index finger on his left hand shot out and poked her forehead several times, driving home his point.

Amina pushed his finger back in warning. It pissed her off that he thought he had the right to put his hands on her. She was timid, but she was no coward. BC was acting out of character. That was big talk from someone who had just betrayed her. His words aggravated her, but his attempt to intimidate her really upset her. Still, she maintained her calm. Amina was enrolled in the self-defense class at the Goode Community Center and could hold her own, but she refrained from allowing her ego to lead her actions.

"I'm going to speak to Abuela and then I'm gone. We're done. I don't need the problems that being with you brings. Live your life and enjoy your new family. I'm good."

With that, she stormed off, only to get a few feet before being violently yanked back.

"Let me go, BC." Her timbre was breathy and soft, but she held her ground.

"Don't act like that with me, Mina. I owned up to making a mistake but we're not breaking up over that. I told you that ain't my baby. Nay isn't like you; she's a community chick, but you? You belong to me."

Amina was doing her best to tear away from him. BC only gripped her tighter. "Stop fighting me!"

"Beni, what're you out here doing? Let that girl go right now!" his abuela demanded.

Her cinnamon skin reddened at the sight before her. Ms. Mary adored Amina. The woman was a jewel. She stood at about five feet five inches and still had all the curves of her youth. She was sassy, sweet, and fearless. Her grandson knew not to disrespect her, or she would tap dance on his butt.

Unlike her grandsons, she was not Puerto Rican but born and raised in South Carolina. She met BC's Puerto Rican grandfather in college. They married and had two children. BC's grandfather died a few years ago, and it had hit them all hard.

"Abuela, I'm just talking to her." Amina noticed how his tone and inflection mellowed when he was speaking to his grandmother.

"She doesn't want to talk to a cheater. She's the best girlfriend you ever had, and she's a good girl, too good for you. You make me sick acting like you weren't raised right.

Now, let her go before I get my broom and beat the brown off your butt. You're not too grown to get a beating. Don't try me today. Anyway, her and Benito gotta get to the community center. You know she's got to work. That girl has been through an ordeal after what happened with Aaron. Stop being a bully and putting on a show for our nosey neighbors," Mary spat as she fisted her hands onto her wide hips. She cocked her head to the left and took another breath before going in again.

"Don't you ever bring that trifling, two-faced hussy Nayelis to my house again. I got papers on that loco girl. Her mind is just useless. That's why you mess with her. I'm telling you, stupid plus stupid just don't work. Now let Mina baby go, and if you ever touch her again, I'm taking my cast iron pan upside your big head," Ms. Mary fumed before motioning Benito to her. When he exited the door, Ms. Mary pulled him into her and kissed him before sending him to Amina.

"Abuela!" BC whined.

"I said what I said. Now get on gone and let Mina baby and Benito go. Leave her be! You better give her time to process what you did. Don't you dare apologize unless you mean it. Just like your father Estephan. You're not a farmer; stop planting your seeds everywhere."

With that declaration, she turned and trekked back into the house, letting the screen door slam behind her as Amina struggled not to laugh. It was not a funny situation, but his grandmother had a way with words that always caught Amina by surprise.

BC hated it. Amina could tell by the annoyed look on his face, but he let her go. There was no way he would say anything because Amina knew Mary was watching them out of her blinds.

"We're going to talk later. I can drop you off," BC offered. His tone was softer now as were his features, but it was not compelling enough.

"The bus is fine." Amina reached out for Benito's hand and they marched off.

Chapter 7

Amina closed her eyes as Hasina played the piano. The ache that she felt at BC's betrayal floated away just like the melody of the song played.

This was her realm. Music was instant manna to her ailment. Hasina had a gift for the piano. The other students were gone to snack time, including Benito. Hasina was one of her younger students and preferred private sessions whenever possible.

Amina accompanied Hasina with a violin. When she played music or taught children how to play, she lived. Music was the motion of her life; without it, the silence was deadly. Silence made her remember what was taken away, but music helped her to remember the better days. Good memories lingered in melodies and concertos. Memories of her mother's beautiful voice. The way her amber eyes danced to the rhythm of the beat. How she kept tempo with the flick of her head. The way her long fingers kissed the black and white keys.

There was something soothing about the music, something so beautiful about the combination of a violin and piano. It was classic; it was beauty; it was hope. Music moved her soul in ways that nothing else could. There was freedom and solace in the notes. There were so many emotions that music could evoke.

Hasina, at the tender age of five, was a piano prodigy. The way her tiny fingers danced on the keys and made such vibrant, hypnotic melodies was entrancing. There was passion in the way she played.

Finally, the song ended, and Amina peeled her eyes open, forcing herself to confront reality. It was unwanted.

Amina wanted to hold on to the memory of her mother longer.

Her dark golden eyes landed on a smiling Hasina. Just like Benito, Hasina held a special place in Amina's heart. She played with a maturity and devotion far beyond her young years. Hasina loved music; the piano brought out another side of her.

Like Amina, Hasina was a diffident child when not playing the piano or the harp. Hasina unfolded slowly. It had taken months before Hasina was comfortable opening herself up to Amina. Through patience, attentiveness, and love, she and Hasina began to make beautiful music.

"Are you ready for your snack?"

Hasina nodded timidly and slid off the piano bench, but before leaving, she turned and hugged Amina.

"Are you okay, Hasina?"

There was something in her embrace that caused Amina alarm. Hasina nodded her head that she was and exited the room.

Concerned, Amina made a mental note to speak with Hasina's grandmother. She did not know the full extent of what was happening in the family. However, it had been confirmed that Amal was sick. She prayed that the child would not lose her mother. That was a club no child should belong. Amina made a mental note to send encouragement to Amal.

Exhaling, Amina picked up her cell and clicked on the iTunes icon and played Lauryn Hill's *The Miseducation of Lauryn Hill*. Her mother adored that album. She played it all the time and said when Lauryn made this album, she was speaking of Kenise's life. Of course, it was also a favorite of Amina's. It was her mother's life soundtrack and the one way she kept her memory alive.

Kenise cultivated Amina's passion for music. Closing her eyes again, Amina got lost in the notes. The day had been aggravatingly long not just physically but mentally as well. God knew she just wanted relief. In less than an hour, she would be on her way home, a place she once adored. Not anymore, though; home was a battlefield, and she was on the losing side. No longer was her ailing alcoholic father there but her verbally abusive aunt who had free reign.

That was why BC was so important to her. After what he did, she felt lower than ever. When her aunt found out, she was going to have a field day. Ever since her father was convicted and sent to prison, Adeya had been unbearable to deal with. Amina honestly did not think that was possible.

Only God understood how insufferable BC's actions had been. He may not have been the best boyfriend, but he was hers, or at least she thought he was. For a young woman who had so much removed from her life, losing something else just seemed to go along with the theme of her life.

Amina thought that as she neared college graduation and having her acceptance into a graduate program would reignite what she lost after her mother's death. Happiness would rule where agony and loss reigned.

What a naïve theory.

Instead, everything felt desolate. Whenever anything good happened there was the astringent aftertaste of defeat. Maybe God never intended for her to be anything more than what she was. Her mother had committed sin. Her aunt told her plenty of times she was paying time for her mother's crime. Her mother's crime was love. Her father's crime was death. She was the curse that was left behind.

Releasing the negative and paralyzing thoughts, Amina mentally reached for memories of her mother and brothers. Finding her way to the piano bench, Amina silenced her phone. Warmth embraced her as her thin fingers glided across the piano. Just like that, she was whisked away to another time and place.

There was an ache in her throat; her mouth wanted to open and belt out a song. Her voice was one of power. Her mother always said she would save lives with her voice. Amina had a vocal range that most would envy, but her father had forbidden her musical passion. He thought that music and the church were evil. He believed that music led her mother into the arms of another man. That man happened to be a trustee at the church that Kenise and Amina attended. He was also in the choir with her mother.

Remembering the past caused Amina to attack the keys. She literally played her despair. Thoughts of her father soared through her mind, followed by uncensored memories of BC. The music became more rapid, singed with agony and defeat, mixed with loneliness. Her mind was so entranced that she didn't notice she had a visitor. She swayed with the music, internally singing, and bemoaning her grief.

Her flow was interrupted by the clearing of a throat. Amina stopped, her eyes gently returning to the present. Seeing that it was Mrs. Goode, she quickly spoke. "I apologize, Mrs. Goode. Sometimes, I get carried away by the music. Is Benito okay? Or is it Hasina? She seemed a little detached today," Amina inquired as she eased off the piano bench. She looked down at her watch to see the time and noticed she was not wearing her timepiece. Was snack time over?

A relaxing smile etched across Mrs. Goode's face, instantly calming Amina. "No apology is required. Benito is fine. The children are being entertained by my husband and son, Jotham. I actually wanted to speak to you about something else."

Amina nodded and watched as Mrs. Goode closed the door for privacy. Her mind was flooded with a million thoughts. None seemed good, but she could not think of anything wrong she had done.

"Congratulations on getting accepted in the PsyD program. I wanted to tell you that when you came by earlier this week. However, it just did not seem like the right time. I can't wait for the music therapy program to begin. It was a marvelous idea you brought to us. Our children, especially our minority and immigrant population, need this kind of counseling. I just thank God that He bought you back to us."

After what happened to her mother, Amina's father yanked her out of church. She only started going back in her senior year of high school. Even now, her father did not know she was attending church. Though, she hadn't been attending regularly over the past year.

Now that he was imprisoned, maybe he would take the news better. A lot of people found God after being incarcerated. If her father ever attended Goode Faith Worship Church, he would love it.

"Thank you." Other than Kalifa and BC's family, no one had congratulated her on her accomplishment.

Mrs. Goode nodded and then sat down on the piano bench. "I need to ask you something. You can say no so please don't feel obligated to say yes. I'd prefer you pray about it before answering."

Amina's eyes widened. "What is it?"

"Sorry, that did sound a tad ominous, and I apologize." She took a deep breath before continuing. "Amal is sick. I know Hasina senses it, even though we do our best to distract her. Most of the time she stays with me and my husband. However, after speaking with Amal, I want her to have someone in her life that can help her through the grief process. Hasina adores you. I know she's timid and doesn't speak a lot, but you two have bonded. I'd like to offer you a full-time, live-in position as her nanny. It comes with full benefits and won't interfere with your current college courses or your doctoral program once it starts."

Whoa, that was a big compliment and even bigger task. The Goode family was wealthy and well known throughout the state of North Carolina and beyond. They could get anyone, like a licensed professional to do this job.

Amina looked Mrs. Goode in the eyes. She had no idea it had gotten that bad for Amal Goode. "Me?"

Her beautiful face lit up. "You. I've watched how my granddaughter is with you. I've observed how you treat all these children. You're patient with them. You listen to them and converse with them. The time you take with each child when you teach them music is aweing. Everyone has noticed. My son will need the help while he attends his wife. They're both good with you being the person that helps with Hasina. Reth would have come himself, but these have been difficult times. He's been distracted."

Understanding what was not being said, Amina nodded. That accounted for their odd interaction that day in the office. When her mother died, her father shut down emotionally. That left Amina, still a child, trying to be an adult. Erasing the memory, Amina's mind went to what Mrs. Goode said about her son. She had no idea Reth Goode would even speak her name. Yeah, she had babysat in the past, but her interaction was not with Reth. Her encounters were always with his parents, a few with his wife, but never really him.

Now, he wanted her to be a full-time, live-in nanny for his daughter. That was just...wow. To know that Reth knew of her existence gave her a chill and piqued her curiosity. "I'll give it deep consideration and prayer. When do you need an answer?"

"Two weeks."

"Okay."

Mrs. Goode let out a relieve moan; a mist of tears lingered in her eyes, but she did not say another word. Motherly, she patted Amina's hand before excusing herself. For some reason, Amina knew in that moment she would agree to do it. She loved Hasina, and if that child were losing her mother, then she would need someone who had already gone through that misery.

∞ ∞ ∞

It had been nearly two weeks since Amina broke up with BC. He finally stopped calling her when he realized she wouldn't answer. Though she knew breaking up was the right action to take, it still stung. She grieved the loss of their relationship, but it was necessary. Mostly, she had been splitting her time between school, the center, and hanging out at the diner to keep her mind busy. She did her best to arrive home as late as possible; however, today was different.

Drained from a busy day, Amina arrived home much earlier than usual. The smell of liquor tainted the air. Fighting to not inhale the stench, as Amina strolled deeper into the house, she noticed the hardwood floor was littered with a rainbow of bottles. Some were empty, some still held an amber or clear liquid, a sign that the drinker was unable to finish drowning her misery. Amina assumed this was the work of Adeya or one of her friends.

Adeya had been more of an issue since Aaron was sentence to four years. She vowed they would fight it. All she did was drink, party, and make a mess. The woman was a forty-year-old teenager.

Even though her heart broke to have a felon for a father, it might just save his life. His addiction was killing him. Now, it seemed that same addiction was being passed down to Adeya.

The house was a complete mess. Sighing, Amina began cleaning up. After working and going to classes all day, she had to come home to deal with this mess. The only blessing was that Adeya was not present.

Padding to the washroom, she started the laundry. Next, she headed to the kitchen and hummed a melody; it was dark, brooding, and painful, the way she would currently describe her life. Seeking out a pencil and music paper to write the notes, her journey was interrupted when Adeya and her friend entered the house.

It was an unwelcome intrusion. Amina's heart sunk. Adeya and Amina's relationship was better when they did not have to interact with each other. Hence, her coming home as late as she could.

"Oh, you're here?" Adeya sneered; her hard, beady eyes glared at Amina. Adeya was slightly overweight with wide hips. She was barely five feet six inches, but her attitude made her appear almost seven feet. With the hateful way she was eyeing Amina, she knew her aunt was about to act a fool.

Only God knew why Adeya hated Amina so much. For the life of Amina, she had no idea what she did to her aunt to make her become so mean and nasty. Adeya was not an alcoholic like her brother, but lately she increased her intake. Whether she drank or not, her demeanor was always the same with Amina.

Often, Amina wondered if her aunt was on drugs due to the company, she kept in addition to her mood swings. Plus, her eyes always looked unsettled and sickly. Instead of responding to her, Amina continued as if she never spoke.

"Pitch, did you hear me?"

That stupid nickname cut like a knife. Colorism was an issue in the Williams family. Being referred to as "Pitch" was like nails on a chalkboard. Adeya called her that to get under her skin. No matter how old she got, it still pained her.

"I think she ignoring you, Ade."

Smacking her teeth, Adeya answered. "Yeah, Mela, I think she is too. That pitch-black spook is disrespectful like that. She thinks 'cause she about to graduate and got into that doctoral program she better than everybody," she huffed, side-eyeing Amina. "Then again, she might be mad because her little boyfriend got him a new little girlfriend. A pretty light-skin girl. I told her ain't no dude wanted her ugly tail. She too dark. Yeah, she got that hair like her momma and them eyes, but what good it do her? What a waste. I heard he got the little girl pregnant too. That's just you reaping them bad seeds your momma sowed."

Mela giggled as if it was the funniest thing she ever heard. There was nothing amusing about Amina's pain or her loss.

The constant belittling and attacks were destroying her. Adeya was a bully and a predator. Her bringing up BC's infidelity was meant to break Amina. For just a few moments, she did not think about it. Now, it all flashed back, not just him and his betrayal but her mother. It burned her soul.

"Well, are you going to be in here, or are you going to disappear? My friends are coming over. I don't want you making them uncomfortable with them Bible verses and watching that television pastor or listening to Christian radio. It's annoying."

Blankly Amina stared at Adeya, her elegant hand fisted in anger. Adeya's friends made Amina uncomfortable. When one was surrounded by evil spirits, one got the Word to fight away the evil. Please believe she was surrounded by demons.

"This is my home, so yes, I'll be here. If you want to entertain your friends, get your own place," Amina snapped, taking them all by surprise.

Any other day she would have not responded. She would retreat to her bedroom to avoid confrontation, but that all changed. Amina read somewhere that being silent was a response; it was giving others the permission to continuously disrespect and mistreat her. Before she finished the thought, her face snapped.

Adeya had slapped the snot out of her. Shocked by the violence inflicted upon her, Amina inhaled a deep breath. It was an attempt to calm herself and not react violently.

She failed.

Everything in her wanted to retaliate. Instead, she took several deeper breaths. She would not allow herself to become the bitter, deplorable woman she saw before her. There was something terribly wrong with Adeya. It only got worse after Amina's mom died.

"It would be best if you took your party elsewhere." Amina's voice was even tone; there was no hint of the fire that was brimming beneath. "Please don't hit me again. Intelligent people use their words to express themselves; only fools use violence. I let you have that one. I won't be so kind if you attempt that again."

Both Adeya and Mela's mouths dropped. They were used to the timid Amina that they bullied at will. Well, not today, Satan; not today. Just as she finished that thought, it was as if her aunt read her mind. Something altered in her aunt's facial features.

Adeya knew that Amina had finally had enough of this situation. The dynamic was shifting, and as her mother used to say, two women cannot share the same kitchen. This house was not big enough for the two of them.

"Oh, you got a little sass in you now," she fumed, leaning back, and cocking her head to the side. Amina remained unmoved. That only infuriated Adeya more.

"You think because you're grown and educated that you can talk to me like that? Huh? You need a beating. That's what yo momma should have been doing instead of cheating on my brother. I got something for that mouth," Adeya raged and then charged Amina. And the fight was on.

It would have been fine if it were one-on-one. Adeya was stout but not stronger than Amina. Her aunt's only exercising was lifting her fork to her mouth. It showed as she huffed and puffed, but she had a python grip. Though Amina didn't want to fight, she had no choice. Amina was a musician, a songwriter, not a fighter. Still, she was going to protect herself.

At that moment, it was as if something else took over. Amina went in and easily got the better of Adeya. Years of pent-up frustration and anger were being let loose, and then Mela jumped into the fight. It was on; it felt like fifteen rounds of a heavyweight bout, but Amina refused to allow them to beat her into submission. She was tired of losing.

"What's going on?!" a random male voice shouted as he attempted to break them up. "Ade let that girl go. Ain't that yo niece?"

"She's rude. All I do for her and my brother, and she disrespected me and then put hands on me."

That was a bald face lie. This woman was so toxic that any interaction with her would lead a person to contact the Center for Disease Control. Adeya was a walking pandemic. Disgusted by her deception, Amina turned around and stormed to her bedroom, packing up anything important. This was an unfortunate situation, and what was worse was that she really did not have a place to go tonight. There was no way she could stay at home. Verbal abuse was one thing, but physical abuse, oh no. Besides, she witnessed her father hit her mother after their relationship started to deteriorate.

There was not a person alive who could hit her, and she would accept that behavior. If her aunt wanted to lie and say she took care of everyone, well, let her. That woman only lifted her finger in violence or to eat and nothing more.

It was Amina who paid the bills, kept the house clean, took care of her father before he was arrested, and cooked the meals. If Adeya wanted to do it, then she could have it. Amina gathered her belongings, preparing to leave.

"You betta leave. Don't come back! We better off without you. Ain't nothing but a slut like your deceitful momma. You ain't even good at that; that's why that boy cheated on your stupid black tail."

"Shut up, Adeya! Don't say nothing like that to that girl. That's yo niece!" the unknown male shouted at Adeya.

"As loose as her momma was, I don't think she none of my kin anyway. I told Aaron she not his."

Amina ignored her taunt, but she really wanted to defend her mother's honor. Everything in her wanted to turn around and go for round two. There was no reason for her to speak ill of a dead woman. Instead of retaliation, she held in the anger and kept marching. Once the adrenaline wore off, the pain started. It was both physical and mental.

A million thoughts roamed through her head. The most important one now was to find someplace safe to rest her head and think. The only place she knew was the diner that stayed opened twenty-four hours. There she could clean up her face and devise a new plan.

By the way people stared at her, she knew her face, and her hair, looked a mess. Amina quickly entered the diner and headed to the bathroom. Even as swiftly as she moved, eyes of concern and confusion followed her. Amina knew she couldn't stay long.

Yeah, she looked unkempt and quickly fixed herself up as best she could. The swelling and beginnings of a black eye were already starting. Her nose was not broken, but there was dried blood caked inside of her nostrils. She could only imagine the bruises forming on her unexposed body parts.

What she needed was a First-Aid kit. Once she cleaned up, she exited the bathroom and then headed out the door of the diner. Amina kept her head down, hoping no one could identify her.

Next, she stared at her cell phone. If she and BC were still together, she would call him. Should she? After fifteen minutes of uncertainty, she pushed her pride aside and called. He did not answer. She waited an additional fifteen minutes and called back but nothing. Seeing that her standing at the end of the parking lot was bringing unwanted attention, she quickly started to move again. There were homeless shelters. Then she thought about Kalifa but did not want to intrude on her knowing her family situation.

The afternoon was quickly dissipating, and the sky darkened. It was probably unsafe to wander alone at night, but she was desperate. Keeping her head down, she lumbered through, quickly making her way to into Walmart. At some point, a banging headache started, so she grabbed some ibuprofen and then a First-Aid kit. Thank God she had her emergency money with her.

Resentment was settling in. Her aunt had no right to attack her. How could BC be so cruel as to hurt her the way he did? What had she done to God for him to send this storm her way? He had her mother and her brothers; why take more? Why make her suffer?

Just as quickly as the pessimistic thoughts entered, Amina dismissed them. It was not right to be upset with God. He had not betrayed her. Her father betrayed her by choosing alcohol over family. Her ex-boyfriend betrayed her for seeking flesh over faith.

Amina was almost desperate enough to call BC's grandmother, but Ms. Mary did not drive after dark, and it was after eight, much too late for her to drive that deuce and a quarter. Sighing in defeat, she headed to the snack aisle. Then she just stopped. The full weight of what had just transpired hit her, and it hit her hard.

She was alone.

A piece of her was scared. Unshed tears outlined her eyes like liquid eyeliner. Exhaustion nipped at her like frostbite. There was no way she and Adeya could ever live together. Not anymore. Tonight, was the conclusion to their testy relationship. Her aunt despised her on a level that Amina could not comprehend or change.

Worst of all, Amina allowed Adeya to make her react in violence. That was something her mother hated. Amina allowed Adeya's words to turn her into someone she was not. It was stupid and careless. Her hands were created to pray, to play music, and to heal. That was what her mother taught her.

She should have just walked away; she always had before. For some reason, her feet refused to retreat. All those years of being called pitch, slut, ugly, stupid, midnight, and disrespecting her dead mother was too much.

"Ms. Amina," a soft voice called.

Amina was so in-tuned to her inner conversation and dread that she barely heard the little voice. Cautiously, she turned, and her eyes went high then fell low. She looked at the small girl before her and a smile fought to make an appearance. Her small arms were wrapped around a unicorn pillow.

It was Hasina Goode. Amina had no idea what the sweet child was doing out after eight o'clock at night. The diminutive, quiet beauty was dressed like Princess Tiana. Her gorgeous curls danced down her back; her big, starlit eyes scanned Amina. A sad expression covered her face. Instantly feeling insecure, Amina wanted to cover herself and run. That was not an option. Besides, there was no one with Hasina, which was odd. She would not leave the child alone.

Fearlessly, Hasina took a step closer and then stopped short as she analyzed Amina's face. "You're hurt." she concluded. Those brilliantly bright orbs darkened in anxiety.

That was a correct assessment. Amina managed to nod as that was all the energy she could spare. The fight had left her some time ago. The remorse and guilt were kicking in now. "Hasina, what did I tell you about leaving me?" a deep tenor voice penetrated the silence, awakening Amina from her frozen state.

"Whom are you speaking with?"

"Uncle Ko, it's Ms. Mina my piano teacher."

His dark russet eyes turned from his niece and fully concentrated on Amina. His face went from curious to acknowledging who she was. "Are you okay?" There was so much genuine concern in his voice that it sounded like a melody to her.

The Goode brothers had that kind of effect on people. Maybe because they were well traveled. They were also well-mannered. It was almost distracting.

Amina quickly overcame the moment as her heart rate increased and her breathing became labored. She needed to retreat, but again her feet betrayed her. With haunted eyes, she watched him observe her. There was no expression of judgment on his face, but she wondered what he was thinking. Probably that he did not want a woman like her being near his niece. Would she lose her job at the center? Would Mrs. Goode still want her to be Hasina's nanny?

There were some members of the church who turned their nose up at her because of the actions of her parents. The Goode family had never acted that way toward her. Especially their mother; she was nothing but kindness and love.

Amina was still in awe that she was hired for the music

SYMPHONY OF GOODE LOVE

position in the first place. She loved music and she was exceptionally talented, but still, it was a shock and an honor. Mainly, she kept to herself and tried not to bother anyone, particularly after her father's arrest. This was probably the longest interaction she had with Kondo ever. Well, that was not true; she had taken a few of his self-defense classes, but nothing since the year that she was trying to free her father.

"Are you okay?" he asked again, this time taking unhurried steps toward her.

Amina attempted to open her mouth to reply, but only tears fell. The feeling of helplessness and defeat overtook her, and she released it.

"You're in good hands, okay? Don't cry, Amina," Kondo comforted; his voice was soft and soothing, almost like a lullaby.

"Do you remember me? I'm Kondo Goode. I help teach the self-defense classes sometimes at the Goode Community Center. This year has been difficult for you, so we haven't seen you as much. I know you're probably more comfortable with my brother JD. You're always so quiet," he concluded. The latter seemed to be him musing more to himself than addressing her.

That was true. Amina kept her distance especially after her father's drunk driving killed a man. However, Jotham was a people person and would not allow anyone to feel left out. It was the pastor in him. Amina was aware of Kondo. He and his brothers were Carolina royalty. All four of the brothers were built like Kushite warriors—tall, sculptured, and dapper with smooth, sienna skin, except for Jotham who was a lighter shade. If that weren't enough, they were extremely intelligent. All of them had graduated from the prestigious HBCU Morehouse College as undergraduates and then attended Ivy League institutions for graduate or professional studies. Their parents always shared their accomplishments as each of them excelled in their chosen careers.

Amina was in awe of the way each brother carried himself. It was to be expected since their parents were genuinely caring God-fearing people. From what she could tell, they were outstandingly gifted, respectful, and well-mannered men.

Amina nodded her head that she knew him. It was not that she was afraid of him; the children at the center adored him. It was just that she was depleted. One part of her wanted to fall into his arms and just weep. Yet, she did not know him well enough to breakdown like that, and secondly, that kind of reaction was not her. At least it used to not be her. So much had happened in the last year, and the past few weeks had her on an emotional overload.

Every tear that fell felt like treachery. She was displaying weakness and neediness, neither of which she liked to do in public. Weakness was not an option for her. The only family she ever had used her vulnerability against her. Now was not the time to be fragile.

Her puffy eyes followed the path that Kondo traveled. As he got closer, he examined her. It was as if they were the only people in the store. There was a focused determination in his glare. Letting herself relax, she allowed him into her personal space. If she remembered correctly, he was a pediatrician, or he was almost one.

It seemed her brain was currently offline. What Amina did note was that Kondo looked a lot like his older brother Reth. They had the same russet eyes and comforting aura about them. From the tender age of ten, she had a crush on Reth Goode, but he was far out of her league then and she was too young for him. Kondo was darn near his twin. Except he did not make butterflies erupt in her stomach. Even BC didn't give her butterflies. God had a great sense of humor.

"Amina, Hasina and I are going to take you home."

Bringing herself back to the conversation, she shook her head. "No. I can't go back," she mumbled. There was no way she could return with her aunt's behavior.

Seeming to interpret her dilemma, he nodded. That focused determination was back in his eyes. Amina's heart constricted a little less. The slight nod of his head let her know he would assist her, and she let him.

Amina followed quietly as Hasina held her hand and they finished their shopping. While wading through the store, some people stared at them and Amina prayed they did not think Kondo harmed her.

When they finally made it to self-checkout, Kondo insisted on purchasing her items. Exhausted from the happenings of the day, she easily relented to his request.

Once they got to his Range Rover Velar, Amina mentally started to drift. Her mind replaying the past week's events as if they were happening in real time.

"Amina," Kondo called out, snapping her out of her reverie. Her amber eyes barely met his, but it was enough for him to continue to speak. "I called my mama to let her know I was bringing you home. She's not at the house right now, but she will be. I don't know who attacked you, but I know you and my mama are close. Maybe you'll feel more comfortable talking to her."

"I'm sorry. I didn't mean to be an inconvenience," Amina finally mumbled. She was drowning in humiliation. Her mind wondered what he was thinking. The entire church knew about her mother's affair. Her father came to the church during the second service and removed her, but not before cursing the entire congregation. It was disgracing behavior.

It was that shame that kept her mute since Kondo assisted her in getting into his SUV. Even years later, there were still members who looked at her with disdain or pity.

"You're fine, sweetheart. I'm happy to help."

Kondo had called her sweetheart twice; sincere

endearments like that had been withheld from her since her mother's death. For some reason, it made her sad all over again. Doing her best not to show the pain, Amina offered a slight grin. He was genuine. His treatment of her was humbling. Her own family did not even care, but he was a virtual stranger, offering her assistance.

Resting her sore head on the seat, she hummed a tune. The music notes swirling in her head were dying to get out. She needed her music paper so she could write them all down. It would be the only way to rest her tired, torn mind.

Chapter 8

Sleep descended upon Amina with a vengeance. Her body was well at rest as if it unconsciously knew that she was safe. The humming of a bird finally woke her from her deep, dreamless slumber. Cautiously, her amber eyes scanned the room. This was not her bedroom and she was not at home. Aching pains surge through her body as she became fully awake. It was a blessing that she was able to rest. Then again, there was a different aura about this home.

The tug of resentment did not linger here. Hurt and agony did not paint these walls. Love was here. It was as strong as the scent of the Lewis Ginter Botanical Gardens in Richmond Virginia. The last vacation she took with her mother was there.

Inhaling deeply, the scent of lavender enveloped her. There was no scent of alcohol, no sea of half-empty bottles, no shouting, or threats from her aunt. For a moment, just a moment, she got a glimpse of her past when her mother was alive. It sent shivers down her spine. It was hard to believe that she was happy once, that she had a family and that at one time she was loved.

Death stole that all away and mocked her hungry heart. Death practically made her an orphan. However, Amina was an adult now and it was time to let the past go, except the past was the present. It loitered in her unhealed wounds. It mocked her image whenever she looked in the mirror; it was the shadow that always followed.

Shaking the feelings of self-pity, Amina allowed herself to take in her surroundings. Replaying the events of the previous night, she could not recall how she had arrived in the bedroom. She could only presume that Kondo brought her here.

Just that quickly, her mind began to wonder what Dr. Goode and his wife must have thought about her intrusion upon their home. They were not judgmental; they were kind people who welcomed her into their home countless times before. It was never like this. Most of those times, she was babysitting, not invading their home because she was kicked out of her own.

Tilting her head to the left, her eyes landed at the opposite end of the queen size bed. There was a purple towel and washcloth, Dove soap, Colgate toothpaste, and a toothbrush, as well as a change of clothing. By the looks of things, it was either nighttime or early morning. Though it felt like she had been sleeping for days, it was probably only mere hours.

Easing off the bed, Amina's size eight feet rested on the wooden floor. The coolness tickled her bare feet. With careful efficiency, she collected the items and entered the bathroom to bathe her battered body.

Turning on the lights she nearly had an attack at how horrible her face looked. It was swollen and she had a black eye; her lips were swollen too. They were large by nature but inflated thanks to her aunt and her aunt's friend. Careful of her bruises, Amina peeled off her clothes and gasped at the sight. Though her skin was dark, some of the bruising was visible.

A feeling of fear overtook her, and she dropped her head. Doing her best not to fall prey to negativity, she mumbled a prayer. As she finished, a song hit her, "The Breakup Song", by Francesca Battistelli. She hummed the lyrics before she entered the shower. Each word made her feel a little bit stronger. Just as the song said, *Fear you don't own me.*

She stayed in the shower until the water turned cold before she finally got out, dried off, and dressed. When she entered the bedroom again, she searched for her personal belongings and wondered if BC had even called her back. They were over, but after all their years together, would he not care a little about her?

Finding her phone, she picked it up and saw nothing. It was an indication of how lonely and an outcast she really was. Making friends was extremely difficult, especially now that her father was considered a murderer. Mostly, she did not trust a lot of people. The last year of her life had been lonely and full of judgment and fear. Life taught her to be cautious.

It was early morning, and she needed to come up with a plan. As she got lost in her thoughts, there was a knock on the door.

Dropping her phone, she quickly went to open the door. There stood Eleora Goode; her radiant smile was contagious. Even though Amina wanted to hide, she offered a soft smile of her own. Then. she dropped her eyes.

Mrs. Goode's robe was wrapped securely around her toned body. She was a gorgeous woman. Her beautiful skin was ageless and the color of deep mahogany. She had soft, vivid eyes. Her features were a showcase of her homeland, Kinshasa, the capital of the Democratic Republic of the Congo. Eleora was proud of her heritage and shared her story of falling in love with an African American missionary, Dr. Chiram Goode. However, back then, he was a struggling graduate student doing mission work. Amina always loved hearing their love story.

Nothing about Mrs. Goode was pretentious or fake. She was sincere and truly a lover of the Lord. She had a godly presence. It gave Amina hope. Eleora inhaled deeply before entering the bedroom and pulling Amina into a motherly embrace. Like a needy child, she fell into the arms of a woman who knew more about her than any other living person. It was not because she confessed anything; it was because Eleora paid attention.

Maybe that was the gift that God gave her because Mrs. Goode, always knew. Amina always hid her true feelings unless she were playing or writing music. That was the only time that she was vulnerable.

"Oh, my dear. When Kondo brought you home, I wasn't here. I was just leaving from visiting some of the church members with Chiram. I want you to know that you're safe here. When I came earlier, you were sound asleep, and I hadn't the heart to wake you. Now, tell me; who hurt you? No one hurts my little Song Thrush."

Amina did not want the embrace to end. She had not had a mother's hug in so long that she forgot how it felt to be held. Today of all days, the anniversary of losing her...it was all overwhelming. Taking a moment to control herself, she gently removed her body from Eleora's embrace.

Exhaling, Amina brought herself to her full height and did her best to be strong. It would take all her strength to share what had occurred in her home. "You have some insight into my home situation. My aunt and I had a disagreement that led to a violent altercation. Normally, I wouldn't fight back; I would just walk away. However, she hit the right nerve and I fought her back. Then her friend jumped in, so it was two against one. She told me not to come back home, that everyone was better off without me."

Eleora shook her head. Multiple expressions crossed her face like a mood ring, and Amina was sure Eleora was upset on her behalf. "That can't and won't happen again. You'll stay here, simple as that."

That was a sweet offer, but Amina knew she could not do that. "I can't accept that, Mrs. Goode. Adeya will tell my father that I started it and upset him while he's doing his time. Besides, today is the anniversary of my mother and brothers' death."

Eleora's face seemed pained by Amina's words. "That slipped my mind. I know that the loss of your mother and brothers is a pain you still feel deeply. I'm here for you, for whatever you need. As I said, you'll stay here."

Amina was about to reject the offer again, but Eleora hushed her. "Later in the morning we'll talk more. Now you need your rest." Once the words left her mouth, she leaned over and placed a sweet kiss on Amina's forehead. "I love you, sweetheart."

Then she exited the room, leaving Amina to her thoughts. Instead of allowing worry to overtake her, she simply prayed herself back to sleep.

When morning came, Amina sat on the bed for a moment as she thought about the state of her life. Feeling somewhat down about her circumstances, she reached for her cell phone with the premise of reading her Bible app. However, she quickly saw she had a missed a call from BC. Just one, though, and he did not even leave a voicemail or text message.

It stung a little. It almost felt like another rejection. It was time for her to admit that they were done. There was no need to go back because he was not good for her. At least that was what she was trying to convince herself, though deep down it scarred her. Add that to her missing her mother and the day was just quickly becoming a repeat of the day before.

Biting the inside of her jaw, she tried to ease the pain. Yesterday was horrible but Amina believed that better days were ahead. Graduation was a few months away. That needed to be her focus, to finish strong and enjoy summer break.

She knew her mother would be so proud of her. Kenise was the best mother any child could have. It was her mother who created her love for music. No matter what Adeya said, her mother was a good woman.

At that innocent thought, a smile graced my face. Smiles did not come often. Throughout her childhood, she smiled and laughed all the time. She and her mother were always singing and playing instruments. Then her mother told her a secret. The secret was Kenise was pregnant with twins, and she was going to name them Zion Kingston and Kingston Zion. She really did love Lauryn Hill. Even Amina's middle name was Lauryn.

When her mother first shared that news, her eyes brightened like the sun and then slowly those beautiful eyes began to dim. If Amina had been paying attention, she would have noticed that the dimming had started long ago.

Her parents' relationship was deteriorating without her knowledge. At her adolescent age, she did not notice the slow fade between her mother and father. She did notice, however, that her father hit her mother, the increased arguments, and the additional meddling of her aunt. At the time, it made no sense to her. Amina was protected and loved by a wonderful mother until one day, she was gone. Zion and Kingston were gone. Her safety and protection were gone.

Death came in uninvited, but by that time her parents were breaking up, and the family was separating, Amina and her brothers were tossed into the middle until the truth was revealed.

A terrible car accident revealed the secrets her mother had hidden. Kenise was with her lover Gavin. They were coming back from the courthouse. They had officially gotten married. Apparently, her parents were never married, all unknown to Amina. The reason she was not with them was because she had a music lesson. Gavin said they were on their way to get her and start a new life. They never made it to Amina. Their new life ended before it could ever begin.

The family was run off the road, and her mother died instantly. The boys held on a few hours, long enough for Amina to kiss them goodbye and tell them she loved them one last time. Aaron wanted the medical staff to keep the boys on life support, but it was not his decision to make. It was Gavin's as he was their biological father. Aaron did not know that— until that day. It was ugly. It had been ugly ever since.

The way Aaron and Gavin carried on was embarrassing. It was something she wish to forget. It troubled her terribly, and it shamed her. All her father said was that her mother was a woman of the streets. He declared that Amina would never be the sinner her mother was.

Then he turned to alcohol full time, leaving her to care for herself before her abusive aunt moved into their home. Adeya's arrival only worsened the issues. Her presence was a trigger for her father and hell on earth for Amina. Now, with just a few months until she graduated, she was excited about her future.

Guilt and fear had been her compass and her reasoning for staying so long. Guilt that she knew something was different about her mother. Guilt that she liked Gavin when he was around because he was peaceful and fun. Fear because once Aaron was released, he would start drinking all over again. He was all she had, but no matter what she said or did, the alcohol was stronger.

Aaron was still livid with her mother. She favored her mother except her skin was darker, much darker. Amina shook; she always had these thoughts on the anniversary of the death of her brothers, and mother. Nothing she did seemed to shake the morose thoughts.

Clearing the memory, her eyes sought out the digital clock to see what time it was. She didn't have class until noon. Sighing, she quickly got out of bed, made it up, and went into the bathroom to clean herself up. If she hurried, she could visit her mother and brothers' grave.

Half an hour later, Amina headed to the breakfast nook. As she got closer to the entrance, she stopped short as she heard the most riveting vocal cadence. It overtook her body like warm honey.

That voice was rich and decadent, hypnotic and melodious with just an edge of an accent. It was alluring. If voices could be paintings, his would be a masterpiece to rival all masterpieces. She wanted to bathe in the vibration of his intonation. Amina could compose an entire symphony around the humming of his timbre. The only person to have that impact on her was Reth Goode.

Dread consumed Amina as she did not want to encounter him, especially in her current state. When she saw him a few weeks back, he seemed not to notice her. There was no way he could ignore how ugly she was now.

Insane. It should not matter what a married man thought of her. She was going to have to pray and repent. This was not the way to conduct herself. Even knowing that, and knowing she was of no importance to Reth, he was the muse to her first love song, the main character in her adolescent dreams. That was wrong to think of him like that, yet she could not stop.

He had an elegant wife that looked nothing like her. Amal Goode had flowing, long, fine hair and perfect light skin. Amina watched her from a distance and attempted to mimic her style and grace, but she was a horrible imitation of the real deal.

"Mama, Baba, Delilah St. John is going to drive me mad. Amal has been sick for a long time, but Delilah was out and about gallivanting to exotic places, uncaring. Now, she wants to be mother of the year and come into my home with her bossiness. That is only upsetting Amal and disrupting my household. My wife needs all the rest and relaxation she can have during this time. I can't deal with her busybody mother."

Amina froze. There was no way she was supposed to be hearing this. It was not her place and she did not want to eavesdrop. She attempted to silently back away but quickly bounced off a brick wall. Without permission, she let out a yelp at the sight of Kondo. He let out a hearty laugh but then apologized once he saw how he'd frightened her.

"Kondo, baby, is that you?" Mrs. Goode's accented voice inquired.

"Yes, Mama, and I have Amina with me," Kondo added and escorted her into the breakfast nook. When she saw that not only Reth was present but also his brother JD, she wanted to melt into the floor. Their stunning eyes quickly assessed her, and she was instantly ashamed. JD's light skin turned beet red, and his normally calm preacher demeanor was overtaken by anger and a frown. It seemed that neither Mrs. Goode nor Kondo had shared what had happened to her.

Amina's head instantly dropped to shield the bruises on her face. Out of all the brothers, JD was the easiest to converse with. He had always shown her respect and treated her well. It burned in her what he might be thinking at the sight of her now.

"Amina, what happened? Did BC do this?" He sat his coffee cup down and quickly hurried her way. There was urgency in his strides, his anger being replaced with concern.

It shocked her that he was aware of who she was dating—no, used to date. Then again, it probably shouldn't have. He was just as observant as his mother. He had witnessed BC picking her and Benito up from the center on occasion. "I, um, it was —"

Sensing her distress, Mrs. Goode quickly came to her defense. "Son let her be. She'll share when she's ready. For now, just know that she'll be staying here for now."

Clearly unbothered, JD was on a mission to get an answer to his question. "Did BC do this or not? That's all I'm asking," JD continued as he scanned her body.

"No."

Out of the corner of her eye, she saw Kondo. "She's good, JD. I checked her out last night. There is nothing broken; they are more surface bruises. There's no internal bleeding. I gave her something for the pain, and then she went to sleep."

Amina stood unmoving as the two brothers discussed her as if she were not present.

JD seemed appeased by his brother's words then returned to his spot and lifted his coffee cup. Still, there was a look of displeasure and worry on his face.

Chiram Goode offered Amina a fatherly smirk and a wink. His sons got their height from him. Chiram was seriously fit and handsome for his age. There were just the beginnings of gray hair around his edges, but it gave him a more refined look. He really looked more like an older brother than the father of four adult sons.

"Sons, let us give your mother and Amina some private time."

The brothers all took turns kissing their mother. They acknowledged Amina as they departed, and she quickly took the proffered chair Mrs. Goode pointed at.

"Good morning," Amina offered, not sure what to say or do. Embarrassment was erupting from her like an active volcano. Having that much attention on her was unnerving.

"Good morning, my little Song Thrush. Would you like something to eat or drink?"

Amina grinned at the endearment Mrs. Goode had bestowed upon her the first time she heard Amina sing. "No, ma'am. I was just coming to tell you I was going to my family's gravesite." Amina licked her lips before adding, "I apologize for interrupting the private moment you were having with your family. I attempted to leave, but I ran into Kondo. I didn't hear much, but you have my word I'll not repeat anything. Also, before I leave, I knew you said you needed to speak with me."

A sweet calmness overtook Eleora's features. "My dear, you didn't interrupt anything. I apologize for keeping you from visiting your family." Eleora paused before continuing. "Have you thought any more about what I asked you about?"

Amina blushed as she recalled Eleora asking her to become Hasina's live-in nanny. It would be an answered prayer after the falling out she had with her aunt and after breaking up with BC.

"I'd love to accept, but do you think Reth, and Amal would approve of me? I mean, after what occurred between with my aunt and my father's incarceration. I just thought you know; you'd rescind the offer. Surely, I made the worse impression with my appearance. Your son must think horribly of me and my family."

Eleora shook her head no as the words bled from Amina's lips. "No, dear, of course not. We would love to have you here; well, you'd moved into Reth's estate. Thank you for accepting. Please don't accept just because of this current situation. If you don't want the position, nothing will change. You're still welcome here as long as you need."

Amina nodded. "I've prayed about it. I want the position."

Eleora smiled graciously and then sweetly patted Amina's hand. "It's decided then. Later, I'll arrange for you to meet with Amal."

Amina nodded in agreement. Then, she offered Eleora a hug.

"Amina, dear, I know you don't have a car and the bus doesn't operate this far out. I can have one of the boys take you to the gravesite and then to school."

Amina nodded. It was too much kindness, but she appreciated it. Normally, BC would take her, but that was no longer an option. "Thank you."

∞ ∞ ∞

Reth rested his throbbing head on the leather couch in his father's study. His other two brothers sat beside him. They were missing Djimon, but he was flying home soon. Reth would feel whole when his brother was home.

Closing his eyes for a moment, Reth released a heavy breath. There was so much on his mind that he just needed a moment. The peace he sought could only be found in his family home. Jotham patted his leg, causing Reth's eyes to flicker open. Sleep had been nonexistent for the past six months when he had to accept defeat. He kept that to himself; there was enough to worry about, and he would not bother his family with his sleepless nights.

"Reth?"

Jotham saying his name sounded like a question and a statement. Jotham had this sixth sense of knowing what a person was feeling without asking a question. Their father said that was one of his spiritual gifts.

"I'm good, JD." That was a lie, but he did not have the energy to share the truth; instead, he changed the subject. "So, what was that in the kitchen? Is it one of the girls you're helping from your street ministry?"

Jotham frowned and slitted his eyes at Reth. His reaction caused Reth to sit up from the couch, an apology on the tip of his tongue. From his brother's reaction, he must have offended him.

"You don't remember her?" Jotham queried.

"No, am I supposed to know who she is? Since everything with Amal, I can't remember anyone. I barely make it to church."

"That's Amina Williams. She teaches music at the center and gives Hasina private lessons. She's babysat your daughter in the past. That's Mama's Song Thrush."

Reth shook his head. He really was out of his mind; how could he forget that? "Wait, she's the one Mama wants to be Hasina's live-in nanny? It just didn't click when she entered the kitchen. With all that swelling, I didn't recognize her."

"She's okay physically. Now, mentally, and spiritually, that's JD's expertise. From what I can tell, she's a good woman. She's just in a bad situation. When I told her that I would take her home, she almost had a breakdown," Kondo recalled.

Reth nodded, the family had a lot going on, and he was unsure if adding another person's drama was the correct move. "I wonder who hurt her. If it's something street-related, we don't need that at the center, and I surely don't want it around my daughter."

Chiram cleared his throat and shook his head, causing Reth look his way. "Baba, what is it?"

"Amina's been through a lot, and I want to stop the speculating and tell you all what happened. Normally, I would agree with your mother and let Amina tell her own story, but since I'm sure she'll be Hasina's nanny, I'll share. It stays between us, but you can tell Djimon," he replied sternly as he sat up in his chair.

"Firstly, her father was recently convicted of felony vehicular manslaughter. He was sentenced to four years, though I think they'll give him credit for the year he served. The young man, Jose Hernandez, died when Aaron hit him. Yesterday, Amina was attacked by her aunt and her aunt's friend. They jumped her because they didn't want her playing her Christian radio and making her aunt's friends uncomfortable. I had no idea of the abuse she suffered. She's hidden it so well. Still somehow, she's graduating from college and has gotten into a doctoral program. God is preparing her for something great," Chiram shared as he leaned back in his chair and continued.

"A few years ago, her mother and twin brothers were killed in a road rage accident. They never found the person who did it. Though she loves her father, she had a close relationship with Gavin, her mother's new husband, and she lost him too. He left North Carolina after the funeral. He wanted to take Amina with him, but since he was not her biological father, he had no case." Chiram shook his head. "Gavin did request that your mother and I keep an eye on her, which we were doing anyway. Amina has a special place in your mother's heart. Amina's a fighter, and she'll be great for Hasina. That young woman has never been in the streets or around the wrong people. That has never been Amina, so don't be so quick to judge, son. She did not create her circumstances, but she's doing her best to survive them."

Reth's eyes widened in shame for his assumption of her and in pain for her loss. Now, he remembered exactly who Amina was. The girl could sing like no one he had ever heard. Even as a child, her voice was beguiling; she had the prettiest smile and most electric amber eyes. She was painfully shy after the death of her mother. It was as if she retreated into herself.

Then she vanished after her father verbally assaulted the entire church. He had not realized that she came back to the church or that she was his child's music teacher. That was just how out of touch he was.

"Amina's father Aaron holds disdain towards the church because he felt it was the church's fault that he lost his family. When the dust finally settled, Aaron wasn't the father of the boys but Gavin. Kenise was never Aaron's wife; they just shared the same last name. Everyone only assumed they were married. That caused an uproar throughout the congregation. Kenise married Gavin; they were in a car accident after. The gossips said it was because of their sin. For a while, the church was divided. I remember," he spoke softly, mostly to himself, as the memories unfolded. That young woman had suffered through great trials, and from the looks of it, she was still suffering.

"It's really scary the way you accurately recall stuff," Kondo replied.

That was a blessing and a curse. "It's good for a judge to remember details. Since Amal has fallen ill, I can honestly say, my recollection has been weak. I didn't even remember the poor girl existed, and she's been an active part of my daughter's life." Then he turned JD. "You seemed really bothered when you thought BC hurt her. Who is he?"

"Well, he used to be a standout soccer player. Everyone thought he was going into the MLS, but he got injured his freshmen year of college. Then from what I've witnessed, he's gotten into the wrong crowd. He's been associated with QCB, also known as the Queen City Boys, but Amina has no clue. He's living a double life. The only reason I know is because of the street ministry that I do."

Reth exhaled. He was not sure what to make of this new information. He knew about the QCB, as he was good friends with the Charlotte District Attorney. He was aware of how dangerous this gang was. Although, he did not know a lot about Amina, he did not want her caught up in a bad situation. That was something he and his brothers had in common, to save those in need. He just prayed that having her as his nanny would not come back and bite him.

Chapter 9

Amina sat nervously in Reth's Jeep Grand Cherokee Trackhawk. Her body molded into the leather seats. When Eleora offered one of her sons to drive her to the gravesite, Amina assumed it would be JD or Kondo, but not Reth. His presence just made her nervous, which was why she kept wiping her sweaty palms on her ripped jeans.

When he asked her if she was ready to go, she scrambled back and forth like a confused squirrel. He had to think that she was all kinds of ridiculous and remedial. Somehow, she managed compose herself and made it to his SUV. By the grace of God, she did not fall on her face, but she kept her head down, mainly, too embarrassed to make direct eye contact with him.

"Are you okay?" Reth asked after moments of silence.

"I'm fine," she muffled.

He nodded, but she could tell that he did not believe her. The response she gave him was standard; it was the expected reply. People always asked, 'how are you', or 'are you okay', but rarely did they care. Besides, it seemed Reth had his own issues to deal with, and she would not add hers to his heavy load.

"My mother said you've accepted the nanny position. It seems that you and Hasina have a great relationship."

Amina lifted her head up but kept her eyes down. For some reason, she did not want to see what his eyes saw when viewing her. Fearing his rejection, she thought of him disapproving of his daughter being in her care was too much.

"Yes, sir, we do."

He laughed. "I'm not so old that you need to call me sir, but I appreciate the show of respect."

She wanted to smack herself in the head. He was older than her but not that much. "I'm sorry. I meant, Mr. Goode, or should I say Your Honor?" Amina quickly amended.

Reth released a light chuckle then added, "It's okay to call me Reth. Your Honor is only required when in court, and I don't think you'll ever have a reason to be in my court."

"Right. Okay." The words came rushing out as she started twiddling with her fingers. No matter how she mentally told herself to chill, she could not.

"Amina, take a deep breath, relax. It's okay. I know you've been through an ordeal. I'm only attempting to make conversation. I didn't mean to cause you stress."

"You didn't."

Again, he nodded, though he seemed skeptical of her response. "So, tell me about you and my daughter."

At that, she lit up. Benito and Hasina were the light in the darkness; if she could keep her mind focused on the positive aspects of life, maybe she could start healing. "I love Hasina. She and Benito are my most favorite young people. It makes my heart smile when I hear her play the piano. She's a little timid, kind of like me, but when she plays the piano, it awakens her spirit. I can see the confidence in her little body as her fingers take command of the keys. She is also remarkable with the harp.

I make sure that each child learns a string instrument. I thought she would have chosen the viola, but she wanted to play the harp. We started out on the mini harp and then she said, 'Ms. Amina, I want to play the big one'. She owned it. The way her eyes shimmer when she learns a new piece, oh, it does something to my soul. Your daughter has musical gifts, and I pray that God helps me to unlock all of them."

Feeling his gaze upon her, Amina finally glanced up and saw his russet eyes glowing. There was love and a bit of pride in his eyes. It was clear that he adored his daughter and was proud of her. It made Amina wonder if her father had ever looked that way when someone praised her. Probably not, her father stopped seeing her many years ago.

"You think highly of my little princess. I'm glad she has such a great relationship with you."

Embarrassed by her reaction, Amina did not reply, choosing instead to stare out the window. They both fell into a comfortable silence until Reth turned up the radio. He had his iPhone plugged into the Bluetooth. Most of his playlist had been jazz, which she liked as well. However, she was not as familiar with the artist he was playing. Then the song "Give Me You" by Shana Wilson came on. That was her song; she loved the pureness of Shana's voice. This song was everything and one of her most favorite gospel tunes.

Forgetting time and place, Amina closed her eyes and allowed herself to drown in the lyrics. It spoke deeply to her spirit. She only meant to hum the tune, her mouth opened, and she lost all control. Amina belted out the song. She was crying out to God.

Singing was the only way she knew to cleanse her soul. Even when she was younger, she used to sing her prayers. Her mother thought it was the cutest thing ever. How she missed those innocent moments.

"Your voice is riveting," Reth's polished, velvety voice intoned. It brought her back to reality.

Her voice had nothing on his, but she kept that to herself. When Reth spoke, it was like witnessing life. The soulful cadence of his voice was almost spiritual. "Sorry."

"Don't ever apologize for sharing your talent. Truly, your voice is a blessing from God. They could use you in the choir. There's healing in your vocals."

Amina blushed deeply, but thanks to her coloring, he would never know. It made her feel priceless that he complimented her. Her inner teenager was bubbling over. She was a borderline fan girl.

Just as he was about to speak again, his cell phone began to ring. It was his wife. It felt as if a tall glass of ice-cold water had been dumped on her face. Shame hit her harder than an avalanche. It was beyond time for her to check her emotions. No longer was she an innocent child with a crush but an intelligent young woman who knew not to covet another woman's husband.

"Excuse me, it's my wife and I need to take this."

"No problem." Amina quickly pulled out her own cell phone and plugged in her earbuds and started to play her own playlist.

It was a short phone call Amina noticed, but he accelerated his speed getting her to the gravesite much faster than she thought he would.

"Thank you. I got it from here. I'll just catch the bus to school. I'll head to the center after that. I can hitch a ride with JD. Again, thank you. Take care, bye," Amina spilled out quickly and shut the door.

Reth watched until Amina was out of sight. What an odd interaction, he thought to himself. Still, he wanted to at least stay to make sure that she was okay, but his wife called him.

Apparently, her mother was working her nerves also. Delilah was a strange woman; well, really, she was simple, a busybody, and a gold-digger. And those were Amal's words not his. Something told him that her recent interest in her daughter had to do with money. God forgive him for thinking that way, but it felt as if she were waiting for Amal to die so she could collect. Unbeknownst to her, there was nothing to collect. Everything that Amal owned, the money from her deceased father, was going to Hasina. Their daughter was Amal's sole heir. Once Delilah found that out, Reth was sure she would disappear into the night, never to be seen again.

Sighing, he put the Jeep in reverse, prepared to drive off, but something told him to wait, so he did. Reth mentally noted to contact Jotham to ensure that Amina was okay. Something about her worried him. Somehow, in the short drive over here, she had wiggled her way into his mind. After what she suffered, it was easy to care about her. Memories of her attending church poured through his brain.

Reth wondered what was going through her head. Was there more happening at home than they knew? Maybe he was overthinking. When his brother said that she was dating a gang member, that really put him on alert. Amina did not seem the type. No, he did know her well, but she had to be caring and goodhearted to be so trusted by his parents. From what he saw, she was too good-natured and meek to associate with trouble. The entire ride she barely looked him in the eyes. At first it bothered him, but knowing that her aunt was abusive to her, the reaction she had toward him made sense.

Due to his tall, muscular frame and no-nonsense demeanor, he could come off as intimidating. He recalled the looks of sheer panic and confusion on her face when she found out that he was driving her. More than likely, she also did not trust easily.

Still, he could not see her dating a gangbanger. A woman

like her, he suspected, would end up dating someone like his brothers. Amina had a bookbag full of psychology and music books. She was quiet and studious. Nothing about her gave off wanting a bad boy.

From the way she sang, that girl had a vocal range to rival Whitney Houston or Yolanda Adams. He was a lover of music. Her voice was like a homeopathic remedy. The richness of it hit directly to the spirit and rooted into his soul. It touched him in ways he was not sure how to articulate. She was an intriguing young woman.

He smirked at her calling him sir, mister, and finally, Your Honor. He was probably no more than a decade older than her, but at least she had manners. It seemed to him that what she needed was a break, a friend, and safe place to process everything she'd recently endured. His family could offer all of that.

Reth looked out of his side mirror and thought about waiting for her until his cell went off again. This time, it was an incoming text from his wife. Letting out a groan, he sped off and headed home.

∞∞∞

Amina's fingers traced the impression of her mother's name on the flat headstone. Then she touched her bothers' pictures on their flat headstones. The twins shared a casket. That was the only thing that Gavin and Aaron agreed on.

"I miss you all so much. Honestly, things are getting worse with the family. Daddy's in prison, and Ade can't stop being cruel. I'm tired of being the dumpster for everyone else's trash." Amina let out a huff before continuing her monologue. "Adeya hit me; like, we got into a brawl. I'm sorry, Momma, but I had to defend myself. Please forgive me for allowing violence to take over. You know that Ade is a different kind of human." Amina paused for a moment before continuing.

"There's more. BC and I broke up. He finally did it, cheated on me or I finally found out. I don't know why I'm surprised. The girl is pretty too. She has light skin the color of butterscotch, nothing like my dark skin. I know you'd tell me that I'm stunning and that my skin is perfect. It's just that the only voice I hear now is Adeya calling me Pitch and midnight. It burns. She always says that I don't belong in the family. She swears Aaron isn't my daddy. Whatever.

"There is some good news. I've been offered a position as a nanny for the Goode family. You know them. They're good people and I'm honored they thought of me. It comes with benefits, so I accepted. I don't know how Daddy will feel about it, but I can't live my life based off the opinions of an absentee father. I want better for myself. I love you, and I love my brothers. Kiss them extra for me, please." She leaned back for a moment and closed her eyes to pray. Then she added, "I'll come back later." She blew three kisses in the sky, praying they reached her family. Then Amina stood up and cleaned herself off before turning to leave.

Feeling lighter, Amina made it about three feet before she halted her steps. Standing in her path was BC. He wore all black with a royal blue bandanna around his wrist. Straightening up her shoulders Amina pushed forward as if he were not present.

"Mami, don't be like that," he scolded as he reached out and pulled her back to him. He turned her around and froze. The frown on his face transformed into concern.

"Baby, who hurt you?" BC growled. He took his index finger and lifted her face as he examined the damage.

Amina yanked her face away. "Don't."

"What'chu mean *don't*? You better tell me something. Who touched you? Was it that dude that was in that Jeep? You letting dude put hands on you? I know you ain't messing around on me," he fumed.

"Stop. One, you and I aren't together. We broke up because you can't be faithful. Two, that's my new boss. I accepted a nanny position. Three, don't act like you care. We both know you don't. You were just using me for your brother, right?" Then she attempted to leave again, but he stopped her.

"Stop being mean; you know that's not you. Now, tell me who hurt you."

"Nobody, I gotta catch the bus to get to school."

"Amina Lauryn Williams, stop all that noise. I'm taking you to school, but you need to tell me what happened to you. You called me, and I called you back, but when you didn't answer, I figured you dialed by mistake. I knew what today was and I wanted to support you."

Groaning, she reluctantly told him what happened.

"Adeya, that old bum drunk, and her girl double-teamed you like that? Nah, I can get some girls to beat her up because don't nobody hurt my Mina baby."

Pressing her lips together to refute his claims, Amina rolled her eyes and lightly chuckled. "Nobody huh? Well, you hurt me, or did you forget?" His action was a lot worse than the bruises she was sporting.

He stared at her for a long time. Until it went from awkward to uncomfortable and a medley of emotions etched on his face, but Amina held his gaze.

Finally, he broke. "Man, you be tripping. You know I would never purposely hurt you. I told you I made a mistake. Like, you can't forgive your man for messing up. Well, whatever; come on so I can get you to school. You know you get right anal if you're late for a class. Then you'll be ticked off at me for that too."

He was right about her not liking to be late for school. Instead of fighting, she allowed him to take her to school.

Chapter 10

A week later, Reth stood waiting at Charlotte Douglas International Airport for his brother Djimon. Beside him were his other two younger brothers. They tagged along for the ride under the guise of wanting to keep him company. However, Reth knew it was more than that. His brothers were concerned about his physical wellbeing and mental state. Even before the incident with him not remembering Amina, they had been concerned. Now, with his mother-in-law hovering around like a vulture, it was taking a lot out of him mentally.

His entire family was concerned, which was why his mother demanded that he get a nanny for Hasina. Her premise for that was to ease some of the stress off him. He agreed, but now that only added to his worry. He had not spoken to Amina privately, but it was on his to-do list. They spoke briefly while he drove her to the cemetery, but it was not the deep conversation he needed to have.

Questions and concerns lingered in his head about Amina. Still, he would accept her because that was what his mother and wife wanted. He trusted their judgment. His daughter adored Amina. Also, Hasina had been practically living with his parents for the past few months. It was time to bring his daughter home full-time.

Reth knew his family viewed him as weaker; he viewed himself that way as well. The fierce older brother of the

Goode tribe finally came up against an opponent that he could not defeat. No matter how many accolades he received, being editor of the Yale Law Journal, a highly sought-after immigration attorney that was now one of the youngest immigration judges in Charlotte, he could not argue or prosecute cancer.

Cancer remained undefeated. It was beyond his legal expertise. Cancer. Six powerful letters were killing his wife, his friend. There was nothing he could do about it. For a man who was used to doing, it made him feel like less of a man to do nothing.

All his life he had been a protector, a fighter for what was right, an advocate for justice. He had done his best to be a great role model for his three younger brothers, but even he had his faults and shortcomings. Defeating death was one of them.

His mother counseled him to pray. God could change anything and take cancer away, but either his faith or prayers were weak. No prayer he prayed had stopped the aggressive and ruthless spread of the cancer.

Death, whether he wanted it or not, was coming. It did not care about the carnage it was leaving behind. It did not care that a daughter would grow up without her mother. It did not consider the physical and mental anguish that Amal had already suffered. Death did not care. It was relentless and suffocating.

That was why his brothers had become his shadow. They sensed that he was not himself and was the reason that Djimon was flying home from London. They worried about him. In the year that his wife had found out the cancer was back, Reth had declined too. He was not outwardly projecting his grief or his shortcomings. He could not. It felt wrong when his wife was the one suffering.

Amal Jamila Goode was in the final stages of life, and death hovered over her like a white-backed vulture patiently waiting to feast. It brought out an ugly side of him. At times, he was short-tempered and easily agitated. Grief was making him unpredictable and difficult to deal with. He knew this but was unable to control his emotions, mostly because he felt like he failed Amal.

His soul hurt.

His heart grieved.

Reth had been grieving for a long time, knowing that Amal was in pain and patiently waiting to die. No part of him could fathom what that was like, to know that death was imminent. It bothered him on a level that only God could comprehend. Yet, he denied God, was angry that God chose to take a mother from her daughter. It all was taking a toll on him.

Their home held the scent of decay, and if he stayed one more second, he would have lost his mind. That shamed him to his core.

How could he run from his dying wife? A wife he promised to protect.

Did that make him a bad person? Was he weak because it grieved his heart to see her broken?

It did; what husband thought that of his wife? Was it wrong that he needed a break? Those were the thoughts that constantly traveled in a loop in his mind.

"Reth, are you okay?" Kondo asked, concern laced in his speech.

That was a question everyone was asking him all the time. Reth turned his dark eyes to his brother's face that showed anxiety and sympathy. Kondo was the youngest of the four brothers and the most sensitive. He and Reth had a special bond.

Reth did not like being dishonest, but the truth was too much to put on his baby brother. It was not his brother's cross to bear. No, he was not okay. More than likely, he would never be. The family did not need to know that. They had no idea the secrets he was harboring. Secrets that were carving out his heart. He had learned to mask his emotions and tell people what they wanted to hear, not the truth. Today would be no different.

Reth turned to his baby brother, his mini me, except for his deep dual dimples. They shared the same sienna skin tone and dark russet eyes. Reth and his brothers were well built and over six feet tall, a trait they inherited from their father. Their dark curly hair was inherited from their mother. Reth kept his short; his brother Djimon often wore his in a man bun, while their baby brother Kondo wore his in two thick, long braids. People often mistook him to be of American Indian heritage. Jotham, the light bright as they teased him, was fair-skinned, and lightly freckled on his nose and just as tall but was more medium-built. He preferred a tapered curly Caesar haircut, and whereas they had dark hair, his was a light amber color. He favored their paternal aunt, Miriam.

Before more words could be spoken, Djimon's voice floated through the air. His brother's accent sounded like a passport. It was as if everywhere he traveled was stamped on his tongue. Djimon had spent the last four months in London for an engineering project he was managing. Now, he had somewhat of a British accent.

Reth could almost hear the church ladies swooning over his brother. They would probably say he sounded like Idris Elba. Allowing a little side smile, Reth's eyes glowed with emotion. He missed his brother, who was the second oldest. He always felt whole when they were all together. Together they were stronger, and though he would never tell them, he needed their strength.

His brother was dressed as debonair as ever in an Ozwald Boateng suit, probably fresh off the runway. Only Djimon would wear a suit while flying; the man loved his fashion.

Without hesitation, Djimon pulled Reth into a deep embrace before greeting him in the traditional Congo Brazza style shaking hands and then touching of the sides of their foreheads, first right than left. When he pulled away, a sympathetic smile graced his face. Then he greeted the other two brothers with the Congo Brazza greeting. Their mother did her best to instill their Kinshasa heritage into them. They all spoke French and Swahili in addition to English and Spanish.

"Are you well, brother?" Reth inquired as the foursome headed to the baggage claim. He rested his arm on his brother's shoulder. They were an affectionate bunch, something they inherited from their American-born father.

"I am. London treated me very well, especially the beautiful African and Jamaican women there," he smirked and wiggled his eyebrows.

"Always the women; you better not let Mama hear you say that," Kondo added as he gently bumped his brother.

Djimon nodded in agreement. "I'm glad to be home, but I hate it's under these circumstances."

Reth nodded in understanding. For just a few seconds there had been a reprieve from what was; at hearing the latter part of his brother's statement, a chill ran through him. It was real. Amal was dying and he could not save her this time. Lord knows she suffered enough; this should not be her ending.

One week had passed since Amina and Adeya had gotten into a physical altercation. The physical wounds were healing, but the mental wounds remained unhealed.

Since that time, she had not spoken to her aunt or father.

Amina planned on going back home to get the rest of her personal belongings. However, she feared what she would find once she returned. Her aunt was not the cleanest person; additionally, her aunt was petty. Who knew if she would have any personal belongings left to collect?

Letting out a huff, she removed the thoughts from her mind. Right now, her concern was meeting Amal. Amina was standing at Amal's hand carved door, mentally preparing herself to talk to a woman she had admired from a distance and wished to emulate. A part of her felt like a fraud. *Concentrate,* Amina whispered to herself as she quietly entered Amal's bedroom.

Silently Amina prayed to find Amal doing well. Eleora requested that the two talk; however, due to Amal's health, it was not possible until now. Frankly, that was a good thing because Amina's swelling had diminished, so she did not look as battered as before.

Today was supposed to be a better day for Amal, and Amina hoped the two would have a fulfilling conversation. A part of Amina felt guilty for even entering Amal's room simply because she spent too much time crushing on the woman's husband. The two had not spoken as much after Amina's father was sentenced, but Amal did send her a card and Bible verses. The woman was darn near a saint. Amina had no business being in her presence. That feeling of being a charlatan came back.

Daily Amina prayed to God to remove the feelings but to no avail.

"Mrs. Amal?" Amina whispered, her eyes scanning the bedroom. The room itself was beautiful: large windows, handsewn curtains, accented chairs, and wooden floors. Still, it looked more like an expensive private hospital room except for a king size bed. There was machinery, medications, a water pitcher, and a recliner.

Whatever ailment Mrs. Amal was suffering was indeed serious. Since Amina accepted the position, one of the documents she signed was a non-disclosure agreement. It was not as if she would share any information she only had Kalifa since she officially ended all communication with BC. He attempted to contact her again once he dropped her off at school, thinking they were getting back together. She quickly reminded him that was not happening. He called, but she blocked him.

"Amina?" The voice was soft and lyrical.

Calmness overtook Amina as she answered. "Yes, it's me. Do you need anything? Mrs. Eleora said you wanted to speak with me, but if you don't feel well, I can come back. You seem so worn out."

"No, now is as good a time as any."

Amina nodded and gaited closer to the bed; there was already a chair awaiting her. So, she sat down and lifted her amber eyes to Amal. She no longer resembled the woman that Amina was in awe and envy of. The woman Amina remembered floated with confidence and always had a ready smile. She had an angelic essence, like nothing bothered her, and Amina envied her ability to make it all seem so effortless. Now, she was so sick that it seemed every movement was a chore. Guilt assailed Amina for feeling jealous of Amal. Silently, she asked God to forgive her immaturity and heal Amal.

A gentle smile finally etched across Amal's face. Her eyes closed for a moment as if she were reliving a memory, and then she shared, "Hasina played the piano for me today. She said it was a piece that you two worked on together. She told me it was my song. It's beautiful. Hasina said it sounds better accompanied with the violin."

Amal's giddiness made Amina grin as well. "She's special. The way her little fingers command the piano keys are amazing to me. I told your husband that Hasina is one of my favorites. I absolutely adore your daughter. She's a blessing."

Amal lifted her pale right hand to her heart, and for a moment, life was restored as she grinned. There was no doubt that she was thinking about Hasina. "Amina, thank you. Hasina is more expressive after she's had a music lesson with you. She giggles, and she tells me all about it. I feel such happiness and joy when I'm with her..."

She paused for a moment, and Amina thought she needed something to drink. Just as she was about to offer, Amal started talking again. "I prayed to God that He would send someone her way. Like Eleora, I too wanted you to be in my daughter's life. I don't know how much you know because my husband is extremely private, but I have cancer. I'm dying. I won't see Hasina grow up. I'll miss all the important moments, but I want her to have a person in her life, a person like you to help her.

"You're probably thinking why you, but I remember you. It tortured my heart when your father took you from the church, but God has plans we don't all understand. I never forgot about you, and I prayed for you. Then you came back and worked with the children.

"The Sunday you sang "Potter" was the day I accepted my fate. I knew God spoke to me about you for a reason." Amal hesitated to catch her breath and then continued. "You've lost your mother and I know that you'll help my daughter, guide her through the grief of losing me. I believe in you, Amina. I've seen what you have not seen. There has always been a light in you. It didn't make sense all those years ago, but it started to when you helped me in church that day. It gets clearer by the day. I pray God continues to work in and through you. You have a gift. You are a gift. I know you no longer sing anymore, but your voice is so beautiful and pure. You have a voice that will change lives. Would you sing for me now?"

Amina started to tear up. Now, Amal was complimenting her and wanting her to sing. If she didn't feel bad enough already, she wanted to evaporate now. Would Amal feel the same way if she knew how long Amina crushed on Reth? Instead, she simply asked, "What song?"

"Tamela Mann's "Take Me To The King". It's a favorite of mine. I honestly love any of Tamela Mann's song. It's the song I want you to sing at my funeral."

At her admission, Amina felt her blood freeze and she choked up. It was one thing to sing it now, but at the funeral too? Amina should not even be there. She was not family; she was just the nanny. Forcing herself to relax, Amina placed her hand on top of Amal's and began to sing. Amina sang with all she had in her and was humbled by Amal's request.

"Thank you, Amina," Amal whispered, her tiny hand lifting to rest on her heart. She turned so that she was facing Amina. "God told me it was you that you would be the one for my daughter and for my husband." With that, she winked and then closed her eyes.

Fear instantly seized Amina because she thought Amal was dead. Amina quickly exited the seat and leaned over Amal, prepared to administer medical attention until she noticed the woman was breathing. With that confirmation, she let out her own breath, and what Amal said came back to her. *'God told me it was you, that you would be the one for my daughter and for my husband.'* What did that even mean? Shaking the thought, she placed a hand on top of Amal's and prayed over her.

Chapter 11

Amina sat quietly in the backseat of Jotham's Chevrolet Silverado 3500HD. They had loaded empty boxes for her to pack her belongings. The Goode family was being incredibly kind and helpful to her during her situation. Amal's words still plagued her.

The two had grown close in a short period, probably because Amina knew that Amal was dying, even though she did not want to accept that. Amina considered Amal a friend. Not only that, but Amal had become a confidant for her, and she for Amal. The two had not spoken about what she said. *'God told me it was you. That you would be the one for my daughter and for my husband.'* Although, it was something Amina couldn't shake. Maybe she was overthinking. All Amal probably meant was that she would be there to usher Hasina through the grief of losing her mother, and in that way also help Reth.

"Amina, are you feeling alright? Kondo and I won't let anything happened to you while you're getting your belongings."

Amina's head popped up, and she glanced at Jotham through the rearview mirror. He had misinterpreted her silence; it was not fear but confusion. It had nothing to do with Adeya. Instead of explaining, she simply offered a smile. "I'm fine."

"It's okay to be a little nervous about returning home," Jotham replied. There was sincerity in his voice and facial expression. JD was empathic and kind. It was refreshing to know men like that were still around.

Amina shook her head in agreement. Honestly, it was not going back home that had her nervous. It was what was happening afterward. Reth wanted to meet with her, and she had no idea what he wanted to discuss. Leaning her head back, Amina closed her eyes as she mentally prayed. However, she must have dozed off because she was awakened by Kondo talking.

"We're here," Kondo announced.

It took her a moment to acclimate to her surroundings, but once she did, Amina did her best to prepare the brothers for what was ahead. "I apologize beforehand. I'm the one who keeps the house clean, so I have no idea what you'll see when we get in there," Amina shared, surprising herself. Clearly, she had grown more comfortable around the Goode brothers because she spoke more around them than ever before. It seemed that the more she was around the family, the more she was able to express herself. Exhaling a nervous breath, she opened the back door and slid out of the truck.

"Don't worry about us, Mina," JD offered and followed her at a slower place, while Kondo looked around and then reached in the bed of the truck for the empty boxes.

Pulling out her key Amina opened the door and was attacked by a foul odor. It smelled like a mixture of sour mop, tuna fish, and spoiled milk. The smell was so potent that Amina wanted to close the door. The familiar feeling of shame covered her flesh. She could only imagine what the Goode brothers thought of her after witnessing and smelling the filth. It was bad enough that her father was in prison, and before that, her mother had an affair with a church member. Could she not just have one day where she did not have to feel abashed?

"It's okay, Amina. We're just going to get your stuff; don't worry about it," Kondo assured her softly; his hand gently lay on her shoulder as a show of support as if sensing her mental breakdown. Leaning inward, Amina allowed herself to gain strength from him.

Letting out a groan as she entered her home, Amina knew she had worked to do. There was no way she would leave the house nasty. Pushing through the trash, Jotham and Kondo followed her back to her bedroom. Past experiences taught her to lock the door, knowing that the only way for Adeya to enter was to break it down. She was too lazy to do that. Hence, the house being a mess and smelling like decaying flesh.

Unlocking her bedroom door, Amina entered, prepared to pack up the rest of her belongings. At least her room remained untouched, and the house odor had yet to claim this space.

"Amina, I'm going to open the windows to let the fresh air in. Then I'm going to call in some more help. I think we should move all your belongings and put them in storage."

Mumbling in agreement, Amina and Kondo got started on packing her things. Unlike most women her age, she had not collected a lot of material possessions in her young life. Anything that was special to her she placed in a safe deposit box at the bank; that was something Gavin counseled her to do.

Unbeknownst to her father, she and Gavin kept in contact. He contacted her monthly and sent her money every three months. Amina told him it was not necessary, but he insisted. Like clockwork, she had money transferred to her bank account from him. She had a PO Box at the post office too, something else that Gavin advised her to do. Amina had never told him about the trauma she suffered for fear of retaliation. She also had yet to tell him about Aaron's incarceration.

Gavin wanted her to come live with him when she turned eighteen. At the time, she could not leave Aaron behind. She now regretted that action. It would have saved her the torment she was suffering. Then again, she would not have been here for Hasina and Amal. That, she did not regret.

God knew what He was doing, and though she did not understand why, He did, and she had to trust that.

"Amina, what drawers are safe for me to open?" Kondo asked.

"Huh?" she queried. He offered her a look that she failed to decipher.

"I don't want to open your undergarments drawer."

Ever the gentleman, Amina blushed. "I took all those items when I left the first time. You can go in any drawer; it's just clothes and music," Amina reassured.

Kondo nodded and got to work. While he was busy doing that, she decided to start cleaning up the front part of the house. She headed to the linen closet and got gloves and went to collect cleaning supplies and began the arduous task of restoring her mother's home.

Amina was so fixated on cleaning out the refrigerator that she had not noticed that JD's reinforcements had arrived.

"Where do you need us?" an accented voice questioned.

Startled, Amina bumped her head on the fridge as she attempted to see who was speaking to her. When she was able to collect herself, she looked up and saw another Goode brother, Djimon.

"I'm sorry, lovely, I didn't mean to startle you. JD instructed me to ask you what you needed assistance with." He offered an easy smile, and just like Reth, he had the same starlit russet eyes. They were nearly identical, except, where his eldest brother was intimidating, Djimon was a flirt. His body language was welcoming, and his sweet smile, enchanting charisma, and endearing personality disarmed her immediately.

"Um, I, well…"

"D, what're you doing?" Reth asked.

Amina snapped her head in his direction. She should have known that JD would call his brothers, but she was not prepared for it. They were sight to behold when all four were together.

Reth was dressed like his brothers, wearing a t-shirt, basketball shorts, and expensive tennis shoes. Even dressed down their attractiveness was not diminished.

"I was asking this beautiful lady where she needed my assistance. Since she's here in the kitchen, I think that's where I'll be too," Djimon hummed and winked at her. Confidence oozed off him. He was smooth.

Amina's golden eyes widened at his flirtatious manner.

"No; we're only here to move her stuff out of her bedroom. You can help by using the tools to disassemble her bed. Don't start your *Rico Suave*; she's off limits. Move on so we can get this done quickly," Reth ordered.

Djimon offered her a panty-dropping grin, showcasing perfectly aligned alabaster teeth. He did not even flinch when his brother called him out. After a moment, probably just to irritate his brother, he exited the kitchen to do as Reth requested.

"Don't worry about my brother; he's harmless, well, most of the time," Reth apologized.

Amina fidgeted and stared like a complete idiot. She was not used to being flirted with, even if he were just joking. Still, she just gawked at Reth until the moment became awkward. "Sorry," she mumbled and went back to scrubbing out the refrigerator.

She heard Reth's feet vacillating, and she was about to say something to him until she heard that voice.

"Who you and why is you in my house?" Adeya's loud, husky

voice contaminated the quiet.

Amina felt her entire body tense at hearing her aunt's voice. It triggered her fight or flight response. Instantly, she knew things were about to escalate to epic proportions. That was the only way Adeya knew how to act.

"Girl, he fine and paid; don't question the gifts." Amina knew that voice belonged to Mela, who probably had moved in since Amina's departure. Just like Adeya, she was a leech.

Rolling her eyes, Amina got up to confront her aunt, but Reth pulled her back behind him. It was as if he sensed the trouble brewing. He confidently strolled to the living room where JD was standing, silently observing the two women.

"Dang, Ade, there's another one. Who y'all?" Mela asked, eyeing Reth and JD lustfully.

Unbothered by the scene, JD offered a winning smirk and introduced himself. "Hey. I'm JD, a friend of Amina's. I'm helping her move out."

At that, Adeya's face turned into a grimace. She placed her thick hand on her hip and rolled her neck as she eyed the two brothers. "Say what? She ain't going nowhere, and even if she was, she don't own nothing here."

That was a bald-faced lie. It was Adeya that owned nothing in the house. Amina stepped around Reth to correct her. "I'm getting the rest of my stuff out of my bedroom and everything else that belongs to me."

Adeya snapped at her and started to march Amina's way, but Reth blocked her. He stood protectively like a wall in front of Amina. That one movement shifted the entire mood in the room. Reth challenged Adeya with his eyes while Mela had the good sense to be silent and sat down on the couch. All Amina could do was observe in silence. She could tell by Reth's stance that he was unperturbed by Adeya's attempt at intimidation.

"Move," Adeya huffed, attitude dripping with just that one

word.

Reth shook he head. "I can't do that, ma'am," Reth's authoritative voice stated. There was a warning in the way he spoke. Though he spoke lowly, somehow, Kondo and Djimon heard it because they came from the back of the house to see what was happening.

"Lawd, it's two more of them." Mela started fanning her face as if she were about to faint. "They got to be brothers or cousins. Amina, girl, you got you a whole chocolate rainbow harem of man. I'm impressed; jealous but impressed. It must be true what they say, the blacker the berry, the sweeter the juice. They bout to be diabetic 'cause you real black," Mela stupidly commented before laughing at her own crude joke.

The room deadened. The ignorance of Mela's vulgar remarks made Amina want to disappear. Every time she thought it could not get worse, it did. Run was all she could think to do and would have if not for the movement of Kondo and Djimon.

Without an explanation or encouragement, Kondo and Djimon stood shoulder to shoulder with Reth. It was like a choreographed dance as JD made his way to be on his brother's left side. In true warrior fashion, they created a barricade between Amina and Adeya. It was the grim look on their faces that suggested they were tired of the absurdity being displayed.

Mela's laughter ceased immediately, and she was now sobering to the fact that they were ill-prepared to deal with the current situation. "Ade, them dudes don't look like they playing."

Full of pride, Adeya turned around and glared at Mela. "Hush," Adeya ordered before turning her attention back to Reth. She took a step back to look Reth in his eyes, but she spoke to Amina.

"Pitch, who you done brought in my brother's house? Huh?

Where you find these thugs at?"

Mela sucked her teeth. "Girl, them dudes ain't thugs. They move different," Mela attempted to whisper, but Adeya ignored her.

"They lying if they said they want you because you ugly. So that means, you must be putting out, just like your whore of a mother. We ain't taking no more bastards in here!" she insulted.

Collectively, the brothers' faces illustrated their distaste and lack of patience with Adeya. The tension was as thick as the fog in Namib desert.

"Enough! Don't you ever speak to her like that again. That's the only warning I'm giving you," Reth snarled. Even Amina stood taller at his declaration.

An evil grin etched across Adeya's blemished face. She started rolling her neck as she spoke. "I'on know you. I can talk to her anyway I want. I ought to call Aaron and tell him his daughter out here whoring." Then she paused as if a thought came to her. "You know what? Y'all can get her stuff, but if you want her, you better pay for her. So, run me my money, and she's all yours."

Foolish and overconfident, Mela giggled before adding, "Get yo coins, sis."

Mortified by her aunt's behavior and Mela's lack of decorum, Amina felt faint. There was no way her aunt just suggested they purchase her. Tears welled up in her eyes. Adeya had stooped to a new low.

The disgust felt among all four brothers permeated the room, and Amina was two seconds from falling apart. Her body started to shiver, and she whimpered, attempting to hold it all in. Amina was losing her battle, and Reth seemed to notice.

"Kondo take Amina to the truck," Reth ordered.

Amina looked up at Kondo, and he reached out for her. This was the second time he witnessed her being a complete mess. Without a fight, she fell into Kondo, and his arms wrapped protectively around her. She was too embarrassed to even glance up.

∞∞∞

Rage tingled throughout Reth's body. Today was not the day to come at him incorrectly. That's exactly what this woman and her friend did. It would never happen again in his presence. Adeya was going to learn today.

When Reth heard the door shut he turned his attention back to the most despicable woman he had ever encountered. Not only was she unattractive on the outside, but her inside was as equally disgusting.

Had his mother not raised him to be a Christian and a gentleman, he might have slapped some sense into her. The person that stood before him was a bully, a coward, and a threat to Amina. The moment his mother decided that Amina would be Hasina's nanny was the moment she became another person for him to protect. Yes, his plate was full to the brim, practically overflowing, but he would never permit anyone to be mistreated in his presence. The way she disrespected her niece was offensive. How dare she imply that he and his brothers would treat Amina in such a way?

"Why?" Reth asked, his voice was at its normal cadence, though he was blistering inside. He did not raise it; there was no point.

"What?" the short stout woman returned, jerking back her head back and placing her hands on her wide hips. There was less surety in her voice now. Though it was apparent that she wanted to seem in charge, she was not. No, she was in his arena now.

Instead of answering her, he just glared at her unblinkingly. That was when he observed the first pop of sweat on her large, acne-scarred face. Unlike Amina, her aunt was not an attractive woman. She may have been in her younger years, but jealousy, bitterness, and rage ate away at her.

Now, he had his answer. This woman was jealous of her intelligent and attractive niece. It was unfortunate. Amina lost most of her family, only to be left with an alcoholic father and an abusive aunt. Though he did not know a lot about Amina, he knew that she did not deserve this toxic treatment.

Hearing his brothers' grunts of annoyance, he knew it was time to speed this along. "Ma'am," he used the term sarcastically, "I'm someone you don't want to offend. I'm the Honorable Judge Reth Goode. I have the ability and the power to make your life incredibly uncomfortable. Amina is not, nor has she ever been, a whore. Watch your nasty mouth when you speak in my presence and when you speak to and about her. Let this be the absolute last time you use that type of language to characterize that young woman." Reth paused momentarily to see if she understood him; apparently, she was still having issues because it looked as if she were about to speak. This was not the time for her to speak. He needed her to listen.

Reth lifted his index finger and waved it side-to-side in warning. "Don't. Your turn to speak has not been granted. I still have the floor." He paused for a moment to ensure she understood him and then he continued. "A while back, it was brought to my attention that you and your friend over there attacked Amina. That upset my family and me. I pondered what type of human being would stoop so low as to attack someone as brilliant, thoughtful, and kind as Amina. Now, I see. Therefore, I've advised Amina to go to the police station and press charges against you for assault and battery, lynching, not to mention your attempt to sell her, and any other charges I feel like adding. Once I've done that, I'll contact her father personally and let him know that you tried to sell his daughter to the highest bidder. Shame on you! Know this: you found the right man on the right day." His russet eyes darken as he glared at her.

Attitude was still written all on her face. During his speech, she seemed to find a backbone. It was clear that she did not want to fall back because her friend was watching them. However, she would be a fool to try him.

"Wha—"

"It's still not your turn, ma'am. Let me finish. I do hate to be interrupted. You've interrupted me twice and it vexes me. That's the judge in me. As I was saying, Amina is under the care of the Goode family for the foreseeable future. We protect our own; if you ever open that landfill you call a mouth to insult her again, you'll deal with me. If you threaten her or raise your hand to hit her, you'll deal with me. I promise you don't want problems with me. You're a guttersnipe and an oppressor. The good news is that your reign ends today. If Amina so much as tells me that you whispered her name incorrectly, I'll be on you like ants protecting their queen. Are we clear? Now, you may speak."

Her sickening eyes enlarged at the meaning of his words. They were not threatening words, simply a promise from a man who tired of ignorance easily. Instantly, she nodded her head in understanding. The puff of anger and attitude dissipated as quickly as it arrived.

"Brothers, are you in agreement with me? Have I left out anything?"

"We're in agreement," his brothers spoke in unison.

Reth lifted a brow to them and then turned his attention back to Adeya. "My brothers and I will continue to complete our task. We're almost done. In fact, it looks like we only need about two more hours; that's when you can return. Now, Adeya you'll leave, and you'll no longer contact Amina. You'll not verbally or physically abuse her. This is your first and only warning. Leave while I'm feeling generous. When you step out that door, don't you even look at Amina," Reth warned.

The woman's eyes began to water; sweat was now covering her body, yet Reth remained unmoved. He was so perturbed by her behavior that his skin was crawling.

"C'mon, Ade. Let's go, I'm hungry anyway," Mela encourage as she pulled on Adeya's arm.

"Oh, and ma'am; yes you," Reth replied, nodding to the woman pointing at herself. "All that I said to her applies to you as well. Understand?"

"I got it," she snapped.

"Make sure that you never forget it."

Reth watched as they stumbled over each other getting out of the door. He followed them, too, just to make sure they did they were told. He watched them drive off then he motioned for Kondo to come back with Amina.

Reth turned around to see his brothers were equally livid. They would speak about this privately later. He was going to see whose name was on the deed of the house. Adeya was about to get a thirty-day notice to vacant. She truly picked the wrong man to battle. He had time today.

"You handled that much better than me. For the first time in my life, I wanted to put my hands on a woman. Don't tell Mama, though," Djimon fumed.

Reth knew that was saying a lot. His brother had almost been ruined by a Gypsy woman. That was the lowest they ever saw him, so for him to say that he wanted to put hands on Amina's aunt showed just how offended they all were.

"I can't believe that really happened." JD shook his head in disbelief. "Amina didn't deserve that. The look of dejection and humiliation on her face hurt my heart. That can't and won't continue."

"We'll discuss it later; right now, let's get her moved out of here and to my place. I can't promise that if her aunt returns that I won't forget she's a woman."

His brothers nodded and went back to work, speaking in low tones amongst themselves when Kondo re-entered with a shattered Amina.

She wore her pain and shame the way others carried their confidence.

It stung.

No one should ever feel that way or be betrayed like that by their family. It stirred something in his soul. If he thought Amina would allow it, Reth would have pulled her into his arms and hugged her.

"Head up, Amina; you have nothing to be ashamed about," Reth counseled.

Cautiously, she lifted her head, but she refused to meet his gaze. If he had been in her shoes, he probably would react the same. "We're almost done; then we can get something to eat, and I'll take you back to my house. Unless you would rather go visit my mother."

She did not reply. He understood. "Just sit down and we'll take care of everything."

Reth motioned to Kondo to help her, and then he went back to her bedroom to start carrying out the furniture that she requested to keep.

An hour and a half later, Amina sat stone-faced inside the diner. It was a blessing that Kalifa was not working today. She did not want her friend to know how scandalous her aunt really was. Still, the incident replayed vividly like a movie reel in her mind. Her body was still reacting to her aunt's taunts. The mortification she endured during that verbal altercation had her mentally paralyzed.

No matter how she tried to rebuild the parts of her that her aunt and father tore down, her efforts never lasted long. The insults were like wrecking balls, the hits like dynamite. They were determined to derail her life. Anything good she tried to achieve they did their best to destroy.

There was no reason for Adeya to behave the way she did. It truly gutted Amina to her core, yet what bothered her more was that Reth witnessed it. All the brothers witnessed her be torn down again. Amina feared that he was going to fire her. The way the Goode brothers must have viewed her now was shattering the little pieces she had left.

Her mind volleyed with what ifs and what she believed they thought of her. It was creating a massive headache. Leaning her head into her hands, she tried to massage the ache away.

"How are you feeling, Amina?" Reth's decadent voice inquired.

"Are you firing me?" Amina blurted, not even hearing his question. Her voice quivered, and the rest of the brothers who were having a side conversation abruptly stopped speaking. All Amina could hear was the pounding of her heart.

It sounded like a combination of African percussion, the Meinl African Bougarabou and Pearl Shakerine. Instantly, musical notes and words burst through her mind like the Victoria Falls in Zambia.

The perplexed look on his smooth, even-toned face let her know he was not expecting her to ask that. "No. Why would I fire you?"

Amina let out a sigh of relief and then briefly glanced around the table. All eyes were on her. Inhaling a deep breath and calming herself down, she answered in a whisper. "My aunt, what she said, and the offer she made. I just thought, you know, I mean..."

Reth and all his brothers shook their heads no in unison. Since JD was sitting next to her in the semi-circle booth, he gently pulled her in to him. "It's going to be okay, Amina. You have all our support," JD replied, and the rest of his brothers replied in kind.

The waitress arrived then and took their orders' once she left, Reth spoke again.

"How long has she been treating you this way? Why did she call you Pitch?"

He had heard the belittling nickname. "She refers to me as that because of my dark skin."

Reth tilted his head to the side as if that were unfathomable. She could tell by the silence that he was not the only one that felt that way. "What?"

"Adeya's life mission is to make my life horrible. No one in the family has my skin complexion. Adeya often says Aaron isn't my biological father, hence her comment about bastards. Often, she reminds me about my mother and how ugly I am because of my skin tone. It's only gotten worse over the years."

At her confession, Reth reached out and placed his hand on top of hers, and her breath caught at his attention. His touch was electric and sent shockwaves throughout her body. Then he withdrew his touch just as quick. Amina feared her reaction offended him.

Reth cleared his voice before speaking. "I'm sorry that happened to you. I can tell you this, and I don't lie; you're beautiful. It's not just your outer beauty; it's your inner beauty too. Don't let the meaningless musings of a bitter aunt depict how you view or value yourself. It's obvious to see that she's jealous of you. You're attractive, intelligent, hardworking, caring, and talented. People like your aunt see a light like that, and they want to dim it because of their own darkness. Don't give that woman or anyone else an ounce of power in your life."

"I agree," JD replied, patting her back.

"Me three," Kondo added, grinning at her. He was even friendlier than JD. There was an ease about Kondo that instantly relaxed her.

"Well said, brother, and Ms. Amina, I also concur. You can ask anybody; we Goode brothers know beauty when we see it. You, my dear, have all kinds of melanin magic. Your eighty percent cacao is good for the soul. You're a dark chocolate goddess. Don't ever stress or be depressed about the hue that God created you with," Djimon cooed, causing Amina to blush. In seconds, they repaired a little of the damage her aunt inflicted.

"There he goes. It looks like we need to protect Amina from the African Casanova. Wait until he starts reciting French sonnets. If that happens, Amina, tell me!" Kondo exclaimed, grinning at his brother.

"D, calm all that extra down," Reth warned, and Djimon just shrugged his shoulders.

"Did I lie, brother?"

"No, you didn't lie," Reth added, showcasing an extremely rare smile that jolted through Amina's core.

At his response, Amina almost choked on her saliva. JD patted her back, asking her if she was okay. It took her a moment to recover, and she nodded. However, Kondo gave her a knowing look that she ignored.

Then she spoke. "Thank you all for your endearing words and for helping me with my aunt. I appreciate it."

"You're welcome," they all chorused.

At that moment, Amina knew she had friends, protectors, and people who really cared about her, and it almost made the humiliation she had to bear worth it. *Dark chocolate goddess and melanin magic*, beautiful—she liked that, a lot. She was about to write a song, maybe call it Cacao Goddess.

Chapter 12

Yesterday had felt like trying to climb out of quicksand. The memories of her aunt's insults floated through her mind, but they did not stick this time. The hurt lessened each time she thought about it. Possibly, that was because how the Goode brothers had her back. No one ever protected her before. Their protection and words inspired her to write new music.

Last night was the first time she stayed at Amal and Reth's home, which was just as gorgeous as them. It took a moment for Amina to realize that all the brothers lived near each other and that Djimon designed each of their homes. Though Kondo had his own home, he stayed with his parents most of the time. They did not live too far away.

Amina found out how close their parents lived as they drove her back to Reth's home. For some reason, the feeling of inferiority she normally felt in the presence of them had also lessened. They had witnessed her shame, seen her bruises, knew some of her past, and still stood beside her. That earned them her fidelity, trust, and respect.

Placing her unfinished composition in her music satchel, Amina prepared for the day. She did not have class today and wanted to do something special with Hasina and visit with Amal.

"Ms. Mina?"

Instantly, a warm smile graced Amina's face before she turned around to see Hasina. This little girl was adorable.

"Come in, Hasina. Have you eaten breakfast yet?"

She shook her head no.

"How about we eat breakfast and visit with your momma?"

"Yes."

Reaching out to grasp Hasina's hand, they trotted to the kitchen. Amina had not been there a short time, but she remembered where the kitchen was, and Hasina had given her the grand tour. Prior to Amina being hired, Hasina explained there was once a cook here, but her father had since sent the cook to his brothers. Hasina thought it was because she was not at home, but Amina was sure it was due to Reth and Amal wanting privacy.

Although Amina was not the cook that Kalifa was, she was good enough. The two started to prepare a light breakfast for themselves and Amal. Once they were done, the duo headed back upstairs with a breakfast tray and headed to Amal's bedroom. Amina prayed she would want to go outside today.

Hasina knocked and they waited for permission to enter. The nurse, Akilah, opened the door and greeted them with a smile before stepping out of their way. Amina was happy to see Amal sitting in her wheelchair and grinned as Hasina zipped toward her mother.

"Mommy, Ms. Mina and I made breakfast. Are you hungry?" Hasina asked as she carefully boosted herself up to sit on Amal's lap.

"Yes, my love."

Amina knew that Amal most likely was not hungry, but the way Hasina's face lit up also let Amina know there was nothing that could defeat a mother's love. For her daughter, Amal would do anything. Amina moved closer, arranging the food on the TV tray so they could all share. She made a protein shake just for Amal.

Amal's eyes glanced at Amina. "Thank you."

Amina nodded knowingly before retrieving a chair. After blessing the food, the trio began to eat.

"How did yesterday go?" Amal queried in a breathy voice.

Amina glanced down and then remembered Reth telling her not to as she had nothing to be ashamed about. Shaking off the embarrassment, she held her head high and recounted what happened, doing her best not to say anything that would upset Hasina, but her attention seemed to be elsewhere currently.

"She did what?"

"I know. I felt so horrible because your husband and brothers-in-law are honorable men, and for her to insinuate something so grotesque and improper hurt."

Amal lifted her frail hand on top of Amina's. "Re is right. There is a light in you so bright that it threatens those who are in darkness. They know the light will always defeat the dark, so their only defense is to attempt to dim the light until it's dark too. I know because in my life, my mother was my darkness. In some ways, we're alike; for me, it's my mother, and for you, it's your aunt. Don't let her win. You have too much to offer. There is an army of people praying for you and who love you, Amina; never forget that."

The sincerity of her conviction, the strength in her eyes, and the kinship in her suffering let Amina know Amal spoke truth. Her advice was heartfelt. Amina felt something overtake her body when as Amal's hand rested upon hers. It felt like a transfer; something supernatural was happening.

It was as if the chains were breaking. The chain of insecurity, the chain of fear, the chain of shame and uncertainty. Although no words left her mouth, not even a sigh, it was as if she and Amal were communicating, as if they felt what the other was feeling. What should have terrified her brought her an inner peace she had not felt since losing her mother.

"Don't go, Amal," Amina whispered.

"I'm not yet, Amina. It's not quite time."

"I mean, just stay. I pray I don't sound selfish, but the warmth, the inner peace I feel right now, I haven't felt since my mother. I owe you so much. I mean, oh goodness, I'm not making sense. It's just that I've admired you for years—your ethereal beauty, the way you conduct yourself, and the it-factor that you possess. The ease you ooze around groups of people. Your confidence. It can't be duplicated; I tried." Amina felt the need to confess to Amal the feeling she had for Reth. It did not feel right to connect on this level and not be honest.

"You're entrusting me with your most precious gift, and you've been so kind to me, and I've sinned against you."

By this time, Hasina was off in the corner playing with the dolls she left in her mother's room. It was almost as if she sensed the two needed the privacy.

"Amina, honey, calm down, and start over. Why do you believe you've sinned against me?"

Even now, she was caring, kind, and considerate. This woman was a saint, Amina thought to herself.

Inhaling deeply and exhaling cautiously, Amina explained. "Please forgive me, but I've had a crush on your husband since I was probably ten. I didn't mean to develop it, but it was just there. Then it grew. Not that he watered it, as he had no idea I existed. It was just the musings of an adolescent mind. He was my first muse. I'm sorry. Then, he was married. I wanted to be upset, but you're all the things I view as beautiful. You hold all the characteristics a man like him deserves. You two look so good together. For a while, I was envious, jealous that my darker skin made me ugly and invisible. Jealous that I would never know the love you two displayed. It was wrong. I know that, but I couldn't stop it. I had no mother anymore, and my father made me feel that being anything like her was immoral. I tried to emulate you, but I failed."

Amal guffawed and what an amazing sound it was. It was light and airy. However, Amina felt a little afflicted that she was laughing at her. As if reading her mind, she quickly shared, "Oh honey, I'm not laughing at you. That's just not what I expected you'd say. I love your honesty. It is so refreshing," Amal gushed before bringing her other hand to rest tenderly on Amina's cheek.

"Amina, you're magnificent in your own way. There is no need to compare yourself to anyone. You're uniquely you and made in His image. Let me share this: what you saw as confidence was me pretending. I was playing the part of wife to my friend. I, too, have insecurities. The only thing I've ever had is beauty or at least that is what I was told. Unlike you, I don't have degrees and never worked a job. My brain was not important, only my body. Sadly, I was raised to be a trophy. For me, beauty came with its own downfall. When a person is viewed as a pretty face, that's all others see. They tend to sexualize you and dismiss your thoughts and opinions. This beauty has often been my curse, my death. That's for another day. On this day, you owe me nothing. Most of my friends have a crush on Reth. He's sinfully dapper, and he's confident and protective. I would be offended if you didn't have a crush on him," Amal teased, causing Amina to laugh as well. Then she got serious.

"I have a secret to confess. Reth was never meant to be mine. I was never supposed be his forever; his forever will come, but it's not me."

Amina's brow furrowed in confusion, but Amal continued. "Amina, I was jealous of you. The little girl with the golden eyes and golden voice. Pipes so powerful that they could evoke emotions out of the sternest of people. The little girl that grew into an extremely attractive young woman. The young woman who came back to a church that mocked her; the young woman who fought through grief and loss, through pain and abuse. The young woman who received a full scholarship to college and a graduate program. The young beauty who loves more than most, who gives her time to children others refuse to see. The woman who has created a music therapy program, who is using her talents to serve God and community. I admire you, Amina. There were moments I dreamed what if I were like her.

"When I look at you, I see bravery and brilliance. You stepped up for me to care for my daughter, Reth, and me. Even knowing how you felt, you still came to us. You're love in its purest form. I saw that in you, and I longed for it. Now, God has seen fit to bring us together. When I leave this Earth, I'll leave in peace because I know they'll be in loving hands."

Amina just stared at Amal speechless. Tears ran like a river from both their eyes. Amina never fathomed that Amal ever had any insecurities. She wondered just how beauty could be a curse, a death, when everyone was obsessed with it. No one brought products to make themselves ugly, but prettier, younger, lighter, more attractive. Confounded, Amina pushed the thoughts aside and concentrated on another thought. It truly pained her that she wasted years being jealous and fearful of Amal when she could have been her friend. Whitney Houston and CeCe Winans' "Count On Me" circulated in her head.

"I'm sorry it took this to bring us together because I would have loved to have had you in my life sooner," Amina admitted.

"God's time is always the right time. How about we go to the music room, and you and Hasina play for me?"

Amina nodded. That she could do; she would play and sing, anything to keep Amal smiling and laughing. However, it bothered Amina that Amal said that Reth was never meant to be hers. What did that mean? Why was she not supposed be his forever, his forever will come, but it was not his wife? Maybe it was her medication, but Amal had made a similar statement before. It was all baffling.

∞∞∞∞

Reth closed his eyes, bowed his head, and began to pray. Yesterday had been more of a struggle for them than he cared to admit. It was a blessing they were able to get Amina settled, and though he thought she would move in next week, having her here now seemed like the best decision.

Last night, he and his brothers shared with their father what occurred between them and Amina's family. Reth also shared his idea of having Adeya removed from the house. She had no right to rest her head in a place where she did not keep up.

Chiram, a man of God and peace, was infuriated about the incident. Reth understood. He still carried some residual anger this morning, which was why he was praying.

It may be a pointless endeavor as he fussed at God for allowing Amal to suffer, for not curing her, and for leaving their daughter motherless. He berated God for the countless afflictions that Amal had to overcome just to suffer all over again. There was nothing he could do to save her. As much as he wanted to be like Job, he was unable to do so. His mind was restless.

Now, he was adding Amina to the mix.

Exhaling loudly, he quickly ended his prayer. It was not that he could concentrate anyway. The growling of his stomach reminded him that he had yet to eat breakfast. Pushing away from his desk, he got up and walked to his office door. When he opened it, the most melodious sounds invaded the quiet mornings he had grown accustom to. It sounded like a piano and a saxophone. It flowed like the Boyoma Falls. His feet remained unmovable as he heard the music change. The saxophone no longer played; it was just the piano. Then he heard her voice. At first, he did not know the song, but as he listened, he knew she was singing "Reckless Love" by Anthony Evans, and her rendition of the song had tears flowing down his eyes.

He felt what she was feeling, heard how she was singing out to God, what he could not express in prayer just minutes ago. He lamented to the Father right there. He was the one that wandered, and God was leaving the ninety-nine to come for him.

∞ ∞ ∞

It was late when Reth found the courage to enter his wife's domain. For hours, he had been lurking in the shadows like a coward. Throughout the past few weeks, he checked on Amal when possible; sometimes, she did not want him around. He understood and respected her request.

Reth admired her strength. In fact, he admired all the women in his life—his mother, daughter, and now Amina. He had observed how Amal and Amina had become fast friends. Whatever they talked about, he did not know, but he felt that Amina not only loved his daughter but also his wife. It was that knowledge that eased the apprehension he had about hiring her. Truthfully, that only added to it. He knew after he met Adeya that Amina was never returning to that toxic household.

At night, when he was sure Amal was asleep, he would apologize to her. He apologized for allowing this to occur. It was his fault. If he had of been there for her years ago, this would not be happening. Then she would be able to have the life she deserved.

Amal had been his friend for years. They grew up together, and she was family to him before marriage. It hurt him to see her like this. When they were growing up and he saw the future, this was not what he envisioned. Back then, he thought JD would capture her heart or possibly Kondo. Reth's ambition was power, not a relationship and surely not marriage.

Easing into the chair that was next to her bed, he placed his large hand atop her fragile one. It was so thin and pale that it resembled a skeleton. This was not the Amal who loved to laugh and often teased him. Cradling her hand, he felt there was still warmth, and that meant she was alive. He let out a sigh of relief. There were good days when he thought she would beat this, like last week when Amina was singing to her, and then there were days like this. Days where it looked like death had come. Amal stopped all treatments, so he knew death was imminent. The tension he had not known was then released.

Next, Reth closed his eyes and began his nightly routine. Just as he was about to speak, he heard the whisper of her voice. It was soft and scratchy, a worn inflection as if it had taken all she had just to speak. That crushed him. His eyes immediately opened and clashed with her tired terracotta eyes.

"Amal?"

There was a hint of a smile that graced her thinning face. Her once beautiful, bountiful head of hair no longer remained. Yet, there was still beauty in her. Cancer could not remove that.

"Re, no more. This is not your fault. Please don't blame yourself for this," she wheezed out.

Reth was about to speak, but she shushed him. He remained silent to allow her to speak her peace. "I want you to promise me that you'll forgive yourself. When I'm gone, you have my permission to tell the truth. We should have never lied." She paused to catch her breath and gather her strength. "Promise that you'll find love. I love you. I always will, but you deserve true love. The kind that I could never provide. We were never supposed to be." She took a deep breath before continuing. "I pray you'll find a woman to share the Goode Love Vow with. It's my prayer that you and Hasina will find someone to love you both. I know that person has entered your life already, and God will reveal her to you when you're ready to receive her love. Promise me that you'll live and not settle for the façade of love ever again. You're a good and honorable man Reth Abioye Goode. Don't ever forget that."

Reth nodded, but he was not sure he agreed with her. He was not good; if he had been this would not be happening to her. Who was this person she was talking about loving him and Hasina?

"Don't be angry with God about anything. He saved me. He allowed you to save me. Now, I get to see the Father and thank Him for all the blessings He graciously bestowed."

Reth did his best to hold his tears. There was peace when she spoke that latter part. A glow illuminated her paling skin. She almost looked like her old self. It scared him because he knew she was ready.

Loveable and considerate Amal. He never pictured life without her. Now, it was all he ever thought about. Even in her last moments, her thoughts and prayers were never selfish. She was a giver, a kind soul who thought of others before herself. That she inherited from her biological father.

"Reth." Her saying his name sounded like a plea but also an ending. He knew that if he promised her this, that she would leave. God knew he did not want her to suffer more.

"One more thing; please take care of my Amina. I have grown to love her. She's my Ruth, and I'm her Naomi. Her friendship is true and loyal. When the time comes, I want you to read the Book of Ruth; read it with intention and you'll see what I have seen."

Reth was not sure what to make of her latter request, but he would do it. "I'm sorry, Amal. I'm sorry it all happened this way. You'll always be my dearest friend. I've never been able to deny you anything. For you, and for Hasina, I'll do as you ask."

Then he leaned over and gently kissed her cheek. "Rest and be well. I'll take care of everything on this side. If you're ready, then I release you, back to the Father that gifted you to me. I love you." Then he pulled her thin frail body into his and closed his eyes.

Chapter 13

It was six in the morning, and Amina beat her alarm going off. Since she had officially moved in, each morning she and Amal did their quiet time together. It was amazing how close the two had become, and they were even closer after Amina shared, she had a crush on Reth. The pair practically talked about everything. Amal even told her that she could invite Kalifa over.

Hopping out of bed, Amina quickly entered the bathroom to wash up and brush her teeth. Once she was done, she put on her robe, grabbed her Bible, and headed to Amal's bedroom. A song was already brewing inside of her.

There was a different vibe in this house. It was unlike what she was accustomed to when she lived with her aunt and father. Here, she had no battles, no need to constantly be on alert; here she felt safe. Honestly, she had not felt safe in ages.

Smiling to herself, she lightly knocked on Amal's door and then entered as she often did. However, she stopped short. Since she had been in their home never had she saw Amal and Reth share a bed. Per Hasina, her parents had separate sleeping quarters. Amina never inquired why because it was not her business.

Seeing the two now, they looked so sweet and comfortable together. It hurt Amina to think that death would separate them. Deeply in her heart, she prayed that a last-minute miracle would happen. It had to because Amal meant so much to so many. Truly she was a caring and loving soul. Amina did not want to see the aftermath of losing her.

Still, she had no right to be gazing at them. It was private, their special memories, and she did not want to intrude. Her body heated in embarrassment as she tried to quietly back out of the bedroom as to not disturb their slumber. Just as she made it to the door, she was nearly hit in the head as Hasina came bouncing in and calling out to her parents.

"Mommy, Daddy, wake up!" Hasina called out as she leapt on the bed.

Apparently, she had not seen Amina, who was ready to disappear.

"*Binti,* come to me; let your mommy rest for now," Reth tiredly whispered in Swahili.

Thinking he was occupied with his daughter, Amina attempted to exit the room unnoticed.

"Amina?"

"Sir? I mean, Reth," she sputtered as she turned around. "I'm sorry. Amal and I usually do our quiet time together. I apologize for interrupting. I didn't know, um… since…. I was just leaving."

Reth nodded, and before he could say another word, she ran out the room and closed the door. She went to her bedroom and prepared for the day. It was later in the morning before Amina returned to Amal's bedroom. This time she knocked and waited for a response.

Reth answered. He was dressed now but not in his work clothes, which consisted of a suit and tie, but in khakis and an oxford shirt. He looked fatigued and sorrowful. For some reason, that tugged at her heart and she wanted to embrace him. "Back again," she smiled awkwardly before adding, "I was just checking on Amal."

"She's resting; today isn't good for her. Maybe you should go hangout with your boyfriend."

Amina swallowed hard. He did not say it rudely, but still the tone hurt her feelings. She did not even have a boyfriend, but it seemed to her that he did not want her in his wife's space.

Reality hit. She was simply an employee, and if her boss wanted her gone, then she had to respect that. He more than likely wanted to spend as much time with her as possible. Today was not the day to feel sensitive about it. It was not about her.

"Absolutely. If you require my assistance with Hasina, just call me," Amina replied and jetted off.

It wasn't until she was outside that she realized she had no transportation. Amina had her permit, but she never took the license exam. There was never anyone to teach her and she always had BC to drive her wherever she needed to go.

At least Reth's family all lived close. Amina could ask JD or Kondo for a ride. That sounded like a good idea. It was best to keep out of Reth's way, she concluded. Amina trekked down the long driveway, through the open gates, and looked to see which brother was home. She saw JD's truck and then made her way to his home.

She quickened her pace and jogged up to JD's door. Still reeling from Reth's abrupt dismissal, Amina calmed herself as she rang the doorbell and patiently waited. Several minutes later, JD opened his door and seemed surprised at the sight of his visitor.

"Is everything okay with Amal?" The alarm in his eyes threw her off momentarily.

It was then Amina realized why he had that look on his face. "As far as I know. Reth just said today was not good for her. He felt it was best I spend time with um, my boyfriend. Thing is, I don't have one, and I don't have a license or a car. I came over to ask if you could drop me off at the diner. Rufus, Kalifa's boss, lets me hang out sometimes during her shift."

"Come in."

Thanking him, Amina entered. She stood quietly awaiting JD to escort her to through his home. It was just as nice as his brother's. Neither seemed the type to display their wealth. JD's house was more of a comfortable bachelor pad. It was open and spacious, decorated in dark grays and blues. From where she stood, she could see the African mask decorating the walls. They were proud of their heritage and culture. Amina appreciated that. Her mother was half-Jamaican and was just as invested in her culture, one unknown to Amina.

"Essentially, my brother kicked you out of the house." JD frowned.

"That's an accurate assessment. However, he was polite about it."

JD smirked and lifted a disbelieving brow. "If you say so. I was about to go to my parents' house for brunch. You can come with me and then we start your driving lessons."

"Wait, what?"

"You can't be a nanny if you can't drive. I'm going to help you get ready to take your driver's exam. Don't worry; I taught Kondo, and he's a great driver."

"Who taught you?"

"Djimon, and Reth taught him."

At that, Amina grinned at him. "You all are really close, huh?"

"They're my best friends. I trust each of my brothers with my life. My brothers will most likely agree that we like it best when we're all together."

"That's great. I miss my siblings. I often wonder what life would be like if the twins had survived. I'm glad you all have each other. When the time comes, Reth will need all of you to help him get through.

"Come on, no more sad talk. We've got things to do."

∞ ∞ ∞

"Breathe, Amina, you're doing fine." JD encouraged as if he was trying to get a stuck cat out of a tree.

Amina had not attempted to drive in years. Once she lost her mother, she vowed never to learn to drive. Then she attempted again, but since her father's incarceration, she was terrified to get behind the wheel of a car.

"JD, maybe that's enough for today." Amina was sweating even though the air conditioner was blasting. She had a death grip on the steering wheel.

"You've got to get out of your head." The calmness of his voice helped relax her.

JD was correct, but that was easier said than done. "I know."

"Well, drive us to the diner. Kondo is meeting us there. We'll eat and regroup."

"You want me to drive?" Her entire body stiffened like a board at the thought.

"Yes, you can do it."

He seemed so convinced that she could that she wanted to at least try. His faith in her was stronger than her faith in herself.

It took them longer than it should have; several people passed them and honked the horn, but JD never rushed her. He was supportive and kept encouraging her. Seeing the diner was like a beacon of light. She parked and let out a sigh of relief.

"See, I knew you could do it."

Amina nodded and exited the car. That was all the practicing she wanted to do for the day.

"I thought that was y'all. Amina how was your first driver's lesson?"

"We're alive."

Kondo cracked up, and then he pulled her into a side hug. "Was it that bad?"

"Ko, she did fine."

Kondo nodded, opened the door for her to enter, and JD followed. Amina shook her head at the brothers. They really were close. During her driving lesson, she found out that Kondo was in his last year of his residency. He was a pediatrician. Amina could just see all the women flocking to his medical practice. JD also shared that his baby brother was a bit of a genius, who graduated medical school in three years. Apparently, graduating early was a trait he shared with his oldest brother, Reth.

They sat themselves at a table, and Amina looked around for Kalifa and waved once she finally saw her.

"Is that Kalifa?" Kondo asked.

"Yeah. Hopefully, we can get one of her off-the-menu meals. My girl is a great cook. She lets Benito order anything he wants. He loves whatever she creates for him."

"How's he doing?" JD asked.

It was an innocent question, but it hit her hard. Amina dropped her head; she had not been as active in Benito's life since she had broken up with his brother. "It's been hard seeing him while not seeing his brother," Amina admitted.

JD put the menu down, and then look at her. "Meaning?"

"I broke up with BC a while back because I found out he got a girl pregnant. Since I'm working as a nanny in addition to school and the center, I don't have the extra time that I once had. My schedule is packed, but I call Benito to check on him. We talk when he comes to the center. Yet, it's not like it used to be, due to BC and I not being together."

JD nodded, and Amina noticed that he and Kondo shared a silent communication. She wondered what that was about but stayed silent.

"Hey Mina, are y'all ready to order?" Kalifa asked.

"Bring me one of your specials. I don't care what it is. I know it'll be good."

"Same for me, beauty," Kondo added, throwing Kalifa a charming smile. His actions reminded her more of Djimon than Reth.

JD went back to studying the menu. "I'll have the grilled bacon chicken club sandwich plate half and half, no mayo or lettuce, and extra pickles. A pink lemonade to drink and a slice of strawberry cake."

"You're eating today?" Kondo joked.

"What? All Mama had was fruit. Had I known that I would've ate at home. I'm a growing man; I need protein—and sugar," he grinned.

Kondo shook his head in laughter.

"What would you like to drink, Kondo? I already know what Mina wants."

"Pink lemonade is good for me as well, thank you."

"You're welcome. I'll have your drinks soon." With that, Kalifa scampered off.

Amina turned to watch her go, a perplex expression her face. Maybe she misunderstood, but it sure seemed like some light flirting was happening between Kondo and Kalifa, and if it were, she was here for it. "Interesting," she mused.

"What was that?" Kondo asked, lifting his silken brows. He

had the softest, prettiest hair. When his hair was unbound, his curls were popping.

Glancing up at him, she replied, "Nothing, I was just thinking out loud."

Then they fell into light conversation about JD's street ministry and Amina's graduation. It did not take long for Kalifa to bring their drinks. They talked more while waiting for their food. Amina excused herself and went to the bathroom. She checked her phone on the way, just to make sure that Reth had not contacted her. He had not. Amina prayed all was well with Amal.

She wanted to check on Amal but remembered the look on Reth's face. He needed time alone with his family, and she would not intrude. After she used the restroom and washed her hands, Amina texted Benito. Guilt assailed her; she really needed to make some time for him.

Once the decision was made to break up, Amina did not think it would impact her relationship with Benito. Unsure of how it was going to work out in the long run, she was not turning her back on Benito. Walking with her head down and mind fully concentrated on texting, she bumped into someone. She had an apology ready, but when she saw who it was, she held it back.

"That's how you do me?" BC asked.

"I didn't see you. Excuse me."

Instead, he held her in place. "Mina, I miss you. Benito misses you. We need to sit down and work this out."

She glared at him, words and lyrics flowing through her mind. Now, she viewed him differently. All those things she praised him for seemed so insignificant. He was just a guy like any other, and he was not after her heart; he simply wanted to use her. Nothing that he could say would make her believe differently. "Benigno Cordero Soto-Calderón, we are no longer together, nor will we be. I'm not interested in dating someone who would cheat on me and make a baby with another woman. Not just that, but a woman who is clearly my enemy. You disrespected me, and I'll not dishonor myself by taking you back. As for Benito, I'll always be here for him. I was just texting him. As far as us, we're not going to ever be what we once were. Maybe down the line, friendship will be possible but nothing more than that. I don't trust you anymore."

That was probably the most she ever spoke at one time to him. It felt good to get all that out.

BC pulled in his bottom lip and the tips of his ears were red. BC nodded his head as if he were weighing her words and his response to them. He lowered his hands to her waist and pulled her close to him. Due to their standing there so long, they were gaining the attention of other customers. His hold on her was making Amina nervous.

"BC."

"Walk with me outside. I don't need these people in my business."

"My food's coming."

"It'll keep; now come on before you upset me. I already don't like how you talking to me."

Amina was about to reply but hushed and followed him out of the diner. She hoped that JD and Kondo had not witnessed any of this. She did not need to jeopardize her job. Her aunt had already made a scene, and she did not need BC doing the same.

BC pulled her toward his car and just looked her up and down. She did not have anything special on. It was just a tan t-shirt dress and sandals.

"Why are you trying to hurt me, Mina baby? I admitted my mistake. I've implored your forgiveness, but you keep saying the same thing. Like, what makes you think you can break up with me? After all I've invested in you, all I've done for you, and all we've been through. How can you throw us away because of one mistake out of years of dating?"

Amina rolled her neck from side to side to relieve tension. She did her best not to knit her eyebrows or show any annoyance with her facial features. BC was really getting on her nerves. How she never saw this possessive controlling side of him before had her stupefied.

"Answer me!" he shouted, causing her to jump and frown her face.

"Chill, BC. You're going to give yourself a stroke allowing your temper to reign like that. I didn't throw you away. Do not try to manipulate the situation to fit your narrative. You threw me away once you decided to have intimate relations with that girl. I'm simply responding to your actions. This is what we call consequences."

His faced balled up and his chest inflated as he digested her words. "Don't do that. Don't come off like you better than me when you know if you had of just gave me what I wanted I wouldn't have messed up. I didn't even want to have sex with that girl, but every time I tried with you, you pulled way. You were acting like you didn't want me."

The lyrics of Lauryn Hill's 'Lost Ones' started flowing through Amina's mind.

"If that's the story you want to tell, then go with it. I'm not to blame for the decision that you made. I would be to blame if I took you back and you did the same thing, which statistically, you will do. Let's end this while we can still be amicable to each other."

His scowl deepened at her response. "You're mine, Mina." He gripped her tighter at that declaration. His body suctioned to hers, making it nearly impossible to move. "I told you that a long time ago. You agreed. So, there's no breaking up. You need a break, cool. I'ma give you that because I hurt you. Don't think it's forever, and don't think you can leave me or mess around on me. From here on out, watch the tone and words you use when speaking to me."

Then he leaned over her and whispered in her ear, "Don't make me have to show you that other side of me. I'm being nice now, but the longer you fight me, the worse it will get."

Before Amina could formulate a rebuttal, she was being pulled back. JD gently placed her back behind him, and Kondo was directly in BC's face. An angry Kondo was all kinds of scary, and Amina was thankful not to be on the receiving end of his ire.

"Not that one," Kondo warned.

With a menacing glare on his face, BC stepped to Kondo. "Man, I don't know who you are, but that's my girl, so move around." BC bared his teeth like a rabid dog.

Immovable and irritated, Kondo narrowed his eyes, daring BC to try him. "Amina doesn't have a boyfriend anymore. Seems he didn't know her worth, so she dumped him." Then he looked back at Amina, "Isn't that right?"

"It is. Just go home, BC. It's over," Amina pleaded. This scene was exactly what she was trying to avoid.

"So, your aunt was right. You replaced me with him? Are you having sex with him? You out here giving him what you withheld from me? That's how you get back at me? I told you if you did that, then blood would be on your hands." His face was so red now that Amina thought he would have a stroke. He was livid. BC was nearly suffocating himself with rage.

Amina's body was shivering she was so frustrated. "No, dummy. You know exactly who they are. We work together at the center. Why would you think I would even—forget it. Just go," Amina spat, which was unlike her. Anger was something she did her best not to give into. She regretted even calling him a dummy. He wasn't dumb, but his accusations were so far off.

He had no right to threaten her friends.

"Whatever, but this isn't over."

"But it is. She's done with you," Kondo warned, sounding just like Reth.

BC waved them off and got into his car then sped away.

"I can't believe my life," Amina mumbled and then turned away and went back into the diner, into Kalifa's awaiting arms. She was thankful that JD and Kondo were present, as the situation would have been much worse.

She had no idea who this BC was. He had never treated her like this before, and it scared her.

Solace, though temporary and fleeting, consumed Amina when she was in the music room. The Goode Center was where she felt most comfortable. Coming in early, she needed to play her violin to clear her mind. Retrieving the violin from its case, she admired it a moment before preparing her mind and body to play. Then, like magic, the melody exploded. Instantly, relief washed over her body.

The music was fast and hard; it was how she felt. BC had no right to conduct himself the way he did, and he threatened her! Never in her life had she dealt with so much drama. When had BC started behaving that way? It was reminiscent of her father's obsession with her mother. That could never happen. Death was the only way her mother was free, Amina refused to allow that to be her destiny.

Then she felt guilty. Reth and his family were dealing with the impending loss of Amal, yet his brothers were thrusted into her domestic dispute. It should not be happening at all. The more she thought the harder she played. Gradually the stress and tension started to melt away. She finished the tune, relaxed her shoulders, and then opened her eyes. Her mind was clearer than it was before she started.

"What goes through your mind when you play like that?" Reth's penetrating voice boomed through the quiet room.

Alarmed by his arrival, her immediate concern was Amal. "Is Amal okay?" Amina's eyes widened in fear. If he said those words, she would be completely lost. So much had already occurred, and there was no way she could deal with that loss.

A genuine smile lit up his face. No man should look that gorgeous. It was distracting. "You have this uncanny ability to never directly answer my questions. However, Amal is as good as can be expected. She was as concerned about you as you are about her. You two have become close."

Amina nodded as Reth continued speaking. "I'm here to drop off Hasina for practice. Also, I wanted to apologize if I spoke too harshly to you this morning. I was in a stressed state of mind and it was wrong to ask you to leave."

Amina was shaking her head before he completed his sentence. "There's nothing to apologize for. I understand. Um, but to answer your question, I play what I feel. Oftentimes, I find it difficult to accurately communicate my thoughts and feelings verbally, so I just play."

Well, she did not have that issue earlier today when she interacted with BC. Her standing up for herself probably surprised him as much as it shocked her. Reth absorbed her words and was quiet for a time. Amina liked how he took a moment before he spoke. It let her know that he meant what he said. He listened to understand, not to respond. "I don't think I've ever witnessed a person be so immersed in the music. It's almost as if you become one with the notes, but it's more than that; you make others feel it too. Amal and I discussed that today. When you play, it's more than the intervals and scales, sounds, and notes; it enwraps the listener, bathing them in the highs and lows, the pitches, and tones. The music comes alive in a way I've never experienced before. Your ability to do that intrigues me."

Then the world stopped turning. Amina just gaped at him. Why couldn't he be available? BC never got her music like that. It was not important to him, but in one moment Reth made her feel unexplainable joy. The more she learned about Reth the more her soul longed to connect to his.

She had no idea how to reply to that. No one had ever told her that her music enwrapped them or made them feel as if they were bathing in the notes. Reth sure knew how to give a compliment. If her skin were lighter, he would have witnessed her entire body flush.

"Amina, are you okay?"

Amina nodded her head, though her mouth was still opened.

"Are you having one of those moments where you cannot accurately communicate your thoughts?"

She burst into laughter. His humor caught her off-guard. The entire interaction had. "Sorry, it's just that no one has ever described my playing that way. It just took me by surprise, is all. It's the greatest compliment I have ever received. Thank you."

"It's the truth. As my brother said, we're honest."

Amina broke eye contact. If she looked at him any longer, her admiration might turn into adoration and he was a married man. She was sure he meant nothing by what he said, but boy was it getting her in her feelings.

To distract herself, she started to fiddle with anything in order not to look at him. "I have to get the music ready for the children. Are you staying to hear Hasina play?"

"If you don't mind. Amal wants me to record her."

"Parents are always welcome."

$$\infty \infty \infty$$

She's uncomfortable, Reth surmised as he watched Amina interact with the children. She was a natural and they adored her. Seeing the way Amina interacted with Hasina warmed Reth's heart.

If this were before Amal, Amina would have caught his attention and kept it. That was something he struggled with. Amina was extremely stunning, and the fact that she was unaware of how beautiful she was made her that much more attractive. It aggrieved him that she clammed up after he complimented her musical talent.

It was true. He loved music. However, there was something distinctive, pristine, and captivating about the way Amina played. Amal told him that in church the day she heard Amina singing a Tamela Mann song and it was as if she floated into the sanctuary. It was an experience for sure. Amina's gift was music. It reached him in a way nothing else ever had.

Reth leaned back and quietly observed her. She was more composed now. Maybe his arrival unnerved her. Though he originally thought it was what he said, he wondered if it had something to do with her interaction with her ex-boyfriend.

Kondo and JD shared with him how BC was aggressive toward Amina. Knowing Amina, she was concerned about his reaction. She had nothing to be anxious about. Amina was not the issue, BC was. If BC were going to be a problem, Reth would address it. No matter what, Amina's place was secured, always. She was family now, and he was protective of his family.

He was already in the process of having that aunt of hers removed from the house. She had been served a thirty-day notice to vacate. It was on his to-do list to contact Aaron

Williams as well as Gavin. Once Amal started to have some better days, he would take care of that.

Amal requested that he take care of Amina, which he would do anyway, but since Amal spoke so passionately about it, he made it a top priority. That's what he was doing now.

He was and would always be a man of action.

"Daddy, watch me play." Hasina's honeyed voice called to him.

He watched her, giving her his full attention. She smiled. Amina was teaching her how to play the viola. Though the piano was his daughter's first love, she seemed to be taking well to her new instrument. Seeing her giggle and interact so easily with Amina calmed his concerned heart.

There would come a day when Amal would not be present, and he wondered would his daughter still smile then. He never wanted her to be sad.

Amina whispered something in her ear that made her giggle, and then Amina kissed the top her head before making her way to Benito.

This must be what Amal sees in Amina. She's just a humble, caring soul that has been through ordeal after ordeal, never allowing her setbacks to dictate her movements. He respected her for that.

Chapter 14

Sickness was in the air, and death was not far behind. Every day felt special as any day could be Amal's last. That knowledge was ripping Amina's heart to pieces. She felt that Amal's time on this side was coming to an end.

It terrified her. It upset her. Mostly, it just pained her. If anyone knew the aftermath of death, then it was Amina.

Grieving Amal's impending death was bringing back the loss of her mother and brothers. Unlike Amina, Reth and Hasina had a great, supportive family. They would get through this trying time; it would be extremely difficult but not impossible. Amina was going to be by Hasina's side for as long as she needed her to be. Reth, too, if he required her support. In a short time, she fell in love with the entire Goode family. They were what family was supposed to be.

Reth's brothers were spending more time at the house. One of his brothers always spent the night, and his parents visited daily. Kalifa had even come by to visit and brought food for the family. They were so thankful and welcoming to Kalifa.

Today, Amina and Hasina were sitting at the table making a musical picture collage of Hasina's family. Most of the pictures were of Hasina and Amal. The idea came to Amina the previous night.

The pair was deeply invested in their project when the doorbell rang. Remembering that Reth's family was in various parts of the house, Amina got up to answer the door when Djimon flew by her. "I got it, goddess."

Amina nodded and turned her attention back to the art project.

"Let me see my daughter!" an agitated voiced yelled, and Hasina ducked down, a fearful look etched on her face. It caused Amina to become alarmed.

"Hasina, what's wrong?"

"It's my other grandma, the mean one."

That meant it was Amal's mother. Though Amina had no interaction with the woman, Reth and Amal did. When Amina first arrived at the Goode household, she overheard Reth talking about Delilah. Amal called her darkness and said she was like Adeya. That unnerved Amina, but no one was going to hurt or upset Hasina or Amal in her presence. Amina was the product of what happened to an unprotected child. That was not going to happen to Hasina.

"Don't worry, I won't let anyone hurt or upset you. It's me and you, right?"

Hasina nodded. A relieved look rested on her face.

The idea of anyone harming Hasina in the slightest rubbed Amina wrong.

"Calm down, Delilah. I didn't say you can't see her. I said she was sleeping. Reth is in there now; I'll escort you upstairs," Djimon replied sternly. It was a tone that Amina had not heard from him. In times like these, most people did not have the patience to deal with ignorance.

Amina worried her bottom lip at Delilah's outburst. Reth demanded that everyone who entered be quiet. He stressed that he only wanted positive vibes around Amal. Amina was sure with the arrival of Amal's mother that would be shattered.

Amina heard their footfalls grow quieter, and then she

assisted Hasina in sitting up and the two went back to completing their project.

"Tell me, why does your grandma's appearance cause you to react like that?"

Hasina gradually looked at Amina until their eyes connected.

"She's not like Bibi Goode. She's loud and mean. I can't do anything right when she comes to visit. She makes me nervous."

Amina knew the feeling. She felt like that around Adeya. Children were not created to be perfect, and they were not little adults. It bothered her that Hasina had to suffer for even a moment.

"Sometimes, she hits me, but don't tell Daddy."

That caused Amina's entire body to go stiff. "Hits you?" At the child's admission, Amina could feel her blood pressure rising.

Hasina nodded. "When I forget my manners or do something wrong. I try really hard, but I can't remember all the time."

The Bible says to be slow to anger, slow to speak, and quick to listen. It was how her mother raised her, but she was absolutely enraged. So much so that she wanted to march up to Delilah and dare the woman to try her. Why would anyone hit Hasina? She was a sweet, innocent little girl. There was no reason for her to be this anxious and nervous. There was no way she was keeping this information from Reth. He needed to know.

Burying her anger, Amina leaned back on the couch and gathered herself mentally. She did not want to upset Hasina more. However, if Reth knew that Delilah had hit his daughter, and Amina knew and did not share that information, he would be livid. Having seen that side of Reth, she did not want to be the eye of his ire. Also, he had a right to know.

"Hasina, your daddy is super awesome. Like hands down one of the best dads I have ever met. I think it would hurt his feelings if we kept a secret like this from him. In fact, I don't think keeping secrets are ever good. It would be best if you shared with your father what you told me. I'll be there with you if you want."

Hasina's face darkened for a moment as if she were weighing her options. She looked a lot like her mother. Her facial expressions were like Reth's. "Daddy won't be mad?"

"Not at you, sweetheart. He loves you so much. All he wants to do is keep you safe and only allow people in your life who love you and protect you."

Hasina nodded and they went back to doing their collage.

About twenty minutes later, Amina was making lunch for Hasina, when her cell phone started going off. Looking at the caller ID, Amina had no idea who it was but answered just in case it was something about her father.

"Hello?"

"Is this Amina?"

"Yes."

"Good afternoon. It's Principal Edwards. I was attempting to get into contact with Ms. Mary, but was unable, and you are the next contact."

"What's wrong, Mrs. Edwards? Is Benito okay?"

"Benito was involved in a fight. It was not his fault; he was defending himself, but he did get hurt. The nurse checked him out and wanted him to go to the hospital, but he's refusing."

"I'm coming." Amina hung up and placed food in front of Hasina before telling her she would be right back.

Several thoughts circulated through her mind as she

powerwalked to Reth's office and knocked on the door.

"Enter."

Relaxing her nerves, Amina entered and saw all the brothers and their father had assembled in the office. For a moment, she feared she had interrupted something important. "Excuse me, I apologize for interrupting. Benito's school called, and he's been hurt. They can't get into contact with Ms. Mary and I'm the next contact. Can I leave to get him?"

Reth facial features softened at her request. "Of course. Where's Hasina?" Reth questioned.

"She's in the kitchen. I was making her lunch."

"I'll go with you and check him out," Kondo offered.

"I'll go tend to my niece," JD added and excused himself.

Amina nodded; she kept forgetting Kondo was a doctor. "Thank you, Kondo. Thank you, too, Reth." JD was already gone, but she would thank him later. It warmed her heart the way they were so willing to serve without being asked.

Reth nodded, and Amina turned to leave with Kondo by her side. Before leaving, Amina picked Hasina up and explained she would be back but had to help Benito. Amina gently kissed her forehead. "I'll be back as soon as I can, Hasina. If you need me, no matter what it is, you call me."

Hasina nodded her head in agreement. She was now sitting on JD's lap and seemed content. Amina knew that she was safe with her uncle. There was no way that Delilah would attempt anything when so many eyes were on her. Still, Amina whispered a prayer. Then she and Kondo left.

It seemed to take forever to get to the school, but the drive was less than half an hour. Kondo assured her that Benito was most likely fine. However, Amina would not accept that until she saw it with her own eyes.

Before Kondo parked his vehicle, Amina was out the door,

running into the school. She knew the layout well. "Where's Benito?" Amina shouted, not caring how she looked or sounded.

"He's in here."

By the time she entered the nurse's office, Kondo had caught up to her with his doctor's bag.

"This is Dr. Goode. He's going to check him out," Amina told the nurse who was checking out Kondo and not being secretive about it.

Benito had a busted lip, a swelling knot on his forehead, and dried blood from his nose. His eyes were red from crying, and Amina was livid. Fighting back her own tears, she watched closely as Kondo began to assess Benito.

Kondo started examining him and asking him what hurt, and when Benito pulled up his shirt, Amina nearly lost it; there was massive bruising.

"What happened?" Amina snapped her neck to the nurse.

"I didn't witness it."

"Where's Mrs. Edwards because this is unacceptable, and somebody will tell me something. He's ten; that doesn't look like injuries done by some other kid; did they gang up on him?"

The nurse turned bright red and went to get Mrs. Edwards. As soon as she left, Amina glanced at Kondo. "Is anything broken? Does he need stitches or x-rays?"

"I know it looks bad, but there isn't anything broken or any internal bleeding. However, I will take him to the hospital if that makes you feel better."

"I trust you, Kondo." Just as those words left her mouth Ms. Edwards entered.

"Who did that to him?" Amina fumed.

"There was a group of boys that did this. Neither Benito nor the other boys would say what started the altercation."

"What are you going to do about this?"

Clasping her hands, Principal Edwards maintained eye contact and answered, "The boys will be suspended."

Amina crossed her arms, unimpressed with the punishment. "We've had this conversation before about his being bullied. It was my understanding that this school district has a zero policy on bullying. When the bullying turns violent, the offending party is supposed to be expelled. That's what your policy states. However, this was a lynching, and I ought to press charges. If it's the same little boys, you better do something about them before he comes back to school. If I find out it's because Benito is Black and Puerto Rican and those boys are white, we're going to have some major issues." Amina was shaking she was so upset. Add what Hasina told her about Delilah, and she was about to lose her religion.

"If he requires any medical attention, we'll be sending the school the bill. In fact, I want a meeting with their families as well. I request a copy of the video because I know you have cameras all over. This is supposed to be a safe school, but he's had more issues here than anywhere else. If you fail to adhere to the policy your school created, please believe you'll be hearing from my attorney. That child did not deserve this treatment or your subpar protection. Shame on you, Principal Edwards. This better be the last time anything like this happens." Then she turned her attention back to Benito. "Come on, sweetie. Dr. Goode is going to take care of you and then we'll call Ms. Mary."

Kondo carefully assisted Benito to a standing position and assisted him walking as the three departed. Feeling completely overwhelmed, Amina started to cry. Quickly whipping her tears away, she got into the backseat with Benito and did her best to comfort him. Confrontation terrified her unless she was fighting for someone else.

As Kondo entered the driver's side he stated, "Remind me to never get on your bad side. You went in, and I was like well, she got that. I didn't know you had in you."

Amina's features soften at his words, her eyes as red as a stop sign. Chewing her bottom lip, she was about to apologize for her uncharacteristic behavior, however, Kondo shook his head. "That's the momma bear in you, and you were one hundred percent right."

Once everyone was settled, Amina asked, "Can we take him to your parents' home? I don't want to impose on Reth and Amal."

"Don't worry about it. My brother won't mind."

Amina hoped he did not.

Kondo took care of Benito, and he was now sleeping peacefully in her bedroom suite. Amina was somewhat more settled than before. Although her face was back to its natural dark chocolate hue, her nerves were still a little rattled. Even after speaking with Ms. Mary, the incident still bothered her. More so because she was ignorant as to what instigated the situation. As far as she knew, the bullying had ended.

Leaning her head back against the wall, her golden eyes followed the path of Kondo. He had been her superhero today. As upset as she was, he had her laughing as he recounted her interaction with Principal Edwards. Amina teased him back about the school nurse that tried to slip her number into his medical bag.

"Did he tell you what happened?" Kondo asked.

"No. He's keeping it from me, but maybe he'll tell Ms. Mary or his brother. Thank you so much for looking after him," Amina finished before pealing her body off the wall to hug him.

Kondo smiled and winked at her before he exited the room. Alone with her thoughts, Amina sat in the middle of the bedroom floor exhausted. Her worry wheel was out of control. The tension was causing her lower back to ache. Amina dropped her head in a silent prayer. Praying usually relaxed her enough to release tension, one of her top three coping strategies she utilized to center herself. Listening to music was her second and writing music was her third.

As she prayed, she hummed a tune she was working on. For some reason, it felt more powerful than words. A knock on her door startled her trance-like focus. Glancing up at the open door, Amina saw Reth standing there. His features were composed, and he remained silent as he motioned for her to come out of the room.

"Is everything okay?" Amina's eyes widened in concern.

Reth offered a side smirk before replying, "You worry a lot, don't you?"

Shrugging her thin shoulders, Amina let out a guilty breath. "I try not to be that way."

"Mmhm. My daughter talked to me today. She shared that you told her it wasn't good to keep secrets from her father." He lifted a brow and his lips barely turned up.

Amina let out a sigh of relief. It warmed her heart that Hasina had a trusting and loving relationship with her father. "She had an unusual reaction to Amal's mother, and I asked why. When she told me the truth, she didn't want you to know. I just reminded her that she had a really great dad who wouldn't be angry if she were honest."

"Thank you."

Amina nodded.

"I appreciate how you care for Hasina. I had no idea Delilah ever hit my daughter, and the revelation shocked and angered me. It's been addressed, and Delilah is aware she is to never touch Hasina again. She also is not staying in the house. I want the women in this house to feel comfortable and safe. Delilah seems to have the opposite effect on everyone."

Doing her best not to swoon at his vow of dedication to his family, Amina replied, "As long as Hasina and Amal are good, then so am I. It's their home; it's my place of employment."

"It's your home too. If you ever feel like it isn't, then let me know so I can remedy the situation."

Unable to school her features, Amina almost swallowed her tongue. She was sure her face was going through so many expressions that he probably thought she was a mood ring.

"Thank you."

He nodded. "Also, my Ma phoned Ms. Mary to let her know about Benito, and she agreed to let him stay the night. Kondo will stay the night to monitor his progress. Ms. Mary will pick him up in the morning."

Frowning at the information, Amina replied, "Oh, I thought she was on her way."

"She was, but my mother requested he stay. There wasn't an immediate need for her to drive all this way. Both she and Benito need their rest."

"That's great." Amina started to turn to leave him, but he called her back. His arms were now across his chest. His demeanor was more serious now. That caused her to hesitate in concern.

"JD and Kondo shared with me about the incident with BC. I understand that you two are no longer together. My brothers stated he was violent toward you. Has he physically assaulted you before?"

Embarrassment flooded her entire being. It was her hope

that the incident, as Reth termed it, would not get back to him. It just made her look irresponsible and immature.

"No. He's just annoyed that I won't take him back. I assure you it won't impact my taking care of Hasina."

Reth waved off the latter part as if it were of consequence. "I'm concerned about you and your wellbeing. If this continues, you're to let me know."

"Of course."

"Alright then, have a good night."

"You as well," Amina replied and watched him leave.

Hours later, Amina was unable to sleep. She got up early and tiptoed to Amal's bedroom. The door was already ajar, so Amina entered. She padded softly to the bed to see that Amal was awake; she was staring at the musical picture collage, and Hasina was nestled into her mother.

"Hey," Amina whispered.

Amal smiled. "Thank you for this."

"You're welcome."

"Rest a while with us." Her voice sounded so strained. Amina did as she requested, and then she started singing softly. That seemed to always relax Amal.

∞∞∞

Reth stared into the dark morning. Dew rested on the ground and decorated the windows. It had been weeks since he and Amal had the conversation about her letting go. He honestly had not been sleeping, so he just kept watch over her. Even though her time was dwindling down, she was happy. Reth knew that was because of Hasina and Amina. That young woman had nestled into Amal's, as well as his bothers', heart.

If he were honest, she had nestled into his heart also. Not wanting to linger on what that meant, Reth buried the thought. Since Amal was dealing with so much, Reth did not share that Delilah had hit their daughter. That kind of information would not help his wife. Instead, he told Amal he felt it was best for her mother to stay at a nearby hotel and then visit. Amal agreed and shared with Reth that just as Adeya was spiteful and uncaring toward Amina, her mother was the same. He and Amal spoke at length about the similarities that she and Amina shared and how God chose the perfect time to introduce the two.

His wife said that Amina was her Ruth. He did not understand that term, but he had been reading the book of Ruth to attempt to understand what his wife meant. He studied the relationship between Ruth and Naomi; he thought Amal was speaking of the friendship, companionship, and loyalty between the two women, not necessarily that Ruth was Naomi's daughter-in-law. It was not a book that he previously paid interest to until now. When he read the book of Ruth, with Amal and Amina in mind, his comprehension of his wife's meaning was becoming apparent.

Quietly, Reth had observed the relationship between his wife and Amina grow stronger. Women that Amal had known for years were not as close as she and Amina. It was a sincere, loving friendship. Reth had not thought that would occur when his mother suggested that Amina become Hasina's nanny. His daughter genuinely loved and trusted Amina. His entire family was smitten by her. Everyone could see how special Amina was, except Amina. Maybe it was humility or maybe it was the haunting lies her father and aunt told her. All he knew was that Amina was rare and exceptional.

He even admired her drive and work ethic. After all she suffered and survived in her life, she loved and cared about others. Amina did not hesitate to put the needs of others before herself. Not only did she have a Ruth spirit, but she had virtuous qualities. Letting out a breath, he decided to visit with Amal.

Leaving his office, he jogged up the stairs and headed to her bedroom. When he arrived, the door was ajar, and he wondered if Hasina had snuck in to be nearer to her mother. Lately, she had been doing that a lot as if she sensed that her mother would soon be transitioning. As he entered the bedroom, he saw not only his wife but also his daughter and Amina. He smiled. It was good that Amal was surrounded by love.

Chapter 15

I t was the wheezing that woke Reth. His heart palpitated as he lunged out of the recliner to get to Amal. Something inside of him told him her time was ending.

"Amal, I'm here; it's okay." He did his best to sooth her while also contacting the onsite hospice nurse on duty.

"It's time, Re. Remember what you promised, okay? Tell your parents and brothers the truth about us. Love again and take care of Hasina and Amina; let them take care of you."

Reth nodded his head, but he was not ready. This was his friend. No, they did not have the traditional relationship of husband and wife. She wanted him to share with his family the truth that he kept buried for years. He would never lie to Amal. If that was her dying request, then he would do it.

"Let me get everyone here so they can say goodbye."

As weak as she was, she managed to halt his movement. "Everyone I need to see is here. I've made my peace with everyone. I'm tired, and I'm ready."

Reth lift his hand to softly caress her face. Just as he did, Hasina woke up, her eyes missing nothing as they landed on her mother.

"Mommy, are you going to heaven now?" It was an innocent question. There was no sadness or hurt in her voice, more of acceptance and understanding that the time had come. For some reason, his daughter's question ripped through him.

Reth choked his tears down. A million times he ran this scenario through his mind. Still, he was unprepared. Yet, Hasina and Amal seemed at peace.

"Yeah, baby. God's calling me home. Remember, we talked about this?"

Reth was amazed at how strong Amal's voiced sounded when she spoke to Hasina.

His daughter nodded. "Amina said I can still talk to you. I'll feel you in the wind, in your flower garden, in the swaying of the trees, and inside of me. You'll be everywhere. I won't see you, but I'll always feel you. You're going to be with the angels watching over me."

Unable to hold back, tears roamed down Reth's eyes as he heard his daughter accept the reality of what was happening. It seemed to comfort Amal as well. Amina had been sweet to explain it that way to Hasina.

"That's right, Hasina," Amina added.

Hasina leaned over and kissed her mother. It was tender and sweet. Reth knew this would be the last time he witnessed this interaction.

Out of the corner of his eye he saw Amina. She placed her hand over Amal's and held it tenderly. "I love you, Amal. Thank you for being my friend, for trusting me, and showing me the true definition of beauty. It isn't a curse; it's a gift from God."

Though Reth could see the life draining from her, there was a lovely smile on her face. "Bye for now, my loves."

Reth leaned back on his haunches and watched Amal close her eyes. God knows she fought a long time. He wanted her to rest; she deserved it. His heart mourned the loss immediately. At the same time, he felt relief for his wife. Peace, as only God could provide, entered the room as her life exited.

"Bye for now, Mal," he whispered as he kissed her cheek.

Reth had gotten lost in the thoughts when he heard the shrilling voice of his mother-in-law. He thanked God that she was not present during Amal's last moments. Amal deserved a peaceful transition.

"Is she dead? Why didn't anyone contact me?" Delilah demanded. "I should have been here."

Reth closed his eyes and took a deep breath. Amal did not want her present, but he refused to share that information. It would only cause strife.

He opened his eyes to witness Amina gathering up Hasina preparing to exit the bedroom. He knew that Amina took her job seriously of protecting Hasina. It was something he appreciated right now.

Gazing at Amal one more time, Reth got up and escorted Hasina and Amina out the door. They came face-to-face with Delilah.

"Who is she?" Delilah seethed. Her bejeweled index fingered pointed accusingly at Amina as if she had not seen her before. That irritated Reth.

"Family," Reth replied dryly, though he owed her no explanation.

"Why is she in my daughter's bedroom? You let her in there and not me?" Delilah screeched like a banshee. Her eyes narrowed in disgust and she balled up her face in anger.

Briefly, Reth wondered where that disgust was when her daughter was suffering and needed her. Fighting his instinct to tell her off, Reth took a calming breath before replying, "They were saying goodbye, and you're welcome to do the same, but don't be rude, Delilah. I'm a man mourning my wife, and I'll not deal with your antics this day," he warned.

Delilah shook her head but held her tongue as she entered Amal's bedroom. Reth did not want to insult her, but he knew how she was. Today was not the day for her to go full Delilah mode. He did not have the patience necessary to deal with her.

Chapter 16

Butterflies flew around Reth as he sat quietly in the flower garden that Amal created. This place was her haven, where she felt at ease. It was beautiful and colorful, like Amal.

A grin eased across his face as he recalled when Amal first got the idea to garden. Amal killed all the flowers within days. Bless her heart but she had no idea what she was doing. However, she was determined. They ended up hiring a professional to teach her. Reth chuckled at the memory.

Now the garden had an assorted array of beautiful flowers from all over the world. This was where he said his final goodbye. Soon enough, the funeral would happen, but he wanted to privately pay respects to his friend, his partner. Even though they were not lovers, there was love between them. They were the best of friends. Amal's trauma and painful secret unified them in a way nothing else could. He was prepared to take her secret to the grave, but she wanted it told. As always, he would respect her wishes.

Deeply connected to his inner thoughts, Reth did not notice he was no longer alone until a dulcet voice spoke his name. "Reth, would you like some breakfast?" For a moment, he thought he dreamed it. However, when the scent of vanilla bean with a hint of coconut floated over him, he knew Amina was present.

From the day Amal took her last breath, Amina had been

by his and Hasina's side. She worked tirelessly and asked for nothing in return. Already, she assisted his mother in writing thank you cards. Even though she was timid and quiet around new people, she interceded if she noticed that he or Hasina were tired of the onslaught of visitors. For that, he appreciated her. It was as if she understood when to be silent and when to speak.

"No, but if you and Hasina are done, I would like some company," Reth answered as he turned to look at her. Tranquility overtook him the moment he laid eyes on Amina. She was dressed in a white sundress that highlighted her black jade skin; innocence radiated from her golden eyes that were adorn with remorse and empathy. A hint of a smile spread across her face as their eyes met. Meekly, she clasped her hands in front of her, showcasing her timid personality. It was not pretend; it was just Amina.

Biting the side of her top lip, she spoke softly. "Your mother has taken Hasina with her. They're having a girls' day. So, it's just us. If you like, I can play you something. I have my saxophone."

Music had always been a way for him to cope with stress as well as anxiety. With the recent loss, he needed a moment of respite. It seemed Amina sensed his need. Thankful for her insight, Reth gestured in agreement.

It did not take her long to come back. With the delicacy of a dancer, she assembled her saxophone and placed her stand in the other hand. Once she was settled, she started to play. The mellow, rich tone flowed over Reth like a serene wind. Wrapped up in the security of the melody, he closed his eyes as the music uplifted him. It was a song he was unfamiliar with, but he liked it. He wondered if it were a song she wrote. Amina was that talented.

Everything about her was majestic. What befuddled him was how she could be filled with so much love and caring for others and lost so much. That was the beauty of her. It made Amina stand out in the crowd. It warmed his heart that Hasina had Amina in her life. There was no one that compared to her. Amal spoke so highly and lovingly about Amina. Now he could see why. For a young woman who had suffered and been denied loving kindness, she shared it selflessly.

When the ballad ended, Reth felt less grieved and more grateful. His russet eyes opened, and he peered into eyes the color of the sun. They were heated and illuminating. She was entrancing and alluring without even trying.

"Did you compose the ballad?"

Blinking her eyes several times, which was something she did when embarrassed, she answered, "I did."

"It's beautiful."

Amina offered a bashful grin that transformed her face. Then she unhooked the saxophone and put in on the stand. Silenced lingered between them, though Reth could feel her quietly observing him.

A myriad of scenarios entered his mind as he pondered what she was thinking as she took him in. However, the wait was short. With choppy uncertain steps, she strolled over to him. She stood directly in front of him, a soft wind caused her dress to sway around her exposed legs. Letting out a breath, she asked, "Reth, would you allow me to pray for you?"

In all the thoughts that circulated his mind, that inquiry was unexpected. Knowing Amina like he did, that should have been his first thought. The sincerity in her voice humbled him. Many people had come and offered their thoughts and advice since the death of Amal, but Amina was the first to request to pray for him.

There was no way he would deny her request. He motioned it was okay, and Amina ease down in a praying position in front of him. With an ease of one who had been praying a lifetime, she clasped her delicate hands around his large ones and beseeched the Father on his behalf. Something unlocked in his heart. It was felt physically on a supernatural level. Something he could not quite name, but he was certain that this was a moment of awakening.

∞∞∞

The day felt never-ending. Reth was relieved that strangers had been replaced by family. His mother brought Hasina back, and Amina was upstairs preparing her for bed. He was grateful for Amal and his mother's insight of how much Hasina needed extra care.

Reth's father was informing everyone that their aunt and uncle as well as their cousin Mahari would not be able to attend the funeral. Mahari was in West Africa on a Christian mission. Miriam was on a faith-based medical mission with Hospitals of Hope. There had been an outbreak that required his aunt's medical expertise.

Miriam was a critical care nurse and dedicated herself to medical missions early on. She had her doctorate's degree in nursing (DNP), and with her extensive knowledge, Reth understood the importance of medical skills. Mahari was an optometrist, bringing sight to the less fortunate.

"They're doing God's work. I know if they were able to be here, they would," Reth replied.

Chiram agreed.

Before his father could speak more on the situation, the doorbell rang. Frowning at the disruption, Reth let out a low grumble. Father forgive him, but he was tired of entertaining people. It was draining in a way he never thought it could be.

"I'll get it," JD offered as if sensing his brother's fatigue.

Reth shook his head in appreciation.

Now, he regretted letting his staff have an extended vacation. At least he had his family to use as a buffer. It was becoming overwhelming.

Reth cracked his neck, easing the tension in his body as he prepared to greet his new guest. When he saw who it was, he nearly had a conniption. It was Delilah, dressed like royalty with an unknown woman trailing her.

Trouble.

Lifting an irritated brow, Reth leaned back in his chair and silently took in the two women before him.

"Son," Delilah gushed, though Reth knew it was for show. She only referred to him as "son" when she wanted something. He was no longer obligated to adhere to her requests. Make no mistake, he would not. Those days ended the moment Amal transitioned.

Sauntering closer to him as if his home belonged to her, she offered what he suspected to be a welcoming smile. It looked odd on her, though, almost forced. "Yes?"

"I've been extremely worried about you. This is my niece Emmarie," Delilah introduced. "Emmarie, this is Reth, my son. That's his father Chiram." She paused and gave Chiram a flirtatious look that had Reth feeling uncomfortable, and then she continued with the introductions of his brothers.

Emmarie seemed a little nervous. Her brown eyes were locked on Delilah while Reth just watched perplexed. Awaiting an explanation for her arrival, Reth casually observed the room. Delilah's attitude had worsened since Amal's passing. At the time, he dismissed it, assuming it was grief and guilt. Now, he was not so sure.

"Nice to meet you, Emmarie," Djimon offered, as did the rest of the family.

The young woman offered a gracious smile. While she was greeting his family, Reth explored her. Like Amal, Emmarie had light skin with long hair that flowed midway down her back. She was thin, well-dressed, and appeared to be submissive. This was Delilah's protégé.

Hiding a smirk, Reth was becoming aware of what Delilah was planning. She had already failed. There had been a miscalculation on Delilah's part. She assumed he would find Emmarie attractive because of the physical attributes she shared with Amal. It did not matter that his wife had recently died. If only she knew he was not attracted to women who favored Emmarie.

"What brings you by?" Reth's mother asked the question that was burning on the tip of his tongue.

Delilah offered Mrs. Goode a sheepish grin. "Well, first off, I would like to apologize for my actions the day Amal died. It was just so hurtful that I was unable to say goodbye. I know it wasn't intentionally done to keep me from my daughter." She paused then; Reth thought possibly for confirmation that her assumption was correct, but no one said a word.

"However, I came tonight to offer my services, as well as Emmarie's. My niece's fiancé died about six months ago. With Hasina losing her mother, I thought it would be perfect for Emmarie to help her deal with the transition of loss." Delilah nodded, doing her best to look innocent and caring.

"Is that so?" Reth deadpanned.

His brothers all glanced his way. The tension in the room was mounting like the beginning of a tropical storm.

Delilah was incredibly transparent. They had not even buried Amal, yet this woman was plotting, probably thinking that since Hasina was her mother's sole heir that she could somehow get access to the finances. Amal's deceased father had left her money, and Reth invested her inheritance, tripling it. Amal had half placed into a trust for their daughter and used the other half for living and leisure expenses. Reth had only found out a few days ago that Amal's stepfather had money in place for Amal as well, which would now go to Hasina. However, Emre and Delilah were separated, and that was something she did not know. Reth knew. Emre spoke to him two days ago, filling him in. This niece was not blood related. Emre's goddaughter who had no close relationship with Amal. There was no way he was permitting a stranger to have access to his daughter.

One had to stay several steps ahead of Delilah. The woman played to win, and she played dirty. He was sure that the arrival of a niece that he had never heard of was a way to get her claws back into him.

"It is, Reth. During a time like this, family needs to be together."

Reth glance at his family, and he noticed the smirk on Djimon's face. JD had his head resting on the couch, eyes closed. It was a sign that he was irritated, and most likely praying to calm his nerves. When his eyes landed on Kondo, he gave him a slight nod. They were in sync.

Then Reth turned his attention back to Delilah. "Hasina has someone. You've met Amina; not only does Hasina have her, but her uncles and my parents have always been active in her life." Next, he turned his eyes to Emmarie. "Thank you for caring, but Hasina has a qualified support system. No disrespect, but you're a stranger to her and my family. I would not feel comfortable, and neither would she."

Fire lit Delilah's eyes. She was fixing her lips for a rebuttal, but like an angel of light, Amina descended the stairs, calling out to him.

"Reth, Hasina is ready for her bedtime story."

Mentally thanking God for the interruption, Reth got up and

serenely strolled toward Amina.

"Why does she address you so informally? Does she live here?" Delilah blurted, her face wrinkling like wet paper.

Curious about her reaction, Reth halted mid-stride and turned around and glared at her. Composing himself before opening his mouth, he asked, "Why?" It was meant for both questions she asked.

"I mean, it's just not proper that so soon after Amal's death, that you, a single man, have an unmarried woman in your household. Not only that, but the way she speaks to you is unprofessional when she's just a servant. Besides, what would people say? It seems she's attempting to take advantage of you."

Kondo let out a dry cackle, causing Reth to look his way. His brothers looked as offended as he felt. JD's eyes popped open, and he glowered at Delilah as if daring her to say something else. The flaming redness of his skin showcased just how upset he was while Djimon's nose flared with agitation. Indignation spread throughout Reth's body. Before he could snap her up, Amina beat him to it. That stunned them all.

"Excuse me, ma'am, but please don't speak on what you don't understand or know. To assert yourself in family business without adequate information only makes you look benighted. Let me enlighten you. I've known the Goode family for many years, possibly longer than you. I consider them my extended family; therefore, I'm not a servant. I'm family. Moreover, I love each person in this family, including Amal and Hasina. Nothing improper has ever occurred nor would it. That's a fictionalized notion created in your overactive mind. Perhaps, you're projecting your own feelings. Let me assure you, I'm not competition. I'm a companion to a child who is mourning her mother. I know what it feels like to lose your mother at an early age. It occurred to me that possibly it's you who seeks to take advantage of Reth during his time of grief.

Although, if that's the case, he's intelligent enough to decipher your motives. Let me be clear; I don't need to scheme; whatever God has for me will be granted to me."

It was Kondo's clapping that yanked Reth from his flabbergasted mental state. It seemed Amina found an adequate way to verbally express herself. His eyes went straight to Amina. It seemed her reaction must have shocked her too. Never had he heard her take up for herself and seeing her do so now elevated his respect for her. That was a part of Amina he had only witnessed tonight. There was a yearning to experience it again. Amina could handle herself. Witnessing her taking Delilah to task made him want to do a celebratory stroll he used to do with his fraternity brothers.

Then with the sweetest expression, Amina turned to him and said, "We need to see about Hasina."

Holding back a chuckle, Reth followed Amina upstairs, leaving a wide-mouthed, affronted Delilah. She was unaccustomed to having someone put her in her place. Amina's clapback was gracious but direct.

"Well spoken, goddess." Djimon commented, and Reth heard a round of laugher followed by the slamming of a door.

Chapter 17

Widower. The word sounded so final and harsh. That one word was as equally alarming as the title of husband and father, courtesy of his former playboy tendencies, but he learned to fulfill those titles. His father was a great man to emulate. The loss of a spouse was different. There was no outline or directions on how to navigate under this new title. For reasons he had yet to decipher, that word plagued his mind last night. He had not thought of it before.

Being a widower signaled the end of a chapter of his life. It also meant that Amal was free and no longer in pain. It should have relieved him. Yet, the guilt and grief that surrounded him was as constant as the air he breathed.

Grief and uncertainty had his mind vacillating between the past and present. Troubling thoughts ranged from what Adrian Jamar Bishop did to Amal to her finally coming to peace with death. A million times he replayed what would have happened had he never introduced her to the man that had broken her. To the man who made her feel her beauty was a curse. A man who disavowed the horrible crime he committed against Amal. He never paid the price for his crime. Amal suffered the shame, the pain, and the denial of the future that she deserved.

Washing away the memory he pressed the creamy medium cigar to his lips. The mellow flavors of cedar, toasted nuts, and nutmeg permeated the air as Reth exhaled the Carlos Toraño 1916 Cameroon Robusto cigar. His size thirteen HTW leather shoes tapped lightly to the sounds of African Jazz great Mulatu Astatke. After burying his wife today, he just wanted to get lost in the music.

Closing his eyes Reth, surrendered to the music. He was purposefully absent from the repast. He just did not want to deal with anyone except his family. Right now, he needed alone time. Delilah had worked his last nerve over the past few days, and the funeral was no better. He was sure everyone noticed her theatrics as she paid her final respects to Amal. Emre and Emmarie had to escort her away from the casket. Poor Hasina melted into his side and paled in shame at Delilah's actions. Hasina's reactions to her grandmother's behavior unleashed a level of fury Reth had no idea he possessed. To keep the peace and not lose his temper, he was securely encased in his office, doing his best to block out what the day represented.

The energy needed to deal with his unwanted guest just was not there. He whispered a silent prayer, hoping that Amal would forgive him. If they had a private funeral where it was just his family, including Amina, he would be fine; however, that was not a choice.

This entire ordeal needed to end soon. Had they been able to, Reth would have left the country if not for his daughter. Their retreat would have to wait until Amina graduated because she was like a comfort blanket to Hasina. If not for her, Reth was not sure how he would have survived.

Over the past few days, people were still coming to offer condolences, food, and unsolicited advice. Some were genuine while others were nosey. He had never shared what kind of cancer his wife had. They asked yet he did not answer. It was not their business.

There was an overabundance of pity and judgment and an under-abundance of empathy and genuine care. They spoke lies and thought he was naïve enough to believe them. Him. Reth Goode, as if he could not smell bull crap when it was being tossed at him. Had they forgotten his occupation?

Worse than them were the husband hunters. They had been floating around the entire year his wife was sick, but he had not noticed. His wife had barely been fresh in the ground, and they were seeking to take her place. Reth was not interested in pursuing or being pursued—at least not by them. His mind was only on the promises he made to Amal.

A knock at the door forced his closed eyes to open. He let out a mental sigh. Part of him wanted to be left alone a little while longer, but it could be his daughter. Though Amina did a fantastic job of entertaining and protecting her, his daughter needed her father. Hasina was his responsibility.

Laying his cigar down, he lifted out of his Bedford Traditional XL Swivel chair and slowly sauntered to the double African oak wood door. Inhaling a deep breath, he opened it to find Djimon and Kondo standing at the threshold. One was holding a plate, probably made by their mother, and the other a glass of sweet lemonade tea. JD was probably speaking to the guests in his absence. That was fine with him. Jotham followed their father into ministry, and therefore, funerals were his expertise. JD had done an excellent job officiating over the funeral. Amina's singing was so beautiful that it had him in tears. Amal would have loved it all. Her funeral was a far greater affair than their courthouse wedding.

Reth offered his brothers a grin. He did love them. No matter how bad a day he was having, and this was a bad day, his brothers were always welcomed wherever he was. It was how they were raised, to look after one another.

Standing aside, Reth let them enter and quickly shut the door. Some people just did not respect or understand boundaries. He hoped that no one was bold enough to follow his brothers to his retreat. They would see a hidden side of

SYMPHONY OF GOODE LOVE

him.

"Wanna talk about it?" Kondo asked as he handed his brother the plate loaded with the ethnic foods of their mother's homeland like Piri Piri Peppers and Poulet à la Moambé a chicken dish as well as traditional American staples.

There wasn't much to say. Right now, Reth was unsure of how to express what he was feeling. "No."

Kondo and Djimon both nodded in understanding.

"Just so you know, Delilah has declared she's staying for a few days. I don't know if she thinks she's staying here or what. The premise is to help you get your affairs in order. However, between the three of us, I smell trouble. You'd think after being left out of the living will and Amina putting her in her place, she would tuck tail and run. I bet she's trying to get Emmarie to take Amina's place. As if that will ever happen. She's been throwing side-eyes at Amina the entire day," Djimon expressed as he helped himself to one of Reth's cigars.

"Amina shut her down most sweetly last time, and I was so proud of her."

Djimon grinned. "She did that. Even Amal would've been proud. When she told her, '...possibly it's you who seeks to take advantage of Reth during his time of grief. Although if that's the case, he's intelligent enough to decipher your motives', I nearly fainted. I like sassy Amina."

Reth smirked at his brother's reenactment. It made him feel good that Amina stood her ground. Delilah was out of line. He warned her to be on her best behavior. Hearing that she was using today of all days to upset Amina ticked him off. Delilah ruined her relationship with her own daughter; she was not about to do the same to Amina or Hasina.

Running his hand done his face, Reth glanced up to his brothers asking, "Is Amina okay? I don't want her to feel threatened. She's had to deal with her aunt and ex-boyfriend in addition to losing Amal. This is her home as well, and Delilah will not disrespect her."

"Amina is fine. She and Hasina went upstairs to take a break. Ma put Delilah in her place for now. I almost thought she was going to slap her because she was flirting with Baba."

Reth shook his head. Delilah was playing with her life flirting with his father. His mother did not accept any disrespect when it came to his father—or her.

"Emre has left I think Delilah upset him too," Djimon shared, patting his brother's shoulder.

"Reth, I know this is a difficult time for you. We're here, you know we love you and will do anything you need," Kondo added.

"I know. Um, Mal wanted me to share something with you all. Something I thought I would take to my grave, but she gave me permission to tell everyone. Later tonight, I need to meet with you all. Let JD and our parents know; if you can get these people out of the house that would be great. I'm going to check on my daughter. "

His brothers nodded in agreement and prepared to exit his office when Kondo turned back around. "Brother, I almost forgot; Binah sent these for Amal."

"What is it?"

"Seeds for the dancing plant. Apparently, Amal reached out to Binah because she wanted to add them to the flower garden. You know that song "I Hope You Dance", the country one? Per Binah, this was Amal's gift to Hasina, her own *I hope you dance*."

Reth was stunned. First the Build-A-Bear and now this. What a phenomenal mother she was in this life and the afterlife. Reth nodded to his brother, and instead of eating, he decided to check on Hasina. His heart was full. Amal was so thoughtful; it made him wonder how Delilah birthed such a magnificent woman.

∞ ∞ ∞

It was after eight p.m. when Reth entered his office. Hasina was asleep with Amina by her side. The way Amina was stepping up amazed him. He was seeing exactly what Amal said all along her. Her resilience was something to admire.

His parents and three brothers were all sitting in his office waiting for him. The guests had finally left, with the prompting of his parents. Delilah attempted to linger. Even Emmarie seemed uncomfortable. Finally, Reth had to ask Delilah to leave. To protect his mental health, he needed her gone. He prayed that she was on her way back to St. Croix. There was nothing for her here.

Halting the mental chaos, Reth made his way to his desk and propped up on the side. He had mentally been preparing himself for this moment since Amal first asked him to share the truth.

"I just wanted to say thank you for all your help and support. I love you all and I thank God for you." His family nodded. "However, what brings us here tonight is a promise I made to Mal. It's something I have kept for years. Amal and I got married at the courthouse; the Goode Love Vow was never done, and I know you've asked why, so here's the truth." He let out a breath and started.

"One day, she came to see me, and I introduced her to a colleague, Adrian Bishop. You've heard me refer to him as AB. The two met and seemed to be friendly. AB was more interested in Mal than she was in him. I didn't know that at the time, but she knew he was not what he seemed. AB and I traveled out of town for an immigration law convention, and Amal came to visit. I was out, but AB was there. During my absence, AB sexually assaulted her."

Silence lingered long enough that Reth was unsure if they comprehended his words.

"What?" Reth looked at his mother who was in tears now. He hated to do this, but it was Amal's dying wish. He was carrying it out. "Yes, she was raped by him. When I returned, she had cleaned herself up, and I knew nothing immediately. It was not until she found out that she was pregnant that she told me the truth. I confronted AB. After I finished with him, he put in his notice at the firm. He denied it all, but I know Mal would never lie. Anyway, she was scared when she found out she was pregnant. Since I did not protect her before, I wanted to protect her after. We got married, and I promised her that Hasina would be raised as my daughter and not AB's child. I signed the birth certificate since she was born during our marriage. I am the presumed father. AB is not dumb enough to ever claim her because he knows the truth will be revealed. He doesn't want it with me.

"Amal and I were never in love the way a wife and husband should be. We had separate quarters. Our marriage was never consummated. We were just two best friends raising our daughter. It's why we never did the Goode Love Vow. Amal wanted me to find my soulmate and then do the Goode Love Vow. Anyway, it was a year later that she found out she had cervical cancer. AB gave Amal an STI."

There, it was out and where he thought he would feel shame, he felt nothing but relief. Looking around at his family, he saw shock and anger, pain and grief written on their faces. It was Kondo who recovered first, got up, and then walked over to Reth and embraced him. Reth sunk into his brother's hold.

"I'm sorry you held this secret for so long, brother. That's something neither you are Mal should have had to carry alone. I admire your strength and the goodness of your heart to protect her and Hasina so fiercely. Just know that after hearing this, I love you more for being the upstanding and outstanding man you are. I stand with you and Hasina always."

Then JD and Djimon followed. They held him close and Reth allowed himself to be vulnerable. He wept like a baby. It was so freeing to finally share the truth with his family.

"Let it all out, brother; you're safe here to let it all go. God will carry you," JD whispered.

"We're with you, Re. We'll always protect you. I'm so sorry you've suffered in silence with this. I don't know how you or Amal did it, but you don't ever have to carry a burden like that again," Djimon added.

"She told me that it wasn't my fault and that I didn't have to keep apologizing. I just felt so guilty because I introduced her to the man who violated her. I've just held that guilt in my heart for so long."

"It's time to release the guilt. The actions of AB are not a reflection of you. You turned something tragic into something honorable. I expect nothing less from any of my sons, but I want you free of this. Don't let it imprison you any longer," Chiram stated and he, followed by his wife, reached out and held Reth.

"You don't have to be strong all the time, Reth, and it's okay to ask for help. It is why God blessed you with three brothers. In this family, we share the load. In this family, no one suffers anything alone," Mrs. Goode lectured.

"I know, Ma. I just could not damage Mal more. I could not share her story until she allowed and even then, I dragged my foot on it. I was supposed to tell you all days ago. I just don't want anyone to ever think less of her."

"We don't, and we wouldn't. We love Amal, always have and always will," his mother cooed.

He nodded his head.

"It's been a long night, son; how about you get some rest? If you like, we can all stay tonight and have a big family breakfast. I think that'll be good for Hasina."

Reth nodded in agreement. He hugged his brothers once more and then walked out of his office and ascended the stairs and went to his bedroom.

Chapter 18

Twirling a loose strand of hair, Amina lay awake, staring at the ceiling. Memories of the past and present merged. Lost in her thoughts she replayed the day in her mind. It had only been two hours since she left Hasina sleeping peacefully with a smile on her face. That smile was because Amal in her wisdom had a Build-A-Bear teddy created and sent to Hasina. The joy in her eyes when she received the gift would forever be imprinted on her brain. Hasina was having a tough day, as to be expected during bereavement. Amal knew this day would come and made a recording of herself for Hasina that said, "I love you, my sweet girl". Even now, Amina was still emotional. It was marvelous to witness the connection between daughter and mother.

Secretly, a part of her yearned to hear the voice of her own mother. After her mother died, her father destroyed every recording and picture of Kenise. Out of anger, he tried to erase her existence. Anything left of hers he destroyed or gave away. Amina was only able to salvage one photo, and she never took it out for fear it would be destroyed too. Today, however, was not about her but Hasina.

Admiration and respect bloomed in Amina's chest when she saw how resilient, confident, and courageous Hasina was. Then again, she was Reth and Amal's daughter. She inherited her fighting spirit.

However, Delilah was intent on making a scene. Without

knowing Amina, the woman despised her. That was apparent the night she accused Amina of trying to manipulate Reth. The disdain rolled off Delilah like tornado winds. Though she said nothing, her actions did all the talking. The dirty looks, the eye rolls, and turned-up nose really upset Amina, but she remained respectful and classy. This was not her first interaction with an adversary.

Releasing the mental tension, Amina put those thoughts aside. Delilah did not deserve to live rent-free in her mind. Instead, she prayed about it and was entrusting it with God. There was nothing else for her to do. Since sleep refused to allow her comfort, Amina eased off the bed and exited her bedroom.

The door had been left open to allow Hasina easy access if she needed her, but it seemed the little piano princess was doing well now. That was comforting to Amina.

Creeping down the stairs, Amina headed to the kitchen to make herself some warm honey Sleepy Time tea. If sleep continued to evade her, she would work on her music. Before graduation, there would be a senior concert. Amina was missing the last pieces of her work until she talked with Amal. Soon her symphony would be complete, and she wanted to incorporate the children at the Goode Community Center in her music class. It was going to be an epic performance.

Graduation was fast approaching, and she could not wait for the summer, to rest and reset. Hopefully, during that time, her father would have a change of heart and allow her to visit him. Right now, she reached out and he did not reach back. That was something she had not told anyone. It was too embarrasing to share that her father, even locked up, was rejecting her.

It was the beeping of the microwave that brought her back to the present. She put a little honey in the mug and set it aside to cool. Then she meandered to the patio doors and looked out into the starlit sky. So many thoughts ran through her mind.

How she missed the innocence of her youth.

Letting out a relaxing breath, she let herself get lost in the quietude of the night. It would help hush the rushing thoughts that would only debilitate her. God did not create her to break her; no, this pain was preparation to fulfill a purpose He had planned from the beginning. That was what she needed to focus on.

"You couldn't sleep either?"

The smooth, deep, unexpected voice should have startled Amina, but instead, it enwrapped her in warmth and affection.

Allowing her eyelids to flutter for a moment she let her heart dance to the melody that always played when he spoke. Reth's vocal perfection was entrancing and enthralling.

Turning around, she leaned toward Reth's direction but made no movement to get nearer to him. He wore simple sleepwear—pajama bottoms and a plain black T-shirt, though they hardly concealed his toned, muscular body. Mentally chastising herself for that thought, she shook it off and redirected her runaway musings.

After all that Reth endured up to now, she thought he had handled himself accordingly. It was much better than the awful scene her father displayed after her mother and brothers died. For that, Amina admired him.

There were remnants of pain and would be for a while, if not always. Loss always changed a person, whether for the better or worse. Amina prayed for Reth and Hasina, prayed the changes that occurred in them would be for the better.

"Would you like some tea?" she asked in a whispered voice. She was unsure why she reacted that way when no one was about.

"I came for something sweeter."

Amina let out gasp but quickly regained her senses. He was

talking to her, not about her. Her face flamed at her behavior, and she mumbled, "God help me."

Either ignoring her response or just not hearing her, Reth continued, "My brothers told me there was some cake from Tamu Bakery. I'm not normally one to give into sugar, but tonight calls for it and Tamu is my favorite," he explained.

Amina smiled and went over to retrieve her tea. "I'll leave you alone."

"Please join me. We haven't spoken as much as I'd like. There's much to discuss."

Amina was clueless as to what he wanted to talk about. Had she done something wrong?

"Stop overthinking, Amina." Then he started cutting himself a slice of strawberry cake. It seemed not only was it a favorite of JD's but also of Reth's.

At his admonishment, she could feel her body flush and was grateful he couldn't see it. "Sorry."

"Don't apologize. Come."

Amina followed slowly, apparently too slowly because Reth reached for her hand to accelerate her speed. Her heartbeat tripled at his touch. It was harmless, and he meant nothing by it, yet it sent sparkles shooting through every crevice of her body. She was going to have to swim in holy water. What was wrong with her?

He stopped at the dining table, pulled out a chair, and directed her to sit before doing the same.

"Um, what's on your mind?"

Reth grinned. "Right to the point kind of lady, huh?"

Amina shrugged her shoulders and kept her eyes concentrated on her tea. Mentally, she prayed that Reth would not notice her odd behavior. There was still an undeniable attraction to Reth, and she felt guilt over it. As a single, pious woman, she should be solely fixated on the Lord and His work. The man God intended for her would find her working for the Lord, not lusting.

"Did you hear me?" Reth asked.

"No, I'm sorry. I've been a little off today."

His face altered; sadness was there now, followed by understanding. "I miss her too."

"Of course, you do, Reth. She was your wife and you had to say a final goodbye; well, final on this side, but you two will be reunited again. Amal was someone who you'd thought would be your forever partner. When people get married, they don't think their soulmate will die anytime soon. I understand losing those that you love. If no one else does, I do."

Their eyes connected and he lifted his index finger and playfully tapped her nose before saying, "Amina the wise, but Amal and I were never meant to be forever. We weren't soulmates; we were teammates."

It was almost as of Reth were someplace else. His confident guard was down, his tone affable, and the stress lines that had attached to him earlier in the day had disappeared. For once, he just seemed mortal. There was a part of her that wanted to pull him into an embrace and hold him until all the anguish of losing his wife disappeared.

Insecurity and fear of rejection glued her to the chair. Though his latter statement had her perplexed, she did not question it, though she recalled Amal saying something similar. Curiosity made her want to investigate deeper, but common sense let her know that now was not the time. They each settled into their private thoughts as he ate his cake and she drink her tea.

"How is Benito?" Reth's strong voice broke through the silence.

Amina respired. "He's better physically. Ms. Mary confirmed

that for me, but he won't tell me why those boys attacked him. However, Kalifa has a theory and I just refuse to believe it."

Placing his fork down, Reth push the plate aside; his thick forearms rested on the table as he gave her his full attention. "What's the theory?"

Twisting her lip, she gazed at him, surprised by his interest. Amina mulled over the conversation she had with Kalifa just days ago. "She thinks it's gang related. Either he was jumped into a gang or somehow did something to piss off gang members. He's only ten. That child doesn't have a violent bone in his body, and he has no reason or interest to join a gang."

"Did you ask him?"

"No." It came out unsure, and she looked at Reth. Although his face was unreadable now, she was sure that he thought there was something to what Kalifa was saying.

"I'm sure you'll do what's best. How is school going? I believe graduation is coming up."

"It is, but I have to finish up my composition this week and turn it in to my professor. Once I get his approval, then I'll be able to perform my piece at the senior concert."

Reth nodded. His russet eyes nearly glowed in the night.

"I can assist with Hasina. That way, you can concentrate on school. My family and I'll be there to support you. Make sure you put your concert and graduation on my calendar. Those are extremely important dates, and you should have family present."

Amina nearly choked on her tea. That was not at all what she expected, but then again, to attempt to know what Reth Goode would or would not do was a difficult task to undertake. It did something funny to her heart that he considered her family. She had long considered his family her family, but to hear him say it so meaningfully meant the world to her.

"Thank you."

"No thanks required. You understand that you're part of this family now. Also, if Delilah St. John disrespects you in anyway, no matter how minor, you tell me. I'll handle her. Her issue is not with you; however, you're an easy target for her. Envy and animosity have consumed her because she expected Mal to leave her money or something she could sell for money. As you and I know, she left everything to Hasina, except for her Jeep, which is now yours."

Amina had forgotten all about that, which is crazy considering she was present at the reading of the advance directive. When her name was spoken and it was revealed that she was getting the SUV, it shocked her. She thought the SUV was Reth's.

Her driving lessons were going well, and JD thought that she was ready to take her driver's test. As if reading her mind, Reth stated, "Are the driving lessons are going well?"

"Per JD, they are. It's easy with him or Kondo present, but I haven't driven alone."

"You'll do well. I believe in you."

Amina eyes widened at his declaration. She had to be misinterpreting him. Every time he spoke, she felt a spark in her heart. She was one kind word away from spontaneous combustion of heart emojis.

"Come, let's get these dishes clean and try to get back to sleep."

Without saying a word, Amina got up and followed him to the kitchen. She took his plate from him and washed their dishes. Reth stood there until she was finished and then escorted her upstairs.

Yep, the spontaneous combustion of heart emojis were coming.

∞∞∞

"Kalifa, I'm cursed by the flesh. Something is terribly wrong with me. I've prayed about it, but I can't shake my attraction to my boss. My goodness, the man just buried his wife last week. All I can think about is how good it would feel to be in his arms," Amina ashamedly confessed.

Kalifa's light caramel eyes blinked several times, as if she were attempting to digest what Amina had just blurted out.

"Wait, so you still have a crush on Reth? I mean, not that I blame you. All four of those brothers are like walking African sculptures. They're educated, motivated, and give back to the community. They don't take any mess. That Kondo puts my heart ablaze."

Shocked by her admission, Amina did a double take. Kalifa had never mentioned Kondo or any other guy, not even a celebrity. She was on another level of concentration, as her mind was on school and creating her own business. Poor Diego was a forgotten memory if he were ever one at all.

"What? He puts your heart ablaze? When did that happen? My best friend who cringes at the sound of Diego's voice. The woman who clams up at male attention is smitten with Dr. Kondo Goode. My goodness!" There was something in the Goode bothers DNA because it made sane women act completely insane.

Kalifa's eyes danced around until finally meeting Amina's gaze. "He's been coming in with his doctor friends. We are open twenty-four seven and he's in his residency, so he has crazy hours."

Though Amina remained silent, her face was extremely active. Kondo was coming to the diner by himself. Was there something brewing between the two of them? Shaking that thought, she needed Kalifa to give her some advice. However, this tea was piping hot.

"What should I do about Reth? Amal was aware of my feelings, and I apologized and asked for her forgiveness. Then the other night, I was in the kitchen, and he came in; then he reached for my hand to escort me to the dining room, and I almost lost my mind. My thoughts were sinful. I'm talking I was staring at his forearm and wanted to caress it. Then, when we went back to the kitchen, I was eyeing how muscular his back is. I never even thought of a back as being sexy. Even when he does not touch me, my body gets all excited. I need to take a swim in some holy water."

Kalifa cackled at that. She was laughing so hard that her left hand smacked the table. That went on for at least another two minutes before she wrinkled up her nose and then tapped her lips with her index finger. "Didn't you tell me that she said that *God told me it was you. That you would be the one for my daughter and for my husband.*"

Amal had said that, and Amina was confused as to what that meant. Surely, she was not giving her blessing for Amina to move in on Reth. What woman would urge another to take her man? Not that Amina had the ability to do it. "I'm not even sure what that means. She also said that she and Reth weren't supposed to be, and they weren't meant for forever. Reth also said something similar. He said they weren't soulmates; they were teammates. I'm not quite sure what to make of it. Even if it meant *that*—Reth doesn't see me in that way. He's a man who needs a woman like his wife. I don't measure up. What do I have to offer an established man?"

Kalifa rolled her eyes and sucked her teeth. "You never told me about that other part. I think you need to talk to Reth and get clarity. However, to answer the latter part, you have a lot to offer: your beauty, intelligence, love, grace, and talent. I can go on and on. Amina, you're a catch, and that's why BC can't let you go. You two never had sex and he's out here tripping. You've got that marvelous, one-in-a-million uniqueness about you. The way you love and care for people. You don't give up on anybody. You see people in ways others discount them. That's why you took so much from Adeya and your father. It's the people like you, who love even after loss, pain, and rejection, that give hope to others. That's just a sampling of what you have to offer," Kalifa replied, before adding, "I don't know much about love and courtship, but love doesn't live on a timeframe. If God has ordained for you to be with Reth, then you'll be with him. You need to stop overthinking everything. It's time to go with the flow and follow faith."

Appreciative of the advice, Amina leaned back in the chair, contemplating. Maybe, she was overthinking. Reth always admonished her frequently about that. Then again, Reth had not given her any reason to believe that he was the least bit interested in her. Yes, he said she was part of the family, but that did not translate to attraction.

Dropping her head in her hands, Usher's "You Got It Bad" was blaring through her brain. It was best to leave it with God and redirect her focus on her schoolwork, jobs, and Benito. If not, she was going to get into a heap of trouble. The flesh was beastly, and if she were not careful, she would fall into a lust pit.

"I'm going to leave that be. After classes, I'm heading over to visit with Benito. Hopefully, I can get him to spill what happened."

"I think it's gang related. I know you disagree, but that's my belief. I hate to say that, but if you've noticed, BC has been wearing a lot of blue and black, and they're QCB colors."

Leaning forward in the chair, Amina's head jerked up in shock. She recalled seeing BC in those colors when he was at her mother's gravesite, but it did not click then. "But BC is a pretty boy; he wouldn't let anyone jump him, and I never saw bruises on him. Surely, he would not want that life for his brother?"

"Bestie, during the last year, BC wasn't around you much. How do you really know? Plus, that's what the streets say. I did overhear BC was at least affiliated with the Queen City Boys through his cousin. I'm sure that night we went out that some of those guys were QCB."

That was news to Amina. "We have to go now."

"We?"

"Yes, you're off today. So, let's go to Ms. Mary's and see what Benito has to say."

Kalifa lifted her slender index finger and tapped Amina forehead. "You do remember the whole jealous, possessive you belong to me act that BC pulled last time you two bumped into each other? I really don't want to witness a repeat. You know I can't fight."

Of course, she had not forgotten. BC had shown out, but this was Benito and he needed guidance and safety. "Benito is worth it. No, you can't fight, but you call dial 911."

The stress lines that were occupying Kalifa's face disappeared, and Amina knew she had won her over. The pair got up and headed to the SUV.

It did not take long to arrive at the house, and from what Amina could tell, BC was not home. She made sure not to park in the driveway so he would not be able to block her.

Closing the car door, Amina and Kalifa made their way to the house. Amina took the lead and knocked on the door. Seconds later Ms. Mary to open the door with a welcoming smile.

Not too long ago, this house was just as much her home as her own. After breaking up with BC, she kind of broke up with his family too. That was the part that hurt.

Amina did not hesitate to pull Ms. Mary into a long embrace. They saw each other in passing, but Amina missed a few church services. Most of her attention had been on Amal and Hasina.

"How're you doing, Mina baby? I know you've been through it with your aunt and my grandson."

Amina slanted her head to the left and offered a reassuring smile. "I'm good, Ms. Mary."

She nodded and motioned for them to enter the house. They sat on the couch and talked a little before Amina asked, "Is it okay if I take Benito for the day?"

Mary's eyes brighten with delight. "That would be great. They called me in to work a shift at the hospital. I was hoping that BC was coming home, but I haven't seen him. I'm at my wits end with that man-child. I'm about to call my nephew Dre to help get BC back on the right foot." She shook her head and then added, "God worked it out and brought you and Kali girl to help me."

Amina grinned good-naturedly and then excused herself as she went to Benito's bedroom. Amina knocked on the door and heard his soft voice say enter. She opened the door and entered. "Hey B."

His loving eyes glanced at hers. His bruises were fading, a faint reminder of what occurred. Questions flowed through her brain, but she knew now as not the time to ask.

"So, I spoke to your grandma, and she said it was okay to take you for the day. Would you like to hangout? I've missed you."

His eyes lit up at the invitation. "Can I see Kondo?"

Amina fake pouted and pretended to roll her eyes. "I think he's at work, but I can probably get JD, and you can meet Djimon. He's cool. I hear he likes to play X Box."

His eyes widened in excitement, and he quickly got off the

bed and put on his tennis shoes. Less than ten minutes later they were off. Amina called in an order at the diner. Since Benito wanted to see Kondo, they were going to drop him off lunch. Kalifa knew his order by heart.

Once they pulled up at the diner, Benito and Kalifa got out to retrieve the order. Amina gave her the money because lunch was on her.

Watching them enter, Amina pulled out her cell phone and texted Reth. She was checking up on Hasina. It didn't take long for after she hit send for her phone to ring. It was Reth's number.

"Hello?"

"Hey, Ms. Mina. Daddy said I could call you."

Relief surged through her. Hasina sounded happy on the phone. They spoke briefly because Mrs. Eleora was over. Just as she was about to hang up, Reth's voice came onto the line.

"How is your music project going?"

"It's coming along, but I'm taking a break to eat and get Benito." She was about to say more when she heard her name being yelled. Looking out the window, she saw her aunt.

"Hold on for a moment; my aunt is yelling my name, and it might be about my dad." Getting out of the SUV, she walked to the middle of the parking lot where her aunt was standing. The two had not seen or spoken to each other since the incident back at the house.

"Pitch!" she spat like she was being murdered, causing Amina to slow her pace. "You black, messy beast; you trying to evict me?"

Amina looked at her puzzled. "Huh? I don't know what you're talking about."

She huffed and yanked paperwork out of her black tote and then shoved the papers at Amina causing her to nearly drop her cell phone.

Perplexed by the paperwork, Amina glanced and spoke, "Adeya, I don't know anything about this. I never filed anything. I haven't even had the time." It was a good idea though; her aunt needed a reality check. She was living in Amina's mother's house that was now her house, rent-free.

"Lies, you stupid slut! Your harem put you up to this; well, you gonna get it," Adeya screeched like a banshee.

Before Amina could prepare herself, something hard hit her head. On instinct, her hands went to her head to sooth the injury, but the blows kept coming, followed by shouting. Amina fell to the ground and balled up her body to protect herself.

It was all in vain as her world faded to black.

Chapter 19

It should not have happened. The phrase replayed in Reth's head like a bad song.

Amina's safety was his responsibility, and he failed her. The look on Hasina's face when she saw them bring Amina back home nearly broke his heart. Hasina's fear was that she was going to lose Amina too. Only an hour ago, he sent his daughter to bed.

Two days Amina had been in and out of consciousness. She had a nasty head injury that required stitches and would most likely leave a scar. Her eyes were swollen shut, and she had a busted lip. Then there were the bruises on her back and legs from where she was shielding blows. According to Kalifa, Adeya attempted to stomp Amina to death.

Yesterday she was released from the hospital, and now, she was asleep again. Reth had not heard her utter one word, only groans of lament and pain.

The rage that surged through him was unidentifiable, animal-like. He was that livid, and he was determined to find a way to make Adeya pay for her violent actions.

Gazing out the window, Reth rocked back and forth on his heels to cool off the growing animosity. He interlaced his hands behind his head while he thought. How was it that he seemed to always fail women in his care? First, Amal with AB and now, Amina with her aunt. It was his fault; he should not have evicted her, or at least let Amina know so she would be aware.

Reth's anger caused him to make sloppy moves. Apparently, he underestimated the deep-rooted antipathy that Adeya had against Amina. It was criminal the way she despised her own niece. Tightness pulled at his chest as unfiltered thoughts circulated in his head. He had not slumbered in days, and fatigue lingered like a starved jackal. Sleep kept nipping and he kept fighting. He refused to leave Amina. As soon as she entered his life, she entered his heart.

A knock at Amina's bedroom door interrupted his mental turmoil. Reth turned around to see his mother and father. Fearing it had something to do with Hasina, he quickly hurried over to them.

As if sensing his uneasiness, his father quickly stated, "Son, Gavin has arrived. He is waiting to speak to you. He wants to see Amina, but with his wheelchair, it'll be difficult to get him upstairs."

Reth nodded knowingly. The accident that stole the life of Amina's mother and brothers, left Gavin paralyzed. "Will one of you stay with her. I don't want her to wake up alone."

"I'll stay with my Song Thrush."

Reth kissed his mother's cheek and thanked her before following his father out.

They arrived at his office, and he saw that his brothers were also present. They were just as upset as Reth was about the ordeal.

"Brothers, Gavin," Reth greeted them before taking a seat in his chair.

"Hello, Reth. It's good to see you all again, but I wish it were under better circumstances. Can you tell me what happened? The media has picked up the story. I saw some cell phone footage, but I don't know the backstory."

Reth's fatigued russet orbs stared directly into Gavin's chestnut eyes, and he told the story, from the moment they found out Adeya had attacked Amina prior to the current one. "So, you see how I am responsible for what happened recently."

Gavin shook his head in disagreement, as did Reth's brother and father. "You're not to blame Reth, believe me. I am. This started long before you."

Reth frowned at the admission but waited for Gavin to expound.

"This started a long time ago. Amina knows nothing of this. Before I met Kenise, I went on a blind date with Adeya. There was no chemistry. I was not attracted to her. However, she seemed to like me, a lot. I told her we could only be friends. I thought she understood that, but I noticed that her interest started to become dangerously obsessive. I had no idea who she really was or what she was capable of. I didn't know that Aaron was her brother. Then Kenise and I started hanging out more. I fell in love. Adeya did not take that well. She loathed Kenise with an intensity that consumed her. It started far before I entered the picture, I think my choosing Kenise over her was the spark that lit the fire." Gavin paused for a moment, as if he were gathering up strength to finish. "The day Kenise and I were run off the road, it was not some random road rage; it was Adeya. I like to think that she didn't know the boys were in there, but hearing how she's treated Amina, she probably did. Adeya does not like competition of any kind."

Reth sat back in the chair, nearly stunned by the revelation. His eyes bounced around the room and he saw his brothers were in the same state of incredulity. Adeya was deceptively dangerous. It was all over unrequited love. She murdered innocent children because a man did not want her. "You left Amina with the woman who murdered half of her family?"

Gavin shook his head, shame evident on his face. Reth was not attempting to guilt him, but he needed to understand why

Gavin felt leaving Amina behind was necessary.

"I wanted Amina with me, but Aaron refused. I should've told the police, but I was so full of grief that I thought it was better to walk away. I had buried my wife and sons. I didn't want to go through a trial. On Amina's eighteenth birthday, I asked her to come live with me, to attend college in Virginia, but she declined. I failed her. I should have fought harder."

"We both did. I promised Amal I would take care of Amina; instead, I led her right into trouble."

"I aim to make it right. Before coming here, I went to the police station and told them everything. Hopefully, they'll charge her with murder and attempted murder. I wish I had done this after the accident."

Reth leaned back in his chair. Exhaustion nearly claimed him, but he fought it off. "Amina needs to know the truth. It's about to be a media circus, especially when they link Adeya to Aaron. He's doing four years for driving under the influence and killing a man," he shared and then dropped his head in his hands, exasperated. "Why can't Amina catch a break?"

∞∞∞

It had been a torturous and tumultuous couple of days once the media got ahold of the video that showed Adeya attacking Amina. They soon linked them to Aaron, and once the police released, they had a suspect in custody for the murder of Amina's family. With Gavin's statement, the police added the charge of murder to the rest of Adeya's charges, all which were currently unknown to Amina.

Today was the first day she was fully awake. Reth's mother and Kalifa came over to assist Amina in showering and getting dressed. Hasina, still reeling with the loss of her mother, had become needier for Amina. Seeing her nanny virtually lifeless stressed her out, which, in turn, stressed Reth out. They needed a break. As soon as Amina graduated, he was taking his family on a vacation to the East African country of Mauritius.

Rolling back his shoulders to release the mounting tension, Reth entered his home with the intention of greeting his family. He also stopped by one of his favorite seafood restaurants to bring supper for them. By now, Reth thought his mother would have brought Amina and Hasina home.

Amina had a doctor's appointment earlier. He believed that she had spoken to Gavin around lunchtime. He wanted to be present for that conversation, but work called. Looking around the house, there were no signs any one was home. Entering the kitchen, he sat down the food and went in search of his family. The house was empty, so he jogged to his bedroom and took a quick shower before putting on his lounge clothing and heading back downstairs. He found his cell phone on the counter and called his mother to get an expected time of arrival. Before she could pick up the call, the doorbell rang. Knowing it was his mother at the door, he ended the call.

Opening the door without verifying the visitor was a dumb move on his part. His lips were fixed to greet his mother but died as soon as she saw Delilah St. John and Emmarie.

Reth fought the instinct to slam the door in her face. Everything about Delilah always rubbed him wrong. He thought after the issue with the advance directive and the funeral that she would not be back. Apparently, he was mistaken.

"Reth, aren't you going to invite us in?" Delilah requested in a syrupy tone that set off alarm bells.

Against his better judgement, Reth stepped aside and allowed Delilah and the woman with her inside. Inhaling a breath, Reth did his best to calm the annoyance tap dancing throughout his body. He was sure that Delilah was up to something, and sooner or later, she would reveal her hand.

Closing the door, Reth ushered the women into the family room. Once they sat down, he asked, "To what do I owe this visit? I thought you went back home."

"I thought about it, and I feel my place is here. I got a sign from God when I saw that the young woman in your employ was savagely beaten by her own family member. I had no idea she was associated with such savages. I said I cannot have my poor, innocent granddaughter around such behavior. I offer my services again."

Reth lifted a frustrated brow. Delilah missed her calling as an actress because she was putting on an Oscar-worthy performance.

"I don't recall accepting the request the first time you offered. My daughter is doing fine in Amina's care. I don't appreciate you speaking out of turn about her. It would behoove you to leave Amina alone, and in the future, I require that you to call before you come to my home unannounced."

The look of sheer trepidation mixed with antipathy was a sure sign that Delilah was wholly unprepared for Reth's response. Reth watched how she took her dainty, jewelry-covered hand and rested it upon her chest. Gone was the fake concern and innocence. He knew she would be unable to maintain the act long. That was exactly what it was. Delilah was a predator and only cared about her needs, but she could also be a chameleon. When it came to him, she met her match, and Reth was not budging.

"I see you're still upset about the way I chose to discipline my granddaughter."

"Not entirely, as we have discussed that. This is about you taking liberties that you have no right to take. If you genuinely care about getting to know your granddaughter, then do that. What you'll not do is use a situation in which you have little to no knowledge about to push your agenda into my life. Next time, call before you come; now please leave. I'm expecting my family soon, and my food is getting cold." The sternness of his voice brook no argument, and Delilah had the good sense to motion for her niece to retreat.

"I apologize, Reth. I know I was not the ideal mother. I know I made mistakes with Amal. I just wanted to do right by Hasina. Maybe one day you'll forgive me and no longer view me as an enemy but as an ally. Everything I do does not have an ulterior motive." With that, she reached for Emmarie's hand and the two sauntered from the family room.

Reth followed and opened the door for them. As they exited, he saw his mother parking her car. Hasina popped out so quickly that Reth wondered if she had been buckled in her seat. She ran into his arms, bypassing or not even noticing Delilah.

"Daddy!" She wrapped her little body around and hugged herself to his chest as he started back the way Hasina ran from. Reth was sure that Amina would need assistance. He halted his steps when he saw his brother Djimon getting out as well.

Djimon was going back to London to complete his project in a few weeks. He wanted to stay to ensure that everything was okay before he left again. Reth appreciated Djimon and the rest of his brothers. They had been a great support for him, making the transition without Amal easier.

"Hey." Reth greeted as Djimon opened the other door to assist Amina.

"Unwanted company?" Djimon questioned as both their eyes followed Delilah and Emmarie, who was in the car while Delilah looked on.

Shaking his head, Reth continued the short journey to Amina. She looked so fragile. The bruises were not as prevalent, thanks to the color of her skin, and the swelling had gone down, but Reth worried about the unseen pain. He had no idea how he would feel if he found out his family member murdered half his family.

"Good news?"

"Ma went in with her, but I think it was a good report," Djimon answered.

Amina lifted her face him and offered a small smile. Reth smiled back and he reached out his right hand to her. His left securely held his daughter. He did not mind her clinginess; she had gone through a lot too.

Amina advised him to not assume that Hasina did not sense or know what was happening, to always make her feelings a priority and talk to her daily. In doing that, he felt as though he and his daughter had gotten closer, but he knew that Hasina adored Amina as well.

"Thank you," Amina mumbled.

"You're welcome." He pulled Amina into his side and assisted her to the house. "I got dinner, but we're probably going to have to heat it back up."

"Okay."

Mrs. Goode got ahead of them and went to open the door. Before Reth entered, he glanced back at Delilah, but she was in her car now. He could feel the blazing of her stare. Turning his back to them, he ushered his family inside and closed the door.

Chapter 20

The warm Carolina sun kissed Amina's exposed legs as she rested on the patio chair. Splayed across her upper body was a sleeping Hasina whose little face was nestled into Amina's neck. She had been her little shadow since the attack, and Amina did not mind at all.

To her left was Kalifa, who had been by her throughout the ordeal. Kalifa's friendship had been paramount in her recovery, as well as the Goode family, and Gavin. Initially, Amina was upset with Gavin for not telling her sooner about the murderess she was living with, but she let it go quickly. Both were grieving back then and to blame him would be wrong and irresponsible. Besides, she was a child then and wouldn't have known how to process that information.

Since the revelation, Amina had hidden herself behind Reth's mansion walls. The only time she left was to go to the doctor and attend school. Her professor accepted her music project that doubled as her final. He seemed impressed with her work. Due to her head injury, although improving, she was chauffeured by someone in the family.

The quiet little life she had, and her cloak of invisibility, altered once Gavin announced the truth. The police arrested Adeya. Once she heard the news, that her own aunt murdered her family, it ripped through her being like a serrated knife. Questions flowed through her head like a river, but there were never any answers.

Kenise and the twins died because Adeya coveted her husband and did not know how to handle rejection. Knowing the truth was a bitter pill to swallow. It was better when Amina believed that it was some random road rage incident.

This woman lived in her home, broke bread with her, knowing that she murdered her mother and brothers. Adeya was a demon.

Now, the entire world knew that not only had her father murdered someone, albeit an accident, but his sister was a murderer too. What would they think of her? The aching feeling in her heart hurt worse than the bruises. Half of her family was dead, and the other half was locked up. She was left alone, feeling empty and inconsequential. With her family's business on the news and in the streets daily, how would parents entrust her with their children?

It worried her that the children would stop coming to the center. People never looked at the whole picture when they did things. Adeya and Aaron's actions impacted her too. She had already dealt with the gossip after her mother's death. How would they treat her now?

Determined not to cry again, Amina blinked several times, inhaled the deepest breath she could, and held it for thirty seconds before slowly releasing it.

"It's going to be okay." Kalifa whispered soothingly, as if her voice would wake up Hasina.

Amina did not look at her. Honestly, she was tired of hearing that phrase. It was not okay, and it would not be for a long time. It felt like constantly being dumped into an active volcano or being left in the eye of a hurricane.

"She murdered my mother and brothers, over a man. I don't think it'll ever be okay."

Kalifa dropped her head. "I…"

"It's fine, Kali. I don't expect you to have the answers. Only

God and time will work out what's happening inside of me. I don't think I can express it properly either. I just, I feel so alone. I literally have no family. I know eventually, I'll forgive Adeya because I must, and even my Dad, but I don't think I'll ever see them again. Deep sorrow fills my heart at that truth, but I can't do it anymore. They'll eviscerate me. I've lost enough in this life; I won't lose me."

Kalifa reached out and wrapped her hand around Amina's. "You don't have to, Mina. This is your life, and you don't owe Adeya or Aaron anything. You've sacrificed a lot for them, and each time they throw it in your face. You're only obligated to take care of you right now."

Amina nodded. Life had been beating her butt for ages. She was tired of losing. With glossy, amber eyes, Amina peered toward Kalifa. "Be honest with me, Kali. What's so offensive about me? Why am I so unlovable, so worthless, that the people who are supposed to protect and love me, use, hurt, and abandon me? Adeya must really loathe me to have taken my family from me and still attack me ruthlessly. Like an idiot, I thought I needed her acceptance. I remember being little and using skin bleach to lighten my skin so Adeya wouldn't call me names. I tried to be perfect so my Dad would see me, love me, and he just kept drinking. Even BC cheated on me. Sometimes, I really wonder why God left me behind. Right now, my life feels like punishment."

Tears began to fall from Kalifa's eyes. "Aww, best friend, you're lovable and worthy. I know it's hard right now. You're dealing with a lot, but you're so much more than what you've survived. It's just that it seems like a lot now, and when troubles come, we tend to follow negative thinking and meditate on the bad stuff. It's a lot of good happening for you as well," Kalifa cooed as she got up and wiped Amina's tears.

Amina knew the words her friend said were true, but they just did not penetrate the wall of agony her aunt's actions had built.

"Amina," the rich, low-toned voice called out.

Sniffling and trying to gather herself, Amina turned cautiously toward Reth. He was standing before her in his suit. He must have recently gotten off work. He tried to be home as early as possible to spend time with Hasina.

"Yes?"

"Let Kalifa take Hasina to bed for her nap, and you and I will speak in my office."

His facial expression gave nothing away, making Amina chew her inner right cheek. Had the time come when he finally had enough of her and was firing her? Surely all this attention could not bid well for his career.

"Amina, stop overthinking," Reth lectured knowingly and then turned to leave.

Amina quickly, and gently, passed Hasina over to Kalifa. Her friend rubbed Amina's back to offer comfort. They were having a silent conversation. Then, the three of them entered the house. Amina went to the left, in the direction of Reth's office, and Kalifa to the right, up the stairs to Hasina's bedroom.

Not feeling as confident as she would have liked, Amina entered the open door, sat down on the leather loveseat, and waited. The beating of her heart felt like a clock ticking, counting down what may only add to her demise.

Reth entered a second later, his suit jacket discarded, his tie loosened, and his sleeves rolled three quarters of an inch. His forearms were on full display, showcasing his commitment to the gym. There was an ease to his facial features; still though, she could not read him. His russet eyes took her in, and she did her best to meet his gaze but failed.

Immediately, Reth sat down beside her and wrapped his arms around her shoulders, gently pulling her into him. As if someone had turned an off and on switch, the tears ran rampantly, and he held her tighter. In all her years of living, never had she felt as safe and protected as she did at that moment. A year ago, she wouldn't have cried in front of him, let alone on him. His arms felt like an electric blanket, calming the chills that assaulted her body.

"Let it all out. I know you're hurting, and if I could, I would take every ounce of your pain and carry your burden. You've the right to be hurt, upset, and feel every emotion you're going through right now. I want you to know that you aren't alone. You have me, my family, and Kalifa. You have the kids at the center, Ms. Mary, and Benito. I know we aren't your blood family, but we're family through the blood of Christ, and that's much stronger." He continued to hold her, stroking her hair. Every defense she had, he disarmed. Amina hungered for this man in a way that words could not describe, and it petrified her.

Leaning into his comfort, she mumbled incoherently. Her mind was temporarily offline, and she was unable to form the vocabulary needed to express herself. However, Reth understood that. Even when she said nothing, he seemed to understand her meaning.

"I overheard what you said to Kalifa. I wasn't attempting to eavesdrop, but I think it was meant for me to hear. For years, the two people who should have loved and protected you, created a deep insecurity in you. They've made you question your worth, even making you feel as if you don't deserve love. I don't like you feeling that way, Amina." He stopped speaking then and eased back, pulling Amina's face up so they were eye-to-eye.

All Amina thought was that she hoped her nose was not running and that her eyes weren't puffy. Those thoughts rapidly exited as she saw the seriousness on Reth's face.

"You're worthy. You're worthy enough to be loved, to be

respected, to be appreciated. Your skin is one of your most beautiful physical attributes. You have the skin tone of my homeland and of power. I know your aunt told you that dark skin isn't beautiful, but that's a lie. You were painted a hue of perfection by God, and God never makes a mistake. Don't ever let me hear you down talk yourself or let others define how you see yourself. Adeya and Aaron's era of terror in your life is over. The power to change, to rewrite your life is in your hands. Their sins are not yours, and their lies are not your truth. Do you understand?"

They were so close that Amina inhaled the breath he exhaled. The scent of citrus lingered in the air. Amina's heart was beating a mile a second as she dreamed of Reth's lips crashing upon hers. They lyrics of Lauryn Hill's "Nothing Even Matters" cruised through her mind. At that moment, she was willing to risk it all. His lips were full, smooth, and inviting. Her eyes zeroed in on them.

Those chocolate lips of seduction lingered just inches away, getting closer until they slightly caressed against hers. Her mind went into overdrive. Everything in her body tingled at the new sensation of his mouth. This was by far better than anything she could imagine. His lips were lyrics serenading her emotions.

Combining the kiss with his words had her exploding with passions she could not define. Her mind went thoughtless, and she deepened the kiss as if she was starved and dying of thirst and hunger. His kiss was her survival. Reth consumed every part of her body, mind, and spirit. He was the maestro, and this was her performance of a lifetime. Every note had to be executed perfectly. Feeling herself descending deeper into the rapture of Reth, he abruptly jerked away, ending the symphony of Goode love she was preparing.

Coolness attacked her wet swollen lips that yearned for the saccharine taste of his for a moment longer. At the realization that he had pulled away, uncertainty began to bloom internally. Had she misread the situation? Was she a bad kisser? Did her breath stink? Did he not want her?

"I'm sorry," they both said in unison. Though for her, she was not sorry. This was what she had dreamed, except for the awkwardness that followed.

Liquid-stained amber orbs glanced into his direction. "Amina, I shouldn't have done that." Reth stood up, putting space between them. For the first time ever, he looked uncertain.

His chest was heaving as if he had run a marathon. It was clear to her that he was struggling. His eyes were clouded, and the conflicted expression on his face let her know that he indeed was feeling that he made a mistake. However, she could still feel the passion of his lips, and the warmth of his embrace. She longed to feel it again.

Bereft of his affection Amina stood up hoping that he would not notice her trembling body or the humiliation she felt at his rejection. Insecurity was back stronger than ever. A man like him would never want a real relationship with her. Besides, his wife had just died. It should have never gone that far. Guilt assailed her next.

Guilt taunted her that she was no different than her aunt and even her mother. Love was not for people like her. The fiery insults of her aunt began to ring in her head; the rejection of her father was close behind. Amina could only blame herself. She allowed her imagination to lead her when she should have stayed planted in-reality and not in fantasy.

Taking a deep breath, she tried to calm her vibrating body. Feeling strong enough to speak, she stated, "It's alright. You were just caught up in the moment. I know you didn't mean it. You would never see someone like me in that way. Excuse me," Amina spluttered, feeling like an absolute fool. Turning quickly, she nearly tripped over her feet as she made a mad dash out of the office as if the hellhounds were chasing her. Not once did she give him a second glance. Before her feet touched the first step, tears were already falling.

∞∞∞∞

A curse was fighting to escape Reth's mouth. He had been a complete knucklehead. This was not how it was supposed to go.

"Mal, this can't be what you meant by taking care of her and letting her take care of me," Reth mused out loud.

Conflicted and puzzled by his own actions, Reth followed the path that Amina took upstairs, but instead of going to her bedroom suite, he went to his own and headed for the shower.

Thoughts rushed through his mind, and he tried to figure out where he went wrong. He just buried his wife, and no, it was not a real marriage; they were not lovers, yet he had remained celibate since they married. Still, Amal was his wife, but his heart yearned for Amina. What kind of man did that make him? He kissed the nanny!

Somehow, he was able to shut that part of his mind off. Amal was his friend, but he was never sexually attracted to her, or her to him. Then, she told him that she knew he had needs and that she was okay with him seeking a relationship outside of the marriage.

That never happened. He could not fathom disrespecting her in that way. His work and family were fulfilling enough, and then came Amina Williams, all quiet and shy, sweet, and enduring, like a quiet storm entered their lives. He did his best not to see her. Amina Williams was not created to be ignored.

She loved the three most important women in his life: his mother, Amal, and Hasina. It all started to shift. No matter how hard he tried to fight the attraction, push her away, she was too magnetic. Guilt ran rampant, coursing through his veins like an infection, because he had feelings for her. Those feelings were secured the day they moved her from her home. The day he declared in his mind that she was his to protect.

Like a coward, he could not admit it. Those feelings were buried deep. However, Amal knew. Though she never said anything directly, she was hinting. Amina had to be the person she was speaking of. Lord knows, she occupied his thoughts; her voice lulled him, and her eyes were pure gold treasure. Amina was created to be treasured, to be his treasure.

For nearly half a decade, he put his feelings and desires on hold. He refused to allow himself that level of love or intimacy because Amal needed him. She was gone now, leaving behind an emptiness. No longer could he hide behind her.

For so long, she took up the woman space in his life. His needs and wants were never a priority, but seeing Amina day in and out, having her concerned about his needs, knowing that she had her own issues, were breaking down his walls. Those walls were being rebuilt by Amina.

Today, when all he wanted to offer was comfort and let her know that she was worthy and loved, he moved too fast. His inability to explain himself made her doubt herself. He was interested in her, and in that way, but their current situation was the problem. How would she feel if he wanted to court her?

Sighing at his own lack of control, Reth turned off the shower and toweled off then applied lotion before getting dressed in lounge wear.

Hopefully, Amina would allow him to apologize to her. It had been so long since he courted a woman; honestly, he was as bad as Djimon was now. He was a bit of a playboy until Amal. Now, at his age, he wanted a wife and more children. Again, something he never contemplated while with Amal. It was never going to happen unless they adopted children. The idea of Hasina having brothers and sisters with amber eyes made him giddy.

Stopping mid-thought, Reth smacked his head. He was most definitely doing too much. He had no idea where that line of thinking had come from.

Opening his bedroom door, he heard his mother's voice. Instead of heading toward Amina, he headed back downstairs to see what had brought his mother over.

"Ma?"

"Hello, my dear," she cooed, kissing his cheek. "Amina called me over and said she wanted to go check on her parents' house and see about Benito, and then she's coming back."

Reth rolled his head to the side. Amina was running.

"What's that look for?" she asked.

Chapter 21

The house was a mess. Right now, so was Amina. She didn't want to think about all that now, which was why she was here.

Adeya was apparently livid by the actions Reth took to evict her. However, it was expected. Adeya was an immature woman and did not know how to deal with not getting her way. She marred the walls with obscenities. Amina traveled the rest of the house to assess the damage. Her father's bedroom was untouched, as was Adeya's, but her bedroom received the full intensity of Adeya's ire.

Thankfully, there was nothing left in there. The windows had been broken, derogatory words were spray painted everywhere; feces had been rubbed on the wall, attracting a family of flies. It appeared as if she took a sledgehammer to the floor, evidence of who she really detested.

This woman had murdered her mother and her brothers and still had malice in her heart for Amina. The rage she must have felt to unleash this amount of destruction. All Amina felt in her heart was sorrow. Clearly, Adeya had untreated mental issues. Every move she made was in response to a man who never did and never would love her. To hurt him, she took his family and his ability to walk, and he still did not want her. Now, she was in prison and there was no way she was getting bond.

Placing her hands on her hips, Amina closed her eyes,

inhaled a deep breath, and released it gently. This predicament was not going to knock her off her square. Refusing to allow the negative thoughts to lead her down the path of insecurity and fear, Amina reinforced her walls and prayed. Once she lifted her head, she felt Kalifa's hand on her shoulder.

"We'll get this back right."

Amina agreed. "I'll take you home. I know you need to get ready for work."

"I already called Rufus and told him I'd come in tomorrow. Roxi is working for me."

Amina smiled. She turned to tell Kalifa thanks when they heard the door open.

Wondering who it could be, they both headed down the hall the door. It was Mela.

"Can I help you?" Amina queried, making a mental note to change all the locks today.

Mela's eyes took Amina in, seemingly shocked by their presence. "What'chu doing here?"

"This is my home. What're you doing here?"

At that, she sucked her teeth and placed her hand on her hip. "Trying to help your aunt. Have you not seen the news? They trying to pin your mama's accident on her. She's facing three counts of second-degree murder. She needs help."

"Indeed, she does, but that help won't be found here. This is no longer her home, nor does she own anything in here. Therefore, there's no need for you to be here."

Mela blinked several times as if she were not aware of whom she was speaking with. Amina officially had enough. Too many people, for too long, had taken from her. To maintain the peace, she suffered in silence. She kept her mouth shut when she should have spoken up, allowing others to control her, and hiding behind her shyness. No more.

Maybe Reth's rejection was the last insult for her. It was tiresome being the one nobody wanted. Banishing the negative thought, she focused on her mother. Kenise did not raise her to be a footstool, a fool, or a coward. Lifting her head high, she met Mela's glare and did not vacillate.

Mela smirked. "Them dudes got you out here wilding and feeling ya self. You all the way turned out."

"If that's all, please escort yourself out. Unless you want me to contact said dudes. I believe you were warned to stay away from me."

Seeming to not want the trouble of dealing with the Goode brothers, Mela did an about face and exited the house.

Kalifa giggled at her quick retreat. "That's how you handle business, all calm and collected. You know what; let's get out of here and have a girls' day and night. I'm talking hair done, new outfits, and going out. Before that, we'll write down what needs to be fixed and then it's fun for the rest of day."

That sounded refreshing and something she had not done in forever. "Right, let me call Djimon to see if he can at least board up the broken windows, and then we can go out."

Amina quickly texted Djimon and sent him photos of the damage. As soon as he read the text, he called her.

"What happened?"

"Typhoon Adeya happened. I just need the windows in my bedroom boarded up, the locks changed, and a do not trespass sign put up. I'll clean it up later. Kalifa and I are going to take a chill day before the long process of fixing this mess up. I can't deal right now."

"I tell you what; we're on our way now. Just wait until we get their and I'll handle it."

"Djimon, that's too much to—"

"Amina, you're family, and we take care of each other. Don't worry about it. JD and I are on our way now."

"Thank you."

"Any time, chocolate goddess."

Giggling, she hung up the phone, and Kalifa looked at her. "He called me chocolate goddess."

"Wait, don't you have a song titled that?"

"The song is Cacao Goddess," Amina corrected, as she and Kalifa went to sit on the porch to wait for the JD and Djimon.

∞∞∞

It had taken them two hours to get their hair done. Amina got a silk press blowout and her hair trimmed. It hung right at the tip of her butt. It transformed her from boring to chic. The women at the salon were complimenting her natural hair and eyes. It was in sharp contrast to what she was used to hearing in the past. In those two hours, she felt exquisite.

Kalifa had bantu knot curls, and they looked incredible on her. Now, they were in the mall shopping for new outfits. The pair had not been to the mall since BC and Diego brought them, and that felt like a century ago.

Following Kalifa, Amina glanced around, window shopping, trying to decide if she wanted to wear pants or a dress. Her wardrobe was nothing to blog about; she kept it simple and always hid herself, but she did not want to do that anymore. God did not create her to be invisible. Amal told her that she was made in His image, God did not hide. The enemy had imprisoned her for far too long. If she wanted to be seen for who she was, she had to start seeing herself too.

Deeply rooted in her mental thoughts, she did not hear Kalifa talking to her, but she did feel Kalifa's hand on her arm. The hold tightened, signaling that something was wrong. Turning to Kalifa, Amina's eyes trailed the same path as Kalifa's. There in the store were BC, Diego, two unknown girls, and Benito. The level of unbothered that Amina felt was soothing.

"Let's get what we want to wear. I'm not bothered by him anymore. My goal is to level up. I pray he's happy and will leave me alone."

Kalifa chuckled, lifted her hand for a high five, and then pulled on Amina's arm as they traveled to another store. Upon entering their latest destination, the sales associate greeted them with a smile.

"Your eyes are gorgeous," the sales associate complimented before asking, "How can I help you beautiful ladies today?"

Amina nodded her thanks, feeling herself blush at the comment.

"We're having a girls' night and need to be flawless," Kalifa answered, causing Amina to grin. It seemed like they were both revealing a new side.

"Come this way; I'll get you ladies right."

Tess, the sales associate, was true to her word. Her expertise was much appreciated; she even helped them to select shoes and accessories and allowed them to use her employee discount. The more they shopped, the more excited Amina became about going out.

As they made their way to the food court, two handsome guys approached them.

"Hello ladies."

Amina and Kalifa smiled in greeting.

"I'm Denali, and this my boy, Kasson. What's your names, beautiful?"

"I'm Kalifa, and this is my best friend, Amina."

"Would y'all do us the honor of eating with us?"

Amina stood still as if she was participating in the mannequin challenge. This had never occurred before. These two guys were attractive, and they approached them.

"Um."

"Are y'all available?" Denali asked, noticing their hesitation.

"No, nothing like that. Sorry, we're a little shy," Kalifa covered.

That seemed to ease the tension. Amina felt Kalifa's boney elbow in her side, and it woke her up. They agreed to eat with the guys, who were full of compliments. The foursome talked for another hour before leaving the mall.

After that, Kalifa invited Amina back to her house so they could get ready for their night out.

∞∞∞

Reth was livid when his brothers informed him about what Adeya did. If she had not already been arrested, she would be now. He quickly called his contacts, while Djimon contacted his, and they got to work fixing the mess that Adeya made. It was more trashed than anything, but she took all her rage out on the bedroom that belonged to Amina.

They had all the door locks changed and ordered replacement windows but boarded up the ones that were broken. Reth decided he would speak to Amina about having the entire house renovated. That way, she could rent the house out and make some extra money.

"It looks better," Djimon stated.

Reth nodded in agreement, his large arms folded, as he looked everything over.

"Brother, what's bothering you?"

Reth scratched his head, not wanting to tell his brothers that he lost control and kissed Amina. He meant to comfort her, not kiss her. Then she kissed him back and it lit a spark in him. He could not even tell his mother what he did. He knew she suspected something, though.

Before he could think of a reply, JD, followed by Kondo, were coming their way.

"I don't know about y'all but I'm tired. I need a nap," Kondo announced, yawning. Reth knew he was tired by the hours he worked at the hospital.

"Tired? I was thinking we could all go out tonight. Reth needs it, and Djimon has to go back to London soon, so I think we need a brothers' night out," JD suggested.

Djimon turned up his lips and side-eyed his brother before teasing, "I don't know if I trust JD to oversee something that important. Little brother is *saved* saved. You know the pastor in him won't let him get too loose. We're about to have a Bible Study on Daniel, apple juice, and peanut butter and banana sandwiches."

"Don't do me like, D. Just because I'm a pastor doesn't mean I don't know how to have a good time. Besides, you know I'm allergic to peanut butter. It would have been almond butter sandwiches and almond milk. You better act like you know!"

Reth chuckled despite not wanting to do so.

Djimon cackled before grabbing JD by the shoulders and patting him. Then, the horse playing began, and to Reth's dismay, Kondo jumped in. Reth just shook his head at their antics.

He let out a loud finger whistle to get their attention. "Knuckleheads, if we're going to go out, we can't be out here cutting up. Let's get home. Hasina is spending the night with her grandparents."

They stopped then and glanced at him. Reth offered them a smile. Maybe this was what he needed—a night out with his brothers to clear his mind and his heart. One kiss had unlocked everything he buried while being married to Amal. Amina was changing all of that.

Chapter 22

The jazz lounge that Kalifa had brought Amina to had been newly renovated. From the outside, it looked like any other upscale club, but inside, it was cozy. The chill vibe helped Amina release the stress of the day. This was a twenty-one and older club, so the grown and sexy were out. Eyes were on both ladies.

Tonight, was amateur open mike night, and Kalifa talked Amina into signing up since two acts had to pull out. They sat at table three near the stage, sipping on pink lemonade and watching a performance.

"So, those guys were really sweet."

Amina nodded, but she had Reth on the brain. She had been mentally imprisoned by his smooth lips, the aegis of his arms, and the firmness of his chest. Her mind went from one extreme to the other. That man was going to be the death of her and then and the one to resuscitate her.

Unable to keep the news to herself, she blurted, "I kissed Reth."

Kalifa jolted as if she had been shot; her pink lemonade sloshed across the table, landing on the floor. "Say wh-what? How'd you leap from crush to kissing?"

With dancing eyes too ashamed to meet Kalifa's, she answered, "In his office; he was being all sweet and soothing, and then it just happened. I was prepared to risk it all. I probably did. I swear I saw heaven, and then he pulled back and I felt his repudiation. I ran out of their faster than a cheetah hunting prey. I'm going to hell, Kalifa." She was going to hell and losing her job.

Kalifa put her drink down and pressed her lips together. "When did you become so dramatic? You're not going to hell."

Amina glanced at her uncertain. "I took advantage of him. He just buried his wife."

Mind temporarily blown, Kalifa processed what Amina told her. "That's a lot to unpack. But um, who initiated the kiss?"

"He did."

Kalifa waved her off. "You're innocent. There's no hell for you. All that is on him, and he needs to ask for forgiveness."

Before she could reply, the host called her name. The pair had been so lost in their conversation that Amina had forgotten she signed up.

Kalifa nearly pushed her out of the chair as if she were going to run away.

Amina wore a crop top and matching fitted skirt. It was sparkling gold, highlighted her complexion, and made her eyes shimmer. As she strutted to the stage, she could hear the catcalls but pretended not to; instead, she focused on the piano and the song.

Sitting down on the piano bench, Amina closed her eyes and tuned out the room. "The song I chose to cover is "I Surrender" by Arlissa. This song encompasses my life or, at least, how I've been recently feeling. I hope you all enjoy it."

Her fingers hit the first key, and she was lost, driven by pain and desire, indifference and love, resentment, and forgiveness. Opening her mouth, she belted out the lyrics. It felt as if it was always raining on her, so she was surrendering.

It was over after this. Losing her family, being abandoned

by her father because that's what he did; he abandoned her for alcohol. Never good enough as the bullies at school never let her forget she was not worthy; neither did Adeya. The blackness of her skin always seemed a sin. Adeya never let a day go by that she did not remind her. Adeya was her most dangerous adversary, the one woman that stole so much joy from her life. Well, she was not stealing more. BC, Nay, and their baby would no longer hold a place in her mind.

Finally, Reth. No, she did not have the poise or prettiness of his dearly departed wife, but she loved him before she knew what love was. Never again would she accept something just to have it like she had with BC. This was her releasing all those toxic, painful emotions. This was her resetting her life. The lies they told would burn this night.

Once the song was over, Amina transitioned from Arlissa's song to Jazmine Sullivan's "Masterpiece (Mona Lisa)". For far too long, she let other people's opinions destroy who she was. This was her public proclamation that was worthy. She was a masterpiece, masterfully crafted by God, created in the image of God. She was good enough: good enough to love, good enough to protect, good enough to be cherished. If her father could not see her value, then so what? She saw it. When she finished playing, the entire club erupted in applause. It was only then she remembered where she was, not in the safety of the music room at school, not the center, or Reth's home. Never had she allowed herself to be so vulnerable so publicly.

Reth side-eyed JD as they entered the newly renovated jazz lounge. Normally, this would have been the best place for him to relax and gather his thoughts. However, tonight was amateur open mike night, so there would be a variety of musical acts. It was all to bring in more patrons, to engage a younger crowd.

"It's going to be a good time," JD assured knowingly.

Reth did not respond. He was still in a foul mood because Amina had not come back home or contacted him. In fact, she called Djimon, and that irritated him all day. Why had she not asked him for assistance? *Did she like his brother more?* Reth quickly shook that thought.

"Come on, Reth. Table seven is reserved for us," JD interrupted his mental musing.

Burying his morose thoughts, Reth followed his brothers to their reserved table, and they quickly ordered drinks and appetizers. They settled in and Reth looked around before turning his attention back to his brothers.

"Do you think we should try to contact Amina's father?" Kondo asked.

"I think it would be best to consult with Amina. After the maelstrom I caused with having her aunt removed from the property, I'd say we follow Amina's lead."

Kondo gave him a thoughtful look before nodding in agreement.

The conversation settled as their drinks and food arrived, and some guy was singing, but his vocals did not compare to Amina.

Reth did that often, compared others to Amina's talent. There was never any comparison. Amina was in a league all her own. Reth tuned him out until the host introduced Amina, silencing their entire table.

"JD?"

"I had no idea she was here," JD responded to the unasked question. By the expression of awe on his face, he knew his brother was telling the truth.

Reth's eyes followed her path. This was not the same woman

that hurried out of his office like a scared kitten. She was all woman, dressed in gold and looking like royalty. Her long hair was straightened, flowing like a waterfall down her back. She sauntered onto the stage like a confident lioness. Reth's eyes traveled each step she took, his heart beating to the sway of her hips. When she sat down on the piano bench, Reth let out a breath.

He frowned at the men catcalling her. The need to protect her, to claim her as his own, nearly undid him. It was as if he was really seeing her for the first time. Amina was stunning.

Reth leaned forward in his seat and watched as she transformed into her performance pose. She closed her eyes, and her nimble fingers rested on the keys. He was jealous of the keys that were able to feel the tenderness of her fingertips. He wanted the same access. Amina was saying something, but Reth could not hear the words. He was too captivated by her essence.

What he heard was her lyrical, dulcet voice amplify throughout the lounge. The dominance her voice exuded cascaded throughout his entire being. The way she mastered her voice and took control of every person in the room was extraordinary to witness. They were puppets and she was the puppet master.

Reth observed the way her body conducted the melody, how she completely lost herself in the music. Amina was elegant grace, a picture of perfection, and he yearned to be the frame.

In her performance, she was letting all that held her down go, and as she ended the song, another melody started. This song he knew, Jazmin Sullivan's "Masterpiece (Mona Lisa)".

Proud to see her in this moment, Reth beamed. It had taken time, but Amina was now seeing herself as so many others saw her. In front of a room of strangers, she was shedding the old and coming into her own. She was a masterpiece, a work of art. Skin like onyx, eyes of gold, hair like silk, and she was a humble soul. In this moment, Amina was incandescent.

As she finished the song, the entire lounge erupted into applause and cheers. Reth stood up, giving a standing ovation. His brothers followed.

"Chocolate goddess did that. Man, oh man, is she looking hot or what? How old is she again?" Djimon grinned, wiggling his eyebrows at Reth.

Reth stopped clapping and turned his full attention to his brother. "Don't even, D. Not that one; never Amina," Reth warned, as he moved his chair out of the way to meet Amina. By her facial expression, Reth could tell that she was amazed, if not a little embarrassed, for being so opened. However, that was what made her such a phenomenal performer. What Amina did with music was rare, and he prayed she never lost that.

Once he arrived near the stage, Amina was descending the stairs. A little teary-eyed, her gaze was locked straight ahead. In was so intense that he followed her stare; he noticed that she was looking at a smiling Kalifa.

Making his way in the same direction, Kalifa noticed him first. There was an expression on her face he couldn't decipher. He put his index finger to his lips. She gave him a slight nod that she understood, Reth continued at a slow pace, allowing Amina to arrive first.

"Kali, I got so lost in the music that I forgot where I was. I'm a little embarrassed."

"That was everything. I live-streamed it on social media; girl, you're blowing up. You need a YouTube honey because you did that."

Amina sucked her bottom lip in as Kalifa showed her something on the cell phone. Still, she had not noticed Reth. He was about to speak when his brother came out of nowhere.

"Chocolate goddess, we've been bewitched by your siren

voice," Djimon cooed, as he rested his arm around Reth's shoulder.

Reth wanted to gut punch his brother for flirting. Instead, his eyes were drawn to Amina. Her reaction at seeing them was one of astonishment.

∞∞∞∞

Stupefied. That was the only word to come to mind as Amina took in the Goode brothers. Never in a million years would she think they would be present, especially Reth. Goodness, did he look handsome in his dark wash jeans and button-down UNTUCKit shirt, rendering her speechless.

"Amina, are you okay?" The magnetism of his voice reset her brain, freeing her muteness.

Blinking her eyes several times, she offered Reth her full attention. "I'm well." Though, her voice seemed to indicate otherwise. Even after her transformation, Reth still had the ability to impact her in ways no man ever had.

A knowing smiled crept across his smooth, sculpted face.

"Come with me, Amina, we need to talk."

Something about their needing to talk made her nervous. The truth was that she had sincere feelings for Reth, wrong or right; she had been enraptured by his essence since she was teen. There was always something about his aura, his soul flame, that lured her to him. Tonight, would be either the ending or the beginning.

Mentally soothing herself to shut down any nervousness, Amina turned to Kalifa and told her that she was going to have a private conversation with Reth. Kalifa lifted a curious brow; her eyes swarmed with accusations and mischief. However, whatever thoughts flooded her mind remained unspoken.

Instead, she nodded her understanding and winked. As she spoke to Kalifa, she could hear Reth speaking to his brothers.

Once she finished her conversation with Kalifa, Amina quickly addressed the other three brothers before permitting Reth to lead her away. Tenseness poured over her body in anticipation as Reth placed his hand gently on her lower back to escort her through the maze of patrons, some of whom were congratulating and complimenting her. Amina was too busy internally imploding to comprehend them.

Words remained unspoken as the pair exited, though there was an explosion of questions and feelings that were seeping through Amina's marrow. The coolness of the air brushed against Amina's flaming skin, causing her to close her eyes for a moment of respite. In just a short period of time, she claimed her freedom from a lifetime of enslavement to the opinions and actions of others. Now, she was in the presence of a man she both admired and adored. The need to express those feelings was overpowering. Behind that need was also hesitation because his heart belonged to another, and his deceased wife did not deserve her disloyalty.

"Where'd you park?"

Reth's voice was like the soothing causing her to open her eyes. Gracelessly, Amina pointed to the left of the parking lot. Her Jeep was parked in the second row. He nodded and then assisted her as they continued their journey to her vehicle. Reaching for the keys to allow them entrance, Reth held out his hand.

"I'll drive. My brothers will ensure that Kalifa gets home safely."

Unsure of her own voice, and still feeling rattled, Amina wordlessly handed over the keys. Reth's free hand then went to her elbow as he guided her to the passenger side and then opened the door and assisted her in. His touch ignited a firestorm inside of her, though she did her best to hide her unraveling.

Either clueless to her reaction, or just gentlemanly enough not to call her out, Reth acted as if nothing was amiss as he closed the door and strolled to the driver's side. Doing her best to dry her sweaty palms, Amina rapidly inhaled and exhaled three breaths. She managed to settle her nerves before Reth entered the Jeep and started it up.

Buckling her seatbelt, she remained benumbed with fear of making a mockery of herself. Past interactions with Reth taught her that she did not respond well to him, always jumping to incorrect assumptions or blurting out responses that needed to be left unsaid. This time, she would allow him to control the conversation.

"Amina."

Jumping at the sound of his alluring voice, she mentally reprimanded herself for her reaction. It was just her name, yet she interpreted so many meanings from that alone, causing her to overreact. This was what he did to her psyche.

"Yes?"

"Your performance tonight was phenomenal. The transformation left me speechless. I think you had every person in that room transfixed by your singing."

Amina allowed herself to smile at the compliment but remained reticent. Exhaling a breath, Reth eased on the brakes as they came to a stop light and then looked at Amina. She felt the focus and intensity of his eyes as if they were part of her being. Whether intentionally or unintentionally, Reth Goode was a magnetic force that pulled her into him, no matter how hard she fought.

"Have I angered or offended you?" he finally asked, more than likely picking up on her strange vibe. His voice was gentle like the flow of dove wings but also unsure. This tone was new because Reth was always confident and in charge. The uncertainty perplexed her.

Harnessing all her courage, she turned her amber eyes and gazed into his. Lyrics erupted into her mind as she studied him. Musical notes unleashed with a passion she had never felt. Reth was walking music genres. He reminded her of neo-soul songs by artists like Musiq Soulchild and India.Arie fused with old R&B loves songs by Al Green and Roberta Flack & Donny Hathaway. Oftentimes, she got lost in his melody. He also possessed the classical captivation of Beethoven-Romance No.2 in F Major. How was she supposed to fight her feelings when he was musical perfection?

Right now, she felt so conflicted; love and shame, anger and longing, acceptance and rejection played tug of war in her mind. He had no idea the thoughts that flowed through her head or the feelings that she felt for him. He had no idea how much authority he exuded over her heart.

"I'm not offended or angry with you, only myself." It was an honest answer that left her feeling exposed. Inevitably, he would ask why.

Still holding his gaze, she watched as he took in her words, processed them, and then prepared to ask a question. However, a horn blew behind them, disrupting the moment.

Minutes later, Amina asked, "Where are we going?" It was not important, but she felt compelled to fill the silence.

"There's this quiet, little place by the lake where I like to go. It's a good place to talk."

It was a vague answer, but Amina did not press for more. Instead, she leaned back and let the music in her mind overtake her. At some point, Amina had fallen asleep because the next thing she remembered was the gentle shake. Fluttering her eyes, she leisurely took in her surroundings before turning her attention back to Reth. His face looked like the rising of the morning sun.

"Join me," he requested.

Blinking off her fatigue, she opened the door and waited for Reth. Seconds later, he was at her side. He escorted her to the rear of the Jeep, and they sat down on the tailgate.

Amina gazed at up at the sky that was sprinkled with vivid stars and a half moon. She was doing her best to distract her mind from Reth's closeness. The lingering, attractive scent of his cologne, however, would not allow her a moment of respite.

The thrashing of her heart resembled the pounding of buffalo escaping from a predator. It was impacting how she was breathing. However, Amina finally regained control over her facilities.

Pulling in her lips, she felt Reth sorting through his thoughts. Still, she remained quiet but stole a peripheral glanced at him. Even in his state current uncertainty, Reth was regal and commanding. He placed his hand on her arm to get her attention, and Amina fully turned to face him.

"I apologize for taking advantage of you. It was obvious that you were distraught about the news of your aunt. I meant to only comfort, and instead, I overstepped my bounds as your friend and employer. You have every right to be upset and disgusted with me. I fully support the #MeToo movement, and I am embarrassed by my conduct and lack of respect. Please forgive me."

Without a second thought, Amina guffawed. Her entire body shook as she laughed. Reth apologizing for something she had dreamed of since she was a teenager seemed to break the tension. Shaking her head, she finally regained control of herself. "Forgive my laughter, but I didn't feel taken advantage of. There is nothing to forgive, as you did nothing wrong or improper toward me," Amina expressed as she observed his reaction. She saw that he looked both offended and relieved. Exhaling a relaxing breath, Amina added, "I felt like it was me taking advantage of you. While the kiss was happening, you pushed away. I felt ashamed, as if I wronged you. Guilt assailed me, especially with you grieving Amal."

In one fluid movement that seemed more acrobatic than a man of his size and demeanor should be able to execute, his hands went from her arm to her face, preventing her from speaking. First, her eyes glimpsed at his hands touching her before allowing her golden orbs to meet his russet ones.

"It seems there has been a lack of communication on both our parts. We've filled in the confusion with our own thoughts. Let me clarify my intentions so we never have this bemusement again."

Amina leaned closer to hear him, and he started to share the history of his relationship with Amal. Finally, everything that Amal said, as well as Reth, began to make sense. It grieved her that Amal, because of her attack, viewed her beauty as a curse. Rape was never about beauty but power. Amina wished Amal were still alive so she could tell her that it was not her fault.

"So, you see, Amal and I were never soulmates. We were never husband and wife in the sense that God intended, but to save her, I would do it all over again."

If she were not already having romantic feelings for this man, she would have fallen in love with him the moment she heard why he married Amal. It was selfless and honorable. To show her gratitude for his sacrifice, she pulled his hand into her lips and gave it a gentle kiss. Hearing the truth allowed her to breathe easily as well as absolve her of guilt. Everything made sense now. Exhaling a slow breath, she licked her lips and cooed, "I knew you were an exceptional man. Amal was blessed to have a man of valor protect her honor and to be a father to Hasina."

Reth blushed, and she giggled. "Have I embarrassed you?" Amina questioned since she had never seen him blush before.

"Well, that's not what I thought you would say, but thank you for the compliment."

"It's the truth. Even when I was younger, I just knew there was something about you." Then, Amina shared the conversation she had with Amal about him. "I've had a crush on you for forever. I just thought someone like you would never see a person like me. So, when we kissed, it was like a dream come true. I know that sounds cliché, but for a woman who has had everything she loved removed willingly or stolen from her, to have something that was unattainable felt like every impossibility was possible. Then, that feeling dissipated when you seemed to regret it. I just felt dismissed. It was a reminder that good things don't happen to me anymore." Flooded with emotions, Amina dropped her head at that admission. Mentally, she chastised herself for being so vulnerable with him.

The feeling did not last long. She felt a warm hand under her chin lifting, her head up. The richness of him was almost too much to bear. "Good things do happen to you. From the moment you entered my life, I saw you, the woman, and it made me nervous. Feelings that I buried began to resurface, and Amal knew that. She knew a woman like you would catch my eye and capture my heart. It unnerved me. Amal, being my best friend besides my brothers, had seen the attraction before me. I was unsure of how to react to those feelings because even though my marriage wasn't a traditional one, I still respected Amal as my wife."

He let out a sigh before continuing, "I've been out of the dating game for a while. In my haste to express my feelings for you, I came on too strong. Never was it my intention for you to feel rejected. I'm clueless as how to navigate this new chapter of my life. I want us to get to know each other and spend time together if that is what you want. There's no pressure and no time limit. We move at the pace best suited for us."

Amina could barely contain herself. This was what it was like to have a conversation with a man about a relationship. BC would never. She almost wanted to pinch herself to see if she were dreaming. Reth Abioye Goode was interested in her. There was so much sincerity in his eyes and body language. If it were possible, she would save this moment in a jar. If this man knew the deepness of her affection for him, just how his presence impacted her, he would know she was ready, set, go. "I'd like that, but if we do this, then I have to move out of your home. I'll still care for Hasina, but I can't live in your house while we get to know each other. It wouldn't be right, so if we do this, we do it the right way."

A mischievous grin spread across his face. He looked more like his brother Djimon now. There was a bit of a flirt in him.

"That expression reminds me of Djimon."

Reth chuckled. "He learned from the best."

"Is that so?" Amina flirted back. She did enjoy this teasing side of him. To see him in better spirits made her heart leap with joy.

Reth shrugged his shoulders. "I was different before I married Amal." He gave her a glance to see her response, but she remained mum.

"Amina the wise, your logic is sound—I agree. I would feel comfortable with you staying at my parents again. I was thinking about getting your house remodeled so that you could rent it out. That way, you have another stream of income, and the house would not sit empty. After the run-ins you've had, staying their alone would worry me. Also, living with my parents keeps you and Hasina close. It's obvious that you two adore one another."

Before she could speak, he took his index finger and tapped her nose. Goosebumps littered her exposed skin. "No, that is not why I seek to pursue you. I know how your mind works. I like you, *mpendwa*, simply for you."

Unable to contain herself anymore she turned into a bubbly, giddy teenager. She had no idea what *mpendwa* meant, too caught up in the moment, she did not ask. Yet, she liked he called her an endearment. "I really like you too." She captured the tip of her tongue between her teeth, feeling timid at her honesty.

"Good, because my intentions are to court you with a purpose. You've only known toxic love from the way your father and Adeya treated you, as well as your ex. They were toxic people, seeking to use you to benefit self. Understand that you are dealing with a man now, and I'm committed to only showing you good love. I'm seeking to encourage your growth, to support your dreams, to be a benefit and an asset to all that God has placed in your heart to achieve. My goal is to magnify all that black woman magic."

The effect of Reth's words exalted Amina. She could have been knocked over with a feather. That edification and declaration lifted her spirit in ways he would never know. Reth was her *Symphony of Goode Love.* He was an instrument she was determined to master.

Chapter 23

R eth pulled out the chair for his mother. As usual, Eleora was glowing with her thick natural hair pulled in a tight bun. She wore a yellow sundress that highlighted her Pilates toned body. When they entered the restaurant, the eyes of men his age ogled her. All he could do was smirk and shake his head. They had no idea how deeply devoted and in love Eleora was with her husband, the same love that Reth and his brothers sought when seeking their wives. A love so passionately entrenched in the depths of God that no distraction could cause either of them to forsake their vows.

Reth's heart was exhilarated as he took in his parents, who were joining him for lunch. Before Amal's cancer returned, this was a weekly occurrence. His parents did this with all their sons, and on Sundays, they had a family dinner. Even though Djimon frequently traveled internationally, his parents made sure to video call him for their lunches. It helped them to remain close.

After ensuring that his mother was comfortable, Reth slid his right hand down his suit jacket and unbuttoned it and he sat down across the table from her. Instantly, he could feel his mother's eyes on him. Not for the first time, he wondered if Amina had shared with his mother about the kiss and his feelings for her. He knew that his mother would question why Amina wanted to return to his parents' home and not his. If that did not pique her interest, he was sure that they noticed the slight alteration in his mood. Being around Amina was changing him for the better daily.

Even though he and Amal's marriage had been one of convenience, a part of him felt his growing feelings for Amina would be viewed as disrespectful to his deceased wife. It was not so much that he was worried about himself but for Amina. If anyone came at her rudely, they were going to deal with him. Amina was sensitive and felt unkindness in a way that he could personally overlook. Still, Reth did what any man would do in his position. He prayed. He had prayed and fasted the first moment he felt his heart unravel at the thought of Amina. He asked God for guidance, strength, and protection of Amina. Though others may disagree, their connection felt God ordained.

It had only been two days since their mutual confession of feelings for one another, yet his co-workers and brothers could see a change in him. His mother's knowing eyes were laser focused on him. Eleora was the only person to make him sweat. Before he was a judge, he was the top immigration attorney with nerves of steel and a legal wit that was unstoppable. As a judge, he was fair but tough. When it came to First Lady Eleora Madiata Goode, he was a little lamb.

"Is there something on your mind?" Reth directed his question to his mother, while his father perused the menu. He was sure he caught just a hint of a smirk. His father knew something.

Eleora lifted a brow, more than likely thinking that Reth was being cheeky, but he honestly wanted her to just speak her mind. The unknowing of what she knew was making him a tad nervous. "My Song Thrush has requested to move back into the house with us. When I inquired why, she said it was simply better that way. Then I began thinking, and I recalled how she asked me to come over because she needed to tend to her house, and you were acting strangely. Did you hurt that baby?"

There was still warmth in her words but laced in warning. The concerned look that his mother was now displaying took him by surprise, reminding him of how defensive his mother was over Amina.

Reth winced at her referring to Amina as a baby. She was far from that; she was his *mpendwa*. Shaking off the need to get defensive, he answered his mother. "I would never hurt Amina, at least not on purpose. I feel that my past and present actions have revealed that. However, that day, Amina was upset about her aunt and the unnecessary attention that was brought to her. You know she's a private person. At the time, she was hurting. I requested that she come to the office so we could speak privately. Before I knew it, I kissed her."

There, it was out.

Eleora gasped and lifted her hand over her heart as if astounded by his actions. His father did not skip a beat; he just smiled at his wife's theatrics. His mother knew him to be a man of control, decorum, and respect. His confession most likely surprised her. His father told him that when he met Eleora, he knew she was the one, and he briefly forgot his manners and kissed her too. At this point, it was a Goode tradition.

"It was not my original intention to react that way, but it happened. Once I realized what I had done, I stopped it. Later, I found out she was more offended that I stopped kissing than the kiss itself. We discussed it and both expressed our feelings for each other. Amina, being far wiser than I, declared that it would be best to move out, stating that if I wanted to pursue her, I had to do it right. I agreed. With the current state of things, I did not want her moving back to her house. We agreed that her moving in with you all would be best; well, I made a strong argument that it would be best," Reth amended. He was concerned about BC and her aunt's friends coming for her. That, he would not have.

At his admission, he saw his mother's facial features ease. "Reth, are you sure this isn't a reaction to losing your wife? I know it was a marriage of convenience but you're still grieving. I just want to make sure you're ready."

That was a legit concern. Reth respected his mother for sharing her thoughts on the matter. "I asked myself that. I've even wondered if it's too soon to feel what I feel, but it isn't. Before Amal's death, she kept throwing hints at Amina and me. It was as if she knew that Amina and I were meant to be. I know how that sounds. I'm a man of logic, but I am also a man of faith, and this feels right. I've prayed and fasted to seek confirmation and I have it. Understand, this is not lust or me using Amina to fulfill emptiness. I'm not hollow. Also, Amina feels the same. For the past two days, we've been talking about God's expectation, our expectations, and our hopes for the future and for Hasina. The two of us went to visit Amal's grave and just talked and prayed."

Eleora grinned approvingly. "I guess it's time."

Frowning in confusion, Reth asked, "Time for what?"

Eleora reached for her Brahmin handbag and revealed an envelope, handing it over to him. "This. Amal gave it to me and instructed me to give this to you at the appropriate time."

Reth reached out for the envelope, flummoxed. What could it possibly be that Amal had not told him before she died? Shaking his head, he placed the envelope into his suit jacket pocket. It would be something that he would read later, privately. After tucking the letter away, the waitress arrived and they each ordered and started talking.

"Amina has much to be excited about. She passed her license exam and is preparing for her concert, it is this week. She seems ecstatic about it," Eleora shared, sipping her tea.

Reth appreciated the change in conversation. "She was practically beaming like a star when she spoke of it yesterday.

She took Hasina with her today while she practiced," Reth added, wondering what the two were up to.

"I'm excited for her. She'll be graduating soon after. I just hate that her father won't be present."

Reth fought the urge to growl. Aaron Williams needed a reality check, but right now, he would remain quiet. Gavin had stepped up in a major way since Amina's attack by her aunt. "I was thinking about taking a vacation once Amina graduates. I wanted to take her and Hasina to Mauritius. I haven't told either of them yet. I think it's what they both need to reset. This past year has been difficult."

"That's a marvelous idea. I agree; maybe we can all go," Eleora murmured, smiling at Chiram. His father winked at her in agreement.

Reth nodded in agreement. The idea of spending time with his entire family was a grand one. They had not taken a family vacation in years due to everyone's conflicting schedules. The trio finished their lunch half an hour later, and Reth escorted his parents to their car before getting into his own and heading back to work.

Once he merged into traffic, his work cell phone started to ring. He answered through the Bluetooth. "Judge Goode here."

"Judge, it's Matt, and he's back."

Growing rigid in his seat and asking no questions, Reth knew whom Matt was referring to.

Amina felt like she was floating instead of walking. That was the aftermath of Reth. A real-life love story was developing between them and it felt so right. Still, she was committed to moving slowly. It was not just their hearts at stake; it was Hasina's too. If Hasina did not approve of Amina and her father, then there would be no relationship. No one would ever accuse her of being a homewrecker.

Filing the thought away, Amina reached for Hasina's hand as the two exited the music room. They were finally done with practice. Thanks to Hasina being homeschooled this year, her schedule was flexible, which worked in Amina's favor.

The pair made it to the SUV, and Amina buckled Hasina into her car seat. The duo was headed to the grocery to pick up items needed to create Reth's favorite dish, Moambe chicken (mossaka). Moambe chicken was a roasted chicken cooked in a thick sauce created from palm nuts extract. They were going to pair it with mashed potatoes, vegetables and chapati—East African bread. For dessert they were making Congo bars were basically like chocolate chip cookies, but Amina wanted to stop by Tamu Bakery to get something else since Reth enjoyed the strawberry cupcakes so much. Hasina was beyond excited to cook for her father. That made Amina excited in return.

Once they were done with their shopping, they were going to pick Benito up from school and take him with them, as they had their music lesson at the center. It was Amina's prayer that she would not have to interact with BC. It seemed that he had lost interest in bothering her. He did not contact her after she was attacked by her aunt. Maybe he understood that he could not rekindle what had no embers.

Pulling her SUV into the parking space, Amina reached for her purse and then opened her door to get out. Next, Amina opened Hasina's door and assisted her out of the Jeep. Holding hands, they journeyed inside, and Amina got a cart. Lifting Hasina up, Amina placed her in the cart, much to her dismay. However, Hasina liked to wander when they shopped, and she did not want to lose her.

"Mina, can I listen to music on your phone?"

Amina nodded and pulled out her iPhone, attached the

earplugs, and handed it to Hasina. Then, she pushed the cart to the meat section. With Hasina occupied, Amina knew this would be a quick shopping trip.

As Amina started to check out, Hasina tapped her hand and showed her there was an incoming phone call. Amina winked at her and reached for the phone. From the number, she knew it was her father's attorney and wondered why he was calling. She made sure to pay him in full.

Reaching for the phone, she quickly hit the button to answer. "Amina speaking."

"Amina, hello. It's Ernest Richards, your father's attorney."

"Yes sir, how can I help you?" she asked as she checked out her groceries.

"Well, your father and aunt have both contacted me about representing her. Currently, she has a public defender, and I guess she is not pleased with her representation."

"I see, but why are you calling me?"

"Your father stated you would pay for it."

Amina almost dropped the phone. Aaron Williams had some serious explaining to do if he thought that she was paying for Adeya's defense team. Not in any life was that occurring.

"I apologize, Mr. Richards, for you wasting your time. I'll not now or in the future provide financial assistance toward the defense of Adeya Williams. She murdered my mother and my brothers. Not to mention, she physically assaulted me and psychologically abused me for years."

There was a pause on the other end, and finally, she heard him breathing. "As I thought. Your father also wants to see you. He said he was unable to contact you but requests that you visit him. I can help assist you with that."

Reality just hit and Amina was no longer floating. Her father finally wanted to see her but only to use her financially to assist his sister. It hurt less when he ignored her. This felt like having a poisoned knifed twisted in her heart. What had she ever done to either of them for her own family to be callous toward her?

"I'll get back with you, Mr. Richards. I'm currently at the checkout..."

There was a brief silence before his soft alto responded. "Of course. Whenever you're ready. I look forward to hearing from you. Bye."

Amina did not reply; she simply ended the phone call. Internally, she was shattering.

Shaking off the shock, Amina bagged her groceries with a speed that would have management offering her a job. She completed her transaction and pushed the cart toward the exit with more force than necessary.

Inside, she was fuming like a volcano ready to erupt. The audacity of it all.

"What's wrong, Mina?" the soft, angelic voice queried.

Blinking her eyes to clear the fury, the sound of Hasina's sweet voice, so much like her mother's, calmed her. With a giant smile, Amina answered, "Nothing, sweet girl."

Hasina nodded and smiled back.

When they arrived at the SUV, Hasina jumped in and Amina unloaded the bags and handed Hasina a snack. She shut the door and pressed the lock before pushing the cart back. On her way back to the Jeep, her steps faltered as she saw Delilah St. John knocking on the back window, frantically attempting to get Hasina's attention.

Today just was not her day. "Father give me strength," Amina prayed.

Mentally cheering that she locked the door, Amina met

Delilah's accusing gaze. It seemed that Hasina was ignoring her. Knowing the vile woman, she would have tried to kidnap Hasina and lie on Amina.

Rushing over, Amina stopped when she was close to Delilah. "Can I assist you with something, Mrs. St. John."

Delilah snapped her head toward Amina like an alligator ready to attack. Amina witnessed the pure disgust plastered on her face, as if Amina were a bad taste she could not remove from her mouth. If Amina had not grown up with a bully for an aunt, she might have been offended. It was clear that Delilah did not care for Amina in the least. Yet, Amina had not lost an ounce of sleep over it.

"How dare you have my grandchild locked in this hot car with no air conditioning?"

There was her angle—creating a fictitious story to suggest that Amina was incompetent. Amina pressed her lips and tilted her head to the side at Delilah's ignorant display.

"I literally just put her in the Jeep while I returned the cart. I'm going to start the car up now," Amina replied calmly and then turned around and started the engine and turned on the air conditioning. Hasina was perfectly fine and drinking the chocolate milk she asked for in the store. Even Hasina was ignoring Delilah.

Delilah was hot on her heels. Amina was doing her best to inwardly pray to keep her calm. Delilah was pushing her last nerve. "I don't like it, and I'm telling Reth. You're no good for my granddaughter or my son-in-law. It should be Emmarie, not you!" she seethed like a dragon blowing fire.

"Okay." Amina went to shut the door, but Delilah prevented it from happening by yanking it open, nearly pulling Amina out with it. The gasped from Hasina nearly caused Amina to forget that Delilah was her elder. "Is there something else?"

Delilah rolled her eyes in frustration when she did not get

the expected response. Amina was not going to fall for it. Delilah then lifted her left index finger, shaking it in Amina's face. "Look here, you little hood hussy. I know that you're after Reth, but you'll never compete with my deceased daughter. She was a beauty queen and raised to be a wife, unlike you. You scream low-class, ghetto schemer. You're just a bed warmer and will never be wife material. The way you took advantage of my dying daughter to get her to give you her expensive Jeep. The way you're trying to keep my grandchild from me. The way you're trying to turn Reth against me. I know your kind. I'll be your worst enemy. You'll not get your claws in Reth or his money. I'll see to that," Delilah spat haughtily and then sashayed off as if she had not insulted Amina's character.

Letting out a deep breath, Amina shut the door and did her best to regulate the beating of her heart. There was so much she wanted to say and defend herself. She should have anticipated this woman's words, but they still cut. It had her thinking old thoughts. Nothing good happened anymore, and when it did, it was destroyed by something bad. "Why God? Why can't I ever be allowed happiness?"

"Mina, Psalm 126:5 says, '*Those who plan in tears will harvest with shouts of joy*,'" Hasina quoted, offering a toothy grin. It was as if the argument with Delilah never happened. To be that innocent and unbothered was a blessing.

Instantly, her punctured heart hummed in appreciation. "Out of the mouths of babes," she whispered.

Her time to harvest with shouts of joy was coming; she just had to hold on a little longer. She had to remember who was in charge—not man, but God. She did not live for the world's approval; she lived for God's. Feeling renewal in her spirit, she pulled out of the of the parking space with hope. Amina reenforced that God had her even during this time of uncertainty. With time to spare, Amina decided to drop off the groceries and then pick-up Benito.

Chapter 24

Amina waved goodbye and blew a kiss at Hasina. JD offered to take Hasina home so Amina could talk to Benito about what was happening at school. Amina told Ms. Mary that she would bring Benito home. They were headed to the Jeep when a whining, nasal voice halted their movement.

Amina turned to see Nay waddling toward her. It was noticeable that she was pregnant, but Amina was flummoxed as to why she was on the woman's radar. BC was not an issue for Amina. She'd moved on.

"Amina, um, can I speak to you for a minute?" When she got closer and saw Benito, she waved at him; he waved back and then dropped his head.

Amina handed him the keys and told him to go wait for her. Then, she turned her attention back to Nay. "I'm not sure what we have to speak about." As she got closer, Amina noticed some bruising on her.

"Look, I know I treated you real rotten, but girl, you gotta take BC back. He ain't right without you. I thought I wanted him all to myself, but nah, he don't do well without you in his life. So, what'chu gonna do about him?"

Was she serious? This was too comical to be reality and Amina nearly burst into giggles. This woman, who had mocked her for years and chased BC when he was Amina's boyfriend, now wanted her to fix him. The audacity of it all...

Smoothing the features on her face to become unreadable, Amina replied, "I'm unclear as to what you think I can do. BC and I broke up. When I leave, I don't go back. He's no longer my concern. You wanted him and now you have him. If you're no longer interested in pursuing a relationship with him, then I advise you to end it. Do not come to me to save you. Have a good night." Amina turned her back to her and sauntered off.

"But he's a jerk now. He wasn't like that when you were dating!" Nay yelled, obviously at her wits end.

Amina shrugged her shoulders but did not break her stride or look back. They were her past, and she was in the present trying to build a future with Reth. To waste an ounce of thought on either of them would be doing too much.

Once she got into the SUV, she winked at Benito as he gave her a questionable glance. That little spectacle was nothing to be concerned over. Offering him a reassuring grin, she started up the vehicle and left the parking lot, leaving Nay behind. She was done.

As they pulled out into traffic, Amina turned her attention to Benito as if the episode with Nay never happened. "How's school going now?"

"Better. I don't have to deal with the boys that jumped me. They got expelled and no one bothers me now."

Amina shook her head. This much she knew because she called the school twice a week. Neither she nor Ms. Mary were able to have a parent conference, but the boys were punished.

"Benito, I want to ask you something, and I need you to be honest with me. Whatever you say, I'll not get angry."

He stopped fiddling with his hands and looked up at her, his eyes showcasing his youth and innocence.

"I will, Mina."

"Okay. What happened that made those boys hurt you? Was it gang-related?"

Amina watched him closely. They were at a red light that took longer to change. His face turned a shade of red, as if he were contemplating how to answer her. Seeming to make up his mind, he shared, "Their brothers are mad at my brother. I don't know why."

"Why didn't you tell me that when it happened?"

"People don't like when you snitch. I was going to let Beni handle it. He told me not to fight but to protect myself, but not to start anything."

Amina nodded. Her heart felt lighter knowing that Benito was not involved in a gang, but that did not mean BC was not. If his association was impacting Benito, then she and BC were going to have some problems.

"I'm sorry that happened to you. It was wrong. Please don't ever keep secrets. There's nothing wrong with telling people who love you and want to protect you what's going on. Promise me, no matter how cool it may seem, you will not join a gang."

He nodded.

"Words, Benito. I need to hear you say them."

"No matter how appealing it seems, I won't join a gang."

Amina smiled. "Good."

Less than thirty minutes later, they were pulling up to Ms. Mary's house. Along with Ms. Mary's car, a Porsche was parked in front of the house. The owner was unknown to Amina, yet the car stuck out in the neighborhood. As soon as Benito saw it, he beamed.

"It's my cousin Dre, but he likes for me to call him Uncle Dre. He's back!"

Unable to contain his excitement, Benito jumped out of the SUV, running toward the house. He had left his backpack and instrument. Amina collected his belongings and followed at a slower pace.

When she finally made it to the entrance, Benito was hugging a man. For the life of her, Amina could not recall Dre; she had heard the name but never had a face to associate it with. He was a handsome man, in a commercial way, probably just under six feet with caramel skin and light hazel eyes. He had a tapered haircut and looked professional and wealthy. However, there was something about him that she could not place. He was almost too much and not in a good way.

Doing her best to hide her thoughts, Amina placed Benito's belongings down and greeted Ms. Mary as well as her company.

"Mina, this is Dre, my nephew. Dre, this is Mina, the young lady who captured BC's heart and the only girlfriend he had that I love and approve of."

Amina flushed with embarrassment but held out her hand to greet Dre. "Nice to meet you, sir."

He lifted her hand to his lips and offered a gentle kiss. "No need to call me sir. Dre is what my friends and family call me. It seems, you're family."

Not knowing what to do, Amina just nodded and removed her hand from his hold. She turned her attention back to Ms. Mary. "Benito was great. My concert is Friday at six o'clock pm. I think he's as excited as I am."

"I am. I'm gonna do a good job," he cheesed.

"I know you will." Then, Amina added, "I should be going. I still have to get dinner on."

Ms. Mary frowned. "They making you cook too?"

"No ma'am. Hasina and I wanted to do something nice for her father."

Ms. Mary nodded her understanding. "Be safe, love. We'll be at your concert, minus BC. I know you don't want him there."

"Why not?" Dre asked. His forehead crinkled in confusion.

"I'll tell you later," Ms. Mary answered before turning her attention back to Amina. "I'm so proud of you. My Mina baby is graduating soon and then off to get your doctorate. You're something spectacular. I pray you never forget that."

The compliment warmed her heart. "Thank you, Ms. Mary." Amina leaned over to hug her. She told them goodbye and headed out of the house. Walking swiftly, she climbed in her Jeep and backed out. As she got on the road, she noticed BC's car pulling up and thanked God she left in time.

He honked his horn to get her attention, but she kept driving.

∞∞∞∞

Something was bothering Amina. Reth arrived home to thick tension. At first, he thought something happened between Amina and her ex, but she explained she had not seen him until she was leaving. He almost left it alone until Hasina told him that Delilah approached them in the parking lot. That let him know the source of what upset her; however, Amina was holding firm that nothing was wrong.

Reth was patiently waiting for the lovely dinner that Amina and Hasina prepared for him to be over. Though she made Congo bars for dessert, she still purchased strawberry cupcakes for him from Tamu. It was thoughtful and sweet.

Delilah still attempting to cause trouble in his family annoyed him on every level. She was a thorn in his side that refused to be removed. Yet, the only outcome she could accomplish was to incite his ire.

At this rate, Reth was tempted to contact Emre St. John and have him collect his wife. The couple was separated, but hopefully he could charm her back home. She would not run amuck in his home or upset his daughter or Amina.

"Daddy, did you enjoy your meal?"

Hasina's lyrical voice, so much like Amal's, pulled him out of his stampeding thoughts. Reth glanced over at his daughter with love filled in his heart. Hasina was the greatest gift Amal gave him. He adored his daughter, her innocence, and her kindness. With a fatherly grin, he replied, "It was delicious, *mndani*. It's the best I've ever tasted, but don't tell your *Bibi*."

Hasina grinned so brightly that it warmed Reth. There was nothing in this world he would not do to keep his baby girl smiling like that.

"I won't, Daddy. I love you too much to get you in trouble with Bibi."

Reth heard Amina snicker. For some reason, this moment just elated him. A part of him wished that Amal could be privy to this as well. Since her death, they had not had moments like this. He treasured every moment of joy he received with Hasina.

The past weeks had been tough for her, but with Amina, himself, and family, Hasina had an outpouring of love and support.

"I love you more."

"I love you to the moon!" Hasina giggled.

Reth rested his hand over his heart. "I love you to infinity."

Hasina's hazel eyes glowed with giddiness. "You win, Daddy. You love me a lot."

"I do. I'll always love you, *binti*."

Hasina nodded and then she looked at Amina and back to Reth. "Do you love Mina too? I do."

Reth saw how Amina froze. A part of him hurt for her. From

the way she was treated after the death of her mother and brothers, Reth knew that love had been brutally ripped from her life.

Amina's current reaction had her golden eyes glancing everywhere but at him. That bruised his spirit. Silently and without judgment, Reth observed Amina as she eased her gaze at Hasina and simpered, "I love you, too, Hasina. You're my little piano princess."

Hasina's entire face burst with unmitigated joy. Then, Hasina turned toward Reth, patiently waiting for his reply. He did not want to make Amina feel uncomfortable or have her question his feelings for her. Strong feelings that made him want to protect and care for her. He did care deeply about Amina. This timid, quiet woman awakened the dormant parts of his heart. Amina had no idea the force that she was. When given the opportunity, he would show her.

Winking at his daughter, he replied, "The Bible tells us to love our neighbors as we love ourselves; of course, I love Amina."

He heard a gasp leave Amina's mouth, and she quickly started to clear the table.

"Hasina, you get one hour of television, and then it's bath and bedtime."

Amina mumbled and she scurried around the table. There was only one time he recalled her reacting this way, and that was when his mother asked him to drive Amina to the gravesite of her mother.

Licking his lips, Reth observed her closely. He was unsure if his remark upset her or made her uncomfortable. Instead of calling her out, he turned his attention to his beaming daughter. Getting up out of his chair, he assisted Hasina who then shot off toward the television. The moment she disappeared, he assisted with clearing the table and entered the kitchen.

Amina was washing the dishes. The way she scrubbed them indicated that something was on her mind. Reth leaned lazily against the counter, his arms loosely crossed, and he waited. He knew the moment she realized his presence because her entire body stiffened.

"Did I offend you by what I said?" Reth asked.

"No, of course not."

With her back still to him, Reth was unsure if she was telling him the entire truth. Although, there was no inflection in her voice that would suggest she was lying. "So, what was that then?"

Letting out a sigh, she dropped the dish cloth and turned to him. "I, well, today was just one for the record books."

Removing himself from the counter, he was upon her quickly. His long-muscled arms rested gently around her waist. "What happened?"

"Aaron's attorney called and said that Aaron and Adeya contacted him about representing her. However, the kicker is Aaron wants me to pay for it. To add insult to injury, Aaron now wants to see me after ignoring my requests for months. I know it's so he can use me financially. It's sad that you have only known me a short time and can protect and care about me, but they've known me my entire life and feel nothing for me. I don't understand why they don't love me. It makes it hard to believe anyone else can really love me, or that love has an expiration date. Once my momma died, Aaron's love for me died too."

Feeling her pain and frustration, Reth pulled her into his chest. The way Adeya and Aaron treated Amina made her question his feelings for her. Their carelessness infuriated him. "I'm sorry that happened today. I want you to understand that real love, agape love, which is selfless love, has no expiration date. Pragma love is enduring love; it also has no expiration date. Adeya and Aaron are noxious, miserable people. They can't offer love because they don't know love. I do. You know that I don't lie."

Reth could feel her nodding in his chest, but he still held her. Her grip on him was just as fierce, and for a moment, he wondered how, in her youth, she dealt with so much loss with no support. Sighing inwardly, he continued speaking, "I know running into Delilah St. John only added fuel to the fire. Whatever you're feeling, fury, hurt, or just confusion, I'm here. My family is here, and we're not going anywhere, Amina. You can trust me to support, protect, and care for you." His tongue itched to say love, but she would not receive that the way he was offering it. Not yet. There was still insecurity there because of her father and aunt.

Amina's arms wrapped tighter around his waist, and the weight of what she carried seemed to transfer to him. It was a load he could handle.

"Let it out, Amina."

"I don't want to see Aaron," Amina whispered.

"You don't have to see him," Reth assured, but Aaron Williams was going to see Reth Goode.

"I'm sorry for ruining your shirt." She tried to move away from him, but Reth pulled her tighter, his lips soothingly pecking the side of her temple. There was a scar there from Adeya's brazen attack.

Reth smirked at her. "It's not ruined, and it's just a shirt. Your feelings are more important than fabric. Let me finish up these dishes and you clean up. You bathe Hasina and we'll double team getting her to bed. I have something to share with you."

Amina nodded, though the worried expression on her face was still present. Silently, she turned and exited the kitchen.

Reth watched her leave and then shook his head, annoyed. Today had been one of those days. Delilah was going to hear from him. This foolish quest she was on would end soon. That was not what caused the tension in his back. It was the phone call that troubled him the most. Soon enough, he would settle that too. Packing the thoughts away for now, Reth shifted his attention to finishing the dishes.

∞∞∞∞

Later that night, Reth and Amina read Hasina her bedtime story and then tucked her in. She was knocked out before they made it to the bedroom door. Amina had given her a full day.

"Follow me, Amina, I want to share something with you."

Reth escorted her to the den. They both sat down. Amina's amber eyes glanced at him somberly. It was apparent to him that she was still upset about the happenings of the day. He hoped what he was about to reveal would lighten her load.

"I had lunch with my parents today. My mother gave me a letter from Amal." At that, Reth observed her features ease. Gone was the tightness around her mouth and the dulling of her eyes. It was apparent to him that Amina genuinely loved Amal.

"Are you going to share what she wrote?" There was hopefulness in her tone.

Reth nodded and pulled out the letter. He unfolded it and started to read it to her. He had read it earlier and already memorized it from beginning to end.

Dear Re,

It's time to let go of the past, of me. If you're reading this, then you either have or are close to doing it. Thank God because you have a stubborn streak. LOL!

All I want for you is to know true love and to be happy. Let yourself love and let yourself love her and be loved by her; I mean Amina. The moment I heard her sing in church when we were praying, I knew. I knew Amina was meant for you and that you were meant for her.

I'm so thankful God allowed Amina to be my friend, my Ruth, and for her to love my greatest creation. Hasina adores Amina as much as we do. Our Amina is something special. The love she has in her, the way she cares, the loyalty she possesses— she's a walking blessing. I love her. I love the joy and happiness that she will bring to you and Hasina. I love that you both will bring the same to Amina. She deserves the best love. She deserves the Goode Love Vow and every good thing.

Don't let what others think stop you two. I am watching from heaven, smiling with so much elation to see the two people I love find love with one another. Tell Amina she is worthy and beautiful. Remind her daily because those who should have didn't. Remind her that she deserves to be loved and respected. Teach her the way you taught me. Re, be open to her, allow her to love and protect you too. Go out on dates, write love letters, act like teenagers in love; you deserve that.

Breathe. For years, you have taken care of me, hidden my secret, and protected me. Now, it's your time. Be happy and be in Him. God told me as I prayed that you and Amina were meant for one another. So be.

Love you, Reth & Amina...

Reth folded the letter and then looked Amina. Tears were streaming down her eyes. However, they were not tears of pain, just awe and love.

Overwhelmed by the letter, Amina stayed silent, almost as if she were absorbing the words that Amal had written. Finally, her voice made its debut. "Amazing. Amal is just an incredible, prodigious soul. I thank God for ever second that He permitted me to be in her presence. Even when she was suffering, she was thinking of us. That's an amazing and selfless woman."

Reth smiled. Amal was indeed a prodigious soul and a selfless woman. "She was, and she said the same thing about you. Come here, Amina."

Amina's eyes widened at his request, but she edged unhurried off the sofa and paced cautiously to him. Amina paused just inches before him. Reth reached out and pulled her closer, causing her to sit on his lap.

Reth turned slightly and gently placed a hand on either side of her smooth face. He leaned over and kissed the trail of tears. He pulled back and rested his forehead on hers. "Your heart is safe with me. You're safe with me. Your family failed you in the past, and so did others. You've become accustomed to people hurting you, using you, and because of their lies, you've accepted that behavior as how you deserve to be treated. That's over now, Amina. I can't undo years of verbal and physical abuse, but you have my word that I'll never violate your trust, break, or isolate your heart, or make you feel less than. I want you. I need you. I want us."

Her body became weightless under his hold. "Me too. I just get nervous sometimes. I get lost in my thoughts, transfixed by the what-ifs. If my own father can throw me away, why would you want me?"

Reth suppressed the gripe he wanted to release. The damage her father inflicted was deeply embedded, but it was curable. "The day you entered my life is the day I started to live. Before you, I was just on autopilot. Life just became a cycle of monotony. Then, there was you. It scared me for a moment. The feelings were unknown to me, buried so deeply inside I thought I was incapable of those emotions. My feelings aren't conditional, and they won't expire. This, you, and I, was ordained by God, and no person or people will alter the course that God has set. I can't undo the pain you suffered, but, baby, I can help you heal. Will you trust me to mend the wounds?"

Reth watched as she closed her eyes to calm herself. He examined her face as she processed his words, weighed the pros and cons. Then her amber orbs opened, shimmering like the Northern Lights. It was specular to witness.

"I trust you, Reth. I trust you with my heart. I trust you to help me heal the parts of me that I've hidden. Will you trust me too? Trust me to care for you without seeking anything in return? Will you trust me to love and protect Hasina? Will you trust that I'm as dedicated to you, to us, as you are?"

Releasing a light chuckle, Reth wanted to kiss her breathless, but that could wait. "Absolutely, *mpendwa*."

A timid smile spread across her face. "I really love the sound of your voice. It's the most hypnotic, soothing sensation to me; it's got the relaxing hum of woodwind instruments with the classical allure of a piano and the cadence of bass drums. You're steady, Reth, and I've never had steady."

Reth knew that she was blushing as she shared that with him. That had to be the best compliment he'd ever received. She had him thinking he was on the level of Barry White and Luther Vandross.

Resting his lips on her cheek, Reth mouthed, "Let me sooth you..."

Chapter 25

The combination of floral scents etched memories of Amal in Reth's mind. The memory of how she started the flower garden that was now flourishing caused him to smile inwardly. Reth and Hasina were going to plant the dancing flowers soon. The enthusiasm she felt about their father/daughter project had rubbed off on him. He ordered a memory stone with Amal's name on it to be placed in a section of the flowers.

"Are you buying the entire flower shop?" Djimon queried, snapping Reth out of his reverie.

Turning slightly to his left, he glanced at his brother who was just seconds ago flirting with the florist. There was no doubt they would get a discount, and Djimon, a new number.

Reth scoffed. "Don't be ridiculous. These are all I need. Calla lilies and anemones are Amina's favorite. Orchids are what Hasina prefers. This is a big night for them. I'm just supporting my ladies."

Djimon quirked an eyebrow, and Reth knew more questions would follow; fortunately, JD sauntered over to them.

"Are pink roses appropriate for my niece?" JD asked, perplexed, looking at Djimon for guidance.

With Djimon being ever the ladies' man, Reth understood why JD went to him for assistance on the matter.

"Yes, pink roses mean elegance, and in the Bible, pink roses signify gratitude and peace. I like that you have a variation of pinks. Hasina will adore them. Get her that bear over there too," Djimon added, following his brother.

Reth let out a sigh of relief. Tonight, at dinner, he was going to tell his brothers his feelings for Amina. Kondo and JD would never question him about anything. They just were not that way, but Djimon had no filter.

Today was about celebrating Amina's achievement. She wrote an entire symphony, and he could not wait to hear it. Hasina was so excited that she was nearly bouncing off the walls at breakfast. She and Amina were at the beauty shop getting beautified for the day.

"Reth, are you ready?"

Reth nodded at Kondo and walked over to checkout. The group purchased well over two hundred dollars' worth of flower arrangements. As they exited the flower shop, teasing each other, their conversation was cut short by the arrival of Delilah.

"Reth, fancy running into you here."

"Not if you're a stalker," Djimon coughed out.

The annoyed groan that left Kondo's mouth was exactly how Reth felt. Delilah had to be dealt with in tiny increments. Too much of her was detrimental to one's mental health.

"If you'd excuse us, Delilah, we have a tight schedule to maintain."

"What's the occasion?" Her hawk-like eyes stared at the flower arrangements each brother held. Obviously, she could deduce that it had something to do with Hasina. However, Reth was not telling her anything.

"We're supporting family at an event," Reth replied and immediately started walking toward Kondo's SUV.

A smirk lightened her face. "Oh, well if you need me to keep

Hasina for you, I can."

"That won't be necessary."

Tenacious or just ignorantly unaware, Delilah kept pace with an exasperated Reth, still attempting to engage him in conversation. Reth had to give it to her; she was one stubborn woman, but he was not the one to push. He had little patience when it came to her.

"Did Hasina tell you that your nanny locked her in a hot car? I had to bang on the window to make sure Hasina was okay."

The allegation halted not only Reth's steps but also Djimon's, who was in step behind him.

Thinking she had achieved her mission; Delilah offered a smug smirk and crossed her arms.

Like always, she had misread the situation. Where she thought she had been victorious, she had just defeated herself. Reth was not going to bring up what she did; however, since she wanted to go there, he was going to go all the way in.

"When I speak, you seem to take it as a joke and defy me. I'll never understand why. I have a little time today. So, I'll engage you. Hasina shared with me that you verbally attacked Amina. She also shared that your outburst frightened her. I'm unsure of what issue or issues you have against Amina, but it ends this day. Let me be clear; I'm not interested in pursuing Emmarie; she's not my type. Additionally, I've grown tired of your incessant intrusion into my life and my family. Amina is my family. You have no right to attack or threaten her. Amina's place in my and Hasina's lives is more secured and fortified than the Vatican Secret Archives. Do not come for her again and do attempt to lie on her name. It would beseem you to stay in your place and go back home. There's nothing for you here."

For what seemed like forever, Delilah stood dejected and dumbfounded. Her mouth gaped like a fish out of water before the waterworks started. Reth remained unaffected.

"Reth, I...I thought I was considered family too. What have I done for you to be so cruel to me? I buried my daughter, your wife. Now, you act as if she did not exist and as if I'm some vagabond. You flaunt that little charcoal gutter floozy around town, letting her drive Amal's Jeep and assume Amal's life. I don't like it. That kind of behavior is disrespectful to Amal's memory. How do you go from my daughter to that burnt urchin? She's not better than Emmarie! It's not good for Hasina to have that low-class stranger in her life."

Reth temporarily suffered from aphasia. Time stood still as Reth took in the real Delilah. She was cruel, jealous, bitter, and ignorant. These were the moments he wished Mahari was present so she could slap some sense into Delilah. It took him a moment to gather his thoughts. He shook off the offensive comments and was ready to speak, but Djimon beat him to it.

"I know this nymphomaniac; gold-digging leech didn't just call our chocolate goddess out of her name. Not this one, who abandoned her daughter and husband to upgrade to another man. Her," he pointed his finger aggressively, "who ignored Amal until she married you, didn't even show up for her ex-husband's funeral. I know better. What won't happen is any Amina slander. I'm not Reth, Delilah, I don't care about your feelings or your age. You disrespect my family and I'll gladly do the same. I've maintained my silence out of respect for Amal, but those days are over. Disrespect her again and see what I do," Djimon snapped.

Reth placed a calming hand on his brother. Djimon was a flirt and a jokester, but when he cared about someone, he could be as vicious as a black mamba. Delilah did not need that kind of problem with Djimon. That he even put her business out like that was enough to let Reth know Djimon was on edge.

With the calmest temperament and most soothing voice, Reth spoke to his brother in Swahili before handing off his floral arrangement to him. Reth watched as his brother got into the SUV before turning his attention back to Delilah. The calmness he showed his brother was gone. He gave Delilah an odious glare. It was at that moment she must have realized her error.

"Because of my love and respect for Amal, I've allowed you far more leeway than you're entitled. That ends right now." Reth looked down at his watch; the time stamp was 1:56 pm. "According to my timepiece, it's 1:56 pm and your time is up. Let me give you a history lesson that you seemed to have forgotten. You used your daughter and paraded her in front of wealthy men for your profit. You placed her in perilous situations due to your own greed. My brother was correct in his assessment of you.

That negligence led Amal to many sleepless, tearful nights. You made her believe her only worth was in her beauty and that her reason for existing was to be a man's trophy. I don't know what compelled you to instill that belief, maybe that was how you were raised. That doesn't matter; what matters is that you failed Amal. You made yourself unavailable to her during some of her lowest and darkest moments. There were times she needed her mother, but you were gone. Instead of dealing with that, you lash out without provocation at Amina because she had the relationship with Amal you chose not to have."

Reth paused before taking a step closer to Delilah and continued, "Amina and Amal loved one other; they developed a strong, unbreakable bond before Amal died. Amal called Amina her Ruth. They were that close. You had every opportunity to be an active mother, and you chose men and money every time. I'll never permit you to do that to Hasina. Let me clarify something. Amina is neither burnt nor charcoal; she's a black diamond. Black diamonds are known for their strength, perfection, and creativity. That's who *my* Amina is.

When God created her, he used the most perfect of colors to create her skin tone. Music is how she expresses her creativity and connects to Hasina and Amal. Her strength is in how she loves. Every week, Amina takes Hasina to her mother's gravesite and they talk. I bet you didn't know that because you can't see beyond your own misery. You're too full of yourself. The acerbity you spew will no longer be tolerated. I'm done with you, Delilah. I can't make you leave North Carolina, but you're no longer welcome in my home. There will be a trespass order against you, and if you continue to threaten and stalk Amina, then we will file a restraining order against you. I warned you, Delilah, but you seem to think you can manipulate me. I think you've forgotten who I am. Don't worry; after today, you won't ever forget."

Delilah shook her head, clearly unprepared for what he told her. Without thought, she reached out to pull Reth back, and he gracefully avoided her touch. "Reth." It was a combination of a plea and a command.

"No. I have given far too much of my time as is. There's no need to continue this conversation. I stand by what I said. There is no negotiation. Goodbye, Delilah."

Reth continued his stroll uninterrupted, ignoring Delilah's existence and desperate tears. Once he got into his brother's SUV, he nodded for him to drive off.

After sharing with his brothers, the encounter with Delilah, he quickly contacted Emre and requested he strongly encourage Delilah to return home. There was nothing for her in North Carolina. All Reth could think about was how Delilah ruined Amal; it was her mother's teachings that led Amal into the hands of someone like AB. To think she was coming for Amina after all she suffered with Adeya. That behavior would never be abided again.

One down, Reth mentally thought. Next on his list was Aaron.

∞ ∞ ∞

Anxiety cloaked as concern exuded from Amina. As she fidgeted with her fingers, her mind ran rampant with what-ifs and all that could go wrong. *Had the children practiced enough? Would they get nervous in front of a large audience? Would she?*

"Stop overthinking," an amorous, mesmerizing voice instructed. The vibration of his voice caressed the exposed parts of her skin. The anxiety that threatened to overtake her yielded at Reth's command. It should be illegal for his voice to have that kind of physiological affect over her.

Swallowing deeply to halt the electricity that shot through her body at hearing his voice, Amina turned to him. His voice matched his suit. Reth was a dapper dresser. He wore a tailored light gray suit, with a mint green button shirt and suspenders. In his hands where a bouquet of calla lilies and anemones. Her favorites, and she was unsure how he knew that.

With gleaming eyes, Amina took in Reth, and watched with bated breath as he swaggered over to her. His enchanting gaze held her captive. So many thoughts and feelings flowed through her. Then he stopped, just inches separating them.

"Breathe, *mpendwa*, you'll do fine. This is your night, so enjoy every second of it. These are for you." Reth handed her the flowers and she sniffed them.

Oxygen exploded in Amina's chest; it was as if his voice resuscitated her. "Thank you. No one has ever gifted me flowers before. How'd you know?"

"I didn't realize that no one had ever given you flowers before. However, I'm observant. Ever since Amal transitioned, you do your quiet time in the flower garden. I noticed you give a lot of attention to the anemones, and I overheard you tell Amal you like calla lilies."

Amina dropped her head in awe that Reth took the time to even note what she liked. This was still new to her. It was difficult to accept that someone made her a priority, that someone was interested in her likes and dislikes. This man, whom she admired and adored, thought enough of her to bring her tranquility. Love, or even to truly have someone care, seemed like an impossibility. It was why she accepted mediocrity from BC. To expect greatness would only lead to disappointment. With Reth, greatness was safe to expect. Every day, Reth raised the bar. With him, worry did not consume her.

The tender touch of his hand brought Amina back to the present. He gently lifted her head until their eyes met. "There's no need to ever be timid around me."

Amina offered a meek smile. "I think you're magic." India.Arie's song floated in her head.

Reth chuckled. His laughter was so mesmerizing. Amina felt her body shiver at his attention. Reth removed his hand and lifted an index finger to tap her nose. He leaned forward and whispered in her ear, "I'm not magic, but I'm your man. It seems you bring out a different side of me."

Then, his succulent lips, which were as delicate as the petals of a ranunculus flower, rested on the side of her neck. Amina's eyes closed involuntary as her skin absorbed the warmth and promise of his tantalizing kiss. Her pulse increased and musical notes danced through her mind.

Amina was on the brink of becoming deliquescent. Call her the Chocolate River from Willy Wonka's Chocolate Factory because Reth Goode's kisses on any parts of her flesh caused every crevice in her body to liquefy. He excelled in making her lose her train of thought. He was sturdy, steady, and rooted so deeply that no matter what negative thoughts she harbored, he defeated them with ease.

When he reached back, Amina caught the scent of his

cologne. Her hand reached out and rested on the side of his velvet cheek, "*Wewe ni muziki wangu.*"

Reth's eyes widened in surprise then he winked. "I'll be your music. Thank you. I better go so you can get ready. If I stay here a second longer, I may be inclined to kiss you breathless."

A flirtatious smile painted her face, as she wanted him to do just that, but she had a performance to prepare for. Nodding her understanding, she watched with yearning eyes as he disappeared.

It took her five minutes to come back to herself and then she got right to work. Exiting backstage, she saw that the children were prepared. Amina decided to use all the children. They were her little orchestra. Benito was going to show off his conductor skills. This was her moment, and she hoped Reth liked it. The Symphony of Goode Love was inspired by him.

Reth strolled down the aisle to sit with his family. As he walked by, someone caught his eye. Shaking his head, certain that he was seeing things, Reth's eyes focused on the figure that was sitting with Mary. He knew that Mary would be present as Benito was participating in the event. Seeing BC with her had Reth perplexed, but that was not the kicker. The kicker was the other man who was present. One he had a history with. The man he ran out of North Carolina. Adrian Bishop.

Rage surged through Reth's body as he surveyed him. When Matt said he was back, Reth had no idea he would see him at this event. Questions charged through his mind. Unable to connect the dots of how AB could be associated with Mary and her grandsons, Reth's feet directed him toward Mary and her family.

Before he could be noticed, he was intercepted by JD. Russet eyes clashed, Reth's eyes illustrating how incensed he was, while his brother's eyes held a warning and a plea for mercy. They had a speechless argument that JD won due to him reminding Reth that this was Amina's moment. It was not a time for retaliation.

Acquiescing to his brother's entreaty, Reth schooled his facial features and continued to the front row where his family was already sitting. Once he sat down, he quickly shared with Djimon and Kondo that AB and BC were present and that they were to keep them far away from Amina and Hasina.

Chapter 26

Amina's floor-length black sheath dress wrapped her body like a second skin. Her hair was straightened, and her makeup was light. Inhaling and exhaling deeply, she was ready. The children were in place. It was time for her to make the introduction. In one hand was her violin and bow. The instrument helped to center her.

The clicking of her kitten heels made melodic music. She reached the microphone and motioned for the curtains to lift. The curtain revealed several faces she knew, but the others she could not see, thanks to the bright lighting. This was by design.

Clearing her throat, she opened her mouth to speak. "Good evening; thank you all for joining us tonight. I have the privilege of sharing the stage with my students from the Goode Community Center. They'll be playing a symphony that I composed.

A symphony is a musical composition that has a full orchestra usually consisting of four movements. There will be an allegro, followed by a slow movement that will lead into a scherzo with trio, and end with a rondo. I'm dedicating this to my Naomi. She lost her battle with cancer, but she'll continue to live in every composition that I compose. The name of this is The Symphony of Goode Love. It's inspired by the man who captured my young heart before I ever understood what love was. Probably before he ever knew I existed. A man who is currently teaching me the different kinds of love. That is what this symphony is about. I hope you enjoy it."

Letting out a sigh, Amina turned around and meandered to her seat. Her heartbeat thumped like a stampede of wildebeests. Amina had made a public proclamation about her feelings for Reth. This was her being vulnerable and trusting him. This was her letting him know he could trust her too.

She winked at Benito to signal it was time to start. Amina played her heart out. She was so proud of Hasina on the piano. Amina closed her eyes and allowed herself to become one with the music. The notes fused into her body; she could feel it overtake her muscles, and she felt freer than she'd ever known. As each movement transitioned so did her body. It was as if she had become the symphony.

Less than forty minutes later, it was over. The most halcyon feeling overcame her. At that moment, something unlocked. The verse that Hasina had shared, Psalm 126:5, 'Those who plan in tears will harvest with shouts of joy', was embedded in her heart.

Rising, she told the children to take a bow as they were greeted with a standing ovation. Amina could not stop the grin on her face. She blew kisses heavenward to her mother, Amal, and two brothers.

∞∞∞

Reth felt his brothers stare as Amina spoke. He had no idea what the symphony was titled or that he inspired it, but it made him feel like royalty. Tingles glided all through his flesh. He had an entire symphony named in his honor.

If anyone knew the constant battles that Amina had to fight, if they knew her story of survival, how guarded she had to be, then they would understand the significance of her sharing what she just did. For Reth, it was her showing him that she trusted him, that she loved him. He felt that in his soul.

When she started to play, his eyes were riveted by the sight of her becoming the music. It was one of the most intimate actions he had ever witness. His heart nearly beat out of his chest. The need to touch her was so pervasive that he had to clench his fist to cement himself in his seat.

Music never affected him the way it did when she played music. Amina gave life to every instrument she played and every song she sang. That was her gift. When the orchestra stopped playing, Reth stood up, applauding, and blowing a kiss at his daughter. The children had done a fine job, but all Reth wanted to do was get ahold of Amina and kiss her senseless.

She had him acting like a teenager. Though he loved and cared for Amal, it was nothing like this. This feeling brewing inside of him must be what his father felt for his mother.

"Brother, you have some explaining to do," Djimon spoke in a sotto voce voice.

Reth knew that was coming. His brothers, like himself, had taken to protecting and caring for Amina. It was easy to do; she was an uncomplicated woman with a pure heart.

Reth gazed at his brother and replied, "Is that so?"

"Indeed, brother. For now, we will concentrate on the other matter at hand."

So caught up in the music, Reth had forgotten about the alphabet boys, AB, and BC, which was regrettable. He was sure one, if not both, would attempt something that would offend Amina and thereby offend him. Though he was a man of God that used his hands to pray, those same hands would slay any predator that attempted to come for his family.

Reth's russet eyes followed as Amina made her way to the microphone again. She looked gorgeous in her form-fitting gown and sleek, flowing mane.

"Thank you all for your support. I wanted to give a special thank you to the parents who were kind enough to share their children with me. Additionally, I want to thank the Goode family. They have been better to me than my own family and have loved and accepted me without condition."

Amina placed a hand over her heart, her voice brittle as she fought not to cry. Then, she turned toward the children. "You all did an excellent job, and I am so proud of each of you. Thank you for your help."

Turning back to the crowd she grinned, before speaking. "Please follow the signs to the refreshments." Just as she was turning to leave the stage, Reth saw movement. It was BC.

∞ ∞ ∞

Amina gathered the children and directed them to their awaiting parents so they could attend the refreshment part of the evening. They were as excited as she was.

As she turned to reach for Hasina, she heard her name. Turning to see who called out to her and when she identified the voice, she nearly mean-mugged BC. The need to roll her eyes and suck her teeth was strong, but she maintained her professionalism. This was not the place to show out. There was no need to anyway. He was her past. They had no future, and he had no power.

"Benito left with his friends; they headed to the other room for refreshments."

BC bit his upper lip before nodding. "I saw him. I just wanted to see you. I miss you."

"It gets easier with time."

He looked offended by her flippant reply. "When did you become so cold, huh? I mean, you're out here dedicating symphonies to people when you wrote me a song like I was the love of your life. What you mean about this man teaching you different kinds of love and about loving him before you knew love. What does that mean?"

With each word that he spoke, his voice elevated. Amina grew tired quickly of his accusations and wanted to end the conversation.

"It means that she's moved on." Reth's hypnotic voice had an edge to it and was hardened with a warning.

BC whipped around so fast that Amina was shocked that he did not lose his balance.

"Who are you?"

"The person she was referring to that is teaching Amina the different kinds of love. I'm the man in her life."

Amina knew right then and there that BC was going to show his butt. BC smirked before taking his thumb and rubbing his nose. He nodded his head as if he were responding to internal stimuli. He pulled up his baggy jeans, a sign he was preparing to battle.

"Don't BC. He's a judge. If you proceed to do what I think, then you'll be arrested. It's not worth it because it won't persuade me to come back to you. We're done. You did your dirt. I chose to move on with my life. You should do the same."

He balled up his face and looked at Amina in disgust. "I'm not good enough now? You're really going to choose him over me? I knew you had daddy issues. I bet you gave yourself to him too. That's why you got a new whip and renovating your house. I see how it is. Adeya was right about you," he seethed.

Appalled and annoyed by his incorrect assumption, Amina watched as Reth edged closer to him. Her body language pleaded with Reth to just let it be. Reth nor his brothers tolerated anyone being disrespectful to her. It was appreciated, but the best outcome was to ignore BC and move on.

"What's going on?"

They all glanced back and saw Dre stomping toward them. Amina shook her head, worried about what was about to transpire. She reached her hand out to Hasina and placed the child behind her.

When Dre's eyes landed on Reth, his entire demeanor changed.

"AB, if this young man is something to you, then I suggest you take him and leave." Tension filled the room so thickly it was nearly impossible to breathe. Reth transformed into warrior mode.

Amina felt as if she was supposed to recognize the name. For some reasons she could not place the name AB. It was apparent, however, that he and Reth had a history.

"I see you still think you run everything. Always coming for another man's woman. Isn't she a little young for you? She's beatific with a body created to be explored. That silken skin is rare. So, I can see why you got into an entanglement with her. She's not the same kind of elegant grace as Amal is. Where is—"

AB did not complete his sentence before Reth was upon him. "Don't you ever speak her name. You don't have the right. Don't you dare say another word about Amina."

The auditorium door yanked open again, and Reth's brothers followed by Dr. Goode hurried toward the commotion. All eyes were on them.

"Daddy!" Hasina shrieked, causing all movement to cease. It was then that Amina realized that BC had pulled out a gun.

Alarmed by his carelessness, Amina exploded. "Benigno Cordero Soto-Calderón, put that gun down now! What's wrong with you?" There was no timidity in her voice. She was livid.

He side-eyed her. "Leave right now with me and I will."

This was an unnecessary escalation. Yet, Amina would do

whatever she had to do to diffuse the situation.

"Young man, there's no need for that; put the gun down and let's have a conversation," Dr. Goode requested.

"Yo, mind ya own business. Come here, Mina," BC demanded.

"Beni boy, it's all good. Me and Reth got an old beef, but there's no need to pull out your gun. Now isn't the time for that," AB snapped bluntly.

"You said—"

"I didn't say shoot somebody, especially over some girl. He's a federal judge, and you aren't built to do federal time. Put that down before you hurt somebody."

BC shook his head. He seemed conflicted, but he had yet to lower the firearm. "Amina is mine; he can't have her."

AB rolled his eyes and sucked his teeth in disgust. Amina held Hasina tighter and started to back away slowly. "Listen, BC, I'll do whatever you want, but just let Hasina and Reth walk out of here. Think about it; if you hurt him, you'll be arrested, and then you won't be around to see your child born or grow up. You're reacting on emotions."

"Go ahead, I'm not going hurt that little girl. I just want you."

"You're not going to harm her father either," Amina added, and BC nodded.

"Don't move, *mpendwa*."

"Amina, do what I said. Dre, get the little girl and hand her over to him so me and my girl can leave."

"My daughter and my lady are staying where they are," Reth replied too calmly.

BC was so focused on Amina that he hadn't noticed the movement around him. In a split second, Kondo was on him and disarmed him as if it were nothing. BC was on the floor before he realized what happened. Hasina took off and ran into her father's arms. Overcome with emotions, Amina slumped into the floor. Her night was ruined.

∞∞∞

Pure, unadulterated rage pumped overtime through Reth's veins. While his brother handled BC, Reth wanted to handle AB. He knew he was not supposed to ever return to North Carolina. The entire state was closed to him. Now, this fool had the audacity to attend an event he was not invited to and start some drama. This idiot had the gall to dishonor Amal's memory by uttering her name. Reth wanted to annihilate his existence. It should be him buried six feet deep, not Amal.

Holding his daughter close to his body, he did not take his eyes off AB. Hatred volleyed between them. Reth's mind was calculating ways he could permanently injure AB and get away with it.

"What?" AB asked, cockily spreading out his arms, daring Reth to make a move.

Without breaking the stare, Reth called out to his mother. "Ma, please come get Hasina and Amina."

He felt his daughter be removed from him, though her little hand reached for his. He could not comfort her now, not when this pervert present.

When Reth could no longer hear his daughter's pleas, he finally answered AB. "You need to leave."

Sniffing, AB flick the side of his nose with his thumb before replying, "I'm here visiting my aunt and cousins. You can't do nothing no more. That was years ago, and you aren't going to use that against me."

Reth smirked at his foolish attempt at bravery. "There is no statute of limitations in North Carolina for sex crimes, so, yes, it still stands."

"Amal's not going to say nothing about it."

Before Reth could stop himself, he punched AB in the mouth with a two-piece. "I told you not to speak her name. I don't like to repeat myself. The authorities will be arriving soon; it's up to you if they'll be taking one or two people to jail tonight."

Reth knew from experience how much of a recreant AB was. The idea of jail, even for a night, was too much for him. He was big and bad when it came to finessing and hurting women. He was no match when a man stepped to him, and it seemed that he shared that trait with his younger cousin. After tonight, neither man would come near Amina again.

The mistake he made with Amal, leaving her at the mercy of this filth, would not be repeated.

"Oh, my goodness, what happened?" Ms. Mary's voice echoed.

Not caring to recount the story, Reth let his father speak to Mary while he went to see about his daughter and his lady. They were all that mattered now.

∞ ∞ ∞

Eyes closed and back erect, Amina sat cross-legged on Hasina's bed while Reth soothed her. Replaying the events of the night, Amina was embarrassed, upset, and confused. The chaos and threats horrified her. When BC pulled out the weapon, Amina didn't know what to do.

The night ended badly with BC getting arrested; AB was examined by the paramedics, and Ms. Mary seemed as if the life had been drained out of her. Poor Benito was clueless and crying. The rest of the people in attendance had no idea what they had missed. Amina was crushed. It was absolute chaos. So many unanswered questions lingered in her mind.

From what little Amina could comprehend, Reth's rage emerged because AB had attacked Amal. He was the person who made her believe that her beauty was a curse. For that, Amina disliked him too. His actions stole a life. Then he mocked Reth about his deceased wife. Whether AB was aware of Amal's death she did not know, but Amina did know it cut Reth deeply. It impacted her to see Reth pained in that way.

Clearly, Reth still held himself responsible for the assault on Amal. Amina did not feel like she had the skills to assist him in letting go. Maybe he wasn't ready. Maybe they were moving too fast. New relationships were difficult on their own, but factor in the past Reth had with AB, maybe, he was not ready for her.

"She's finally asleep," Reth whispered, lulling Amina out of her trance.

Glancing over at Hasina, Amina scooted up and kissed her cheek then she eased off the bed and exited the room. Reth was right behind her. His hand connected with her arm, slowing down her retreat.

Unsure of why she was running from him, Amina stopped, but her thoughts kept moving. She feared what might happen due to BC's actions tonight. That would be enough for anyone to throw their hands up and surrender. His daughter's life and his own had been in danger because of her past.

"Talk to me, Amina; your silence concerns me."

Running her free hand across her neck, Amina's mind oscillated between answering him and just leaving the situation as is. There was so much that occurred in such a short amount of time. Honestly, she was still dealing. "I'm just...it freaked me out to see BC pull out a gun all because he wanted us back together. Then, I keep thinking what could've happened to you or Hasina. I wonder what type of trauma witnessing that could cause. Without meaning to, I brought an adversary in your life and possibly put AB on the trail of Hasina. The results could be devastating."

His face softened and his palm rested on the side of her cheek. "It's alright."

Amina shook her head to refute the claim. "I'll understand if you don't want to…"

Refraining from cursing, Reth instead moved his hand to gently massaged Amina's back before bringing his hand to the nape of her neck. "Don't do that, Amina. Don't even complete that sentence. Just because something happens unexpectedly, good, or bad, doesn't mean it impacts what we're establishing. You told me you trust me. So, baby, trust me. What happened tonight was unfortunate, and once we've had a moment to deal then we can talk about it. I'm not going anywhere, Amina."

Instead of replying she simply fell into his arms and embraced him. "Thank you." She felt Reth's lips as they kissed the top of her head.

"Get some rest; you're staying here tonight. I'm going speak with my brothers."

"All right, good night, *mpenzi*."

His chest vibrated with a low growl. "Who has been teaching you Swahili endearments?" he cooed. She had just called him lover.

"Hasina and JD."

"I like it, though, I'm concerned about my daughter being aware of such. Good night, *mpendwa*."

She beamed at him and then went to her bedroom.

Chapter 27

The scent of apprehension and infuriation plastered the path Reth took to enter his study. Emotions ran high after what BC did. Anger and accusations littered the night. His brothers had been awaiting his arrival for more than two hours. It took time to reassure and relax a terrified Hasina. Not to mention how Amina shutdown once escorted out of the building. His need to care for them was stronger than anything.

Due to the undignified actions of the alphabet boys, the family was unable to sit down for an evening meal to celebrate the success of Amina's concert. More than anything, that irritated him the most because she was elated to share her work. Now, her performance was tainted by the actions of two men who had no business being in the same atmosphere as Amina.

Suspiring, Reth entered his study, prepared for the questions, confusions, and possibly, judgment. As soon as his foot touched the floor and he shut the door, Reth felt six pairs of russet eyes upon him. Fortifying his walls, he braced himself for whatever they asked or accused. Once he turned to face them, all he saw were mirrored reflections of what he felt. Relief rushed through him. They were on the same page.

"Brothers." They all nodded at him in greeting.

"I know I asked this before, but are you sure you're all right? You punched a new face on AB, and you refused to allow me to examine your left hand." Kondo's tone was soft and understanding, exonerating Reth of any guilt.

At the mention of his left hand, his predominant one, Reth noticed the swelling and bruising. Prior to his brother speaking about it, he had forgotten about his injuries. "I'll let you take a look later," Reth answered before strolling over to his desk to retrieve a cigar.

"They're gone," JD spoke up as his sock-covered feet were burning a hole into the African handmade area rug.

Reth paused, thinking he had misheard his brother. "I'm sorry, what?"

Letting out a breath, JD replied flatly, "Hasina saw a commercial about lung cancer and linked you smoking cigars to getting lung cancer. She then disposed of, well, hid your cigars. Her explanation was she had to save your life. I meant to tell you that earlier, but with all the excitement, it slipped my mind."

Reth did an about-face, his heart racing at the thought that Hasina was worried about him dying as well. It never occurred to him the affect that his occasional smoking would have on his daughter. It disheartened him that Hasina thought for one moment he would die of cancer too.

"I see."

"She--"

"I'll just say what we're all thinking. How does Amina's ex-boyfriend link to Amal's attacker, and why were they present at her senior concert? What caused said ex-boyfriend to pull out a firearm to end your life? Does it have anything to do with the secret relationship you're having with Amina? I think that about sums it up," Djimon interrupted.

Those were the questions burning his brother's tongue. A brother who should be asleep as he had an early fight to catch back to the UK.

Shaking his head, Reth padded to the empty chair and eased down; he was exhausted. It didn't hit him until now. Steepling his hands, he winced at the discomfort of his left hand. "Firstly, D, I was not secretly courting Amina."

Djimon scooted to the edge of the couch, ready to refute him, but Reth waved a hand to silence him. He knew how his brother was once he got on his soapbox. Reth was still the eldest brother, and his brothers respected that.

"As I said, I was not secretly courting Amina. It's none of your concern who I choose to court. Yet, because I know that Amina has a special place in the heart of our family, tonight I was going to share with you all that we have decided to enter into a courtship. No, it has nothing to do with me grieving and searching for a replacement for Amal. It isn't lust or trivial yearning. What I feel for Amina is beyond that. I would never disrespect her in that manner. I pray one day she'll marry me and be a mother to Hasina, but we're taking our time. As my brothers, I love you each dearly and respect your thoughts, but Amina is the one for me."

At that admission, Kondo grinned knowingly; JD seemed understanding, and Djimon's face creased with concern. Reth suspected it would be that way.

"Don't you think you're moving too fast? Courting versus dating, and with the nanny at that," Djimon questioned.

Maintaining a calm demeanor, he replied, "I don't. She's no longer the nanny. For nearly half a decade, I was in a nontraditional, consensual marriage to save my friend. In an instant, I would do it again. For the last year after, Amal found out the cancer had returned, I mourned her impending death. During that time, she would drop hints about me preparing for a life without her, seeking my helpmate, my soulmate. Of course, being the loyal man that I am, I wanted to hear nothing of it, and then came Amina. The hollow crevices of my heart started to fill. The dormant places started to come alive with bliss and hope. Amal could see that, and she did her best to nourish that, while living and after death. I care not what others think of how I should or shouldn't move forward. I prayed to God; my Father answered, and Amina has my love, fidelity, and protection for as long as there is breath is my body. I'm not asking for acceptance, only understanding. Brothers, do you understand?"

"I do," JD replied. "I understand that you denied yourself for years to protect a person you love, and now you have the opportunity to finally receive what you have given. Not to say that Amal didn't love you, but it wasn't the love of a wife and husband. I'm happy for you, brother. You're right; what other opinions may be is of no consequence. God's permission trumps man's thoughts every time. You have my support always. Just be gentle and patient with Amina. Also, know that I love you, but if you hurt her, I'll forget at least for the moment it takes for me to beat the proper out of you that you're my brother."

Djimon howled in laughter, breaking the tension, followed by Kondo who was guffawing so hard that he dropped his head in his hands. "It's always the pastors wanting to throw hands. You're supposed to use your hands to pray, not slay your brother. Don't be a Cain; be an Abel," Djimon teased but quickly regained his senses and turned his attention back to Reth. "I agree with JD; don't break Chocolate Goddess' heart. She's lost her entire family to death or the system, and I just want to make sure we do right by her. That's why I asked if you thought you were moving too fast. I apologize if that came off accusatory or judgmental. It wasn't. If you're both happy, then so am I."

Reth nodded in understanding and then turned to Kondo, intent on shifting the conversation. "Kon, I never thanked you for saving my life. I appreciated the swiftness you used to disarm him."

"I wanted to do more because I owed him a beatdown. I had to be chill because Hasina was present. You're welcome. What're our next steps in dealing with the dummy duo? You'll not be alone in this Reth. We have your three sixty."

That was true; they were raised to take care of each other; three sixty meant back, sides, and front. He knew his brothers had him on all sides. So would Mahari, their cousin, if she were home.

Chapter 28

Mauritius

Three weeks had passed since the incident that occurred at Amina's school. Djimon had gone back to the UK to complete his project. Amina had reached many important milestones—graduating with honors and passing her driver's license exam—and now, the family was going to Mauritius in East Africa. Reth did not tell her until after her graduation, and she was beyond ecstatic. Never in her life had she ever traveled abroad, so this was the best graduation gift she could have ever wished for.

"Did I do well?" Reth asked as he escorted her and Hasina through the deplaning. The grin he had on his face was enough for her to know that he was aware that he had done an excellent job.

"This is glorious. I've officially graduated. I have my driver's license. I'm entering my dream doctoral program, debt-free, thanks to all the scholarships I've been awarded. I'm being courted by the most amazing man, and now, I get to vacation in another country with all the people I love. You did better than great!" Amina all but screeched. Never in her life had she felt so relaxed and free.

"My ladies deserve this. We're going to have the best time."

Amina was sure of it. It had taken a full thirty-two hours with two layovers to get here, but Amina did not care. It was magical from the moment they arrived at Charlotte's international airport.

Traveling had been difficult for Hasina, who was knocked out and held protectively in her father's arms, but Amina had been too hyped to sleep, and when she did, it was for short periods of time.

Now, they were here. Reth took the lead, holding Amina's hand, followed by his parents and JD and Kondo. A grin stayed on Amina's face as she took in all the sights as they hurried through the airport.

They quickly retrieved their luggage and headed to the awaiting van Reth had ordered for them. As soon as Amina made it outside, she felt at home. This was a vacation with people that genuinely cared about her. Amina closed her eyes and offered a prayer of thanks to God.

Mauritius was a warm seventy-eight degrees and beautiful. A tropical oasis, with low humidity, which her hair appreciated, and a light breeze, which her body bathed in. Reth was going to have to drag her away. The entire vibe here was different yet historical. Honestly, she had fallen in love with the island after spending most of the flight researching its history.

Mauritius had gained its independence back in 1968. According to her research, there was a history of slavery, and it was colonized by the Netherlands, France, and Great Britain. The languages spoken on the island were French, Creole, and English. Per history, when the soldiers came to tell the people they were free from slavery, they assumed they were going to be enslaved again and jumped off the cliff. That part saddened Amina. Yet, she understood that kind of desperation.

The island bounced back, though. It was incredibly diverse with many different ethnic groups. What she was most interested in was the music. The Mauritius music genre was Sega, which was a fusion of Seggae and Bhojpuri. Its origins came from the music of slaves, their descendants, the Mauritian Creole, as well as Madagascar and mainland Africa. Amina could not wait to hear the music live, which was rich and deep in culture. Amina was also fascinated with the instruments they used: the ravanne, the triangle, and the maravanne. The ravanne was a large tambourine-like instrument, while the maravane was a shaken idiophone. It was her hope to purchase some of the instruments and teach the children how to play.

"Mina!"

Jolting at the sound of the musical timbre, Amina glanced up and saw that Reth was waiting for her. "Sorry, I got lost in the moment." Reth just smirked and assisted her into the van.

The ride did not take long as the conversation among the group never ceased. Amina leaned back and enthusiastically took in all the sights. This time last year, she was falling into a depression because she worried about her father and had to deal with Adeya and her abuse. Then there was the inconsistency of BC. If anyone told her that she would be hired as a personal nanny for Reth's daughter, befriend Amal, and then fall madly and deeply in love with Reth Goode, she would have thought they were delusional. God knew and He was helping her find her peace of mind. Lauryn Hill's "I Gotta Find Peace of Mind" exploded in her mind and unable to control the flow, she opened her mouth and started singing. For her, the song represented leaving BC and walking into the present and future with Reth, a man of God, a man of truth, and a man of love. Now, she was comfortable being in her skin and accepting who God created her to be, thankful to God for allowing her a man like Reth.

Fingertips tickled the nape of her neck, and Amina leaned into the security of Reth's touch and kept singing. His touch only amplified her voice. Then his lips nipped at the shell of her ear, sending flaming tingles throughout her body. She did not lose the tune of the song or miss a note.

"I love your voice, *mpendwa*. You're my peace of mind too."

Yeah, she loved this man.

∞∞∞

On day two of their island stay, Amina and Hasina were running through the water. Reth watched them and found himself feeling lighter in their presence. Being with Amina allowed him the safety to just be. Reth had never been in love, and he never thought it could be a possibility. After marrying Amal, he accepted what was. If she could not be happy and marry the man of dreams, then neither should he. Now, with Amina, everything was possible, and he wanted it all. Craved it.

His russet eyes trailed the lovely, dark umber skin that shone like black jade. Licking his lips, he watched the perfection of Amina. A pearl white bikini adorned her toned physic. She caused a bit of a stir in her bathing suit, and Reth almost requested she wear something else, but she had been controlled most of her life, limited to do as she pleased due to her family that he deemed her captors. So, if she wanted to wear the bikini, he was not going to make an issue of it. Vacation or not, if any man approached her, he was going to show up and show out. Amina brought out an entirely different side of him.

"Daddy, come play with us!" Hasina shouted as Amina lifted her up and spun her around. The joy on her face lit Reth's heart afire. All he wanted was for Hasina to have the best of days for as long as she lived. This vacation was about resetting and moving forward.

"I'm coming, *binti*."

As he was preparing to join them, he heard feminine laughter behind him. Turning around, he saw both of his brothers heading his way with two women. Frowning in curiosity, he watched JD and Kondo with interest. They were supposedly jet skiing, but it seemed they were getting friendly with the locals or possibly tourists. With those two, it was never any telling. They were in vacation mode, which meant the ladies were fair game.

"Daddy?" Hasina called out again. Instead of interrogating his brothers, he turned back to his ladies and ran toward them.

Later that evening, Reth and his family, except for his parents and Hasina, sat down to eat. The day had been full of adventure and fun. Now, it was date night. Reth had not been able to take Amina out as much as he wanted due to their scheduling, but he wanted each day and night they spent to be about them progressing their relationship. This was going in the right direction and he wanted to keep it going. Losing Amal reminded him of how precious life was and how uncertain it could be. Therefore, he was not going to waste one second in his courtship with Amina. He was a man on a mission—to conquer and keep her heart.

Reth noticed that Amina was giving Kondo strange glances. He was unsure what it was all about. From what he could tell, Amina was having a magnificent time. When she was not playing with Hasina or flirting with him, she, his timid *mpendwa,* would engage the locals. Reth had not told Amina yet, but he was taking her to see a Sega performer so she could hear live music.

"Reth, do you know anything about these food dishes? I think I want to try Mauritian Biryani and the Farata."

Impressed by her pronunciation and accent, Reth nodded in agreement. "I think those would be great choices. The Mauritian Biryani is made up of basmati rice, and it's favored with saffron, cumin, mint, cinnamon, and cloves. There's lamb and potatoes and other vegetables. The Farata is a tasty flatbread."

He turned his attention back to the menu to decide what he wanted to try. "You know what," the girl who was hanging off Kondo started, "if we knew you had another brother, we would have brought our friend Makayla. She loves a tall, well-built brotha. Well, if she wasn't punch drunk. Ooo, she gonna be upset she missed this treat." She wiggled her eyebrows and winked her eyes.

Feeling the wind from Amina's menu being placed down, Reth turned to her, thinking she was attempting to get his attention. It seemed that her eyes were intensely focused on the woman who had just spoken.

"Why would you do that?" Amina asked, her head cocked to the side. Her response shocked Reth, and his brothers as well. The entire time the women had been present, Amina had said little to nothing to them. Reth figured it was due to her shyness around new people.

"Huh?" The woman's eyes drooped as if realizing she may have spoken out of turn.

"You said if you knew they had another brother, you would have invited your intoxicated friend. My response is why?"

JD dropped his head, looking for something nonexistent, while Kondo pretended to look ahead, studying some random artwork. Intrigued, Reth gently leaned back and observed in silence.

"Well," the woman giggled, for the life of Reth he could not recall her name, which was bizarre because he was excellent with names, but these two women failed to hold his interest long enough to remember, "Kondo said he had three brothers." It was as if she expected that to be the answer.

Amina let out a dry cackle. "I'm aware of how many brothers he has. However, there is a total of three here, brother number four hasn't arrived yet and may not be able to come. Therefore, it can be deduced that if you brought your friend, she would be the odd person out because he," Amina pointed a Reth, "is unavailable. I just wanted to clarify that for you. I know you've consumed a lot of alcohol and maybe you forgot that tidbit of information," Amina finished with a face so serious that Reth wanted to chuckle but seeing this side of Amina told him to refrain from doing so. His lady was putting these women in check in such a classy way. He liked it more than he would ever admit.

"Uh oh," JD whispered shouted, causing the woman sitting beside him to stare in confusion.

The girl's eyes nearly popped out of her head, while Kondo pulled his lips in to prevent himself from cackling, but he quickly lost that battle.

"I meant no disrespect."

"Mmkay!"

Reth lifted his hand and gently massaged the nape of Amina's neck. That seemed to be a calming spot for her. He leaned over and spoke softly in her ear, "You better let her know I'm all yours."

Amina giggled at his playfulness, a side of him that he had only recently released. Just as he was about to kiss her, the waiter came and took their order.

Kondo's friend excused herself, and the other young lady did as well. Once they were gone, Reth asked his brothers what their names were.

"Tisha is the one Amina politely went off on, and the other one is Kaleeha," Kondo replied.

"Sis, did you have to read Tisha like that?" Kondo asked; tears still watered his eyes from his laughter.

"Nah, Kon, she went Boot Bae, remember when that woman

was trying to walk up on dude and his girl put her leg out. That's what Amina did, except with words. She was like that one is unavailable," JD reenacted.

Amina shrugged her shoulders at their teasing. Reth could see the growing confidence in her. "I just wanted clarification. It was not my intention to read anyone."

Reth grinned. "Mina just letting it be known I'm not available and not to disrespect us in that way. You completely shocked me, but in a good way. I like it!"

Amina dropped her head shyly.

"Nope, don't act shy now. You were ready to boss up a minute ago. Wait until I tell Djimon the Chocolate Goddess has shown out. She out here ready to drop weaves and kick girls in their knees behind her man."

"Y'all stop teasing her like that." Just as the words left his mouth, the women returned.

"Thank y'all for hanging out with us, but our girl called, so we're going to head out. See y'all around." The duo turned quickly and exited.

"Dang, sis out here running off potential."

"I saved you from disaster, and you're welcome."

They all laughed at that and enjoyed the rest of the night.

Chapter 29

Reth and Amina held hands as they strolled down the beach. Every day felt like a real-life fairy tale. Amina fell more in love with Reth. For her, the entire vacation had been magical and uplifting. In all her years of living, she had never witnessed good love, kind love, or enduring love. There were no examples ever set forth for her. All she knew was that this man, who held her hand and tended to her heart, had unlocked something inside side of her. Something that only he could grow. Reth allowed her a safe place to just flourish.

The night was cool and relaxing. They had an exceptional week on the island, one filled with laughter, excitement, cultural learning, and a deeper connection to God and one another. The time spent together let Amina know that Reth was the right one for her. With him, she was comfortable to communicate with words and music. There was no fear when it came to speaking up for herself. Being comfortable in her own skin and knowing that Reth was for her and about her allowed her a level of confidence and contentment she lacked before. Amina loved the woman she was developing into. It was someone she admired and respected.

"What are you thinking?" Reth asked, his fingers playing in her hair like a musician playing the guitar.

Glancing over her shoulder at him, they had long stopped walking. Reth's right hand was wrapped around her waist as he pulled her into him. Her shorter form fit perfectly into his larger frame. "I'm thinking that I feel so secure and cared for by you. After my mother died, I lost that and now with you, I've found it again."

Amina placed her hand on his forearm. It was one of her favorite parts of him. Closing her eyes, she listened to the music of his heartbeat. It was strong and powerful, meditating her spirit.

"I want you to always feel that way." He pecked the side her face. "I've one more surprise for you."

Opening her eyes, she looked at him in awe. "What else? This has been the best vacation slash graduation gift I've ever had."

Reth grinned and pretended to pop his collar. "That's good to know. However, I know you wanted to hear some live music, so I arranged for a private concert. They call her the voice of the Indian ocean."

"Really?"

"Yes, it's starting soon, and I know you don't want to miss anything."

He did not have to tell her twice. They continued walking until they arrived at the private concert, and it was everything she dreamed it would be.

Amina's eyes glistened in fasciation as she listened to the music and watched the dancers. They were wearing traditional A-line or two-piece Sega dresses. Colorful and flowing, they allowed the dancers to execute each move freely without constriction. Now, she knew why Reth had her wear one. She looked like the dancers. Lulled by the energy, Amina got up, mimicked their dances, and sang, too, even though she didn't know the words. She just let her body be free.

When the song ended, the women complimented her dancing and she thanked them before returning to Reth. She pulled him into a tight embrace. "I want to stay here forever,"

Amina told him, nearly breathless.

Reth tapped her nose with his index finger before kissing her gently on the lips. Pulling her face closer to his, he rested his forehead on hers. "I'll bring you back anytime you want. It warms my heart to see you so happy. Your delight is contagious. I want you to always feel this free, secure, and loved. I love you, Amina Lauryn Williams. I love every inch of you and the woman you are blooming into."

Amina placed her hands over his, staring intensely in his eyes. "I love you. Can I tell you a secret?"

"You can."

Maybe it was something in the air, but Amina was just putty in Reth's hands. She wanted to share every secret, every triumph and thought. "The night I spent at your parents' house, after Adeya and I fought, I heard your voice; it was so soothing and alluring. All I could think was I wanted to bathe in the vibration of your vocal cadence. I still do."

Reth chuckled at her honesty. "My dear, you amaze me." He leaned in and kissed her again. "In due time, you will bathe in the vibration of my vocal cadence; that's a promise."

Returning to the Queen City, Reth had a pep in his step. The vacation had been invigorating. It was refreshing to witness Amina's transformation and to be the person she shared her innermost thoughts with. Amina did not like to talk much, but when she did, it always rocked him to his core. The fact that she wanted to bathe in the vibration of his vocal cadence had him seriously thinking about buying a ring and hitting up the marriage drive-thru in Las Vegas. His goddess deserved far better than that.

Hearing her say she loved him made him feel like a schoolboy. It was so refreshing to be in a relationship that had potential for growth. It felt good to know she wanted to protect him like he protected her. It was not until Amina entered his life that he saw what he was missing and what he needed. Nothing and no one were about to disrupt what they were building.

Hence, the reason he was entering the prison to visit with Aaron Williams. There had not been anymore communication from the attorney who called Amina previously. Reth entered the private visitation room that was already occupied by a guard and Aaron. He had this meeting planned before his family vacation.

Once he entered, Reth felt the anger and confusion that Aaron emanated. If it were an attempt to intimidate Reth, it failed. He was raised to fear no man, only God. Allowing a hint of a smirk, Reth smoothed out his suit before reaching for the empty chair.

Aaron's sunken, lifeless eyes followed every movement that Reth took. His face showed his sorrow. This was a man who had been using alcohol to avoid his past, and now, all those emotions and feelings he buried were haunting him relentlessly. It looked as though it was eating him from the inside out. The past has a way of being a parasite when one chose to ignore it. This was the product of it.

Sitting down, Reth nodded to the guard to leave them alone. Once the guard left, Reth and Aaron just glared at each other. Aaron finally spoke first. "Who you?" His voice was just as weathered as his eyes. It was thick as if something were caught in his throat.

There was no indication that he recognized Reth. It was not as if Aaron was as active in church as Kenise and Amina. In fact, he only came on the holidays, until that day he cursed the entire congregation. The way some of them treated Amina, like she was an outcast, deserved it.

Never one to back down or mince words, he answered, "I'm Reth, the man courting your daughter."

At that, Aaron sat up and his eyes bulged; his brows lifted, baffled. "What happened to the Puerto Rican boy that was sniffing around?"

"He's gone. He was not good enough for her."

"I agree with that. Look like you got some money. Whatchu want with her? I mean, why are you here and not her? I told my lawyer I wanted to see her."

Biting his tongue to control the urge to hand Aaron the beatdown he deserved, Reth chose the nonviolent option. "About a month ago, your attorney contacted Amina about paying for Adeya's lawyer fees. As you can imagine, that upset her. She could not understand how her father could be so uncaring, knowing that his sister not only assaulted Amina but also murdered her mother and brothers. I must admit, it has me perplexed as well. So, enlighten me."

Aaron closed his eyes, inhaled deeply, and then slowly exhaled. He shook his head and finally gazed at Reth. His entire demeanor had changed, and Reth wondered what he was about to hear. "You're one of them Goodes, ain't chu? You look like that pastor Chiram Goode. I see y'all still after my family. Turned my wife out and now coming for my daughter. I knew she was back involved with ya kind," he spat.

"That's incorrect and you know it. I'm here to try to understand why you and your sister mistreated Amina even after she has done so much for you."

There was a brief silence. Reth seized the moment to analyze the man before him. It seemed Aaron was one to blame others for his misfortune. His inability to accept responsibility for his actions would continue to be his downfall.

"This ain't the life I wanted for Mina or me. I'm a product

of my environment. My father was a mean, abusive drunk and philander. He didn't really mistreat me, but my momma got a lot of his anger. His cheating took a toll on Momma. Adeya is a product of one of his countless affairs. Her mother didn't want her and left her on the porch for my mother to raise. My daddy didn't believe Adeya was his, even after the DNA test proved that she was. My daddy actually despised my sister." Aaron shook his head, recalling a memory.

"He was cruel to her. Crueler than she was to Amina. Told her she was too ugly to be his child. My mother told me it was my responsibility to look after Adeya, so I did. Even when she bashed Kenise. I know Adeya is why Kenise left me for another man. I can't abandon my sister; every other man in her life already has. I know that Amina is my daughter. She's got a kind heart like my mother. I honestly grew to dislike my mother because of how she let my father treat her. Adeya wasn't like that; you broke her then she would fight back. Amina's a pushover. That's weakness. That boy Mina used to date walked all over her. She followed him around like a little puppy, as if he were her savior or something. Just like Adeya, I just wanted her to toughen up."

Rapidly blinking at the revelation and excuse used to justify abusing Amina, it took Reth a full three minutes to gather his thoughts. His assessment of Aaron was accurate. Reth was appalled. His fist was itching to punch some sense into this man. "I thought when I came here there would be something to salvage. That you would accept responsibility and apologize to your daughter. I see you're still an extremely selfish and childish man who does not have the insight or the bravery to grow up. Your daughter is the toughest person I know. She survived the death of half her family, abuse, and neglect from you and Adeya, and still she rises. Know this: Amina is cared for and well-loved by me and my family. Don't contact her again, through your attorney or otherwise. She'll not financially support you or your sister. You never deserved

Kenise and you sure as hell don't deserve Amina. This was your one opportunity to do right by your daughter."

Aaron's dead eyes lit with fire at the truth; it was apparent he interpreted it as an insult. For people who survive on lies, the truth could be traumatic. "I loved Kenise."

Reth shook his head. "You were envious and obsessed with Kenise. It was your lack of action to remove Adeya out of the home that led to her death and the abuse of Amina. You won't ever get the opportunity to mistreat her again. I hoped for a better outcome, but then again, I thought you were a better man. It's a mistake I won't ever make again. Oh, and the house you once lived in, the one that Adeya tried to kick Amina out of, belongs to Amina. You're not welcome back. I suggest whenever you're released that you seek a new residence. That old one is closed to you, and so is Amina. She has a real man in her life now, and I don't play about her. A problem with me is not what you want. I'm just a judge five days a week, but when it comes to protecting the ladies in my life, I'm one hundred precent savage." Reth knocked on the steel table and winked at Aaron.

Aaron growled and started to act like a rabid animal, but it had no effect on Reth. He simply exited with the same confidence as he entered. Another one down. As soon as he made it outside his phone vibrated. He glanced down and saw it was a text from Delilah.

Chapter 30

Amina was in the music room at the Goode Community Center; silence painted the walls, as Amina was alone. Today's task was cleaning the instruments. Seeing her reflection in the brass instrument she had cleaned; a smile lit her face. True happiness and excitement filled her internally, and it made her skin shimmered. Being in love, being accepted, and feeling safe was something that Amina thought would forever elude her, but here she was, basking in all those sensations that once seemed foreign and unattainable.

The vacation had done wonders for her mentally and spiritually. There was no fear of the other foot dropping left. Sighing in contentment, Amina put up the instrument and headed to the piano. There was a song in her heart, one she wanted to write for Hasina based on Psalm 126:5, which she entitled it, "Hasina's Psalm".

Just as she was completing the chorus, her cell phone started to ring. Reaching over to retrieve it, Amina saw that it was Benito, and that concerned her. Since their return to Charlotte, Amina had been unable to contact Benito. She suspected it was because of what happened at her concert. However, she did not blame him or Ms. Mary. They were innocent.

"Hello?"

"Mina, can you come get me?"

"Sure, where are you?"

"At the mall."

"Okay, go to the food court and I'll be on my way."

Without a second thought of how Benito got to the mall, Amina rushed out of the center to her SUV and took off breaking, the speed limit to get to Benito. Parking haphazardly, Amina jumped out of the vehicle and marched across the street to enter the food court. Panic took over when she did not immediately see Benito. She kept frantically searching until she heard someone whisper her name. Benito was hiding behind the trashcan.

"Benito, why are you hiding and whispering?"

Edging out from his hiding place, he jogged the short distance to Amina. "I snuck out the house and took the bus so I could play at the arcade with my friends. While we were there, those boys that jumped me came in with their brothers. I ran before they could catch me." His eyes were as wide as a full moon.

Shaking her head in understanding, Amina reached for his hand, prepared to escort him out of the mall and to the center. That was the safest place to take him. As they exited the automatic doors, Benito pulled to a stop, causing Amina to stumble forward.

Amina side-eyed Benito, confused.

"That's them, Amina."

Following his gaze, she groaned. Not only had Benito spotted them, but they spotted her and Benito too. Letting out a sigh, Amina reenforced her hold on Benito and kept moving as if the four males were not shooting daggers their way.

Unfazed, Amina paid them no attention. After Adeya attacked her, Kondo made sure to give her private defense lessons. Though violence was the last resort, she was prepared

317

to fight for Benito.

"Hey, retard!"

"Run to the Jeep and lock the doors, Benito. I'll handle this." Their calling him that slur had Amina beyond heated. The last time she checked, Benito was in school, and it was their two little brothers who got expelled, so they were the stupid ones.

Benito snapped his neck at Amina as if she lost her mind. "Go call for help."

Benito kept his same speed and did not let her hand go. "Benito," she pleaded.

"No, I'm not leaving you."

Amina heard the heavy footfalls of the guys then they were quickly surrounded. It was as if they did not care that they were in broad daylight.

"Excuse me, but you fellas are in our way," Amina politely replied.

"The little retard got my brother and his friend expelled."

Amina whipped her head around to the average height guy talking. He was thinly built and tatted on every inch of his body, making his white skin appear green. "His name is Benito. Also, he did not get anyone expelled. Your brother and his friend violated school policy and therefore had to deal with the consequences of their actions. I'll not permit you to put a hand on Benito. It would be best if you four continue on and mind your business and allow us to do the same."

Mr. Tatts face balled in disgust as he spit on the ground, an inch away from Amina's flip-flopped feet. "I ain't got an issue wit ya, but him and his brother, we got beef."

Amina took a step closer. "Benito is off-limits."

He flicked his nose and let out a humorless chuckle. "I'on hit girls, but my bro Teagan don't care."

Benito yanked his hand out of Amina's and stood in front of her. Amina placed her hand protectively over his chest.

"Mina? Amina, is that you?" Bash called out.

Amina let out a sigh of relief at the sound Bash's voice. Wherever Bash was, he traveled deep. "Bash." Her tone was one of recognition and pleading.

Seeming to comprehend their dilemma, Bash, followed by five more guys, made their way over to Benito and Amina. "These inbred fools bothering you, Mina?" Bash questioned.

"Actually, they were harassing Benito. I was trying to get him to safety when these four attempted to accost us," Amina explained, her eyes narrowing as she glared at the wannabe thugs.

"Accost?" Nic repeated.

"It means to address someone aggressively," Amina explained.

Nic grinned and replied, "You sexy and smart." Then, he turned his disturbing glare at the four who seemed a lot less confident know. Honestly, so was she. There was something strange about Nic.

"Y'all don't ever learn, do you Edward Dale Chesterfield and Teagan Andrew Baxter? I let y'all slide once, but that won't happen again. Mina baby and Benito are QCB-protected, so you know how this gonna end. There won't be any more inbreeding." That was all Bash said, and all four of the guys looked as red as a stop sign.

"Nic, gone head and walk them to Mina's ride." Nic nodded at the order and started to escort Amina and Benito to her Jeep.

"Mina, why you do my boy BC like that? You know that girl most likely ain't even pregnant by him. You out here doing my boy bad. I mean, the least you coulda did was holler at me. They say you out here dating a geriatric," Nic teased.

Amina cut her eyes at him but did not respond to his ignorance. Reth was all man and far from old. No matter how bad her situation was, Nic would never be a possibility. It did not take long to get her SUV, and she unlocked the door to allow Benito to get in. When she looked back at to where the guys were all standing, mall security decided to finally show up. It seemed that Bash knew them because they did not stop and kept on driving.

"Tell Bash I said thank you," Amina replied.

"What about thanking me?" Nic asked, stepping into her personal space and sandwiching Amina between her car and him.

"Back up, Nic."

"Thank me first." A wicked smirk revealed itself, reminding Amina of why she kept her distance.

Before she could speak, the clicking of a camera gained her attention. There stood Delilah St. John with her phone in one hand and shopping bags in another. Amina thought the woman had left North Carolina for good. Apparently, she was incorrect. Today was going to be one for the books. This woman had it out for Amina.

"I knew you were a low-class hussy. Not only are you chasing Reth, but you have a man on the side?"

Amina frowned, confused. In what world would Nic be her man on the side?

"That's the man that tried to kill Reth and my granddaughter. You think I wouldn't find you? You set my son-in-law up. He's going to know about you."

Clearing her mind, Amina pushed Nic to the side with the strength of a man ten times her size. She glared at Delilah. "I'm not a low-class hussy. My name is Amina Lauryn Williams. I'm a child of God, and I'll not allow the evil spirit that has consumed you to get an inch of my soul. I don't know what you expected to accomplish here, but Amal would be extremely disappointed in the way you've conducted yourself since her untimely death. Reth has told you on several occasions to stop this interference, yet it seems you refuse to adhere to his warnings. You're wasting your life being fixated on Reth and me. You can't stop or rewrite what God has spoken to be, and for your information, he's not BC. Now, be on your way!"

"Ooh, you done made Mina mad, Ms. Lady. I'm Nic and I ain't a side dude or the dude that shot at'cha your people," Nic instigated.

"Nic, let's roll!" Bash hollered, causing everyone's attention to turn. Nic winked at Amina before heading toward Bash.

Thankfully, Delilah started to walk away, but she was steady typing on her cell phone.

Hopping into the SUV, Amina backed out and then zoomed out of the parking lot, and she swore that she saw AB. Shaking from the events of the day, Amina had no idea how everything went from smooth to rocky in less than an hour.

"Mina, are you okay?" Benito asked worriedly.

"I will be."

The news that Amina found out today had her stressed to the max. Never had she ever suspected that Bash was a gangbanger. He did not give off thug vibes. However, the swagger, the voice change, the attitude that he displayed when addressing those guys was a side of Bash that she never saw. It seemed Kalifa was right. Were Diego and BC also QCB? If she were under QCB protection, what did that mean? Lord, and after all that, Delilah was still on a rampage to end her and Reth's relationship.

Doing her best to simmer down and control her emotions, Amina about jumped out of her skin when her cell phone went off. "Hey."

"*Mpendwa*, where are you?"

His voice was like instant manna to her frail mental state.

"*Mpenzi*, I'm leaving the mall with Benito. Reth, so much happened. My nerves are frazzled. I was heading back to the center."

"Come home."

Amina didn't even ask if he meant his parents' house; she knew he meant his. That he considered it her home too, even though she lived with his parents made her smile.

∞∞∞

Benito had worried himself to sleep by the time Amina pulled up to Reth's house. As soon as Amina opened the car door, Reth came out of the house.

"Benito's asleep; I was about to wake him up."

"I'll get him; just pull your Jeep into the garage."

Thinking that request a little weird, she waited for Reth to get Benito, and then she pulled her SUV into the garage. It was then that she noticed that Reth's sedan was not parked. His SUV was there. Not thinking too much about it, Amina entered the house.

As she was removing her shoes and putting her purse down, the front door opened, and JD followed by Kondo came rushing in.

Alarmed, Amina asked if they were okay.

"Where's Reth?"

"Probably upstairs, Benito and I just arrived. What's going on?"

Their reply was halted by Reth entering the room. Now that Amina got a good look at him, she noticed that he has changed his clothes, and it looked like his left hand had more bandages on it. There was slight bump on the side of his forehead.

"Reth, what happened to you?"

"I was run off the road; nobody was hurt except my car has some damage."

"What!" Amina shouted, running to him to assess for unseen injuries. "Are you okay? Did you let Kondo check you out?"

"I'm fine, but I'm more concerned about you." He gestured for his brothers to take a seat, and he rested his hand on Amina's lower back to guide her to the couch.

"Tell me what happened with Benito."

Taking a deep breath, Amina recounted the entire story.

"Who is Bash?"

"He's Diego's older brother. Diego is BC's best friend. It's seems without knowing that I've associated myself with the Queen City Boys." Amina's voice lowered on the latter part.

Reth's right hand massaged her scalp before his fingers slid through her natural hair. His touch, like always, soothed the stress that was about to overtake her. Leaning forward, Reth kissed the side of her forehead. They all sat in silence for a while until Amina remembered that she and Kalifa had plans.

"I have to go meet Kalifa," Amina announced as she turned to Reth.

"Invite her here; after what occurred today, I'm uncomfortable with you being out alone."

Not wanting to add to the worry of the day, Amina agreed. In just a short time, because of her, Reth had been through a lot and she did not want to add to it. Smiling at him, she gently caressed his chest and eased off the couch to call Kalifa.

∞ ∞ ∞

Reth watched until Amina was gone and then turned his attention back to his brothers. Without speaking a single word, they were all on the same page. Nodding his head, his brothers followed him to his study. As the lumbered together, Reth quickly called Matt to do a little research for him. He wanted everything on QCB. Something told him that he needed to dig deeper into AB. He was working on a theory. The conversation was brief.

The clicking of the office door pulled him out of his deep contemplation.

"What're you thinking?" JD asked, folding his arms, his eyes bright with anger.

"I think AB is more dangerous than I first believed. I think he didn't know about Amal's death but came back to Charlotte because of Ms. Mary having issues with her eldest grandson. When he found out that Amina was linked to me, I believe he saw a way to manipulate BC and try to come for me. Revenge was always his downfall. Most likely, he'll try to use Delilah if she doesn't try to use him first. As always, people underestimate me. It's the whole 'we're Christians so we must be pushovers' myth. Obviously, they don't know the God we serve."

JD grinned. "I'm going to keep my ears to the streets and reach out to some of my connections. I really don't like Benito or Amina being in the middle of this. I don't think QCB would ever hurt them, but their enemies won't care."

Agreeing, Reth was about to sit down when the doorbell rang. Knowing that his daughter was with his mother and Amina was in the house, Reth had no idea who could be at the door.

Jogging to halt the incessant ringing, Amina beat him to the door.

"Yes?"

"Is Reth here?" the feminine voice queried.

Not recognizing the voice, Reth made the short distance and stood by Amina's side.

"I'm Reth, and you are?"

The woman handed him an envelope. "You've been served." Then, she jetted off.

Dumbfounded, Reth glanced at the envelope as if it was a foreign object. Who in the world would have him served? Quickly opening the envelope, he pulled out the paperwork and held a curse. Delilah had the gall to sue him for custody of Hasina.

"What's wrong, Reth?"

"Delilah."

Chapter 31

A week later, Reth was still livid that Delilah had the gall to sue him for custody. She had no claim; it was frivolous and annoying, but it still had to be settled.

"Relax, Reth," Amina murmured, her soft hands massaging the tight muscles in his back. She had the most calming effect on him. Amina's presence was the physical embodiment of lavender. That's how soothing she was, and when she sang to him, he was nothing but Playdoh in her hands to shape as she willed.

"Sing me a song; that always helps me relax."

"What would you like to hear?"

"Surprise me."

He almost moaned as she placed pressure to his lower back. He might need to pay for her to get some advanced training in massage therapy. Like the magic that she was, Amina started singing India.Arie's "Brown Skin". That was not the song he thought she would choose. His body molded to the lyrics of the song as well as her touch. The anger he felt toward Delilah melted with each note that she sang. He was completely consumed by Amina.

Reaching behind him, he seized her hand, causing her to stop and give him a puzzled look. He just smirked as he directed her nearer to him as he sat up. Passion and yearning cascaded through his body like venom, and he knew she felt it to by the way her pupils dilated. Reth was man accustomed to taking care of others and pushing his own needs aside. Amina did not let him do that; she took care of him also. It unlocked his defenses and made him remember that he had needs too. Lifting her hand, he gently kissed the inside of her wrist.

The sexiest thing about Amina was that she had no clue how sexy she was or the power she had over him. It was that reason that he did not pursue charges against BC. The boy was stupid in love when he lost the best woman he would never have again. That was a mistake that Reth would never make.

"You're stunning," Reth rasped as he kissed a trail up her arm. Her body trembled at his attention, and he pulled her into him, using his hands to cup her face as he lightly kissed her lips.

Amina gasped, surprised by his forwardness, he suspected. That did not halt his need to consume her.

"Reth."

"Mm?" he responded between kisses. Amina tasted better than the strawberry cupcakes from Tamu.

"It's getting late. I should be getting back to your parents' place."

"Stay here tonight."

"I…"

He cut her off by deepening the kiss. Then, he felt her slipping away. Opening his eyes, he saw how flushed she was. Her lips were swollen by his action. He felt embarrassed at his lack of control. "I'm sorry. I got carried away."

"No, it's not that. I always enjoy kissing you. That was intense, but I just, are you sure you're okay?"

"Why wouldn't I be?"

"The past week has been daunting. You haven't really expressed your feelings, but I can tell that things were bothering you. That's why I offered the massage. You're always taking care of my needs, and I want to do the same for you. Sometimes, I feel like you hold back. I can handle it. I don't want you to feel like you can't share your thoughts with me. BC used to that and then either got mad at me for having no outlet or wanted to make out and..."

"Stop. Don't do that, Amina. Don't ever compare me to your ex. We're not the same." Reth's tone was gruffer than he meant it to be. By the crestfallen expression on her face, his response hurt her feelings.

"I'm sorry. I didn't mean it like that. You two don't compare at all. It's just that I'm limited in my experience, but I didn't mean to upset you." Amina words were rushed, a sign of her being nervous. Fidgeting with her hands, Amina took a step back from Reth, and he instantly felt the distance. "I should go. I'm going to check on Hasina and then head out."

"Amina," he called out to her, but that seemed to make her speed up. Mentally chastising himself, Reth followed her path.

Once he arrived upstairs, Reth watched as Amina entered Hasina bedroom. He knew his daughter was asleep because if she were awake, she would have been downstairs with them. At least twice a week, Hasina slept in the bed with him, which was an improvement since Amal's death.

The door closed as Amina exited Hasina's room; her entrancing golden orbs locked with his. Instantly, he wished he had not spoken harshly to her. He'd rather be getting lost in her kisses and holding her.

"I'm sorry for how I responded. My need to touch you overrode my common sense, and I allowed my jealousy to speak."

"It's okay." The reply was short and a lie. Not a purposeful lie, Amina was not that kind of person. To her, it probably was okay; she would find a way to explain his behavior, which was unacceptable.

"It wasn't okay, Amina. You have a right to tell me that. I love you. I know you love me. We're together; we're friends, partners; you're my beloved. As your man, I should never make you feel as though your thoughts are concerns don't matter. Thank you for caring enough to notice when I need you. Thank you for being brave enough to call me out. Never, my love, accept my mediocrity. If I say or do something that upsets, you need to let me know. Just like you, I'm inexperienced in relationships too."

Amina dipped her head, her shyness peeking through. It only lasted a second before she lifted her head up and strode toward him. Hugging him tightly he released the fear that was creeping into his heart.

"I love you, Reth. Even when we have disagreements. I know your heart. I'm here for you too. We'll get through all of this. One day, when we're old, we'll laugh about it all. I really should go because if I stay, I might awaken love too soon." She kissed him gently and then padded back down the stairs.

Reth shivered. She felt it too. He chuckled at her quoting Song of Solomon. At this rate, he was going to have to put a ring on her finger.

∞∞∞

As Reth and his brothers entered the sanctuary, he heard Amina's voice. She was performing morning worship. Amina was singing Shana Wilson's song "Give Me You", and as always, her rendition pierced his soul. Her voice was indescribable. Whatever her emotions were, she used them when she sang. The entire congregation stared in awe of her.

As she ended the song, a chorus of applause erupted. Amina placed the microphone back on the stand and stood back in line with the rest of the singers. As praise and worship concluded, Amina trekked to the back of the church and sat down.

Perplexed by her action, Reth attempted to get up, but his brother stopped him. He followed Kondo's gaze and saw Delilah followed by AB entering the church. Just the sight of them had him heated. Seeing them together should be no surprise, but if Delilah knew that AB savagely raped her daughter and still associated with him, she was dead to Reth.

"Don't react, Reth. They came here for a reason, so don't fall into the trap they created. Let God handle them. Whatever He has in store is far better than anything you could think up," JD warned.

Turning his attention away from them, he allowed his mind to get lost in the service. After prayer and tithing, Sister Jaylynn got up to make the announcements and opened to the floor to visitors. Delilah stood up and Reth prepared himself for the worse. This woman had some nerve.

"Good morning. I'm Delilah St. John, the mother of the late Amal Kennedy-Goode. I met some of you at her funeral. Today, I wanted to come and support my granddaughter Hasina." She paused for a moment and rested her hand on her chest as if she were overcome by grief. AB handed her a handkerchief, and she dabbed her eyes. "Sadly, since the death of my daughter, I've been unable to spend the time I wanted with my granddaughter and even my son-in-law. It's come to my attention that my daughter's nanny has sought to use my son-in-law's grief to her benefit. I hear that her mother was the same. Not only that, but she put his life and the life of my granddaughter at risk. I—"

Reth stood up before he could stop himself. Some of the congregation was covering their mouths, already whispering the gossip. Others were scowling at her audacity. There was no way she was going to change and control the narrative.

"Enough, Delilah. Don't speak lies in the Lord's house."

She turned her evil-spirited orbs toward Reth. "Is it a lie that you took that girl on vacation to play mommy to my granddaughter? The same girl who has not one, but two family members incarcerated for murder. The same woman who was dating some thug that pulled a gun on you; isn't that true? I just caught her with another man at the mall."

Reth shook his head, disappointed as he watched Amina crumble. The pain and embarrassment she must be feeling made him want to go to her. Instead, his mother did. The rest of the family and Kalifa were glaring at Delilah. Kalifa stood up and went to get Hasina to remove her from the scene, and Reth was grateful to her.

"Lies, Delilah. If you genuinely loved Hasina and Amal, then you would know that the man who entered with you is extremely dangerous. He's the cousin of the man that attempted to harm me. It seems your priories and judgment are lacking. Your intent was to make baseless accusations and cause a ruckus. Your attempt to embarrass and shame Amina only makes you look bad. The people here know Amina. They know the goodness of her heart, the love she had for Amal, and her dedication to not only Hasina but to all the youth in this church. So, stop Delilah. Let it go. Your absence from Hasina's life is by your own design, just like your absence from Amal's life. Do not come into God's house infesting it with deception and confusion. If you want to praise God, if you need guidance and direction, then stay, but if your reason for being here is to berate and create drama, then you'll leave. We don't do that at Goode Faith Worship Church."

"You better preach, big brother," Kondo mumbled loud enough for Reth to hear.

The congregation applauded. Reth hated to share any private information like that. There was so much more to say, but he had to be dignified.

Having enough decency to sit down, everyone turned their attention back to the pulpit while Reth sat down but kept an eye on Amina. His mother was ministering to her, so he would wait.

$$\infty\infty\infty$$

The internal burn almost made Amina want to run out the church. This was so close to the mess that happened to her mother that Amina felt as if she would not survive. History would have repeated itself if not for Eleora's firm hold on her. Not only her, but the senior ladies of the church also came to her aide. The burning rescinded.

"It's all right, baby. The light of God that glows in you, that's what scares her. Don't you ever forget whom you belong to, and don't ever let the misguided define you. God made you for a divine purpose, to fulfill a purpose, and sweetheart, you will," Eleora prophesied.

Tears glossed her eyes but did not fall. Amina received Eleora's words. She was no longer that lost, lonely little girl. Getting herself together, Amina released the fury and asked God to enter. With grace, she got up, thanked the ladies for their support, and sauntered down the aisle to the microphone stand she had used earlier. With her head held high and her eyes and mind clear, she was going to speak, and everyone was going to listen.

Taking the deepest breath, she ever took, she swallowed her fear and released her faith. "Good afternoon, family. I'm a person of few words. I usually use music to express myself. As a child, my voice was silenced, and I thought it held no power. However, I'm reminded today how powerful speaking can be. I'd like to apologize for the display that just transpired. It's not what my friend Amal, my Naomi would have wanted.

Those who knew her knew her grace, restraint, love, and respect. Before my friend died, she and I had several honest conversations. We learned that we had a lot in common.

Most of you know my history; a few months ago, it played out on the local news, therefore, I won't rehash it. I'll say this: my aunt, for reasons I can't comprehend, verbally and physically abused me. When I shared that with Amal, she told me that my aunt was my darkness. Amal said that people in the dark can't defeat the light, so they try to dim that light." Amina paused for a moment and dropped her head to calm the emotions that was rising. Lord knows she missed Amal. Amina felt a hand on her. Reth, his brothers, and mother were all behind her. "I've had a lot of people try to dim my light—my father, my aunt, the tormentors at school, and even some people here in this congregation. Amal had people that wanted to dim her light too. Two of them are present today. In both our lives, those people were winning. Those light stealers made me question my beauty because of the darkness of my skin. They made Amal think her only worth was in her beauty. The light stealers made me question my value. Insecurity flourished in me, like confidence for others. For too long, I didn't see myself as worthy; I saw waste. When I needed a safe place, it was withheld from me. I was left on my own, too young to be unprotected."

Blinking to hold back the tears, Amina continued. "My mother raised me to forgive. Forgiveness allows for healing and renewal. So, Mrs. Delilah, there is something malicious in your heart. I'm not being disrespectful, just honest. There is a reason you have spent more time accusing and berating the people that love Amal than spending time with Hasina. I'm not anyone's enemy. I never set Reth up to be harmed nor would I ever. I'd take any blow to protect him and Hasina.

I'm sorry Amal died. I prayed for a miracle up until she took her last breath. My heart broke when she transitioned. I love Amal. I don't know if she knew how wonderful she was, but she helped me. I know we all deal with grief differently. However, what you did today wasn't grief; that was an attack on a family that loves your daughter and granddaughter and to a person you don't know but chose to judge. I'll—no," Amina shook her head. "we'll pray for you, Delilah. We'll pray the poison out of your heart. May God's peace release the guilt or whatever has caused you to act out in this way.

Your words almost hurt me, but your allegations are twisted and unfounded. Nothing you say will ever belittle me because I know who I am in Christ. My light is powered by His Everlasting Light. Due to my love and respect for Amal, I won't turn my back to you. I won't use your lowest moments against you or berate you. This incident can be forgotten and forgiven. It's up to you. As a Christian, I'm called to love my neighbor, and I try hard to do that. Let this be a lesson learned and a moment of change."

As soon as Amina finished speaking, Delilah hopped up and marched out of the church as if the hounds of hell were on her. With a devilish smirk, AB was right behind her. Ignoring their departure, Amina turned her attention back to the congregation. "If it's all right with you all, there's a song on my heart."

Amina made her way to the piano, sat down, and started to play "Reckless Love," Anthony Evans' rendition. As she played, peace seeped through her before she opened her mouth and belted out the song. As it ended, Amina felt tiny arms wrap around her, and she knew it was Hasina. The entire congregation was on their feet, clapping and crying. Amina knew they must have felt it too. The Spirit was in the church strong. Delilah wanted to cause strife, but it did not work that way. Pulling Hasina into an embrace, Amina kissed her cheek.

"I love you, Hasina."

"I know. I love you too."

Chapter 32

Amina got out of the chair and padded through Amal's garden. There was a lot that had occurred in the two weeks since the church episode. The family had not heard from Delilah or AB. Ms. Mary called last week to say she was taking Benito and BC back to Puerto Rico. The police had no suspect in Reth's hit and run, but they were working hard to find the culprit. Though, Reth seemed too calm about it all. Amina figured he knew more than he let on.

Changing direction, Amina paused as she felt him. Her eyes closed in anticipation of his touch. Reth's footfalls got closer until she felt his warm muscled arms wrap like a bow around her hips.

He had been so affectionate after that night she gave him a back massage. Relaxing her body, she melted into his hold and a smile eased across her face. This feeling never got old. What she loved about Reth was that he knew what she needed without her ever asking.

"Are you okay?" His alluring voice was heavy with concern.

"I am. How about you?"

"Now that I have you in my arms, I feel great. Are you ready to go to my parents' house? Djimon is on his way, as well as my Aunt Miriam, Uncle Nadir, and cousin Mahari. They're excited to finally meet you," Reth gushed, turning Amina around to face him. "You're so breathtakingly beautiful."

"Thank you. I have to match the dashing man at my side." Amina winked. The more comfortable she became in her skin, the easier it was for her to flirt with the man she not only admired but loved.

Reth bit on his bottom lip and pulled it in as his eyes scanned her from head to toe.

"What are you thinking, Mr. Goode?"

"You'll find out later. Now, come on so we won't be late. You keep looking the way you're looking and we're going to have a shotgun wedding."

"What?" Amina giggled.

Reth just chuckled and escorted her out of the garden.

∞ ∞ ∞

Christian hip hop blared as Reth, Amina, and Hasina arrived at his family's estate. Amina found herself bobbing to the music as Hasina took off wFhen she spotted a woman who looked to be around Amina's age.

"Who is Hasina running to see?" Amina turned and asked Reth.

His eyes followed her daughter, and then he smiled. "That's Binah. She sent the dancing flower seeds. Binah, Mahari, and Amal were close. She's like an aunt to Hasina. I didn't know she would be here. She's a dancer. It's rare that she comes home."

Before Amina could respond, she heard "Chocolate goddess" and knew it was Djimon. She missed him terribly. Grinning, Amina went to welcome him with a hug. Djimon just smiled. Reth was right behind her to do the same before playfully scolding his brother about getting too close.

"The Khoury clan is right behind me, and..." His voice

trailed off as something or someone caught his eyes. There was a change in his facial expression that alarmed Amina momentarily. "Brother, is that Binah?"

Before Reth could confirm, Djimon was off. Amina watched as Reth shook his head.

"Retty, I've missed you," a model-like woman squealed. Amina assumed it was Mahari. She had smooth brown skin, flowing ebony hair, and the most illuminating eyes.

"Hari, I've missed you too." Reth embraced her and then turned back to Amina. "Hari, this is Amina, my *mpendwa*."

Mahari's excitement burst. "It's a pleasure to meet you, gorgeous. I've heard nothing but wonderful things about you. I can see the happiness that you bring Retty. I'm overjoyed that he has been able to find love. Welcome to our family, and I hope we'll become best friends."

Taken aback by the easy welcome and kindness, Amina could not stop the goofy grin that had overtaken her. She thought that Reth's extended family would eye her with suspicion because of Amal's place in their hearts, but that was far from the truth. "Thank you, Mahari. I'm sure we'll be great friends."

Mahari nodded and then introduced her parents. Before long, the entire backyard was full of family. Gavin had arrived with his family, and Kalifa had just arrived. Amina ran to embrace her.

"How're you, Kali?"

Smiling, she assured Amina she was fine. Amina was not sure about that. In the past month, something seemed off about Kali, but due to Amina's increased responsibilities, she had been unable to pinpoint the issue. Knowing that now was not the time to get into it, Amina left it alone and headed back to the table.

"Mina, will you play my song?" Hasina asked.

"We'll have to go into the house to play the piano." Hasina nodded, grinning.

"Let me tell your daddy, and then I'll play for you." Amina and Hasina traveled over to Reth, who was with his brother, cousin, and Uncle Nadir. Excusing herself, Amina told Reth she was taking Hasina inside to play her song.

"What song?"

"Mina wrote me my own song, Daddy. It's called Hasina's Psalm," she giddily replied.

Lifting a brow, Reth glance at Amina and she could not help but to blush. "Can we hear the song too?"

Shaking her head in agreement, Amina reached for Hasina's hand, and they all entered the house. Hasina joined Amina on the piano seat.

Amina turned toward their little audience. "This song is based on Psalm 126:5; there's a story behind it. Hasina and I were in the car, and I was having a rough day. I called out to God and asked why. My little piano princess reminded me of this verse, so I titled it Hasina's Psalm." Winking at Hasina, Amina began playing the song. Hasina swayed from side-to-side, smiling. As the song came to an end, the family applauded. After taking their bow, Amina was greeted by hugs and compliments.

"That was beautiful, Song Thrush. You'll have to record that for me," Eleora grinned.

"I will."

Reth wrapped his arm around her and picked up Hasina as they all went back outside to eat. Good music, food, and conversation flowed easily. Taking in her environment, Amina knew she never wanted to lose this. Kissing the top if Hasina's head, her sleepy eyes opened just a fraction before closing. Amina held her tightly and sang another lullaby.

"Oh my gosh, Amina, you're so good with her," Mahari lovingly admired.

Amina grinned timidly at the compliment. As she was about to respond, Reth called her name. Glancing behind her, she saw him standing on the dance floor, motioning for her to join him. Before she could decline, Kondo popped up and reached out to retrieve Hasina. Passing her to Kondo, Amina slowly ambled toward Reth. For some reason, her entire body was tingling with anticipation. This was almost reminiscent of the scene she had with BC, except this time, her heart was safe, and she trusted Reth.

Teeth glowing like diamonds, Reth reached his hand out to her. "Dance with me."

"No, Retty," she teased. Of course, she would dance with him because her most favorite place to be was in his arms.

"Aht," he wiggled his index finger. "I'm your *mpenzi*, your music, your muse; don't call Retty, I only allow Mahari to call me that horrid nickname."

Amina moved closer to him and laughed in the safety of his chest. "It's so cute, though."

"You've been warned," he teased and then snapped his fingers.

"Are you Thanos?"

He dropped his head sideways before asking, "What's with the jokes today?"

Just as she was about to tease him more, Luther Vandross' "Endless Love" started to play. Amina's eyes popped to his, seeking to understand why he chose this song. Seeming to understand the unasked questioned, he replied, "I know how music speaks you. This song represents how I feel about you." Reth pulled her tighter and started to sing in her ear.

She melted like butter, rested her head on his chest, and sang with him. The entire world disappeared; there was only Amina and Reth and she was lost in him.

"Open your eyes, Amina, and look at me," he requested.

His russet orbs captivated her without effort. Just like the lyrics, she would be a fool for him.

"I love you, Amina. I know our relationship did not start traditionally, but I would not change one thing. I've watched you grow from timid girl that wanted to be invisible into this magnificent masterpiece. You're my endless love. All I know is when you entered my life, I knew love was real. You've given a man like me, who buried all those feelings, the opportunity to create the kind of good love that my parents have. Thank you, Amina. Thank you for trusting your heart and seeing something in me."

"Reth, baby, that was beautiful. I'm speechless." Her hands cupped his face as she stood on her tippy toes to kiss him. Words weren't necessary, actions were. This man that she had adored for years, just declared his love for her so effortlessly. It made all the pain and loss worth it.

"Hey now, children are here!" Djimon shouted, reminding Amina of manners.

Coming back to reality, Amina took a step away from Reth and turned to tease Djimon, but instead of seeing just him, she saw the entire family. Everyone was smiling with their cell phones out. Perplexed, Amina watched as Hasina, who seemed sleepy just minutes ago, came strolling toward Amina with a contagious smile.

Something was amiss. Watching curiously as Hasina passed by Amina who turned around to see what was happening. She saw Reth on one knee, thinking he fell. Amina offered to assist him in getting up.

"Are you okay? How'd you fall?"

That made everyone laugh, except Amina.

"Well, there was this beautiful woman named Amina Lauryn Williams who entered my life. She took my breath away and made me fall in love with her."

"Smooth brother," Djimon encouraged.

"Amina Williams, will you marry Hasina and me?"

Unable to speak or form a thought, she could only stare at him. Her hand clasped over her mouth as her body started to tremble.

"Breathe, mpendwa."

"You want to marry me?"

"Yes."

"Brother, she's supposed to say yes, not you," Djimon teased.

The loud smack that Amina heard must have been his mother trying to shut him up.

"Yes, I would love to marry you and Hasina. I love you both more than anything."

Amina watched in amazement as he placed the cushion cut black diamond on her finger.

"I chose a black diamond because it symbolizes passion and strength; it represents enteral, unchanging, and flawless love. In my eyes, you're a black diamond. You're strong, flawless, and passionate. My love for you will be enteral and unchanging. That's how you make me feel."

Huge tears ran down her face, blinding her as she kneeled in front of him. Overcome by his honesty, she pulled Hasina into them and leaned in to kiss him. "Thank you for seeing me, loving me, for protecting me and for helping me find my voice. I thought I lost everything when my family died, but God saw fit to bless me with a new family. I'm so grateful for the both of you."

The family applauding brought them back to reality. Amina

was quickly embraced by the entire Goode family.

"My best friend is getting married!" Kalifa shouted.

"What's going on here?" Delilah's accented voice ripped through the celebration.

∞ ∞ ∞

It takes a highly ignorant and bold woman to enter the premises of a home she was not invited into and then question what she interrupted. Still, because the moment was too beautiful to be tainted, Reth refrained from his normal reaction to Delilah.

"Can we help you?" Reth asked tightly, holding Amina's hand. Delilah would not take from this moment.

"I apologize for interfering with your family event. However, I received a letter from Amal, and I would like to speak with you."

It was silent; no one said anything, but everyone was staring at Reth, awaiting his move. "Speak, Delilah."

"I meant privately."

"I'm aware, but I don't trust you, so if you have something to say that requires my attention, you speak here or you don't speak at all."

Amina yanked on his arm, causing him to look her way. "Hear her out."

Mulling it over, Reth finally agreed. "You can thank Amina, but she, my parents, and brothers will be present."

"As you wish, and thank you, Amina."

Less than five minutes later, the family congregated in the den, while everyone else continued celebrating. Now that Reth had a moment to take in Delilah, he noticed just how different she looked. Her face was pale; bags lingered under her eyes, and her normal high-end attire was replaced with sweatpants and polo shirt.

Holding the letter firmly in her hand, she looked at Reth. "Are Adrian and AB the same person?"

Reth hated to hear his name, but he nodded yes.

"He raped Amal; he's Hasina father."

"I'm Hasina's father, but he's her sperm donor. AB sexually assaulted Amal. My family knows all about it. I shared it with them after Amal's death, as she requested."

The hand holding the letter started to tremble. When Delilah started to speak, her voice was weak and broken. "I've been a fool. I didn't know. What have I done?" It seemed she was speaking to herself and, therefore, Reth remained silent.

"You married her to keep her safe, to protect her and Hasina."

Reth nodded.

"She explains it in the letter, along with how much she adored Amina. I...I dropped the lawsuit; it was just to get your attention and try to control things. Your family has always been good to my daughter and her father. You were there for her when I left her, when her father died, when she was attacked, and when the cancer came. I wasn't. After her death, I realized just how careless I'd been. I wanted a chance to do it right, but of course, I didn't. I let my jealousy consume me. I tried to use Emmarie to replace my daughter, but it didn't work. Your heart already belonged to another." Delilah sighed; it was as if the fight just left her. "I've been wrong for a long time. I have a lot of mending to do, but please know that I'll not be an issue anymore. Emre has summoned me home. I think it's best I get counseling and better myself so that I can start a relationship with Hasina."

Clasping his hands together, Reth kept his gaze on her. "Why were you with AB?"

"He approached my table one night while Emmarie and I were dining. I thought he was a handsome young man and encouraged Emmarie to get to know him better. I didn't know his history. Had I known, I wouldn't have entertained him."

Reth already had Matt on AB. It seemed AB was in some shady business. If Emmarie were smart, she would distance herself from AB before he ruined her life, just like he attempted to ruin Amal's.

"Well, I'm glad you know the truth now. If you'll excuse us, we're celebrating, and I would like to get back to my family."

Cleaning her face with a napkin she retrieved from her purse, she quickly spoke. "Right, I've taken enough of your time. Again, I sincerely apologize for my behavior. I hope you'll forgive me. Especially you, Amina. I've been unjustly relentless in my verbal attacks. It won't happen again."

"We know," Djimon snapped.

Nodding her head, Delilah got up and escorted herself out, leaving the family to speak among themselves.

"Amal out here leaving everybody these Aaliyah four-page letters and didn't even leave me a sticky note," Djimon teased, causing everyone to laugh. It broke the tension. That was why Reth loved his brothers; they were always better together.

Reth looked over at Amina; she still had the same smile on her face as when he proposed. "Are you happy?"

"Beyond measure. I'm going to marry my dream man, the only man I ever prayed to have."

Reth placed his hand over his heart, his face completely flushed. "I thank God that He chose you for me. I love you, Amina."

"I love you more!"

Epilogue

6 months later

Kalifa and Amina entered the restaurant that was hosting her rehearsal dinner. Tomorrow, she would be Mrs. Reth Abioye Goode. Amina could not believe they were able to plan and execute a wedding in six months, but with Reth's family, as well as Gavin's wife Lelah, they had pulled it off without a hiccup. Of course, Reth wanted a wedding in six days.

It was amazing what had happened over the course of six months. Gavin legally adopted her, making it clear that she did have a father who wanted her. In the newspaper, Gavin made sure that it stated he was giving away his daughter. It felt good that she was wanted and that he was determined to walk her down the aisle. He had a new high-tech chair that would allow it.

As the pair entered, Kalifa halted, causing Amina to do the same. Following her friend's gaze, she saw Kondo engaged in conversation with his arm around a woman unknown to her. Twisting her lips sideways, she felt her calm demeanor transition into something harder.

"Kali."

Shaking her head, almost as if to remove the scene from her mind, she turned to Amina and smiled. "Let's celebrate. My bestie is about to be a wife."

Amina shared in her excitement but still she worried about friend, not only because of Kondo entertaining another woman but because something was going on with Kalifa. Whatever it was, she was keeping it to herself. Instead of voicing her concerns, she pulled Kalifa into a warm embrace.

"I love you, Kalifa, and I'll always have your back no matter what. Even though violence is never the answer, for you, I'll slap the fire out of that girl and Kondo; just say the word."

At that, Kalifa howled, and that got everyone's attention.

"That's why I love you."

"What's so funny?" Djimon asked.

Rubbing Kalifa's back, the two turned toward the others. "Nothing, just a joke between friends."

With tears of humor still lingering in her eyes, Kalifa and Amina made their way to the reserved seating for them.

Reth's shimmering russet eyes followed every step that Amina took. She kept her gaze on him. She grinned shyly as he licked his lips adoringly. Tonight, she wore a fitted, strapless cream dress and gold jewelry. Her long hair was in a goddess halo braid.

"Somebody better call the fire department; I can feel the flames from the intensity of his stare. That man is on fire for you," Kali whispered.

Giggling, Amina replied, "The only person who can contain that fire is me!"

Kalifa let out a fit of giggles. They were really showing out.

When Amina got close, Reth stood up and met her; Hasina right behind him. "Beautiful, alluring, breathtaking, awing, queen of my heart, maestro of my soul, I've missed you," Reth's mesmerizing voice whispered in her ear.

Falling into him she, allowed her body to succumb to his touch. "Sophisticated, son of royalty, hypnotic like the old

Motown sound, captivating as a French minuet, my personal symphony of Goode love, king of my heart, holder of my soul, I've missed you more. Tomorrow, I get to be yours forever."

"*Mpendwa*, you're going to make me break our no kissing promise until tomorrow at the wedding. I'm already on pins and needles. I can call the justice of the peace."

She laughed and shook her head. "Be patient, Abioye."

His eyes grew with hunger as she called him by his middle name. Whenever she called him that, it did something to him. Biting his lower lip, he shook his head. "You know what it does to me when you call me Abioye."

Feigning ignorance, she looked at him innocently. "Fine, come sit down." He attempted to pout, but Amina was not buying it. Once they got situated, Hasina sat on Amina's lap, eating, while Amina spoke to Kalifa and Reth. Amina noticed every so often that Kalifa's gazed landed on Kondo, who really had not acknowledged Kalifa, which upset Amina.

Turning to Reth, whose attention was already on her, she asked who the woman was that Kondo brought. "She's an old medical school friend of his. I forgot that he asked if he could bring her. Is it a problem?"

Placing a loving hand on his thigh, she nodded no. Though she wanted to know more about the woman, she would not ask Reth because he would want to know why. Right now, Kalifa would not appreciate her business spoken about. Instead, Amina just enjoyed being surrounded by love.

Her mind went back to a few months ago when Adeya contacted her through Mela. It seemed that Mela had shown Adeya the announcement, and for some reason, Adeya thought that would help her. When she found out that Amina wanted nothing to do with her, she fell back into threats and intimidation. Reth went to the district attorney, and they tackled on more charges. Amina promptly changed her number. She was done with the Williams family. After Reth shared with her what Aaron said, she knew their relationship was irreparable. She was working on forgiveness, but they would never be in her life. Gavin would be the father she needed and the grandfather to Hasina and any other children she had. That chapter in her life was closed.

"Are you ready, Amina?"

Amina heard Kalifa's voice but was unable to answer, as she did not hear the question. "What?"

"Your speech. You wanted to present Reth with the Goode Love Journal."

Nodding her head, she tapped Hasina to signal she was getting up. Lifting Hasina, she gently placed her down in the seat. Picking up her glass, she tapped it with a knife to get everyone's attention.

"Evening, family, friends, and friends of friends. Thank you all for coming to our rehearsal dinner and doing such an excellent job. I appreciate it. Anyway, tomorrow is our big day, and my fiancé will perform the Goode Love Vow. Tonight, I wanted to share something with him. When I first laid eyes on Reth, he had no idea I existed. I was a teenager with a crush. Even then, I knew he was my soul flame; something about his light attracted me even back then. During that time, I started a journal. I call it the Goode Love Journal. Since our engagement, I have been rewriting it because my youthful penmanship has greatly improved." Everyone laughed and Amina waited for them to calm again. My last entry came tonight, as I'll be presenting this journal to Reth as one of his wedding gifts. She turned to him with love in her eyes, and Kalifa placed the journal in her hand. Clearing her throat, she began to read.

This is my vow; this is the truth. Dear Reth, how I adore you.

I need to bathe in you. From the first time I saw you, my heart was yours. Your heart song, a tune that I have on constant repeat.

Synching with the beating of my heart, soothing like the strings of a violin, as classic as the serenade of a symphony. God made you for me.

Countless times, I've yearned to bathe in your vocal cadence, to dance to the vibrations of your timbre. The depth of your voice is intoxicating—so sensual and invigorating. Your vocal sound is warm like bourbon, thick like a chocolate milkshake, and just as sweet. The way your voice moves me, I can't adequately define, but it will come in good time. When God created you, He created a masterpiece so good, perfect, and complete.

I know He created you for me.

You represent His best artistry.

I crave to swim through your mahogany skin. Yes, I'm saved, but the sight of you makes me want to sin. You're worth the wait, and your heart I'll win.

Amazing, phenomenal, and brilliant don't seem the right adjectives to illustrate the man that is you.

You have the body of a Kushite warrior, made stronger by what you've survived. My mind replays secular songs like Your Body Is A Wonderland, Brown Skin, and Ego, but your body, your soul, is so much more. It is created to protect, to withstand any threat, stronger than any mountain, unshakable and embedded in the foundation of Him. No decision you make is ever on a whim.

You have a mind like King Solomon, understanding wisdom, and His word before the world. A man like you is beyond valuable; I feared once you were beyond me, but God whispered we will be.

You have the loyalty of John the Baptist and the courage of Daniel. You possess the fearlessness and strength of Samson, the integrity of Joseph, and the truth must be said; Boaz got nothing on you.

I know this to be true because God created you for me.

First, as my friend. God needed to remove the negativity that

349

had isolated me. When my rebirth was complete, my Father spoke it is time to be.

I bathe you in and breathe you out, inhale your scent and repeat. I need you to feel what my love is about.

I connect to your soul and let all my insecurities go. In you, I feel safe, unafraid, protected, respected, and loved.

You're the finest treasure that I've ever seen, the first to ever be granted to me. We're soul-to-soul bonded by the Father's eternal glow and all I want to do is grow old, forever love you, and never let you go. This is my vow. This is the truth. For forever and ever, my dear Reth, I'll love you.

As soon as she completed the last part, the room erupted and Reth swept her up in his arms. "Amina, read it to me again." The emotions on his face let her know that he felt every word she wrote. It was beautiful to witness.

"I bet a thousand dollars, after tomorrow, we'll have nephew in nine months, Djimon tried to whisper, but the familiar slapping sound let Amina know that Mama Goode heard him.

"Ow, Ma. That hurt. Baba come get your wife. She's throwing hands and they're not holy."

Ignoring him, Amina kept her focus on Reth.

"Tomorrow night," he promised, and Amina blushed.

Staring at herself in the mirror, Amina was stunned. She looked like royalty. Her gorgeous lace, sleeveless, backless white sheath wedding dress was beyond admiration. Her something old were the diamond earrings that Mrs. Goode had gifted her. She had worn them on her wedding day, and Amina would give them to Hasina one day. Her dress was her something new. The something borrowed came from Amal, who bequeathed her Miss. North Carolina tiara. This was her last gift, and it brought tears to her eyes. Amal was something wonderful. Her something blue was the garter that Kalifa had chosen. Lastly, because Kalifa was a stickler for the rules and took being Maid of Honor seriously, there was a sixpence in her shoe. How her best friend found it was beyond her, but Amina had it.

"Song Thrush, you look lovely. I'm so elated that you're my daughter. I love you, honey. I pray that God blesses you and Reth with years of happiness, love, and beautiful children. I always knew you were special. You've overcome so much to be here. I want you to know that whatever the battle maybe small or large, I'll always have your three sixty. You, my dear, are as much mine as my sons and granddaughter. No matter what, don't you ever forget that God created you to do great things. I love you."

Holding in her tears, Amina widened her arms to embrace her mother-in-law. "Thank you. It was your prayers that covered me. It was your love that guided me, and it was home that saved me. Just so you know, I got your three sixty too."

Mama Goode kissed Amina's hand. "Let's go. Gavin is ready for his moment, and my son is about to run in here to claim you if we don't get to moving."

Amina giggled and followed Mrs. Goode.

The doors of the church opened, and Amina floated down the aisle. Gavin held onto her as he escorted her down. The church was packed with family, church family, Reth's fraternity brothers, and colleagues. Amina was dazzled. In attendance were also some well-known, who's who of North Carolina high society.

Once she made it to the end, Reth met them and shook Gavin's hand. "I'll treasure her forever, Gavin. Your daughter will always be safe with me."

"I know she will."

Gavin kissed Amina's cheek before handing her off to Reth.

Dr. Chiram stood before them, but before it started, JD broke rank to pray. That simple action warmed Amina's heart. She was inheriting a wonderful family. Finally, after so much, she belonged. She was wanted. She was loved.

When it was time, they both recited their vows, and then Amina waved Hasina over. "Sweetness, I wanted to give you something too."

Kalifa walked over and handed Amina the necklace she purchased for Hasina. It was a piano locket; one side had a picture of Amal and Hasina, and the other, held a picture of Amina and Hasina. "Piano princess, this is my vow to you. I, Amina Lauryn Goode, take you Hasina Jamila Goode, to be my daughter. To love and to cherish, from this day forward, no matter the situation. I'll forever be your confidant, your Northern Star, your place of safety, according to God's holy ordinance, and thereto, I pledge thee my faith. This is for you. You, my dear, will always have your Mommy; Amal is with you always." Amina placed her hand over Hasina's heart. "You carry her there. I'm here too. I love you to infinity." Leaning down, Amina kissed Hasina's forehead. Amina could hear the sniffling. Reth had no idea she was going to do that, just Kalifa and Reth's parents.

Glancing up at her husband, she saw his tears. He did not seem surprised by her outpouring of love for their daughter. Turning back to Chiram, who was wiping his own eyes, Amina nodded for him to continue. "At this time, Reth will share the Goode Love Vow. Then, I'll let these two kiss one another," Chiram teased.

Picking up Hasina, Reth turned to Amina, love evident in his eyes. "Last night, my wife professed her love for me. We've said our vows, but in the Goode family, we take it a step farther. This started with my great grandfather, Theodore

David Goode. He looked back. "Brothers, come."

Led by Djimon then JD and finally, Kondo, they all stood by him. JD was to his left, Djimon to his right, and Kondo at his back. They all placed a hand on him in unison, their eyes on Amina. Affection oozed through her marrow as Reth reached for her hand. They were all connected. Hasina placed her hand on her father's arm to complete the connection.

"Dearest, Amina, beautiful, alluring, breathtaking, awing, queen of my heart, maestro of my soul, skin like onyx, you're every dream dreamt, and every prayer prayed. I have found the one whom my soul loves. I vow that we will share the unity and connectivity of Adam and Eve. I'll pursue your heart like Jacob sought Rachel. As the head of this household, I'll set the standard. We'll trust in God like Isaac and Rebekah; we'll build a foundation of trust, faith, and courage. God will bless this marriage as He did with Abraham and Sarah. There will never be doubt; not once will you question my love for you or my dedication to this marriage, nor of our Father who ordained and anointed us. I pray our union will be like Aquila and Priscilla—a godly marriage that showcases the love that Christ has for the Church.

It is my honor to be your husband and to have you as my helpmate. It is my pleasure to protect you, to provide for you and our family. It is my duty to promote your dreams and endeavors. Ephesians 5:25 states, 'Husbands, love your wives, even as Christ also love the church and gave himself for it.' My dear, you're more than my wife; you are my beloved, my gift from God, my rib, the mother of our future children, the mother of our daughter. You're my calm on a chaotic day. You're sweeter than any strawberry cupcake from Tamu Bakery. You're the music to my soul, my endless love. As your husband, and head of our family, I'll always place God before all things. Together, we will be enwrapped in the true blessings God wants to bestow upon us. I'll respect and cover you like Joseph did Mary. I'll be Aquila to your Priscilla, King Abasurelo to your Esther, Elkonah to your Hannah, Boaz to your Ruth. I'll be Isaac to your Rebekah, Jacob to your Rachel, and Adam to your Eve. As Solomon said, 'I'm my beloved and my beloved is mine,' Father in heaven, thank you for sharing your beautiful ebony queen with me.

With God leading us, no matter the battle, we will get through. *Mpendwa*, my beloved, this is my vow, the Goode Love Vow; when you enter this family, you enter Goode Love. Djimon, Jotham, and Kondo will hold me responsible, and you, dear wife, will always be supported, loved, and protected." Then, he looked to each of his brothers, and by order of birth, each bother walked over to Amina.

"Goddess, welcome to the family. You're my sister, and I vow to protect you, love you, and pray over you. If you need anything, never hesitate to ask." Then, Djimon balled his fist and tapped his heart three times.

Next came Jotham. "Sister, welcome. Know that from this day, not only do you have Reth, but you also have all of us. I love you; I'll protect you, and I'll pray for you. In Romans 12:9-10, 'Love must be sincere. Hate what is evil; cling to what is good. Be devoted to one another in love. Honor one another above yourselves.' This I'll always do. As your brother, it's my honor to have your three sixty. We're beyond blessed to have you in our family." Like Djimon, he balled his fist had tapped his heart three times.

Lastly came Kondo with the sweetest smile showcasing his double deep dimples. His beautiful hair was unbound, his silken curls soft and bountiful. "You came into our life so quietly. I'll never forget seeing you in Walmart so afraid yet so brave. I knew then you were a warrior woman. Even though you didn't see it or feel it, I did. I knew the moment my brother fell in love with you. I'm thankful you two found each other. Welcome to the family, sister. You'll always find safety and love in these arms. When you married my brother, you inherited three brothers. I know you loss Kingston and Zion, but God has given you more. We're not replacements but additions. Never again will you be isolated or alone because you'll always have us. We'll ensure that Reth lives out every word he vowed." Balling his fist, he tapped his heart three times, "In the name of the Father, the Son, and the Holy Spirit. This is our vow to you, Amina Goode. You're in good hands now and always." He leaned and kissed her forehead before returning to his brothers.

Reth placed Hasina down and she went right to Kondo, a gleeful smile on her face as she toyed with her necklace. Reth dapped to Amina. Removing his handkerchief, he wiped her teary eyes. She was overcome by their show of love and fidelity to her. Those Goode men were something spectacular and in their own league.

"Kiss her, Daddy!" Hasina squealed before Chiram could speak. The audience giggled at her exuberance.

Grinning, Reth pulled Amina in and let his lips speak the passion he felt for her.

The End

Coming soon: Kalifa and Kondo's story.

About The Author

Y. Deonna is a native of South Carolina, and at an early age, she discovered her love of reading and writing. As a youngster, she was fascinated by how authors created exciting and uplifting stories and knew she would one day do the same.

Y. Deonna completed her undergraduate education at Carson-Newman University and her graduate education at the University of Pittsburgh #H2P. It is her desire to fuse together her education, faith, and advocacy to create empowering stories that engage, educate, and elevate readers. Writing novels are part of her ministry and advocacy.

Additionally, she is a victim advocate, social worker, and works with domestic violence and sexual assault survivors.

For more information
https://linktr.ee/ydeonna
Email: authorydeonna@gmail.com

Y. DEONNA

IG: @bluetygrezz
Twitter: @CrownedRuby

Book Catalog

Author Y. Deonna

Standalone Books

Deception Has A Name BWLM

Her Mistake, His Masterpiece BWWM

Healing A Bitter Heart

Warring Between Faith & Flesh: No Fairy Tale Ending

Series Books

Battle Scarred Love 1 BWWM

Battle Scarred Love 2

<u>Stolen Virtue</u>

A Virtuous Theory

Theory of All

Symphony of Goode Love

Connect:

Email: authorydeonna@gmail.com

Join the new Facebook group to be in the know

IG: bluetygrezz

Twitter: @CrownedRuby

Facebook page: fb.me/Authorydeonna

Join the mailing list